DEMON ROAD

ALSO BY
DEREK LANDY

DEREK LANDY

DEMON ROAD

HarperCollins *Children's Books*

First published in hardback in Great Britain by HarperCollins Children's Books 2015
This edition published in Great Britain by HarperCollins Children's Books 2016
HarperCollins Children's Books is a division of
HarperCollinsPublishers Ltd
1 London Bridge Street, London SE1 9GF

Visit us on the web at www.harpercollins.co.uk

Derek Landy blogs under duress at www.dereklandy.blogspot.com

1

ISBN: 978-00-0-815692-3

Typeset in Joanna MT Std by Palimpsest Book Production Ltd,
Falkirk, Stirlingshire

Printed and bound in England by
Clays Ltd, St Ives plc

MIX
Paper from
responsible sources
FSC
www.fsc.org   FSC™ C007454

FSC™ is a non-profit international organisation established to promote
the responsible management of the world's forests. Products carrying the
FSC label are independently certified to assure consumers that they come
from forests that are managed to meet the social, economic and
ecological needs of present and future generations,
and other controlled sources.

Find out more about HarperCollins and the environment at
www.harpercollins.co.uk/green

Laura J —

I introduced you to scary movies, the books of Stephen King, and the myriad delights of horror.

You introduced me to StarKid.

I have still not forgiven you.

1

Twelve hours before Amber Lamont's parents tried to kill her, she was sitting between them in the principal's office, her hands in her lap, stifling all the things she wanted to say.

"We don't stand for troublemakers in this school," said Mrs Cobb. She was a fleshy woman in her fifties who wore a necklace so tight that when her neck quivered and her face went red, Amber expected her head to just pop off, maybe bounce on the floor and go rolling underneath her massively imposing desk. That would have been nice.

"There is a reason we have been placed in the top three educational facilities in the great state of Florida," Cobb continued, "and do you know what that is? It's because we run a tight ship."

She paused for effect, as if what she'd said needed to be absorbed rather than merely tolerated.

Cobb inclined her head slightly to one side. "Mr and Mrs Lamont, I don't know you very well. In previous years, there has been no reason to summon you here. In previous years, Amber's behaviour has been perfectly adequate. But your daughter has been sent to my office three times in the past month for altercations with other students. *Three times.* That is, I'm sure you'll agree, beyond the pale. Speaking plainly, as I feel I must, her behaviour this semester has worsened to such a degree that I am, regrettably, forced to wonder if there might have been some drastic change in her home circumstances."

Amber's mother nodded sympathetically. "How terrible for you."

Her parents were, as expected, completely calm in the face of overwhelming stupidity. That specific type of calm – detached, patient but at-times-veering-into-condescension – was pretty much their default setting. Amber was used to it. Cobb was not.

Betty Lamont sat in her chair with perfect posture and perfect hair, dressed smartly yet demurely. Bill Lamont sat with his legs crossed, hands resting on the understated buckle of his Italian belt, his fingers intertwined and his shoes gleaming. Both of them good-looking people, tall, healthy and trim. Amber had more in common with Mrs Cobb than she did with her own parents – Cobb could, in fact, have been Amber in forty years' time, if she never found the discipline to go on that diet she'd been promising herself. The only thing she seemed to have inherited from her folks' combined gene pool was her brown hair. Sometimes Amber let herself wonder where it all went wrong with her – but she didn't ponder that mystery for very long. Such pondering led to the cold and darker places of her mind.

"It gets worse," Cobb said. "The parents of the other girl in this… *fracas*, we'll call it, have intimated that they will report the incident to the local newspaper if we do not take appropriate measures. I, for one, refuse to see this school's good name dragged through the mud because of the actions of one troublesome student." At that, Cobb glared at Amber, just to make sure everyone present knew to whom she was referring.

"Can I say something?" Amber asked.

"No, you may not."

"Saffron's the one who started it. She picks on anyone who isn't as pretty and perfect as her and her friends."

"Be quiet," Cobb said sharply.

"I'm just saying, if you want to blame someone, then blame—"

"You may not speak!"

Amber answered her glare with one of her own. "Then why am I here?"

"You are here to sit and be quiet and let me talk to your parents."

"But I could let you talk to my parents from somewhere else," Amber said.

Cobb's face flushed and her neck quivered. Amber waited for the pop.

"Young lady, you will be quiet when I tell you to be quiet. You will respect my authority and do as you are told. Do you understand?"

"So I'm not allowed to speak up for—"

"Do you understand?"

Her mother patted Amber's leg. "Come on now, sweetie, let the nice old woman speak."

Cobb's eyes widened. "Well, I think I have identified the source of the problem. If this is how Amber has been raised, I am not surprised that she has no respect for authority."

"Naturally," Bill said, as composed as ever. "What's so great about authority, anyway? It takes itself far too seriously, if you want my opinion. You have a little problem that you blow all out of proportion, drag Betty and myself across town for a meeting we're obviously supposed to dread, and here you sit at your ridiculously large desk like a mini-despot, assuming you wield some sinister power over us. Betty, are you feeling intimidated yet?"

"Not yet," Betty said kindly, "but I'm sure it will kick in soon."

Amber did her best not to squirm in her seat. She'd seen this enough times to know what was coming next, and it always made her uncomfortable. Her parents had only so much tolerance for people they viewed as irritations, and the level of punishment they doled out depended entirely on how they were feeling on any particular occasion. The only thing Amber didn't know was how far they intended to take it today.

Cobb's unremarkable eyes narrowed. "Obviously, the apple hasn't fallen far from the tree. I can see where your daughter gets her attitude."

Mrs Cobb was now little more than a lame wildebeest, the kind Amber had seen on nature documentaries. Her parents were the lions, moving through the long grass, closing in on both sides. Cobb didn't know she was the wildebeest, of course. She didn't know she was lame, either. She thought she was the lion, the one with the power. She had no idea what was coming.

"You've just said, essentially, the same thing twice," Bill pointed out to her. "Added to this, you seem to talk entirely in clichés. And we've been entrusting you to educate our daughter? We may have to reconsider."

"Let me assure you, Mr Lamont," Mrs Cobb said, sitting

straighter and smoothing down her blouse, "you will not have to worry about that any longer."

"Oh, excellent," Betty said happily. "So you'll be leaving the school, then?"

"No, Mrs Lamont, it is your *daughter* who will be leaving."

Betty laughed politely. "Oh no, I don't think so. Bill?"

Bill took out his phone — what he half-jokingly referred to as the most powerful phone in Florida — and dialled a number.

"We do not allow cellphones in the Principal's Office," Cobb said.

Bill ignored her. "Grant," he said, smiling when the call was picked up. "Sorry to be calling in the middle of the day. No, no, nothing like that. Not yet, anyway. No, I'd like you to do me a favour, if you would. The principal of Amber's school, you know her? That's the one. I'd like her fired, please."

Faint fingers of a headache began to tap on the inside of Amber's skull. So this was how far they were willing to take things today. All the way to the end.

"Thank you," said Bill. "Say hi to Kirsty for me."

Bill hung up, and looked at Cobb. "You should be receiving a call any moment now."

Cobb sighed. "This isn't amusing, Mr Lamont."

"Don't worry, it's about to get decidedly funnier."

"I have made my decision. There is no arguing—"

Bill held up a finger for quiet.

Cobb was obedient for all of four seconds before speaking again. "If you're not going to talk rationally about this, then I have nothing more to say to you. It is unfortunate we could not work out our—"

"Please," said Betty. "Give it a moment."

Cobb shook her head, and then her phone rang. She actually jumped.

"I'd answer it," Betty advised her gently. "It's for you."

Cobb hesitated. The phone rang twice more before she picked it up. "Hello? Yes, yes, sir, I'm just... what? But you can't do that." She turned her face away. She was pale now, and her voice was hushed. "Please. You can't do that. I didn't—"

Amber heard the dial tone from where she was sitting. Cobb sat frozen. Then her shoulders began to jerk, and Amber realised she was crying.

Amber felt queasy. "Bill," she said, "maybe we don't really have to get her fired, do we?"

Bill ignored her and stood up. "Right then," he said. "Amber, we'll let you get back to class. You're working at the diner later, aren't you? Try not to eat anything – we're having duck tonight."

Her folks headed for the door, and Amber looked back at Cobb, who stood up quickly.

"Please," Cobb said, wiping the tears from her eyes. "I'm sorry. You're obviously very important people and... and Amber is obviously a very special girl."

"Very special," said Bill, one foot already out of the office.

"I'm sorry I didn't recognise that," Cobb said, hurrying out from behind her desk. "Special students deserve special treatment. Latitude. They deserve latitude and... and understanding. Leeway."

"Leeway, latitude and understanding," Betty said, nodding. "They've always been our touchstones for a happy life."

"Please," Cobb said. "Don't have me fired."

"Well, I don't know," said Betty. "It's really up to Amber. Amber, do you think Mrs Cobb should keep her job?"

There was some part of Amber, some sly and distant part, that wanted to say no, that wanted to punish her principal for her shrillness, her pettiness – but this was a part that wasn't thinking of Cobb as a person. No matter how much Amber may have disliked the woman, she was not prepared to ruin her life just to teach her a lesson.

"Uh yeah, she can keep it," Amber said.

"Thank you," Cobb said, her whole body sagging. "Thank you."

"Wait a second," Bill said, stepping back into the office. "Mrs Cobb, you accused us of being bad parents. If you want your job back, you're going to have to do more than just apologise."

"Oh yes," Betty said, clapping her hands in delight. "You should beg for it."

Amber stared at her parents in shocked disbelief, and Cobb frowned.

"I'm sorry?"

Betty's smile vanished. "Beg, I said."

Amber had been wrong. She thought she had known the full extent of her parents' punishments, but this was a level beyond. This was vindictive, like they were running out of patience on some scale no one else could see. This was something entirely new.

Cobb shot a quick glance at Amber, then looked back at Bill and Betty. "Uh… please," she said quietly. "Please can I keep my job? I… I beg of you."

Bill shrugged. "Yeah, okay." He swept his arm towards the door. "Shall we?"

They left the office, left Mrs Cobb standing there with tears running down her face, and walked the length of the corridor without speaking. Right before her parents turned right, for the parking lot, and Amber turned left, for the classrooms, Bill looked at her.

"This girl you had the 'fracas' with," he said, "Saffron, right? Wasn't she a friend of yours?"

"When we were kids," said Amber, her voice soft.

He nodded, considered it, then walked away.

Her mother patted Amber's shoulder and looked sympathetic. "Children can be so cruel," she said, and followed her husband.

2

THE HEADACHE THAT HAD been building since lunch finally struck by the end of school, driving thin needles of pain deep into Amber's temples. She popped a couple of Tylenol and, by the time her shift at the diner was half over, the pain had faded to a dull throb somewhere at the back of her skull.

"My folks are getting weirder," she said.

Sally looked up from the magazine she was reading. "Sorry?"

"My folks," Amber repeated as she wiped the table. She did her best to sound casual. "They're getting weirder."

"Is that possible?"

"I didn't think so. But do you know what they did today? They were called into my school and they made my principal cry. She literally shed tears. She was begging and everything. They... they traumatised her. It was so messed up."

Sally shifted position, leaned back on the countertop in her red and yellow Firebird Diner T-shirt, and looked thoughtful. "That," she said eventually, "is awesome. I would have loved my folks to have made my principal cry when I was a teenager. When my two start high school, I want to make their principal cry. I hated mine. I hated all my teachers. They always said I'd never amount to anything. But look at me now, eh? Thirty-three years old, no qualifications, and a waitress in a crappy diner with a neon Elvis on the wall."

Amber gave her the thumbs up. "Living the dream, Sally."

"Damn right," Sally said. "And hey, at least your parents are taking an interest for once, right? Isn't that something?"

"I... I guess."

"Listen to me. Just stick it out for another few years and then you can go off to college somewhere and build a life for yourself."

Amber nodded. New York, she figured, or Boston. Somewhere cooler than Florida, where the air alone wouldn't make her sweat.

"My point is," Sally continued, "wherever and whenever you decide to start your own family, you can do it *right*." She gave a little grin. "Okay?"

Amber could never resist one of Sally's grins. "Yeah," she said. "Okay."

"Attagirl."

Customers came in, and Sally put a spring in her step as she walked to greet them. "Hi there!" she said brightly. "Welcome to the Firebird! Can I show you to your booth?"

Amber watched her, marvelling at how natural her sudden cheerfulness seemed. A smile from Sally could turn a bad mood on its head – it was a phenomenon that Amber had witnessed on multiple occasions, and it rarely failed. The customers smiled back and they exchanged a few words and Sally led them to a booth by the window. Even though the Firebird was the third most successful fifties-themed diner franchise in the state – and Amber had no idea where that statistic had sprouted from – Wednesday afternoons were always slow. On slow days, it was policy to sit as many patrons by the window as possible in order to entice people in. Hungry people liked eating with other hungry people, it seemed. Amber had never been able to understand that. For as long as she could remember, she had always hated people watching her eat. She didn't even like eating meals with her parents.

Although, if she was to be honest with herself – and if she couldn't be honest with herself, then who could she be honest with? – their inherent weirdness might have had something to do with that.

Her parents were odd. Amber had known that for quite some time. Ever since she could remember, it was like they shared a private joke that she'd never been let in on. She loved them, of course she did, but she'd always felt like an appendage. She didn't complete the family because the family didn't need her to be complete. Bill and Betty Lamont were so perfect for each other that there were no gaps left for Amber to fill.

Two guys walked into the diner, both in their late teens. Joking and chatting, they stood at the PLEASE WAIT TO BE SEATED sign and only looked at Amber when she smiled and said "Hi!" in her perkiest voice. "Welcome to the Firebird. Can I show you to your booth?"

"Don't see why not," said the first guy.

She smiled again and turned on her heel, making sure to keep the smile in place. She wasn't pretty like Sally, wasn't tall like Sally, wasn't captivating like Sally and certainly did not look as good in her yellow shorts as Sally did, but, even so, there were so many mirrors in the diner that to lose a smile at any point could mean a drastic loss in tips. She stood by the booth in the corner and her two customers slid in on opposite sides of the table.

"My name's Amber," she said, taking her notepad from her back pocket, "and I'll be your waitress this evening."

"Hi, Amber," the first guy said. "My name's Dan, this is Brandon, and we'll be your customers."

Amber gave a little laugh. "What can I get you?"

"We're keeping it simple today. We'll take your cheeseburger deals. The whole shebang."

Amber marked the orders down. "Two cheeseburgers with the works, two fries. No problem at all. And to drink?"

"Coke," said Dan.

"Coke it is."

"Actually, no," said Dan, "I'll have a strawberry milkshake instead."

"One strawberry milkshake, gotcha. And for you?"

Brandon didn't look up from the menu. "Do you have 7-Up?"

"We have Sprite," Amber said.

"That's nice," Brandon said, raising his eyes to her slowly, "but I didn't ask if you had Sprite. I asked if you had 7-Up."

Amber's headache started to spike again, but she kept her smile and smothered her words. She needed this job. The *Dark Places* convention was in a few months and tickets were not cheap.

"I'm really sorry, we don't have 7-Up," she said brightly, like she'd just been told she'd won a bunny in a raffle. "Would you like Sprite instead?"

Brandon took off his glasses and cleaned them. "If I had wanted Sprite, I'd have asked for Sprite, now wouldn't I?"

"Please excuse Brandon," Dan said, grinning. "He's in one of his moods. Brandon, out of all of the drinks that they have here, which one do you want?"

Brandon let out a heavy sigh. "I suppose I'll have a milkshake."

"Okay then," Amber said, pencil at the ready. "What flavour?"

"Well, I don't know. What flavour do you recommend?"

"I've always loved chocolate."

"Then I'll have vanilla," Brandon said, and put his glasses back on.

Dan was trying not to laugh at the antics of his buddy. Amber stood there and smiled. "Sure thing," she said. "Can I get you guys anything else?"

"If we think of anything," said Dan, "we'll be sure to ask."

Amber smiled and left them, fighting a swirling tide of nausea. She got through the swinging doors to the kitchen and leaned against the wall for a moment, waiting for the feeling to subside. When she was sure that she wasn't going to pass out or puke, she gave in the order and stood beside Sally, both of them making milkshakes.

"What are your guys like?" Amber asked, ignoring her surging headache.

"Two businessmen," Sally said, "slumming it, flirting really badly with me and destined to end up with sauce splattered down their shirts. What about yours? The one in the glasses looks cute."

"He's a tool."

"But not that cute," Sally said quickly. "In fact, if you had let me finish before interrupting, you would have heard me say he looks cute, but, on closer inspection, he's obviously a tool."

Amber grinned. "You were going to say that?"

Sally nodded. "If you had just let me finish, instead of babbling on like you always do."

"I am a babbler."

"Yes, you are."

Amber placed the milkshakes on a tray, took a deep breath, and went back out.

Brandon watched her walk over, and Amber tried for a smile. It wasn't convincing, but it'd do. She didn't care about the tip anymore – all she wanted was for these two guys to leave, to take their bad vibes with them, and allow her to wallow in whatever sickly unpleasantness had been threatening to engulf her all day.

"Now then—" she started, but the headache sent fresh needles of pain straight to the back of her eyes and she winced, and the tray overbalanced and the milkshakes slid sideways, toppling off the edge and smashing to the ground.

The sound of breaking glass swept the headache away, and as Amber's vision cleared she could see that the milkshakes had gone everywhere. They'd drenched her sneakers and splattered the cuffs of Brandon's jeans.

Dan howled with laughter, but Brandon glared at her, heat rising in his face.

"Oh my God," Amber said. "I am so sorry. I am so incredibly sorry."

"You…"

"I'll get this cleaned up. I am so sorry."

"You stupid fat pig."

Amber froze.

"You clumsy, ugly little troll," Brandon said. "You did that on purpose."

"I didn't, I swear—"

"You dumped it over me on purpose."

"It was an accident."

Sally hurried over, mop already in hand. "It's okay, no big deal, we'll get this—"

Brandon jabbed a finger at Amber. "She did it on purpose."

Sally laughed. "I'm sure it was just—"

"I want her fired."

Sally stopped mopping, and her laugh turned to a bemused smile. "She's not going to be fired for dropping a tray, all right? It happens all the time. How about this? Your meal is on the house."

"Our meal is on the floor," Brandon said. "Where's the manager? I want to speak to the manager. I want this fat pig fired."

Sally's face turned to stone. "Get out," she said. "Both of you. Out. You're not welcome here."

Dan held up his hands in mock-innocence. "I didn't do anything," he said. "I was just sitting here. What did I do wrong?"

"You picked the wrong friend," said Sally. "Go on. Out."

Brandon kept his gaze fixed on Amber. His face had gone pale and rigid, like he was about to dive at her. Dan had to practically drag him to the door.

Sally stood there with her hands on her hips. "Wow," she said when they had gone. "What a couple of tools. You okay, honey?"

"I'm fine."

Sally patted her shoulder. "They're morons. Don't listen to a word they say."

Sally helped Amber clean up the mess. The two businessmen sneaked glances whenever they could, and Amber couldn't blame them. Even mopping the floor, Sally was pretty. She didn't get red-faced with the exertion like Amber did, and her hair didn't fall out of its ponytail, like Amber's did. She even looked good in the Firebird T-shirt.

Amber tried her very best not to look at her own reflection in the mirrors, though. She was in a bad enough mood already.

The rest of her shift dragged by. When it ended, she pulled on a fresh T-shirt and shorts that weren't yellow, said goodbye to the cook and to Sally, and stepped out on to the sidewalk. It was already getting dark, but the heat was waiting for her, and her forehead prickled with sweat as her lungs filled with warm air. She'd spent her whole life in Florida, been born and raised in Orlando, and she still reacted to the heat like a tourist. It was why, despite having a big, two-storey house to call home, her bedroom was on the first floor, where the air was fractionally cooler, especially on a day like today, when the clouds were gathering. Rain was on its way. Lightning, too, most likely.

Amber had a fifteen-minute walk home. Other kids would probably have been able to call Mom or Dad for a ride, but Bill and Betty had very firm ideas about what independence meant. Amber was used to it by now. If she was lucky, she'd get to the front door before she got drenched.

She crossed the street and slipped down the narrow lane that led to the dance studio she had hated as a child. Too uncoordinated, that was her problem. That and the fact that the dance teacher had hated her with startling venom. Amber was never going to be as pretty as the pretty girls or as graceful as the graceful girls, and she had come to terms with that, even as a kid. Her dance teacher, however, seemed to take issue with it.

Amber got to the badly painted sign of the ballerina and the curiously eighties hip-hop dancer, and Dan and Brandon turned the corner in front of her.

They were talking about something – Dan was chiding Brandon and Brandon was looking pissed off – but when they saw Amber they went quiet. Amber stood there, her legs stiff and suddenly uncooperative, and another headache started somewhere behind her eyes.

Brandon grinned. There was nothing friendly in it.

Amber forced her legs to work again, and she took the lane to her left. They walked after her. She quickened her pace through the growing gloom.

"Oink, oink, little piggy," Brandon said from behind her.

Amber broke into a run.

They laughed, and gave chase.

She plunged out of the lane and cut across the road, slipping between the back of a laundromat and an attorney's office. Immediately, Amber realised this was a mistake. She should have headed towards the pizzeria where there would have been people, and light, and noise. Instead, she was running across an empty lot and finding herself out of breath. A hand closed around her jacket and she cried out, twisted, got tangled in Dan's legs, and they both went down.

She landed heavily, painfully, with Dan sprawling over her.

"Oww," he laughed, rolling over. "Owww, that hurt."

Amber got up and backed off, rubbing her hands where she had skinned them as she fell. The headache was a thunder cloud inside her skull. Goosebumps rippled. Her stomach churned.

Dan stood, panting, and Brandon jogged up to them, taking his time.

"This isn't funny," Amber said.

"It's not meant to be," said Brandon.

"Why'd you run?" Dan chuckled. "We wouldn't have run if you hadn't run. Why'd you run?"

"Let me go," said Amber.

Dan swept his arm wide. "We're not stopping you from going anywhere. Go right ahead."

Amber hesitated, then stepped between them. They loomed over her on either side. She took another step, started walking away, but the moment her back was turned Dan was right behind her, on her heels.

She spun, her vision blurring for a moment. "Stop following me."

"You can't tell me where to go and where not to go," Dan said, suddenly angry. "This is America. Land of the free. Don't you know that?"

She could taste copper in the back of her mouth. "Leave me alone," she said dully.

"We're not doing anything!" Dan yelled, right in her face. She flinched away from him.

"Admit what you did, little piggy," said Brandon, circling her. "Admit that you spilled that milkshake on me on purpose."

"I swear, it was an accident."

"If you admit that you did it on purpose," said Dan, the reasonable one once again, "then we'll go away."

He was right in front of her as he spoke, but he sounded a

hundred miles away. She had to end this now, at once, before the blackness at the edge of her vision overpowered her and she collapsed.

"Okay," Amber said, "okay, I did it on purpose."

They nodded, like they had known all along. But they didn't leave.

"You made me look like a liar," said Brandon.

Amber tried focusing on Dan. "You said you'd go away."

"Jesus," he said, making a face. "Don't be so frikkin' rude."

"Okay," she said, "I shouldn't have done it. I'm sorry. It was stupid. I'm very sorry. Please let me go home."

"For the last time," said Dan, "*we're not stopping you*. We're not *stopping* you from doing *anything*. Why is that so hard for you to *understand*? Are you really that *dumb*? Are you really that *stupid*? Stop treating us like we're the *bad guys* here, okay? *You're* the one who threw that milkshake on my friend. *You're* the one who got us kicked out. *You're* the one who ran. *You're* the one who made me fall over. My knee is *bleeding*, did you know that? But am I *complaining* about it? Am I making a *fuss*? No, I am *not*. But *you*? You won't stop turning this whole thing into some big frikkin' *drama*."

"I don't..."

"What? What was that?"

"I don't feel well."

Her knees started to buckle and she reached out to steady herself, grabbing the front of Dan's shirt. He grimaced and pushed her hand away and she stumbled, and then Brandon was there, grabbing her, straightening her up—

—and then he hit her.

The pain was nothing compared to the violent storm in

her head, but his fist rocked her, sharpened her, and she saw him look at his own knuckles, like he was surprised that he had done it, and then everything was moving very quickly and when she felt a hand on her face she bit down hard and heard a howl.

Her vision cleared. Brandon's horrified face swam into view. She hit him back, as hard as she could, and his jaw came apart around her fist.

A moment stretched to eternity.

She watched her fist.

It was weird – in this gloom, her skin almost looked red.

A deeper red than the blood, though, the blood that exploded in glorious slow motion from the wreckage that had been Brandon's face. Was she doing this? Was this happening? In that moment, that luxurious moment, Amber found the time to wonder if she was imagining this part. Surely this was some sort of bizarre hallucination, brought about by adrenaline and those increasingly painful headaches.

There was no headache now, though. There was no pain of any sort. Instead, she felt… wonderful. She felt free. She felt…

Powerful.

Time started to speed up again. Blood splattered her T-shirt and Brandon hit the ground and, now that she could perceive normal sound once more, Amber registered his gargled screaming. Both hands were at his face and he was crawling frantically away, leaving a trail of blood as he went. Dan backed off, staring at her, his face white and his eyes wide and utterly, utterly terrified.

She had done that. The blood and the screaming and the

shattered bones. It had been no hallucination. She had done that.

She raised her blood-speckled hand. Normal skin again. That was good. Normal was good.

Something in her mouth. Something that tasted of copper. She spat. Brandon's finger hit the ground.

Amber turned and ran.

3

THERE WAS BLOOD ON HER HANDS.

Not in a metaphorical, figurative sense, although of course there was that, too, but in an actual, physical sense, there was actual blood on her actual hands, and it was proving surprisingly difficult to wash off. Amber scrubbed furiously, looked at the result, and then scrubbed again. It occurred to her, not for the first time, that her hands were quite small. If the rest of her body could have been in proportion with her hands, then maybe she wouldn't have been such a target. These were the thoughts that occurred to her as she was scrubbing the blood away.

"Amber?" came her mother's voice from beyond the bathroom door.

Amber looked up at herself in the mirror above the sink – wild-eyed and panicked. "Yes?" she called, keeping her voice as steady as possible.

"Is everything okay?"

"Everything's fine," Amber said. "I'll be out in a minute."

Amber listened to her mother hesitate, then walk away down the hall.

She turned off the faucet and examined her hands. For one ridiculous moment, she thought they were still bloodstained, but then she closed her eyes and shook her head. The frantic scrubbing had turned them both red-raw, that's all it was. No need for her imagination to be going into overdrive on this one. There was enough to freak out about as it was.

She put the toilet seat down and sat, taking deep breaths, and examined the facts. Yes, she had seriously injured that guy, but she had been acting in self-defence and she had been outnumbered. She really couldn't see how the cops wouldn't be on her side about this – if only she hadn't injured him quite so dramatically.

Amber frowned. What was his name? The name of the guy whose face she'd destroyed?

Brandon, that was it. She was glad she remembered it. For some reason, it felt important that she remember his name after what she'd done to him.

She hadn't meant to do it, and she hadn't a clue how it had happened. She'd heard stories about adrenaline, about what it could do to the human body. Mothers lifting cars off toddlers and stuff. It was, she supposed, *possible* that adrenaline had granted her the sheer strength to shatter bones on contact, and anyway how much strength would it *really* take to bite through a finger?

The very thought made her want to throw up again.

She stood, and examined herself in the mirror. Her skin was pale and blotchy and her hair was a tangled, frizzy mess. Her eyes – hazel, with flecks of gold, and the only part of herself she didn't hate – were red-rimmed from crying.

She went to her room, changed her blood-splattered T-shirt

for a top that the lady in the store had said would flatter her figure. Amber wasn't so sure she believed her, but it was a nice top, even if it didn't look especially good on her. She realised her hands were trembling.

She sat on the edge of the bed. Of course they were trembling. She was in shock. She needed help. Advice. Comfort.

For the first time since she was a kid, she needed her parents.

"Ah hell," she muttered. It was worth a try.

She heard them in the kitchen, putting the finishing touches to dinner. Amber crossed the hall, walking with heavy, leaden feet. The house was filled with the aroma of duck, cooked to perfection, and usually this would have her belly rumbling. But the only thing her belly was doing now was housing a whole load of fluttering butterflies. She tried to remember the last time she'd talked to her parents about anything important. Or the last time she'd talked to them about *anything*.

She couldn't.

Her mouth dry, she stepped into the kitchen. Bill was checking the duck in the oven. No sign of Betty. Amber could feel her courage begin to falter. She needed both of them in the room at the same time. She couldn't do this with only one. Could she? Or was this a condition she was setting for herself purely to have an excuse to back out?

And, just like that, her courage deserted her.

Relief sapped the rigidity from her joints and she sagged, stepped backwards without Bill even realising she'd been standing there. She walked back to her room. Maybe she could bring it up over dinner, provided there was a lull in the conversation. The *two-way* conversation, of course, as

Amber was only rarely asked to contribute an opinion. There probably wouldn't be a lull, though, but even if there was this was hardly an appropriate topic. After dinner, then, or later tonight, or—

Amber stepped into her room but Betty was already in here, the blood-splattered T-shirt in her hands.

"Whose blood is this?" her mother asked.

Amber searched for an answer that wouldn't come.

Betty dropped the T-shirt on the bed, crossed over to her, and took hold of Amber's arms. "Are you hurt?" she asked. "Did someone hurt you?"

Amber shook her head.

"What happened?" Betty asked. "Tell me, Amber."

"I'm fine," Amber managed to say.

Her mother looked deep into her eyes, like she'd find the truth locked away in there.

"It's not my blood," said Amber quietly.

"Whose is it?"

"At the Firebird. Some guys."

Betty let go of her and stepped back. "How many?"

"Two. They followed me. They *attacked* me."

Betty had a funny look on her face. "Amber, sweetheart, what did you do?"

"I did nothing," Amber said, her words suddenly rushing out. "I defended myself. I did nothing wrong. They were abusive customers. We asked them to leave. I saw them when I was walking home and they chased me. They attacked me, Betty. Two against one."

"You defended yourself? Are you okay?"

"I'm... I'm fine. Really."

"And how are they?"

Now Amber squirmed. "Um, I don't... I don't know. One of them, I... I think I broke his jaw. And bit his finger off."

"You bit his finger?"

"I bit his finger *off*."

"Oh, sweetheart," Betty said, taking Amber into her arms. Amber stiffened. She didn't know when her mother's arms had last embraced her. "And you're sure you're not hurt?"

"I'm sure. The adrenaline just... I'm fine."

"Has this happened before? This surge of strength?"

"No," Amber said, wondering how long she had to stay like this. "First time."

"How are you apart from that? How are you feeling? Headaches? Nausea?"

"A... a little. How did you know?"

Betty broke off the hug, and looked at her daughter with actual tears in her eyes.

"Betty?" Amber said. "Mom? Are you feeling all right?"

Betty laughed, a nervous laugh that she cut off sharply. "I'm fine, Amber. I'm just... You've been through a traumatic experience and I'm... I'm relieved you're okay."

"Are you going to tell Bill?"

"Of course." Betty smiled, then, the most beautiful smile Amber had ever seen her wear. "Don't you worry. He's going to want to hear about this. So are the rest of them."

Amber frowned. "The others? Betty, no, please, I don't want anyone to—"

"Nonsense," said Betty, waving Amber's objections away with one hand while the other took her phone from her pocket. Her slim fingers danced lightly over the keys and in mere moments a group text had been sent.

They sat on the bed while they waited for the others to arrive. Betty asked Amber about school, about her friends, about her job at the Firebird, and she listened as Amber spoke. It was a new sensation for Amber, talking about these things to her own mother. For the first time since Amber could recall, Betty seemed actually interested in her and the life she was leading. She nodded and smiled, probed deeper where needed, and, when they heard the first car pull into the driveway, Betty came forward and kissed the top of her head.

"You make me so proud," she said softly.

Tears came to Amber's eyes, unbidden, like a burglar breaking into her home, and proved just as shocking.

"You let the others in," said Betty. "I'll help Bill with dinner. Good thing we chose a big duck."

Amber waited until Betty had left before rubbing her eyes. Her knuckles came away wet. There was a curious tightness in her chest that made her breathe funny. She stood up, took a moment to calm herself. She couldn't be sure, but she suspected that this was what it meant to have a loving parent. It was proving to be an unsettling experience.

The doorbell rang and she answered it. Two of her parents' closest friends, Grant and Kirsty Van der Valk, lived only five minutes away, so she wasn't surprised to see them arrive first. What did surprise her was the smile that Grant wore, which was as broad as his chest.

"Hey, kiddo," he said, giving Amber a hug. He'd never called her kiddo before. Never hugged her before, either. He smelled of expensive aftershave, applied with restraint.

He stepped back, still smiling. He had hair that had always reminded Amber of Elvis Presley's in his later years – though the sideburns were not quite as ridiculous. "How'd it go with that principal of yours today? Your dad told me you spared her job. You're a better person than me, you know that?"

"That was never in any doubt," said Kirsty, taking her turn for a hug. If Grant was Elvis, then Kirsty was Pricilla — beautiful, red-headed and so wonderfully *vivacious*. Today that vivaciousness was directed solely at Amber. "How are you?" Kirsty asked softly, like this was a conversation just between them. "Are you feeling okay? How long have you been having the headaches?"

"Not too long," Amber mumbled, starting to get a little freaked out by all this. Did she have a brain tumour that everyone knew about but her?

Then Kirsty's eyes widened. "Good God, that smells amazing. Did you help them cook?"

Amber tried a smile. "They don't let me near the oven," she said, and led them into the living room, where they were soon joined by Bill. As they chatted, he stood by Amber's side with his arm round her shoulder like the proud parents she'd seen on TV.

Then the doorbell rang again, and Amber excused herself. Neither of her parents had any family, so this tight group of friends had long since become a substitute. She supposed, in a way, they were her aunts and uncles, though they treated her with the same cool detachment she'd grown used to.

She opened the door and was immediately swept off her feet.

"Hello, beautiful!" growled Alastair.

Amber didn't know how to react to this. Her feet dangled. Alastair laughed and set her back on the ground. Like her parents and the Van der Valks, Alastair Modine was older than he looked. He had an easy, smiling face behind all those bristles, and was more casual than the others, preferring jeans to suits and rolled-up shirtsleeves to a collar and tie.

"Heard you got in trouble at school," he said, whispering it as though it was a secret. "I knew you were a troublemaker from the first moment I saw you. You were only a few hours old, but I knew. I knew." He took a moment to look at her. "You look more and more like your mom every day."

Amber smiled politely, even though she knew this was an outright lie. Betty was beautiful. Amber was plain. Betty was statuesque. Amber was not. These things she knew.

A third and final car pulled up in the driveway. "The others are in the living room," she said.

Alastair glanced back at the car, then gave Amber another smile and went to join his friends.

Amber stood in the doorway, watching Imelda walk up as the rain started to fall. Her blonde hair was styled and immaculate. Her clothes were perfectly coordinated. Her make-up was flawless. This was all to be expected. Imelda Montgomery was a living, breathing example of a woman who had every box ticked. All except for the smile. Imelda had a pretty face that begged to smile – and yet Amber had never seen her genuinely happy. Not even when she'd been married to Alastair.

"Amber," Imelda said as she stepped inside.

"Hi," Amber said, and that was the extent of their conversation. It was all Amber expected. Imelda made even her parents look affectionate.

They moved into the dining room, and Amber ate dinner

with her parents and their friends. They drank wine and she drank Coke. The last time she'd eaten with them had been three months earlier, on her sixteenth birthday. Until tonight, she'd never seen them in such a good mood. Well, apart from Imelda who, in fact, had looked even grumpier than usual. But that was Imelda. She was a special case.

Amber hadn't invited any of her friends to her birthday. Her true friends, her *real* friends, were all online anyway, on fansite messageboards and forums. She didn't need to meet any of them in the flesh. Online, she could pretend to be popular and funny and interesting, and she didn't have to worry about disappointing anyone when her smile didn't light up the room. Online, nobody cared about the wattage.

She endured questions about the possibility of boyfriends and the casual drudgery of school and she was just beginning to enjoy herself when she remembered the taste of that boy's blood in her mouth. Her appetite vanished abruptly, and she pushed the food around on her plate while the others talked on. Despite what Betty had said earlier, they didn't discuss the burst of violence that had darkened Amber's day. She was grateful for this.

"You look tired," Betty said, leaning across to her.

Amber nodded. "I think I'm going to have an early night, if that's okay."

"Of course it is," said Bill. "Leave your plate — we'll clean up. You get to bed — you've had a big day."

"The biggest," said Grant.

The others nodded and smiled their understanding — only Imelda appeared annoyed. More than annoyed, actually. Practically agitated.

Amber was too tired to care about that now. She stood, noticing for the first time that no one else had even touched their dinner, and smiled and said, "Goodnight."

She got a hearty chorus in response, and she went to her room, closing the door behind her.

Rain pelted the window like machine-gun bullets. Outside it was hot and wet, but here it was air-conditioned cool, just the way she liked it. She wanted to go straight to bed, even though it was just after ten, but she also needed to talk about what had happened to her today. She logged on to the *In The Dark Places* messageboard.

The Dark Princess said...
Hello? Anyone on?

Mad Hatter99 said...
Princess! Where u BEEN, girl?
snuggles up closer for a hug

The Dark Princess said...
Been busy with school n stuff. Having a REALLY strange day.
You seen BAC recently?

Mad Hatter99 said...
Me too! U missed the convo yesterday. What u think of Tuesday's ep?
She was on earlier. Had some role-play stuff going on. Y?

The Dark Princess said...
Just need to talk to her. Nvr mind. Too sleepy to wait up. Nite nite x

Mad Hatter99 said...
Nooooooo! Don't leave me!

Amber logged out of the messageboard and lay back on her bed. Taking off her clothes was far too much effort. Brushing her teeth seemed a ridiculous waste of energy. She could barely keep her eyes open. She heard her parents and the others talking, but couldn't make out the words. There was laughter. Excitement.

Her phone rang, buzzing against her hip. With numb fingers, she pulled it from her pocket and held it to her ear.

"It's me," said Sally. "Just got a call from Frank. Two cops came into the Firebird ten minutes ago asking about you."

Faint alarm bells rang in Amber's head. "What'd they want?" she asked groggily.

"You," said Sally. "They said you attacked those guys from earlier. Did you? They said one of them's in the hospital."

Groaning, Amber sat up. "Did Frank tell them my name?"

"Of course he did, Amber. They're cops. What happened?"

The doorbell rang. Amber hung up, slipped her phone into her pocket while she stood. The room spun for a moment. When she was sure she wasn't going to fall over, she walked with Frankenstein feet to the window.

There was a patrol car in the driveway.

4

THE CHATTER IN THE house died away, replaced by a new, unfamiliar voice. A man's voice. Official-sounding. Amber wished she wasn't so tired. If she could only get her brain in gear, she'd be able to explain herself. She was sure she'd be able to make the cops understand. She took a few deep breaths to clear her head, and walked unsteadily to her door. She opened it. If they wanted her to emerge with her hands up, they were going to be disappointed. She was far too tired to lift her arms.

From the sounds of things, the others had stayed in the dining room, and Bill and Betty had taken the cops into the living room to talk. Amber stayed close to the wall as she moved, in case she needed the support. She got to the family photo in the hallway – the only framed photograph of the three of them – and stopped. From here, she could look across the corridor, through the open door.

Two officers of the law stood there in full uniform, talking to her parents. The cops were saying something, but Amber couldn't focus enough to make out the words. She didn't know why she felt so tired. They all stood in the centre of the room, watching each other. Amber shuffled her shoulder along the wall, then stopped again, concentrated on what the cop was saying.

"…just need to speak to her, that's all."

"Amber's not feeling well at the moment," Bill said. "Maybe if you come back tomorrow she'll be strong enough."

"Mr Lamont," the cop said, "I understand what you're doing. Please don't think I don't. Your daughter may be in trouble and you want to protect her. I get that. I do. But you're doing her no favours if you don't let us speak to her."

Despite her drowsiness, Amber felt her insides go cold.

"My husband isn't lying," Betty said, sounding upset. "If you'd just call Chief Gilmore, I know he'll vouch for us and for Amber. Whatever you think happened I just know *didn't* happen."

"We're not calling the Police Chief, we're not even calling this in, until we've had a chance to speak with Amber," the cop said. "We have two young men who swear that she assaulted them."

"One sixteen-year-old girl assaulted two men?" Bill said. "And you're taking them seriously? You're actually wasting your time with this nonsense?"

"We'll get this whole thing cleared up if you'll just let us speak to her."

Bill put his hands on his hips and shook his head despairingly. Betty looked at him.

"You are such a perfectionist," she said. The upset she'd briefly displayed had disappeared.

"I just like it when things are neat," said Bill. "This… would not be neat."

"I'm sorry, what wouldn't be neat?" one of the cops asked. But Bill and Betty ignored him.

"This is a special day," Betty said. "A wonderful day. For sixteen years, we have waited for this day. What's happening now is a minor inconvenience. That's all it is."

"Mrs Lamont," one of the cops began, but Bill talked over him.

"It's already in the system," he said to his wife. "Already logged."

"No, it isn't," Betty answered. "That one said they haven't even called it in yet. Gilmore will make it go away. He's done it before, and for the money we're paying him he'll certainly do it again. You might have to drive their car into the marshes later on tonight, just to confuse their colleagues, but why not?"

The officers glanced at each other.

Bill looked at his wife and smiled. "You're serious, aren't you? You really want to do this?"

"Yes," said Betty. "I really do." She took a coat from the back of the couch and put it on, pulling the sleeve down past her wrist and wrapping it around her hand.

"Uh, excuse me?" said the cop.

"So which one do you want?" asked Bill.

Betty nodded to the cop closest to her. "That one."

"Fair enough," Bill said, shrugging. "I'll kill the ugly one."

"Hey," said the big cop, but his next words were muffled by Bill's hand covering his face.

Only it wasn't Bill's hand. It was red, and tipped with black talons. Bill's face was red, too, but different, altered, and he was bigger, taller, suddenly towering over the cop, a red-skinned monster with black horns curling from his forehead, like a ram's horns.

The demon that had taken Bill's place slammed the cop's head against the wall. The head crumpled like an empty soda can.

The cop's partner jumped back in shock, scrabbled at his holster for his gun, then remembered Betty and turned just as she changed. One moment Betty. The next a monster. Tall. Red. Horned. Her fist went right through his chest, popping out the other side in a spray of blood. The cop gurgled something that Amber couldn't make out. Betty opened her hand, letting go of the sleeve, and withdrew her arm from both her coat and the cop's torso.

Amber ducked back as the dead cop collapsed.

"Well," she heard Bill say, "that's done it."

Betty laughed. It was her laugh, all right, but it was coming from the mouth of a demon.

The door between the living room and the dining room opened, and Amber inched forward again to watch Grant lead the others in. They stared in shock at the carnage.

Kirsty covered her mouth with her hand.

Bill turned to them. "We can explain."

Kirsty rushed forward. "That's my coat! What the hell, Betty?"

Amber's knees went weak.

"Can we talk about your coat later?" said Grant. "Right now can we talk about the two dead cops on the carpet?"

"I'll call Gilmore," said Bill. "We'll get it all smoothed over. This is not a big deal."

"They're cops!"

Bill-the-demon waved a hand. "We got a bit carried away. We shouldn't have done it. Happy? It's low key for Betty and me for the rest of the night, we promise. We kill Amber, and that's it. No more killing for the week."

Amber's stomach lurched and suddenly she was cold, colder than she'd ever been.

"I really am sorry about your coat," Betty said to Kirsty. "I'll buy you a new one."

Kirsty shook her head. "It was limited edition. You can't get them anymore."

Amber slid sideways, forgetting how to walk, forgetting how to breathe. Her feet were heavy, made of stone, dragging themselves across the floor towards her bedroom while the rest of her body did its best to stay upright. She fell through her doorway, down to her knees, turned and reached out, numb fingers tipping the door closed. Her mouth was dry and her tongue was thick. Something was happening in her belly and she fell forward on to her hands and knees, throwing up on the rug she'd had for years. She didn't make a sound, though. She heaved and retched, but didn't make a sound.

Her parents were monsters. They had grown horns. They'd killed cops. Her parents – and their friends – were going to kill her.

Betty had drugged her. That's what she'd done. A sedative or something, served up in the food. No, the Coke. Amber looked at the mess on her rug and wondered how much of the drug was congealing down there.

She reached out, hand closing round the bedpost, using it to pull herself up, steady herself, stop herself from toppling sideways. She had to get out. She had to run. She started for the window and the room tilted crazily and she was stumbling towards it. She threw herself to one side before she smashed through the glass, instead banging her elbow against the wall. It hurt, but it didn't bring her parents running. She was so thirsty. There was a bottle of water on her nightstand, but it was all the way across the room.

Dumb, numb fingers fumbled at the window. Stupid, dumb thumb jammed against the latch. Dull teeth bit down, drawing blood from her lip. The pain was sharp, sharpened her for a moment, and her thick, stupid, unresponsive fingers did what they were supposed to do. The latch squeaked, moved, and she braced her forearm against the sash of the window and pressed in and up, using her whole body to slide the window open. Then her legs gave out and she fell, cracked her head against the sill on the way down.

Amber lay with her eyes closed, blood pounding in her ears like drumbeats, like footsteps, like knuckles on a door.

"Amber?"

Eyes opened.

"Amber?" Betty said from the hall. "Are you okay?"

No answer would mean the door opening, Betty looking in. An answer, then. An answer.

"Yeah," came the word, awkwardly, from Amber's mouth. More followed. "Tired. Sleeping." Each one clumsy on her tongue.

The door. The handle. The handle turning, the door opening. Bill's voice from somewhere else. "Where do we keep the stain remover?"

The door, closing, and then Betty's footsteps, walking away.

Amber turned on to her side, then got on her hands and knees. Stayed there, breathing, gathering her strength. Without raising her head, she reached for the sill. Grabbed it. Hauled herself up until she got an arm out. Grabbed the sill on the other side. Pulled herself up off her knees, got her head out of the window, into the heat and the air and the rain.

Amber fell to the grass, her legs banging off the window frame. They'd find her like this. She hadn't escaped. She couldn't rest, not like this. She had to get away. Had to keep moving.

Amber was crawling now, along the wet grass, through the dappled shadows of the trees. She had to get away. She had to crawl faster. Had to get to the road. Get to the road, get into a car, drive away. Escape.

The ground beneath her changed, got harder. Not grass. Not anymore. Darker. Harder. Smoother. The road.

Approaching footsteps, hurrying through the rain. They'd found her. They'd found her already. Her arms were weak, no strength left. Her body lay down. Her mind... her mind... where was her mind?

Shoes. High-heeled shoes on a wet road, right in front of her. A voice. A woman's voice. She knew that woman's voice.

"Hello, Amber," said Imelda.

5

Amber awoke in a room that was not her own. Clean lines and no clutter. Heavy curtains kept the dark from escaping into the morning light. Moving slowly, she pulled the covers off and stood. She was in her underwear. Her clothes were neatly folded on the dresser. Clean and dry. She crept to the window, parted the curtains, and looked out over Lake Eola. She frowned. An apartment in the city overlooking Lake Eola. She didn't know where the hell she was.

But she was alive. That was something, at least.

Amber grabbed her clothes, put them on. Her phone was gone. She started to reach for the glass of water by her bed, but stopped, remembering the Coke. There was a bathroom, clean and polished, looking like it had never been used, and she drank from the faucet and wiped her mouth. Then she went to the door, put her ear against it, heard nothing.

She opened it, hesitated, and stepped out.

The apartment was vast, impressive, and utterly devoid of personality. It looked like the penthouse suite of a hotel. Everything was clean and in place. Every colour matched, every curve and line complemented the curves and lines around it.

It had all been designed to cohere, to fit, to belong. There was a designer kitchen to her left, all gleaming metal with a huge breakfast island, and a balcony to her right, a view of the city beyond, all glass and palm trees, and ahead of her was the way out.

She was halfway to the door when she noticed Imelda standing in the living room, her back to her. She was on the phone, listening while someone spoke.

Amber reached the apartment door, opened it silently, and stepped out into the corridor. White walls. She moved up to the corner, and peered round.

At the end of the corridor was the elevator, the door to the stairwell, and a window. Standing at that window, looking out over the skyline, was a tall man in blue jeans, black T-shirt and battered cowboy boots. On the side table behind him there was a mirror, a bowl of potpourri and a shotgun.

Amber stared at the shotgun.

She pressed herself back against the wall and closed her eyes. She was breathing too loud. She was breathing too loud and he'd hear her, she knew he would. She peeked out again. He was still looking out of the window. The shotgun was still there.

She had no choice. She couldn't go back, and she couldn't stay where she was. She had to do something. She had to move forward.

Fighting the urge to break into a sprint, Amber took small, slow steps. She got to the side table without making a sound, then picked up the shotgun. It clinked slightly on the table and the man turned from the window. He was good-looking, somewhere in his mid-forties. His black hair had hints of grey. His narrow eyes were calm.

"You should put that down before it goes off," he said.

"Get out of my way. Get out of my way or I'll... I'll shoot you."

"Your hands are trembling," he said. "Give it to me." He reached his left hand forward slowly and Amber took a single step back and then there was somehow a pistol in his other hand, and he was aiming it right at her head. "Now you're really scared," he said. "Now you want to run screaming. That's perfectly understandable. But I'm not going to move. You're not getting past me."

"Please," she said, the shotgun shaking badly in her grip now. "They're trying to kill me."

"Then why aren't you dead?" he asked. "Put the shotgun back on the table and go back inside the apartment."

Tears ran down her face. "Please don't make me."

"Put down the shotgun."

"I don't understand what's going on."

"I'm not the one who's going to explain it to you. Either shoot me or put down the shotgun."

Amber shook her head, but found herself putting the weapon on the side table, anyway. The man slid his pistol into a holster on his belt before picking up the shotgun.

"Probably wasn't even loaded," she said quietly.

"No, it was," the man responded. "You would have cut me in two if you'd pulled that trigger. Go back inside, Amber. Talk to Imelda."

She didn't have much of a choice. Amber walked back the way she'd come, hesitated at the apartment door, and then walked in.

Imelda saw her, held up a finger for Amber to wait.

"We're keeping tabs on all of her friends, aren't we?" she said into the phone pressed to her ear. "Exactly. I wouldn't worry about this, Kirsty. We'll find her. It's only a matter of time. Okay, I've got to go. I want to check out the principal of her school." She listened. "Because after that wonderful display yesterday, she knows for certain that the principal isn't in league with us. Yes, I am clever. I'll call you if I hear anything. Bye now."

Imelda hung up. "Want some breakfast?" she asked, walking to the kitchen. She poured orange juice into a tall glass and placed it beside an assortment of croissants and pastries. Then she looked back at Amber and waited.

"What's happening?" Amber said.

"It really is a long story," Imelda said.

"There's a man outside with a gun."

"That's a friend of mine, Milo Sebastian. You don't have to worry about him. You have to worry about your parents."

"What's wrong with them?"

Imelda managed a smile. "You think they're behaving oddly? That's just because you don't know them very well."

"They're demons. Monsters."

"Oh, Amber… We're *all* monsters. Metaphorically, I mean. The whole human race. We hate, we kill, we do terrible things to each other and to the planet. But we are also, in *our* case, *actual* monsters. With horns."

"I really don't understand any of this," said Amber. "Please just tell me what's happening."

"I'm going to explain everything. But to start with I'll have to show you. I'm going to change now, all right? I'm going to turn into… well, into a monster, just like your parents. And I want you to remain calm. Can you do that?"

Amber swallowed, and nodded.

"I'm not going to hurt you. I just want to show you."

"Okay."

"You're sure?"

"Yes."

"Okay. Once again, I want you to remain calm. You're perfectly safe."

Imelda's skin turned red and her teeth grew sharp and she had black horns and it all took less than a heartbeat.

Amber screamed, picked up a potted plant and threw it, but it fell short and smashed to the floor.

"You killed Henry," Imelda said, dismayed.

"*Help me!*" Amber screamed.

"You're panicking," said Imelda.

"*You're a monster!*" Amber screeched.

"This is not news to me."

Amber sprinted for the door.

"You tried that, remember?"

A wave of pain swept through Amber, making her stagger but not fall. She pushed herself away from the door and ran for the window.

"What, you're going to jump?" Imelda asked. "Really? We're on the thirty-fifth floor."

Amber grabbed a cushion off the couch and held it out with both hands.

"I'm not entirely sure what you mean to do with that," Imelda admitted.

"You're a monster," Amber said, her voice cracking.

"Yes," said Imelda. "And I hate to break it to you, sweetie, but so are you."

Amber looked at her hands. Looked at how red they were. Looked at the black nails that had pierced the cushion she held.

"Oh my God," she said, feeling how her tongue brushed against teeth that were somehow longer than they had been a moment earlier. Her head swam. She raised her hands, felt horns. "Oh God. Help me. Please..."

Imelda the Monster walked forward slowly. "Amber, I need you to calm down..."

Amber backed away unsteadily, leaving a trail of floating feathers in her wake. She began to cry.

"Stay away from me."

"You asked me to help you. I'm helping you."

"Stay back," said Amber, voice breaking.

"Okay."

"Help me."

"Make up your mind," said Imelda with a faint smile.

"Please, just... why do I have horns?"

"Because you're like me," said Imelda. "You're like your parents, and Grant and Kirsty and Alastair. You're a demon, sweetie."

The word stuck in Amber's mind like a bone in her throat, so that she barely registered Imelda darting towards her until it was too late to do anything about it.

"Sorry about this," Imelda said, and punched her into unconsciousness.

6

AMBER STIRRED FROM HER dreamless sleep, waking without opening her eyes. She snuggled down deeper into the pillow, slowly drifting off again, and then she remembered where she was and what had happened and she sat up so fast she almost fell out of bed.

Back in the bedroom in Imelda's apartment. The curtains were open now. The day was bright and warm. She examined her reflection in the mirror on the wall. She looked normal. Her hair was a mess, but that was the full extent of the damage.

It had been real. She knew it had been real. She'd had horns. She'd grown them as her skin had turned red and her nails had turned black – just like she had before she'd pulverised Brandon's jaw with a single punch. She'd grown them just like Imelda had grown them. Just like her parents had grown them.

But no. No, that couldn't be right. There had to be an explanation. A reasonable, logical, real-world explanation.

She stood. She was fully dressed, in T-shirt and shorts and sneakers. That was good. She left the bedroom. The man with the guns sat on the couch, his long legs crossed, reading a tattered paperback. Milo Sebastian, she remembered. He looked up at her, then went back to reading.

"Where's Imelda?" Amber asked.

"Out," he said.

She waited for him to furnish her with more information, but apparently he wasn't much of a talker.

"Out where?" she pressed.

"Out with the others."

A wave of alarm rushed through Amber's veins. "My parents? What's she doing with them?"

"Pretending to look for you." Keeping a finger on the page he'd been reading, he folded the book closed and raised his eyes. "You can wait for her here. She shouldn't be too much longer."

Amber hesitated, then took a few steps further into the room. "Don't suppose you'd let me go, would you?"

"You've got nowhere to go to," Milo replied. "The cops can't help you. Chief Gilmore can only afford his luxury condo with the money they pay him. Your parents, and their friends, are very powerful people. You must know this."

Amber didn't reply. She didn't mention the ease with which they'd had her principal fired.

She went to the couch across from where Milo was sitting, and sat on the edge, knees together and hands in her lap. "Do you know what's going on?"

"I'm not the one to talk to about this."

"So you *do* know. You know they're monsters, right? You know Imelda is a monster? And it doesn't bother you?"

"Does it bother you that you're just like her?"

Amber shook her head. "I'm not. I'm… I don't know what

happened or what drug she gave me, but I'm not like her. I'm not like them. They're monsters. I'm normal. I mean, I think I'd know if I were a monster, right?"

He looked at her, didn't say anything.

"Why do you have all those guns?" she asked.

"Your parents might start suspecting that Imelda isn't being honest with them. She asked me to make sure no harm comes to you."

"You're here to protect me?" Amber stood up suddenly. "So I could walk out of here and you couldn't stop me?"

Milo opened the paperback again, without fuss, and resumed reading. "Try it and see."

Whatever rebellious fire had flared inside her sputtered and died at his tone, and Amber sat back down. "Do you know where my phone is?"

"Destroyed."

Her eyes widened. "I'm sorry?"

He kept reading. "It's the easiest way to track you."

"But that was my *phone*."

"Best not to make calls. Or send emails. Those are the kind of things that would lead your parents straight to you."

"And how do you expect me to… to… to do *anything*? I need my phone, for God's sake. I need…" She faltered. She needed her phone to go online, to talk to her friends. She needed that now more than ever.

Milo didn't seem to care. He had gone back to reading his book. A western, judging by the cover. Amber had never read a western. She couldn't imagine they were any good. There were surely only so many stories you could tell about cowboys and shooting and horses before it all got boring, even for those who liked such things. How many times could you describe a saddle, or a saloon, or a desert plain?

Still, it was something. He liked books and she liked books. There was common ground there.

"Ever read *In The Dark Places*?" she asked.

Milo didn't look up. "No."

"It's a really good series. It's been adapted into a TV show. They're on Season Three right now. You should read them. They're all about these star-crossed lovers, Balthazar and Tempest. She's a Dark Faerie and he's an Eternal. That's, uh, that's what they're called. He's got an evil brother and her parents are nuts and she's just been possessed by the ghost of her ex-boyfriend. It's set in Montana. They sometimes have horses on the show."

"Horses are nice," Milo said, in a voice that indicated he wasn't paying her the slightest bit of attention.

Amber glowered and stopped trying to make conversation.

They sat in silence for another ten minutes, and then Milo's phone buzzed. He checked it, and stood.

"She's back," he said, tucking the western into his back pocket and picking up the shotgun. He left the apartment, and Amber immediately leaped up, scanning her surroundings for an escape route.

After a few moments, she sat back down.

She heard the faint *ping* of the elevator arriving, and then low voices as Imelda and Milo exchanged whatever they had that passed for pleasantries. Thirty seconds later, Imelda came in.

Amber sat back into the couch, her arms folded.

"I'm sorry," was the first thing Imelda said.

"You hit me."

"You were screaming."

"Not when you hit me."

"If it makes a difference, I'm pretty sure you were going to faint, anyway."

"So why didn't you let me faint?"

Imelda hesitated. "I should have let you faint. I'm sorry." Her apology apparently over with, Imelda walked into the kitchen. "Have you had anything to eat?"

Amber didn't answer. She was starving, and thirsty, but to respond was to forgive, and she wasn't prepared to do that yet.

Imelda made herself a cappuccino without trying to engage her again in chit-chat. When she was done, she came over, sat where Milo had been sitting. She took a sip, placed the delicate cup on the delicate saucer on the delicate coffee table, and sat back. "You need to eat something," she said. "I can hear your stomach rumbling from here."

"That's not hunger. That's anger."

"Your belly rumbles when you're angry? I didn't know that about you."

"There's a lot you don't know about me."

"Well," said Imelda, "that's not strictly true."

"You've barely ever *spoken* to me."

"That doesn't mean I don't know you. Your parents kept us all very well informed – and they know you a lot better than you think."

Amber looked at her in silence for a moment. "What did you do to me earlier? My skin and... What was that?"

"You know what that was."

Amber shook her head. "No. I'm not like you. I'm not a monster like you. What did you do to me?"

"I didn't do anything. You were born that way."

"I wasn't born with red skin, Imelda. I wasn't born with frikkin' horns."

"No, but it was inside you."

Amber glared. "Show me, then. Go on. Change. Transform. Go demony. I want to see it again."

"Amber, I don't think—"

"Go on," said Amber. "I wasn't really expecting it the first time. Now I'm ready. Let's see you in all your glory."

Imelda sighed. "Fine," she said, and stood, and her skin reddened and her features sharpened and her horns grew, and Amber shrank back instinctively.

There was something about the very shape of Imelda now, the way the horns curved, the way her face – once a pretty face, now a beautiful face – caught the sunlight, there was something about all of it that sent a shiver down Amber's back. This was the shape that nightmares took, deep in the darkest parts of her subconscious.

"You can do this, too," Imelda said. Her teeth were pointed. She was taller. Her shoulders were broader. Her clothes were tighter. Her top had come untucked. "You just decide you want to shift, and you shift."

"Is that what you call it?"

"Shift, change, transform. You can come up with your own name for it, if you want."

"I don't want. I don't want to shift. I don't want to be a monster." Amber realised she was shaking.

"It's really not that bad," said Imelda. "You get powerful. You get stronger and faster and you feel something inside you just… alter. It's like you're becoming the person you were always meant to be."

"Not person. Monster."

The smile on Imelda's face faded. "Monster," she said. "Yes." She reverted to her normal state, and tucked in her top. She looked almost embarrassed as she sat back down. "Well, there you go, anyway. That's how it's done. If you're ready to listen, I'll tell you how it started."

"You're not going to let me leave, are you? So go ahead."

Imelda took another sip from her cup. "I've known your parents since I was your age."

"I know," said Amber.

"No, you don't. I met your parents when I was sixteen years old. They were already courting."

"Courting?"

"That's the old word for dating. Which is probably an old word for whatever it is you call it now. We met Grant a year later. Bill befriended Alastair at Harvard, and Kirsty was added to the group after Bill and Betty got married."

"Bill didn't go to Harvard."

"I think it's safe to say that you don't really know your parents, Amber. Is it safe to say that?"

A strange feeling overtook Amber, a feeling of being adrift, cut off from everything she had thought she knew. "Yes," she admitted softly.

"I'm telling you this so that you'll know that we were all friends by the time the world welcomed in the New Year… of eighteen hundred and ninety."

"I'm sorry?"

"I'm one hundred forty-six years old, Amber, and your parents are three years older than me."

Amber didn't have anything to say to that.

"Bill and Alastair met some interesting people at Harvard," Imelda continued. "There were all kinds of clubs and societies back then: curious people looking to expand their horizons. They started out by merely dabbling in the occult, Bill and Alastair. And they drew the rest of us in."

"What do you mean by occult?" Amber asked. "You mean like black magic?"

"I mean *all* magic. Or as much magic as we could do, anyway. There were limits to the levels to which we could rise. I… I have no excuses for the things I've done. I let myself be swept along, but Bill and Betty… This was *all* they thought about. Early on, Bill came to us with a story he'd heard, of a deal with a being called the Shining Demon. In exchange for a tribute, this Demon would grant power, strength, magic and, if you obeyed the rules, eternal life."

"By turning you into demons yourselves?"

"You're skipping ahead," said Imelda, "but yes."

"Why would you want to be turned into demons?"

"Did you not hear what I said? About the power and the strength and the eternal life?"

"But you'd be monsters."

Imelda gave her a soft smile. "Look at me. Do I look like a monster? We can hide. We're very good at it. But you interrupted me. Bill came to us with this story he'd heard. We got interested. We wanted to know if it was true, and if so how we could get a deal like that for ourselves. It took us years, piecing together the different clues, following every lead…"

"And then you met the Shining Demon."

"We were told about a book. *The Blood-dimmed King*, it was called. We tracked it down to this magician in Boston, and we stole it. The Blood-dimmed King is a devil, or the Devil, or the King of Demons or… something. He goes by many names, and he has these Demons who interact with people here on Earth – Demons with a capital D. The Shining Demon is one of them. The book detailed how we could make contact."

"How did you?"

"It was a ritual. It took months to prepare. So many requirements to meet, things to arrange. We couldn't eat for four days beforehand. Couldn't drink for two. It was hard, arranging everything. Almost impossible. But we did it. We managed it. And we made contact."

"Did it look like you?" Amber asked. "You know, monster–you?"

Imelda shook her head. "He was… he was something else. But the book said that one of the most important rules was not to look at him. You avert your eyes. I only caught glimpses. The first thing I noticed was the smell. We were in a basement. Dark. Cold. And then there was this smell of sulphur. It got stronger and stronger until… One moment we were down there, just the six of us, the next this light started to burn, right in front of us, and he kind of grew out of that light. We all looked away immediately."

"And you didn't sneak a peek?"

"All I can tell you was that he glowed. He shone." There was a strange look in Imelda's eye. Almost wistful.

"And he offered you a deal," Amber said, a little louder than necessary.

Imelda snapped out of it. "Yes. He offered us power. Power enough for seven people."

"But there were only six of you."

Imelda went quiet for a moment. "That's right. He told us

what we'd have to do. The terms and conditions were… unexpected. Half of us – Kirsty and Grant and myself – wanted to walk out right there and then. But in doing so we'd break the circle and… well. He would tear us apart. So we stayed. And we listened. And, in the end, we agreed."

"To what?"

She cleared her throat. "The Shining Demon would give us power enough for seven people. So two of us would have to have a child. That child would grow up, and their power would manifest at some stage in their sixteenth year. They'd become as strong as we were. Just like you."

"Okay," said Amber. "And then there'd be seven of you. What was wrong with that?"

"It was what was expected in return, Amber. Some Demons want souls. The more they have, the stronger they get. The stronger they get, the stronger the Blood-dimmed King becomes. But the Shining Demon didn't want souls from us. He wanted a jar of blood from each of us. Our blood, which had magic in it already, spiced with… more magic."

"And how did you spice your blood?"

Imelda's eyes locked on Amber's.

Seconds passed.

"You're looking at me like you're expecting me to figure something out," Amber said, "but I have no idea what it is you're hoping for."

Imelda held her gaze. "Your parents had a son."

Amber's eyebrows rose. "I have a brother?" She'd dreamed of having a brother or a sister, someone to talk to, to share with, to alleviate that awful feeling of loneliness that would creep up on her whenever the house got too quiet.

"Your parents had a son," Imelda repeated. With emphasis on the *had*. "He reached his sixteenth birthday. A few months later, he started having headaches, started feeling sick, and then his power manifested."

"Yes? And?"

"And we killed him."

Amber paled. "What?"

"The Shining Demon explained it all to us, down in that cellar. He told us how we'd have to absorb the seventh's power, how that would make our blood more potent, how that would be a suitable tribute."

"You killed my brother?"

"We killed him," Imelda said. "And then we ate him."

7

THE WORLD DULLED.

"No," said Amber in a soft, soft voice.

"Our demon forms made it easy. Made it far too easy."

Amber shook her head. "You can't have done that. Please, Imelda, tell me you didn't do that."

"We could never let the children reach the stage where they'd realise what they were. It was too dangerous. Too unpredictable. We got stronger with each child we consumed, but each one was born with a strength to rival our own. You're the only one I've seen actually get a chance to shift."

"Was... was I going to be eaten, too?" Amber was suddenly standing. "They were going to eat me? They were going to kill me and eat me? My own frikkin' *parents*?"

"Please sit down."

"I don't think so!"

"Fine," Imelda said, sounding tired.

"So go on! Tell me what you did to my *brother*."

"We killed him and we ate him, and he made us stronger," Imelda said. "We each gave a pint of our blood, which was practically sizzling with power by that stage, and by then Kirsty and Grant were expecting."

"No," Amber said. "No, you can't. None of that happened. That's sick."

Imelda didn't meet her eyes. "Once their son reached his sixteenth year, once we'd eaten him, it was my turn, with Alastair, and we ate my child when she turned sixteen, and then it was back to Bill and Betty."

"You took turns? What was it this time? Another brother? Maybe a sister?"

"It was a girl."

Tears rolled down Amber's cheeks. "I had a sister. I had a sister and you killed her."

"Yes, we did," Imelda said, pulling at a tiny loose thread on her sleeve. "Every sixteen years, the seventh's power was recycled through us, making us stronger, and then the surplus was available again for the next child."

"So that's what you've been doing?" Amber asked. "For, what, the last hundred years?"

"We make it a point not to grow too attached to our children. It's the only way to stay sane."

Amber laughed. "Sane? You think this is sane? This is the most insane thing I have ever heard! This is nuts! It's sick and it's wrong! It's evil! You're saying my parents are—"

"Psychopaths," said Imelda, looking up at her. "Yes. Pure psychopaths. The others, they *became* psychopaths. They let the power corrupt them, eat away at their consciences. But Bill and Betty, they were born that way. They just hid it until they didn't need to any longer."

"So everyone's a psycho except you," said Amber. Her

fingernails – still ordinary fingernails, thank God – were digging into her palms. "That's what you want me to believe now?"

"If I'm a psychopath," said Imelda. "why haven't I killed you? The others aren't around. If I killed you now... ate you... I'd absorb all of your power. I wouldn't have to share it with anyone. So, if you really do think I'm the same as your parents, why are you still alive?"

"I don't know," Amber said. "Maybe you're trying to talk me to death. Or maybe, because the Shining Demon demands a jar of blood from each of you, having me all to yourself would break the terms of your deal."

Imelda smiled. "I'm breaking the terms already by keeping you alive. But I admire your logic. You're always thinking, aren't you? That's what I've always loved about you, Amber."

"You've never loved *anything* about me," Amber said. "Before this, you barely spoke to me."

"I couldn't do it anymore," said Imelda. "I couldn't pretend anymore. Not like the others."

"So how come you're different?"

Imelda hesitated. "The last time I had a child, something went wrong. I'd tried to remain detached from her, but I couldn't. The moment I held my newborn baby in my arms I knew... I knew I wasn't supposed to feel this way."

"You loved her."

"Yes."

"But you still killed her."

"*Alastair* killed her. I tried to run. I tried to take my daughter and escape, but Alastair knew what I was planning. He promised me that if I returned he wouldn't tell the others. I was scared. Confused. Weak."

"So you brought your daughter back to be killed."

"Yes."

"And let me guess — you felt bad about it."

Imelda looked up. "This stops here. With you. I've spent the last ten years building up my courage. I'm sorry I was never kind to you, but it was too risky. I was afraid the others would see what I was planning. Alastair, especially. He knows me the best. But now I'm going to break the cycle. You're going to leave with Milo. Tonight. I'll be joining you as soon as I can, but you have one chance to get out of this alive, and Milo knows where to start."

"You're sending me away? But you can't. This is my *home*."

"Is it? What exactly do you have here, Amber? Friends? Really? Are you going to stay because of school? Because of your job at the diner? These things are enough to make you stay?"

Amber swallowed. "Then where am I going?"

"Milo knows. I don't."

"Why wouldn't you know where I'm going?"

"Because if your parents figure out that I'm helping you," said Imelda, "they will torture me until I tell them everything. If I don't know where you are, I can't betray you."

Amber stared. "But... but then what'll happen to you?"

Imelda hesitated. "Your parents are very ruthless people, sweetie, and they're not going to pass up the opportunity to absorb more power."

"They'd eat you?"

"And if I'm very, very lucky? They'd kill me first."

8

MILO CAME IN AND Imelda talked to him at the far side of the apartment in a low voice Amber couldn't make out. He nodded occasionally and replied, and barely even glanced Amber's way.

She busied herself with looking through the bag Imelda had given her. A few items of clothing and underwear, everything in her size. She dug a little deeper, found a bag of toiletries. Dug deeper. Found a bag of money.

Tens, twenties and fifties in tightly packed rolls. Her eyes widened. There must have been thousands in there. Tens of thousands. A hundred thousand?

All the essentials that anyone would need to go on the run.

Milo and Imelda came over, and Amber stood to face them.

"It's time to go," Imelda said.

"I don't want to," Amber announced.

"I understand that," said Imelda, "but it really is for the best. Milo will keep you as safe as he can and keep you out of sight as much as possible. We're paying him for this – ten thousand a week. Take it from the money I gave you."

"You're not listening to me. I don't want to go."

"I am listening to you, but you've got to listen to me, too. I know what your parents are capable of."

"You can hide me here."

"They'll check here," Imelda said. "Alastair is already looking at me strangely. He's got his suspicions. It's only a matter of time before he stops by for an unannounced visit."

"Maybe he doesn't want to hurt me, either. Have you thought of that? Maybe he's like you. Maybe he's sick of it."

Imelda shook her head. "I wish that were true."

"Ask him!" Amber said. "Talk to him! Talk to my parents! Maybe they'd change their minds if you talk to them!"

"Sweetie, no…"

"Have you tried?"

"I haven't," Imelda admitted.

"Then you don't know, do you? You want to send me away when I might not even have to go. I know my parents, too, all right? I know what they're like. Talk to them. They're weird, but they're practical. All you need to do is reason with them."

"Amber, Bill and Betty aren't going to change their minds," said Imelda. "They're furious. They're desperate. They haven't slept. They haven't stopped searching."

"They're worried about me."

"They're worried you've *escaped*. Sweetie, you saw them. You heard what they said. If they find you, they will kill you. You have to trust me on this."

"So that's it? You think you can hand me a bag of clothes and a bag of money and send me off somewhere? I don't even know where you're sending me. I'm not going, you understand? *I am not going and you can't make me!*"

Imelda glanced at Milo. "She's not usually like this."

"And who the hell is *he*?" Amber almost shouted. "You're sending me off with a strange man I don't even know? How is that a good idea?"

"I trust him."

"He was going to shoot me earlier! And you want me to get in a *car* with this guy? For how long? How long will all this take?"

Imelda hesitated. "I don't know. Maybe… two weeks?"

"*Two weeks?*"

"Or three."

"*What?*"

"It's the only safe way. You'll have to get yourself some more clothes and things, but that bag will do for now."

"We really need to get going," said Milo. "I want to be on the road before dark."

Amber held up her hands. "Okay, okay, listen to me. Just listen, all right? That's your idea. That's the plan you came up with. So now I have a plan. Milo here goes home. He goes home and he plays with his guns and he's happy. And, while he's being happy, you and me get in a car and we drive somewhere nice and we never look back."

Imelda shook her head. "I told you, I can't go with you."

"Why? Why can't you come with me? Jesus Christ, you're the only person I know who isn't trying to kill me."

"It's better for you if I stay, honey. I can keep an eye on what they're doing. If they're close to finding you, I can steer them away."

"You just don't want to be around me."

"That's not true."

"Of course it is. The only reason you're helping me is because you feel guilty. You don't give a crap about me – if you did, you wouldn't be handing me over to him."

Imelda shook her head. "That's not true."

"Well, there we have it – we have two plans. Your stupid plan where I go with some lunatic called Milo, and my good plan, where you and me go somewhere far away, with mountains and trees and maybe a log cabin. We'll go to Montana. It's cool in Montana. We won't have to live in this constant *heat*."

"Let's have a vote," said Milo. "I vote for the stupid plan and so does Imelda."

Amber glared at him, then redirected the glare at Imelda. "Why him? Who is he? What does he have to do with all this?"

"I have my own history with Demons," Milo said. "I'm as qualified for this job as anyone possibly could be."

"So you've made a deal, just like my parents did? Bad people make deals with Demons – bad people who like to eat their children. Have you ever murdered anyone, Milo?"

"Amber, that's enough," said Imelda.

"You want me to get in a car with this guy—"

"Yes," Imelda snapped. "I do. Because I can't be there and he's the only one I know who'll be able to protect you. He's also the only one I know who'd be willing to protect you. Amber, this is messed up. Don't you think I know that? And don't you think this is breaking my heart, sending you away? I've finally been able to tell you the truth, after years of being too afraid, and instead of showing you all of the love I have for you, love that I've had for you since the day you were born, I have to send you away and pretend to be just like the others. I have to pretend to care nothing for you, Amber. I have to pretend to see you as nothing more than our next power boost.

This is breaking me, sweetheart. This is ripping me up inside and I don't know how the hell I'm not falling to the floor in tears, but I'm not. Because I have to be strong. For you. And you have to be strong for me. Because you're the only person in this world that I love, and if anything happens to you I'll... I'll..."

"I'm sorry," Amber said quietly.

"Oh, honey," Imelda said, pulling her into an embrace. Amber didn't know what to do for a moment. This wasn't the quick hug of Grant or Kirsty, or the picked-up-off-the-ground hug of Alastair. This was something else. This was genuine, and Amber found herself lost as to how to respond.

But she gradually wrapped her arms round Imelda and hugged her back, and she didn't even notice the tears that were spilling off her cheeks and soaking through Imelda's blouse. She felt Imelda cry, and realised she was crying herself. This one hug was the warmest, most sincere physical contact she had ever experienced, and she didn't want it to ever end.

9

Rain mingled with the tears on her face as Amber got into the SUV.

Milo had parked it round the back of Imelda's apartment building. They didn't want Amber in plain view. They didn't want her walking across the sidewalk for a few seconds because that was a risk they couldn't afford to take. Their paranoia was affecting Amber. She waited until Milo had the back door open, and then she ran through the heat and the rain, practically dived in. Milo threw a blanket over her and closed the door.

He got in the front, started the engine, and as the SUV was pulling out on to the street Amber realised she hadn't said goodbye to Imelda, and a sliver of anguish pierced her heart.

She made sure she wasn't about to cry, and then pulled the blanket back.

The SUV's exterior may have needed a wash, but the interior was clean and smelled of polish. Milo struck her as the type to maintain his vehicle in perfect running order, and she realised that she wouldn't have been surprised to learn that the dirt and the dust on the outside were nothing more than camouflage.

They drove without speaking for five minutes. Amber resisted the urge to speak. She wanted Milo to get uncomfortable in the silence. When the clock on the dash showed 8pm, she sat up, but kept the blanket wrapped round her head like a shawl. To her irritation, he looked perfectly comfortable.

"So where are we going?"

Milo moved into another lane. "We're going to see a friend of mine. He might be able to help."

"Help how?"

"We're hoping he'll have some ideas on how to evade your parents."

"You're *hoping*? Imelda said there was a plan. Hoping for ideas does not sound like a plan. Who is he, this friend of yours?"

"His name's Edgar Spurrier," Milo said as they slowed at the lights. "He used to be a journalist. His investigations took him deeper and darker than any respectable news agency was willing to delve, so now he's a freelance… something."

"So he's unemployed, basically."

They started driving again. "He prefers the term 'freelance something'."

She frowned. "Was that a joke?"

Milo shrugged.

"Where does he live?"

"Miami."

"That's, like, three or four hours away. Why aren't you more organised? Why isn't he here? Or why can't you call him? I'd loan you my phone only, oh yeah, you *destroyed* it."

"No phone calls, if we can help it," said Milo, totally missing Amber's subtle jibe.

"I have a new plan," she said, sitting forward. "Turn around.

Take me to Montana. That's where they film *In The Dark Places*, so I'd be able to just hang out, watch them film, and I have plenty of money now so I could afford to rent a cabin there until all this dies down."

Milo glanced at her in the rear-view. "This isn't going to die down."

"No, I know that, I just—"

"I don't think you do," said Milo. "This isn't a problem that's going to go away, Amber. Your parents aren't going to change their minds. Your life, as you knew it, is over. You have to leave behind your friends and family. There's no going back."

"I *know* that," she insisted, though even she was aware how unconvincing she sounded.

An accident on the turnpike delayed them, forced them into a slow-moving convoy that crawled through Miami's sprawl of Art-Deco architecture. The rain was heavier here. Neon lights bounced off the wet blackness of the asphalt. It would have been beautiful if Amber hadn't shrunk away from every car that passed them, just waiting to see her parents' faces staring out at her.

By the time they pulled up outside Edgar Spurrier's crappy condo, it was past twelve and fully dark. The humidity closed in on Amber the moment she left the confines of the SUV. The rain eased off slightly, but the clouds were still heavy. Lightning flickered like a badly placed bulb and in the distance she heard thunder.

Edgar's condo was not air-conditioned. A large fan hung from the ceiling and threatened to move the warm air around, but couldn't work up the energy to do so with any degree of conviction.

Edgar himself was a tubby guy with blond hair that hung limply to his shoulders. He had an easy smile and nice twinkling eyes, and beneath his shorts his legs were surprisingly hairless. He handed Amber and Milo a glass of iced tea and took one for himself, then they all sat in his mess of a living room. Books and papers competed for space with notepads bursting with scribbles. No pizza boxes or empty beer bottles, though. Edgar may have been disorganised, but he was no slob.

"Milo has already briefed me on your situation," Edgar said, settling back into his chair. "You've got yourself into what we in the trade call a pickle, Amber. Milo could have taken you to a dozen so-called occult experts around the country and they would have sent you away with useless advice and a headful of mumbo jumbo. Instead, he brought you to me, where deals with the Devil are something of a specialty. The Shining Demon is one of my particular areas of interest."

He paused, and Amber felt the overwhelming need to fill the silence.

"Okay," she said.

That seemed to satisfy him. "Now then," Edgar continued, "your particular quandary is that running isn't going to work."

A bead of perspiration trickled down Amber's spine. "It isn't?"

"It isn't," said Edgar. "Your parents will eventually find you. It's inevitable. I'm sure Milo will explain this to you later. They will find you and they will kill you. So you need to be proactive, am I right? You need to take the fight to your parents."

Amber hesitated. "Uh yeah, except, I mean, I don't want to *actually* fight them."

"No, no," said Edgar, "you don't want to physically take

them on, not at all. I'm not suggesting that for a minute. But you want to take the *figurative* fight to them, agreed?"

"I guess."

"You can't spend the rest of your life *running*. You can't spend the rest of your life *hiding*. Because, if you do, the rest of your life will be very short indeed. So you need an alternative. If I were in your position, what would I do? I've given this a lot of thought since Milo approached me. A lot of thought. But only this morning did the obvious course of action occur to me." He sat forward. "Amber, what you're going to need to do is talk to the Shining Demon *yourself*."

She blinked. "I'm sorry?"

"Not going to happen," said Milo.

Edgar held up a hand. "Hear me out."

"Not going to happen, Edgar."

"Just hear me out, buddy, okay? Keep an open mind about this. There's nothing we can do to stop her folks from wanting to eat her. There just isn't. Consuming her flesh is the only way they can grow stronger, and the only way they can pay the tribute they owe. Because, don't forget, they *do* owe that tribute."

"We haven't forgotten," said Milo.

"So there's nothing we can do there," Edgar said, leaning back in his chair. "If you don't want to talk to the Shining Demon, what does that leave us with? You could go after them. Take them out. Kill them before they kill you."

"I don't want to kill my *parents*," Amber said, aghast.

"They want to kill *you*," said Edgar. "You're going to have to reconcile yourself with the facts here, Amber. This is life or death we're talking about. It's kill or be killed."

"She doesn't want to kill her parents," Milo said. "So we're not killing her parents."

"I figured as much," said Edgar. "I'm a pretty smart guy, remember? You may have thought I was sitting here looking pretty, but what I was actually doing was going through all the options and throwing out those that were a no-go. I threw out everything except the one I started with – Amber here summoning the Shining Demon, sitting him down and having a chat."

Amber glanced at Milo. He wasn't saying anything, but he didn't look happy.

"So that's my idea," said Edgar, talking straight to Amber now. "You explain how unfair all of this is. You didn't ask for it, after all. You are an innocent party, caught up in your parents' diabolical machinations."

"Why would he care?" she asked.

Edgar chuckled. "Good question. And of course you're right. The Shining Demon isn't going to give one whit about any of that. He's a capital D Demon, after all. He likes it when innocent people suffer. That's kind of his thing." Edgar sat forward. "But you, my dear girl, hold a special appeal. The Shining Demon is notoriously picky about who he appears to. He'll only do a deal with someone if they pique his curiosity. But here's the thing. You, Amber, are enough to pique *anyone's* curiosity."

She suddenly felt uncomfortable. "Why?"

"You're the demon offspring of demon parents," Edgar said. "But whereas your folks are demons by circumstance, you are demon by *birth*. That makes you, technically, a purer form of monster – if you'll forgive the description. You have also, by virtue of being alive right now, potentially compromised their original deal, which will certainly have got his attention."

"So summon the Shining Demon and say what?" Amber asked. "'Hey there, please could you change the terms of my parents' deal?'"

Edgar shook his head. "The terms are unbreakable, there's no getting around that. But he could make it so that your parents and their friends never find you. He could make it impossible for them to hurt you. He could do a hundred things that would ruin your parents' plans and make eating you redundant."

"What would I have to do in return?"

Edgar shrugged. "Seeing as how your parents and their friends were going to eat you and then give him their supercharged blood, it stands to reason that he'd want to get that same energy some other way. Sending you out to harvest souls is a very common method of payment."

"I'm not killing anyone. I'm not doing that."

"Very well. If those are the terms of the deal he offers, you just say no. No harm, no foul. But he might not want you to kill. There might be something else."

Amber raised her eyebrows. "Could I offer him my demon side? Is that possible?"

"Even if it were, I doubt that would entice him."

"I'm not going to give him my soul," she said, a little sharply. "It's mine and he's not getting it."

"Sounds reasonable," said Edgar. "Not to worry, however – I do have a suggestion of my own. You're unique enough to summon him and, if you offer him something equally as unique, you might just find yourself with a deal."

"What do you have in mind?" Milo asked.

"The one that got away," Edgar said. "It's a story I was told by a very dangerous man, name of Dacre Shanks. You heard of him?"

Milo shook his head. Amber didn't bother.

"Dacre Shanks was a particularly nasty serial killer back in the late sixties, early seventies. This small-town Sheriff's Department eventually tracked him down, in 1974 I think, and went in all guns blazing. Shanks fell in a hail of bullets. Couldn't have happened to a nicer guy. Anyway, I met him a few years ago, and he told—"

"Wait," said Amber. "You just said he died in 1974."

"He did," Edgar said, nodding. "But before the cops closed in on him, he'd already made his deal with the Shining Demon."

"He's still alive?"

"Technically? No. But he's still around. Last I heard he was in his hometown of Springton, Wisconsin, happily killing a bunch of teenagers, but that was fifteen or so years ago. If you can find him, he might be able to help you."

"You want us to ask a serial killer for help?"

Edgar shrugged. "It's a scary world – you got to be prepared to meet scary people. Dacre Shanks qualifies as a scary person. He's up there with Elias Mauk and Leighton Utt... maybe even the Narrow Man. Outwardly, charming as all heck, but... well. Serial killer, you know? I met him through a mutual acquaintance and arranged an interview of sorts. The man just wanted someone to talk to, and he talked a lot. I got some very graphic descriptions of what he'd done to his victims, some very disturbing insights into his mind... We talked about death, about how it felt when those bullets riddled his body, about what happened after. Milo knows what I'm talking about, right?"

Milo said nothing, and Amber frowned.

"And we talked about the deal he'd made with the Shining Demon," Edgar continued. "How he summoned him, what the terms were, how he found out about him in the first place. And he told me a story I'd never heard before, and I thought I'd heard all the stories about our shining friend. He told me about a man who'd made a deal – I don't know the circumstances surrounding it, but it was a deal like any other – and then welched on it. The Shining Demon granted him whatever he wanted, but, instead of paying him back in the agreed-upon fashion, this guy skips town, and the Shining Demon loses him. And the Shining Demon *never* loses a mark."

"What does this have to do with me?" Amber asked.

Edgar smiled. "If you can find this guy, you can offer his location to the Shining Demon in exchange for getting your parents off your back."

"You know where he is?"

"Haven't a clue," Edgar said, almost happily. "Shanks wanted to talk, sure, but he was pretty cagey with the things he had to say. You'd have to ask him yourself. You might like him. He's got some pretty funny stories. They'll give you nightmares, but they're still pretty funny."

"Uh," said Amber, "I don't really want to talk to a serial killer."

Edgar chuckled. "You'll be perfectly safe. Milo here will look after you."

Amber glanced at Milo. Just how dangerous *was* this guy?

"Why don't you come with us?" Milo asked. "You know him, he knows you, you can make the introductions."

"I'd love to," said Edgar, "but he said he'd kill me if he ever saw me again."

"Why?"

Edgar shrugged. "The conversation turned sour – what can I say? Serial killer, you know?"

10

EDGAR WENT TO FETCH the paraphernalia Amber would need to summon the Shining Demon, and the moment he was out of the room Amber looked over at Milo.

"I'm doing it *now*?"

Milo shrugged.

"Imelda said it took days of fasting and loads of preparation."

"There's more than one way to summon the Shining Demon," said Milo. "Sometimes you don't even have to summon him – he'll appear right when you're at your most vulnerable."

"Milo, I don't know…"

"If you don't want to do this, say so. We'll find some other way."

"Is there another way?"

Milo didn't answer.

Amber slowly clasped her face in her hands and dragged her fingers down her cheeks.

Then she sat forward. "So what do I say? How do I greet the Shining Demon? Do I call him sir, or lord, or master?"

"He's not your lord and not your master, so you don't have to call him anything. Relax, okay? You don't have to be so nervous. Talk to him like you'd talk to me, but don't agree to anything other than the terms *you* want. Ignore everything he says that isn't on topic. He'll try to trick you. Listen to *every* word he uses, because he uses them for a reason."

"You're not making me any less nervous."

"Sorry."

"Do you think this is a good idea?"

"It's the best one we have."

"That's not saying a lot, though, is it?"

"No, it's not."

Amber sat back. Her insides were in knots. "What do you think Imelda will do when she finds out I actually *met* the Shining Demon?"

"That all depends on whether this plan works."

"How do you know her, anyway?" she asked.

"How does anyone know anyone?"

"I don't know. They meet?"

"There you go," said Milo. "We met."

Edgar came back in. Amber didn't know quite what she had been expecting – maybe a robe, or a ceremonial dagger, or a box full of candles with pentagrams moulded on to their sides. She wasn't expecting a large leather pouch, shaped like a deflated balloon.

"It's a gunpowder flask," Edgar said proudly, handing it over with something approaching reverence. It was heavy, filled to its leather stopper with what felt like sand. "Persian, nineteenth century, made from a camel crotch."

"Ew."

Edgar chuckled. "Don't worry, the camel's long dead."

"Still ew."

"See those engravings on the hide? Those intricate little engravings? I don't know what they are. Pretty, though, aren't they?"

"There's gunpowder in here?" she asked.

He shook his head. "Something far more powerful. Far more valuable, too. The only reason I'm letting you use it is because I couldn't get it to work myself."

Milo frowned. "You tried summoning the Shining Demon?"

"Everyone wants something," Edgar said, a little sadly, "but I just wasn't interesting enough for him to bother with. Story of my life, huh? But, if this will work for anyone, it'll work for Amber, and then I can finally find out if it was worth the money I paid for it, or if I was scammed. Y'know, *again*."

"How do I use it?" she asked, handing the flask back.

Edgar cleared a space on the coffee table and laid it down, then sat. "You pour the powder in a circle around you, making sure there are no gaps. You put a match to it. It catches fire. That's it."

"It's that easy? And then the Shining Demon will appear?"

Edgar hesitated.

"What?" Milo asked, suspicion in his voice.

"The Shining Demon doesn't do that anymore," Edgar said. "Appearing, I mean. You can't make him come to you. Instead, you go to him."

Amber went cold. "I what?"

Milo frowned. "She what?"

"I couldn't get it to work, so I just have to go by what the guy who sold it to me said, all right? You put a match to the circle, and when it's lit you... arrive."

"Where?" said Milo.

"Wherever the Shining Demon is," said Edgar.

"Hell?" Amber asked, her voice small.

"Maybe. But don't look so scared. It's absolutely fine. You'll be perfectly safe."

"It doesn't sound perfectly safe," Milo said.

"It is, though. She'll be in no danger whatsoever. As long as she doesn't step outside the circle."

"I don't like this," Amber murmured. "Will you both be with me, at least?"

Edgar made a face. "We'll have to stay here, I'm afraid. Them's the rules. But you don't have to worry about a thing. You'll meet the Shining Demon. You'll explain your situation. You'll offer him the guy who welched on the deal in exchange for a way to protect you from your parents and their friends."

"And only that," said Milo. "Do not deviate from the script."

"That's a good point," said Edgar. "The Shining Demon likes to talk, by all accounts, and he might try to get you to agree to something you really shouldn't be agreeing to. Keep it simple. If he likes the terms, he'll accept them. If he doesn't, douse the flames and you'll come straight back. Do not step out of the circle. I cannot stress that enough."

"What if he pulls me out?"

"He won't be able to touch you so long as you stay where you are. Also, for your own wellbeing, it's probably advisable not to look directly at him." Edgar got to his feet. "There. I think that's everything."

Amber looked up at him. "I still have, like, a billion questions."

"A little knowledge is a dangerous thing," said Edgar. "You'll be fine. Come on, you can do it in the backyard."

He took the powder flask and walked out to the kitchen. Milo got up, helped Amber stand. Her legs felt weak.

"Am I actually going to do this?" she asked.

"You can change your mind at any time."

She expelled a long breath. "I can't believe I'm going to actually do this…"

They went out back. The dark yard was modest, with a small pool that needed a serious skimming. Whether the sweat on Amber's face was from the humidity or the trepidation, she couldn't be sure. The rain had stopped, which allowed the cicadas to start singing again. Edgar led Amber to a patch of crabgrass and handed her the powder flask and a battered matchbook with a picture of a staircase on the front.

"All set," he said.

She looked to Milo for instruction, but he just stood there, cool in the heat. Expecting either of them to correct her at any moment, she undid the stopper on the flask, crouched down, and began to pour.

The opening was small, and the fine black powder came out in a thin, steady stream. The warm breeze made the grasses ripple, but the powder flowed straight down like it was a perfectly still night. Amber turned 360 degrees, making sure not to leave any gaps, and when she finished she stood in the small circle and plugged the flask with the stopper. She held it out to Edgar, but he waved it away.

"Hang on to it until you're done," he said, and she hung the strap over her shoulder so that it dropped diagonally across her chest.

She took a match from the matchbook and crouched again.

Her mouth was dry. Her hands were shaking. She needed to pee. She looked up at Milo.

"See you when you get back," he said.

Amber ran the head of the match across the sandpaper strip. The match flared, and with shaking hands she put the flame to the powder. It lit instantly, expelling a stench so violent it made her head turn. The fire spread from the point of contact in both directions, and she stood and watched it surround her. When the flames met and the circle was complete, the flames turned blue and she was indoors now, in a castle, its vast walls constructed of hewn stone, its ceiling too high to see, its thick wooden rafters swallowed by shadows.

In front of her were five arched doorways with corridors like the fingers of a splayed hand. Tapestries hung on the walls, depicting various acts of depravity, their shock value immediately shamed by the even more gruesome images captured in the stained glass of the long windows that sliced through the wall above.

It was cold here. The sweat that had layered her body in the Miami heat was now making her shiver. Her breath crystallised in small clouds. She thought she was alone until she heard the giggle.

Someone was standing in the dark area between the doorways. Lurking.

"Hello?" she called. Her voice didn't sound like her own. It sounded like the voice of a scared child. "I... I see you. I can see you. Hello?"

The shape didn't move.

From somewhere, from elsewhere, came the sound of

screaming, a chorus of pain carried to her on the wind. It was gone almost before it had registered.

"Hello," said the shape.

It came forward, into the light. Tall and thin, a genderless thing, wearing a patchwork robe that may have been a gown. Heavy make-up, black and badly applied, rimmed its eyes, while its thin mouth was smeared with red lipstick. The foundation it used covered the entirety of its bald head in a thick grey-white that may have been ash.

"Are you the Shining Demon?" asked Amber.

The curious thing gave a high-pitched titter, covering its mouth with long-fingered hands.

"No, no, no," it said in its curious voice. "No, no. But he knows you're here."

"Where am I?"

Another titter. "In his castle."

"Is this hell?"

"To some. What's your name?"

"Amber."

"Hi, Amber. I'm Fool."

"Hi, Fool."

"Do you want to play with me?" Fool asked. "I know lots of games. Do you want to play Who Can Scream the Loudest? I'm very good at that. Or maybe Who Can Bleed the Most? I bet you'd win. I'll give you a head start, if you'd like."

"I don't think so."

"Step out of the circle, Amber."

"I'm sorry, I can't."

"Sure you can," said Fool, moving closer. "Step out of the circle."

Fool smiled. Its teeth were small shards of coloured glass sticking out from bloody gums.

It turned its head suddenly, its eyes narrowing. From one of the corridors came a glow.

"He's here," Fool whispered, and without giving Amber another glance it sprinted from the room.

Amber fought the urge to run, even though every instinct in her body was screaming at her. She watched as the glow got brighter, then turned, lowering her head while her hands shielded her eyes. The room was suddenly lit up. From behind her, the light tread of bare feet.

"You seek an audience with me," came a voice. Male. Hushed.

"Yes," she croaked out, closing her eyes. "I'm… I…"

"I know who you are, child. I know why you're here. You seek protection from those who would harm you."

She nodded. Her mouth was so, so dry. "My parents. And their friends."

"I know them, too," the Shining Demon said. "So eager. So ruthless." His brightness soaked through her eyelids. It hurt. "You are the first to have escaped their platter. The first to find your way to me."

"I need your help."

"But of course," said the Shining Demon, and she could hear the smile in his voice. "I am the only one who could possibly help you. I am your only hope, am I not? Come, Amber, let me show you my castle."

"I… I was told to stay in the circle."

"Mmmm. Yes. Wise, I suppose."

"Where are we?" she asked. "Is this hell?"

"Questions, questions," said the Shining Demon. "Such an inquisitive species, the living. The dead have no need for questions. The dead are quite content in their gentle ignorance." He was walking now, circling the circle in which she stood. Amber didn't speak. She had the feeling he wasn't finished.

"This is his kingdom," the Shining Demon continued. "The one known by many names. My dark and terrible master."

"The Blood-dimmed King," Amber said.

"One of his names, yes," said the Shining Demon. "This is his kingdom, but we are in my castle. You are my guest, Amber. I assure you, no harm will befall you if you take one simple step…"

She turned away from the sound of his voice. "I'm… I'm sorry, I can't. I'm just here to make a deal."

Silence. And then, "Pity."

She licked the dryness from her lips. "Can you help me? Can you take back the power you gave them?"

The Shining Demon came to a stop somewhere to her left. "Your parents, their friends, they have ideas above their station. Ambitions. Some might say blasphemies. But a deal is a deal – I cannot break my part any more than they can break theirs. I cannot take back their power, or alter the terms of the bargain I made with them. But there may still be a way for me to help you. What are you willing to give in return?"

She swallowed. "There's someone you made a deal with, years ago. He cheated you."

"Nobody cheats me, child."

"This one did. You gave him what he wanted and then he ran. He never held up his end of the bargain. Do you remember him?"

The Shining Demon paused for a moment. "I know the one you speak of."

"I can find him. I can find him for you."

"Do you know where he is?"

"No, but I can find out. I think I can find out."

"Interesting," he said.

"Do we have a deal?"

"If you do find him, Amber, then we will talk of deals." Bare feet on stone. He was walking away.

"No," she said.

A sound, like the sharp intake of breath, whistled through the room.

"No?" he echoed.

She had the feeling she had just committed a serious breach of demonic etiquette, but carried on regardless. "I want your word that we'll have a deal if I bring him to you."

"Is that what you want? Truly?"

"Yes," she said, with what she hoped was steely resolve.

He moved closer. "A time limit, then," he said. "How long will you need?"

"Uh... six weeks?" she said, doubling what Imelda had suggested.

"You have three," said the Shining Demon, and Amber did her best not to grimace. "Twenty-one days. Five hundred and four hours."

"And... and then you'll protect me from my parents?"

He was standing right in front of her now. "I cannot alter the terms of the deal I struck with them, but, if you bring me this man in the time allotted, I will alter *you*, Amber. Your blood will be poison. To consume you would mean death."

"But I'll be all right, yes?"

That smile, appearing again in his voice. "Your blood will be poison to everyone but you. You have my word. Do I have yours?"

"I... I guess. What's his name? The man who cheated you?"

"I can give you no more help. I am extending my hand to you — shake it, and we will have a deal."

"I... I can't reach out of the circle," Amber said.

"Come now," the Shining Demon responded. "Tradition must be upheld or the bargain is not binding."

"I was told not to leave the circle."

"You are still standing in it, are you not?"

Amber bit her lip, then slowly reached her hand out.

The Shining Demon grabbed her hand and twisted, and Amber cried out and screwed her eyes shut tighter as he pressed a fingertip into her wrist. It burned.

"Five hundred and four hours," said the Shining Demon as he moved his finger. "If you fail to bring this man to me in the allotted time, your soul is forfeit."

"No!" Amber cried, trying to pull away. "I didn't agree to that!"

"Those are the terms," the Shining Demon said, and released her so suddenly that she nearly stumbled out of the circle.

She turned away from him, clutching her right hand as she cracked her eyes open. The number 504 was burned into the inside of her wrist, a mark, a brand that was already hardening into a scar. The pain faded quickly. "I didn't agree to this," she said. "I didn't—"

A wind rushed in from all five corridors, a dank wind that

brought with it hints of rot and sickly perfume and overripe fruit and human waste, and the wind extinguished the circle of fire and Amber was outside again, in Miami, and Milo was rushing forward to catch her as she fell.

11

Milo woke Amber before five, stirring her from a fitful sleep. She had dreamed of demons and horns and the castles of hell, and she had dreamed of her parents chasing her. She had dreamed of herself as a monster, drenched in blood.

She turned over in her cot and cried silently.

When she had showered and dressed, she joined Milo in the kitchen. He'd made himself a coffee, and poured a juice for her. They drank in silence, listening to the soft sounds of snoring that drifted from Edgar's bedroom. He had gone to sleep like an excited schoolboy after quizzing Amber about everything she had seen and heard. Her entire experience was now on paper, told through the crazy scribbles and hieroglyphics that was Edgar's handwriting.

Everything except the time limit, the number that was now burned into her wrist. She wasn't going to embark on this journey with Milo already viewing her as a screw-up. If she could come away with only one thing from all this craziness, it was going to be the respect of the people around her.

Her wrist ached slightly, and she glanced at it. The numbers now read 500.

Four hours gone already.

Amber pulled her sleeve down quickly to cover it, as Milo laid the map he was perusing on the countertop. "Wisconsin," he said, tapping the old, creased paper. "And right here is Springton, Dacre Shanks's old hunting ground. It's about fifteen hundred miles from here. We'll be taking I-75 for some of it, but we're going to be doing our best to stay away from traffic. Your folks will be pulling out all the stops by now, and we don't want to be spotted by any of their people."

"How long will it take?"

"Twenty hours of driving, maybe twenty-two, if we were taking the quickest route. But because we're not... I don't know. Add another six hours on at the least. Twenty-eight hours on the road, driving eight hours a day, is a little over three days."

"We can drive more than eight hours a day," said Amber. "I've got my learner's permit: we can alternate."

"We won't be alternating."

"Why not?"

"Because I'm the driver," said Milo, in a tone that suggested finality, "and we're taking my car, and, while I'll be able to travel longer at the start, it's going to quickly average out at eight hours a day of driving time. You don't have to know why. You just have to know that those are the rules."

"Whatever," she muttered. Three days to get there, maybe a day to find Shanks and talk to him, which would leave her with seventeen days to find the man they was looking for and deliver him to the Shining Demon. Plenty of time.

"We'll need to change vehicles before we leave Miami, though," Milo said.

Amber frowned. "You think my parents know what we're driving already?"

"It's not that," Milo said, shaking his head. "For a trip like this, we need a special kind of car." He took her empty glass, and washed it and his mug in the sink. "I'm also going to need an advance on the money, by the way."

"How much?"

"Five grand ought to do it."

"Right…"

He looked back at her. "You think I'm going to abscond with it?"

"No," she said quickly. "No, not at all, it's just—"

"You don't know me," said Milo, putting the mug and glass down to drain. "Imelda does, but you don't. You don't know if I'm trustworthy."

"She trusts you."

"But you don't. And why would you? I've done nothing to earn your trust. Handing over five grand to a guy you've just met and whom you don't yet trust would seem to be a stupid thing to do."

"So I shouldn't give you the money?"

"No, you should," he said. "I'm just pointing out the corner you've been backed into. Trust me or not trust me, you're going to give me the money because you don't have a choice."

"I'm confused," said Amber. "Is this a life lesson I should be making a note of?"

"Something like that."

"I don't suppose you're going to tell me what that lesson is, are you?"

"You'll never learn it if I just tell you," Milo said. "Ready to go?"

"Uh yeah, OK," she said. "Should we say goodbye to Edgar?"

He frowned. "Why?"

"Because that's what people do. They say hello, how are you, goodbye, and they say thanks for your help."

"Edgar doesn't need any of that." Milo folded the map, and Amber watched how it shrank into a neat little packet. She'd never have been able to do that so cleanly.

It had stopped raining. They got into the SUV, and she passed him a money roll. He flicked through it, counting the five thousand, and nodded. She lay across the back seat, the blanket over her once again. Milo turned on the headlights and they got back on the turnpike. The roads were still quiet.

It was warm under the blanket. Amber yawned, closed her eyes. She wasn't going to sleep. Sleep meant bad dreams. Sleep meant monsters. But when she opened her eyes and sat up they were pulling up outside a dark house somewhere in outer suburbia, the sky only just beginning to lighten, birdsong threading the pale air.

"Grab your stuff," Milo said.

They got out and took their bags from the back. Amber stood holding hers while she watched Milo go round to the passenger side. He opened up the glove compartment, took out a gun, and clipped the holster on to his belt. Then he closed the door, pressed the fob, and the SUV beeped and locked.

"Are you a cop, or something?" she asked.

"No," he said.

He walked into the darkness between two houses. He didn't tell her to follow him or to stay, so she hoisted her bag over her shoulder and she followed. They came to the side door of a garage. Milo took out his wallet, searched inside it for a moment, and came out with a key. He opened the door and went inside. Amber waited a few seconds, then followed.

He shut the door after her, and locked it. Amber stood in complete darkness. The window had been boarded up. Milo moved around her.

"Is there a light in here?" she asked.

"No," he answered.

She dug into her shorts, came out with the matchbook that Edgar had given her. She struck one and light flared.

A long table against one wall contained all manner of tools and engine parts. She could suddenly smell oil, like the curiously sweet aroma had been holding itself back until she could see what she was smelling. A car covered by a tarp took up most of the space in the garage.

"You took his matches, huh?" Milo said, putting his bag on the table.

"Oh. Uh yeah. I forgot to give them back. I didn't think it'd be a big deal."

"Don't worry about it," Milo said. "I took the powder flask."

Her eyes widened. "He paid a lot of money for that. Isn't he going to be mad when he finds out?"

"Don't see why he would be," said Milo, moving to the tarp. "It works for you and you're going to need it again, with any luck. Why would he be mad about that?"

"Because it's not mine."

"Edgar doesn't care about things like ownership. He doesn't even own the condo he's living in."

"He's renting it?"

"He's stolen it."

Amber frowned. "How can you steal a condo?"

"By pretending to be the son of the elderly owner so that you can ship her off to a home for the infirm."

She gaped. "That's horrible!"

"Not really," said Milo. "The owner used to be a nurse who mistreated her patients. Edgar made sure everyone in the home knew about it, too."

"Oh," said Amber. "Well, I guess that's okay, then."

Milo pulled back the tarp, revealing a black car, an old one, the kind Amber had seen in movies, with a long hood and a sloping back.

"Nice," she said.

He looked at her sharply. "Nice?"

She hesitated. "It's pretty. What is it?"

"It's a 1970 Dodge Charger, and it is a *she*."

"Right," said Amber. "She's very nice, then."

Milo walked round the car, looking at it lovingly.

"The reason we can only travel eight hours a day," said Amber, "is it because your car will fall apart if we go longer?"

"You see any rust?" Milo asked, not rising to the bait. "Storing an old car in this humidity is not generally a good idea, not for any length of time, let alone twelve years. But she's different. She is pristine. Under the hood there she's got the 440 Six Pack, three two-barrel carburettors and 390 horses. She's a beast."

"Yeah. Words. Cool."

His hand hovered over the roof, like he was unsure as to whether or not he should actually touch it. Then he did, and his eyes closed and Amber wondered if she should leave him to it.

"You, uh, really love this car, huh?"

"She was my life," he said softly.

"Yeah. This is getting weird."

He opened the door, paused, and slid in. Sitting behind the wheel, his face in shadow, he looked for a moment like just another part of the car. She heard the keys jangle and she backed away from the hood. If the car really hadn't been started in twelve years, she doubted anything was going to happen, but she didn't want to be standing there if it suddenly blew up.

And yet, when Milo turned the key in the ignition, the garage reverberated with a deep and throaty growl that rose through the soles of Amber's feet and quickened her pulse. It was impressive, she had to admit that.

Milo flicked the headlights on and they shone blood-red for a moment, before fading to a strong yellow.

"Cool," she whispered, and this time she meant it.

12

THEY STUCK TO RESIDENTIAL roads as much as they could on their way out of Florida, staying off the expressway and I-95. Like she'd done in the SUV, Amber had to lie on the back seat, covered. She closed her eyes, but didn't sleep – not at first. Instead, she listened to the Charger. It creaked when it turned. It seemed *heavy*. There was no confusing it with its modern counterparts, cars that acted as cocoons against the world around them. To ride in a modern car was to ride in a deprivation tank – to ride in the Charger was to ride in a streamlined behemoth of black metal. *A beast*, as Milo called it.

Amber examined her hand, tried to remember what her claws had looked like. She was a beast, too, of course. A monster. Not a monster like her parents, though. They were predators – heartless and lethal. No, Amber was the prey, all innocence and vulnerability – except when she had her claws out.

The way she had punched that boy – Brandon, his name was Brandon – hadn't been weak. She probably would have killed him if she'd hit him any harder. She wondered if she *could* have hit him harder. She wondered how strong she was. She wondered what she looked like. Imelda was more beautiful as a demon than as a person. Her parents, too, had been taller and stronger and more beautiful. Amber wondered if the transformation would have the same effect on her, and found herself wondering what she'd look like taller, and slimmer, and prettier. She hoped her eyes didn't change, though. She liked her eyes.

She woke when they reached Homerville, across the state line in Georgia. Milo gave her a baseball cap and told her she could sit up front if she pulled the cap low over her brow. The further they got from Miami, he said, the safer she'd be. It was midday now. They passed through Pearson, and then Hazlehurst, and then Soperton — all brown grass and tall trees and identical houses with mailboxes by the road — and not one word was spoken the whole time.

"Thanks for doing this," Amber said to fill the silence.

Milo nodded, didn't say anything.

"I know I'm paying you, and this is just a job, but I didn't thank you earlier. I should have."

He didn't say anything to that, either.

A few minutes passed before she said, "Is this what it's going to be like the whole way?"

He didn't take his eyes off the road. "What is this like?"

"You know," said Amber, "the silence. The awkward, heavy, awkward silence."

"You used awkward twice."

"It's very awkward."

"I like to drive in silence. It lets you think."

"What do you do when you're done thinking? Or if you've got nothing to think about? Does the radio work? Maybe we could put on some music."

"But then we wouldn't be in silence."

She sighed. "You're really not listening to me."

"I like to drive in silence," said Milo again. "You're paying me, but this is my car and, since I like to drive in silence, we drive in silence. That's just the way it is."

"Even though it makes me uncomfortable?"

He shrugged. "If you can't stand to be alone with your thoughts, maybe there's something wrong with your thoughts."

"Of course there's something wrong with my thoughts. I'm going through a very tough time."

"We all go through tough times."

"My parents are trying to kill me."

"We all have issues."

"Maybe I'm suffering from post-traumatic stress. Did you think of that? Did Imelda? No. She just offloaded me on to you and now here we are. I probably need major psychiatric attention and you won't even let me listen to calm, soothing music. I could have a breakdown at any moment."

"You seem fine to me," said Milo, not taking his eyes off the road. The endless, straight, monotonous grey road.

"I'm a demon," she said.

"Like I said, we all have issues."

Amber glared. "Talking to you is like talking to a... a... Whatever."

She folded her arms and directed her glare out of the window. She didn't intend to go to sleep.

She woke to farmland and trees, a full bladder and a rumbling stomach. "Where are we?"

"Outside Atlanta," said Milo. "You can go back to sleep if you like."

She sat up straighter, pulled her cap off. "No. If I sleep any more, I won't be able to sleep tonight." The thought struck her. "Where *are* we sleeping tonight?"

"We'll find a motel."

"It better be a nice one. I've seen motels on TV and they look horrible." They approached a gas station. "Can we stop here? I'm starving. And thirsty."

"There's a bottle of water in the glove box," said Milo, and didn't slow down.

She gaped as they drove by. "*Seriously?* Why didn't you stop? I need food!"

"We're going to be stopping in an hour or so to fill the tank – you can eat then. It's going to be the first full tank she's had in twelve years."

"Is that so? Well, isn't that lovely? I am really, really happy for your *car*, Milo, but what about me?"

"Your parents and their friends, with all their vast resources, are searching for you. I'm not going to stop this car unless I absolutely have to. Now drink your water."

She punched the release for the glove box. It popped open and a bottle of water rolled off the stack of maps into her hand. She looked at the gun in its holster, sitting quietly in the light cast by the small bulb, and closed it up.

"I also have to pee," she said, twisting the cap off.

"Hold it in."

Right before she took a swig of water, she scowled. "I'm not sure I like you."

Milo shrugged. That annoyed her even more.

The water soothed her parched throat, but she didn't drink much of it – her bladder was full enough as it was. "We must have driven more than eight hours by now, right?" she asked. "We've been on the road since before seven. It's almost five now. That's, like… ten hours."

"It took you a disturbingly long while to add that up."

"Whatever. So why can you only drive for eight hours?"

"On average."

Amber sighed. "Why can you only drive for eight hours *on average?*"

"Because that's my rule."

She looked at him. "You're not a sharer, are you? Okay, fine, let's keep this professional. Let's keep this employer and employee. Let's talk about, like, the mission. What do you know about this Dacre Shanks guy?"

"Just what Edgar told us."

"What do you think he'll be like? Do you think he'll be nice?"

"There are no nice serial killers."

"Well, I know that," said Amber, "but he's not going to kill us on sight or anything, is he?"

"Don't know." Milo took a small iPad from his jacket. "Look him up."

She grabbed it off him. "*You're* allowed to have internet access, but I'm not? How is that fair?"

"Because your parents have no idea who I am, whereas they've undoubtedly got their eyes on your email account."

"Oh," she said. "Oh yeah."

She tapped on the screen for the search engine and put in Shanks's name.

"Dacre Shanks," she read, "the serial killer known as the Family Man. Oh God, do you know what he did? He kidnapped people that looked alike to make up a perfect family. Then he killed them all and started again. Says here he killed over three dozen people before he was shot to death, most of them in and around Springton, Wisconsin. We're actually going to try to talk to this guy?"

"All we need him to do is give us the name of the man who cheated the Shining Demon."

"And why should he give it to us when he didn't give it to Edgar?"

"Because Edgar posed no threat," Milo said. "Whereas we do."

"Do we? He's a serial killer who, like, came back from the grave. I know you've got your guns and you're really good at being horrible to people, but do you seriously think you can threaten him?"

Milo frowned. "I'm not horrible to people."

"Really? You really don't think you're horrible to people?"

"No," he said, a little defensively. "I'm nice. Everyone says it."

"Oh man," said Amber. "People have lied to you. Like, a lot. But even if we could threaten him – is that a good idea, to threaten a serial killer who's come back from the dead?"

"I've threatened worse."

"Worse how?"

"Just worse."

She sighed. "Fine. Don't elaborate. How are we supposed to find him, anyway? What if he isn't in Springton anymore?"

"We'll find him," said Milo. "We're on the blackroads now."

"The what?"

"Guy I knew once called them the blackroads – roads connecting points of darkness, criss-crossing America. Stay on the blackroads and you'll eventually meet every unholy horror the country has to offer. It's a network. Some people call it the Dark Highway, or the Demon Road. It's never the same route twice and there are no maps to guide the way."

"Then how do you know we're on it?"

"I've travelled it before. So has this car. You get the feeling for it."

Amber looked at him for a quiet moment. "Sometimes I think you just make stuff up."

13

MILO PULLED THE CHARGER up to a pump at a truck stop and Amber was allowed out. She stepped on to the forecourt and stretched, arching her spine and feeling it crack. The afternoon wasn't much cooler than the afternoons she'd endured in Orlando. It was hot and the sun was bright and the air was laden with moisture. A truck roared by on the road, rustling the trees on the far side and kicking up mini-tornadoes of dust that danced around Amber's bare calves.

The place was pretty run-down. Desperate blades of grass surged from cracks in the ground like drowning men in a sea of concrete. A long building with a sagging roof and dirty windows identified itself as a Family Restaurant. The letter E was missing from the sign outside, turning EAT HERE into EAT HER. Amber turned her back on it.

Beyond the fence there was corn, miles of it, and a clump of sorry-looking forest behind the truck stop itself. An old Coca-Cola billboard was rusting and peeling on a metal strut.

"Hey," said Milo, and she turned and he tossed her the baseball cap over the roof of the car. "Head down at all times.

Just because you can't see a CCTV camera doesn't mean it can't see you."

She pulled the cap low. "You really think my parents would be able to find me here? In Florida, okay, they probably have cops and officials doing whatever they want, but we're not in Florida anymore."

"Your folks have been around for over a hundred years," Milo said, sliding the nozzle in. "Let's not underestimate how far their reach spreads."

The gas started pumping and Amber headed round the side of the station, following the sign for the restroom. The clerk, a bored-looking guy in his fifties, didn't even glance up as she passed his window.

The restroom was empty and relatively clean. The early evening sun came in through the three windows up near the ceiling. Amber chose the only cubicle with a toilet seat, and when she was done she washed her hands in the sink. The mirror was dirty but intact, and she took off her cap and looked at her reflection. Butterflies fluttered deep in her belly.

You just decide you want to shift, and you shift, Imelda had said. Amber decided she wanted to shift, but her body ignored her. She tried again. She tried to remember how it had happened in Imelda's apartment, how it had happened when she'd bitten that finger off, but she couldn't even come close to replicating those feelings.

Did she even want to? What if she shifted and she couldn't shift back? What if she became stuck as a demon, unable to revert? No matter how much she tried to cover up, someone was bound to see, and then word would reach her parents and they'd come after her, the predators after their prey.

Amber looked into her own eyes. She hated being the prey. She commanded her body to change and this time it obeyed.

The pain blossomed and she cried out, and even as she was doing so she was watching her reflection. Her skin darkened to a glorious red in the time it would have taken her to blush. Her bones creaked and throbbed and her body lengthened — her legs, her torso, her arms. Her feet jammed tight in her sneakers. She was suddenly tall, suddenly slim. Her face was longer, her jawline defined, her cheekbones raised and sharpened. It was still her face, but her features were altered. Her lips were plumper. Her brown hair was black now, and longer, the tangles straightened.

Dizziness, an astonishing wave of vertigo, nearly took her to the ground. She gripped the edge of the sink, kept herself standing, unable and unwilling to look away from the beautiful demon in the mirror.

And she was beautiful. Her skin, though red, was flawless. Her teeth — pointed now, and sharp like fangs — were white and straight. Her raised cheekbones changed everything. Only her eyes had stayed the same. She was glad about that.

And, of course, there were her horns. Black horns, like ribbed ebony, curling out from her forehead and sweeping back. Breathtaking to behold.

Although her shorts looked shorter on her longer legs, they were now baggier, and threatened to slip off her hips. She pulled the neckline of her T-shirt to either side, revealing hard black scales that travelled across her shoulders.

She looked at her hands. They were small no more. They were good hands, strong hands, not small and weak like they had always been. Her fingernails were black, but there was something else, an itch in her fingertips. She curled her right hand and her nails lengthened to claws so suddenly it actually frightened her. She gripped her right wrist with her other hand, not trusting this new and alien appendage not to suddenly attack her. She concentrated, and the claws retracted at her command.

"Awesome," she whispered. This was how it was meant to feel, she was sure. Shifting was supposed to make her feel strong, and powerful, and confident. Not scared, not like she'd been in Imelda's apartment. Not panicked, like she'd been when she'd smashed that boy's jaw.

Brandon, she reminded herself. *His name was Brandon.*

Then the door opened, and a broad woman in a trucker's cap barged in, making it halfway to the cubicles before she even noticed there was somebody else there.

Frozen, they looked at each other with wide eyes. Then the trucker spun on her heel. Spun to flee. Spun to call the cops. And with the cops would come her parents.

"No, wait!" Amber said, lunging after her. She caught the woman before she reached the door, pushed her a little harder than she'd intended. The trucker slammed into the wall.

"Sorry," said Amber, "sorry, but—"

The trucker took something from her belt. A clasp knife. She flicked it open and Amber held up her hands.

"No, wait, I'm sorry, please—"

But the trucker was too scared, too adrenalised, to listen. She rushed forward and Amber backpedalled, losing track of the knife. Immediately, she felt her skin tighten. Her hip hit the sink and the trucker stabbed her right in the belly.

Amber gasped, more from shock than pain. She expected the pain to follow. The trucker stabbed again, and again.

Still nothing.

Amber got her hand up, dug her fingertips into the trucker's face, and forced her back. Her other hand grabbed the woman's knife hand, gripping the wrist, keeping the blade away from her. It suddenly became clear to Amber that all she had was strength. She had no idea what to do next.

The trucker was more streetwise. She slammed her free arm on to Amber's elbow and punched her. It wasn't a particularly strong punch – she was obviously right-handed and she'd been forced to punch with her left – but her fist still connected with Amber's nose and tears still came to Amber's eyes. Anger flared, and she pulled the trucker in and threw a punch of her own. Her fist, which had grown black scales across the knuckles, collided with the trucker's jaw and sent her spinning into the far wall. The knife fell as the trucker hit the hand-dryer, its roar filling the room.

The trucker regained her balance, her eyes focusing once more. Amber stood across from her, only dimly aware that she was snarling. The woman broke for the door.

"I said don't!" Amber shouted. The trucker got to the handle and was pulling the door open when Amber reached her. She got a hand to the woman's head and bounced it off the door, slamming it closed. Amber pulled her back like the trucker weighed no more than a child, and threw her against the cubicle wall. It caved in under her weight and the woman crumpled to the floor. The hand-dryer deactivated.

Amber stood over the trucker to make sure she wasn't getting up. After a moment, Amber frowned, and knelt by her. She felt for a pulse. Couldn't find one. Alarmed, she rolled the woman on to her back, only then noticing the steady rise and fall of her chest. Amber checked the pulse again, searching for a few seconds until she found it.

She stood, and lifted her shirt as she turned to the mirror. Her belly was covered in those black scales, like armour. Even as she watched, though, they were retracting.

The trucker moaned.

Amber bolted into the sunlight. A car passed on the road and she dropped to her knees behind a pallet of chopped wood wrapped in plastic. When the car was gone, she was up, running bent over, making for the shelter of a parked truck, then the trees beyond.

She plunged into the shade and kept going, the trees quickly becoming a wood. Her horns bounced off a few low-lying branches and she ducked her head as she continued, following the sounds of water. She walked for a minute or two, and then light dazzled her eyes. For a heart-stopping moment, she thought the Shining Demon had come for her, but it was only the sun glinting off the surface of a slow-moving river.

Amber looked back. Listened. No sounds of pursuit. No cries of alarm.

She lifted her T-shirt again. The black scales were gone. Her belly was flat, toned, and uninjured.

She pulled off her clothes, left them in a pile and examined herself. Her arms, though red, were devoid of any black scales. She could see her muscles now, rolling beneath her skin. She held her right arm up and curled it, popped her bicep, and laughed out loud. She was strong. She was seriously strong. She had a strength that belied even her new and impressive muscles.

When she'd punched the trucker, scales had grown up over her knuckles. That time, their growth had been natural, instinctive. This time, she closed her fist and concentrated. The skin around her knuckles tightened, and black scales pushed their way, painlessly, to the surface. She focused on her hand now, and felt the skin tighten and watched the scales spread.

She held both hands out. Black scales grew, covering her hands and forearms. She looked down at herself. Her feet were now encased in them. Then her legs. Her belly and her chest. Her neck. Amber took a breath and closed her eyes and felt her face tighten, and the scales grew to cover her head.

She opened her eyes. Her eyelids hadn't grown scales, and neither, thankfully, had her nostrils or mouth — though when she tried opening her mouth wide she found she couldn't. She tapped her fingers between her horns and along her scalp, feeling the scales that had flattened her hair.

She walked to the river and gazed at her own rippling image.

Clad in her armour, she smiled.

She turned her fingers into claws, taking a moment to appreciate just how big, and how monstrous, her normally small hands had become. Then she went to the nearest tree, hesitated, and drew her fingernails across the trunk, leaving four deep grooves in her wake.

She did it again, faster this time. Then again. And then she slashed at the tree, carving out narrow chunks. If she could do that to a tree, what could she do to a person?

The thought disturbed her, threatened to dim her smile. But she shook it off, stepped back and leaped, her hands digging into the tree, and she climbed like she was born to do it. The tree swayed outwards and she went with it, until she was hanging over the river. Practically upside down. Amber laughed, exhilarated. Even her feet seemed to be digging in. Then she made the mistake of glancing at them.

Her feet were misshapen things, her toes as long as her new fingers, and every one of them curled around the tree.

The shock, the panic, the idea that she had deformed herself beyond repair, shot through her and her feet returned to normal and so did her hands. She fell, crying out, twisting in mid-air and then landing in the water.

The scales retracted as soon as she was submerged. When she'd regained her wits, she powered to the surface, already calming. She trod water for a bit, waiting for her heart to stop hammering so hard, then lengthened out and swam for the far side, marvelling at how effortless it all was. A few strokes and she was there. She turned, swam underwater the whole way back. Her fingers brushed silt along the riverbed.

Amber spent another few minutes just swimming. Skinny-dipping. She laughed as she did the backstroke. She'd never been skinny-dipping in her life. She'd never thought she'd ever get the chance. She never thought she'd ever have the confidence. And now here she was, in all her red splendour, in a river somewhere in Georgia. Were they still in Georgia? She wasn't even sure. That just made her laugh more.

The laugh died when she got the feeling that she was being watched.

She looked around. She could see no one in the woods on either side of the river, but the feeling didn't go away. She swam back, hesitating before pulling herself out of the water, then moved up on to the grassy bank towards her clothes.

She was halfway up when she saw the face staring at her through the foliage.

14

AMBER DARTED BEHIND A tree, as much to hide her nakedness as her black horns. Behind cover, she cursed silently, and immediately started looking around for an escape route. There was no way she could get away without being seen. Her only hope was that the person, whoever it was, would be freaked out enough to run away, but not freaked out enough to report the sighting.

She saw the face again in her mind. Shaggy hair – light brown. A boy. No, a young man. Maybe eighteen or nineteen.

"Hello?"

Amber stiffened.

"Hello? Miss?"

She shut her eyes and didn't reply. Silence, she decided, was her best option at this point.

"I know you're there," the boy said. He had an accent. English? Scottish? "I saw you run behind the tree. You know I saw you. I don't get why you're pretending you're not there."

No. Irish. That was it.

"This is getting a little bit silly," he continued. "This is like when my little cousins play hide-and-seek and they close their eyes because they think that makes them invisible. You... You're not closing your eyes, are you?"

Amber hesitated, then opened her eyes, and cursed silently again.

"I didn't mean to peek," he said. "My name's Glen. Glen Morrison. I was just passing, and... Well, no, that's not strictly true. Sorry, I don't want to start off on a lie, you know? The truth is, I've been sleeping here for the past few nights. In these woods. I'm temporarily between abodes, and my financial situation is not what one might call robust. I don't want you to get the wrong idea, though. I'm not lazy. I didn't come over to your country to scam the system or anything like that. I do have prospects. Well, I *had* prospects. It's a very long story, and I wouldn't want to trouble you with—"

"Glen," Amber said.

There was a pause, and then, "You're talking!"

"I am," said Amber. "Glen, I'm naked."

She could practically hear him nod. "I noticed. I mean, oh God, I mean I couldn't help but notice that you were... that you had no... that you were, uh... oh man, what's the word?"

"Naked," Amber prompted.

"Yes, thank you. Naked. You are naked, yes."

"And since I'm naked, Glen, I find having a conversation with a complete stranger a little weird. You know?"

"Oh, I do," Glen said, with an assurance that made it sound like it was a situation he found himself in regularly.

"I'm not sure that you do, Glen."

"Probably not," he admitted. "But, if it makes you feel any better, you don't have anything to feel embarrassed about."

"You're not helping, Glen."

"Sorry. I like your horns, though. Is that rude? Can I say that?"

"Glen… would you please go away?"

"Oh," he said. "Oh. But… Yeah. I mean… right. Sure. Of course. You're naked. You want to be alone. I come along, you feel self-conscious. Obviously. That's natural. That's perfectly natural. I'm intruding upon your special me time."

"And when you go away," Amber said, "could you please not tell anyone about this? About me?"

"Sure," he said, sounding disappointed. "Okay. Well, I suppose I'll just… head off, then."

"Thank you," Amber called.

She waited to hear his retreating footsteps, then waited a bit longer.

"Glen," she said, "are you still there?"

"Yeah," he answered. "Listen, I don't want you to think any less of me, all right? But… but I may need to check your clothes and steal any money you might have."

Amber's eyes snapped wide. "What?"

"I just don't want this to make things weird between us," he said, and then came the sound of rustling fabric as her shorts were lifted off the ground.

"Do not rob me," she called.

"I'm really sorry."

"Do not frikkin' rob me, you little creep!"

"I feel really bad about this."

She pictured him rifling through her pockets, his grubby little hand closing around the roll of cash she'd put in there. She concentrated on growing those scales again, and felt her skin begin to tighten. Then she heard a sharp intake of breath. Glen had found the money.

The scales didn't cover her entire body but they did enough to protect her modesty. Anger boiling, she lunged out from behind the tree, but her horns got tangled in the branches and her feet flew from under her, and she crashed heavily to the ground. She felt some of the scales retract. Glen stared down at her, open-mouthed.

"Wow," he whispered.

She snarled, showing him her fangs, and his eyes went wide. He dropped the money and spun, but Amber was right behind him, faster than he could ever hope to be. She grabbed the collar of his jacket and he shrieked as he was launched backwards.

"Do you know what I've just done?" she growled as she stalked after him. "I've just broken some poor woman's bones in the gas station. I threw her around like she was nothing and then I went for a goddamn *swim*. You think I'd hesitate for even one moment before I ripped your throat out for *robbing* me?"

Glen scrambled back on all fours. "Please, I didn't mean anything!"

"You meant to steal from me."

"I'm starving!"

She leaped, landing on top of him in a crouch, her right hand closing round his neck and pinning him to the ground. "Not my problem."

He looked up at her, tears in his eyes, and those tears just made her angrier. She wanted nothing more than to grow talons, to feel them slice into the soft meat, to sink her teeth in, to feel that warm blood flow down her...

She blinked. Wait, *what?*

She loosened her grip. The impulse to tear his throat open was rapidly receding.

"Are you going to kill me?" he whispered.

"No," she said dully, and stood. "No, I'm... I'm not going to kill you. I wanted to. I was going to. But..."

"I wouldn't worry about it," he said. "Something's going to kill me sooner or later. Most likely sooner, to be honest. If I had a choice, I'd prefer it to be you."

Amber took a few steps back, then turned, walked to her clothes. She let her scales retract fully as she pulled them on, ignoring the uncomfortable feeling of dry fabric on wet skin. Still frowning to herself, she sat on a log to wipe the soles of her feet before putting on her socks and sneakers.

"Your clothes don't fit you, y'know," Glen said.

He was tall and skinny, scruffy but not bad-looking. He bent to pick up her roll of money and she bared her teeth. He walked over slowly and held out his hand.

Amber finished tying her laces and stood, taking her money without a word and stuffing it back into her pocket.

"You should probably invest in a wallet," he said.

"Shut up, Glen," said Amber.

He nodded. "Yeah. That's fair."

She turned away from him, hiked her shorts up to her waist, and started walking back towards the gas station.

He caught up to her. "Can I ask a question, though? What are you?"

"What do I look like?"

"Honestly? A demon."

"Then there you have it."

He nodded. "You'd think that'd shock me, right? Meeting a

demon? A few weeks ago, it would have, but my life has taken a pretty weird turn lately, so I've adopted a policy of complete and utter credulity in all things. It saves everyone a lot of time. These days I don't ask for proof or reasons or anything. I just accept. That doesn't mean I'm not curious, of course. I'm very curious. I mean, look at you. A real live demon, just walking around. Do you live down here?"

"Down where?"

"Here. In the woods."

She frowned. "Are you stupid? Why would I live in the woods?"

"Well, I just thought, y'know…"

"Stop following me."

"Okay. Right. But can I ask another question? Why do you have money? How do you buy stuff?"

She stopped walking and turned to him. "How do you think I buy stuff? I walk into a store and say I want something and I pay for it."

He frowned. "You walk into a shop like that?"

She remembered her appearance. "Oh," she said. "No. This is new. I'm still getting used to it. I keep forgetting I have horns."

"They are magnificent," he breathed, staring at them.

"Eyes down here, Glen."

"Yes, sorry." He blushed. "You're… Sorry. You're just the most beautiful girl I've ever seen. Like, prettier than most actresses and models, even."

Amber grunted, and started walking again. "This isn't the real me."

"No, it is," Glen said, matching her pace. "Like, you're

beautiful in a way that I've never seen before. Everything about you, your face, your horns, your amazing teeth, your skin that's my favourite shade of red, your legs, your body, your—"

"You can stop anytime now."

"I'm not scared," he said. "You might think I'm scared of you because you're a demon and most people would be scared of demons, and that's why you put up this wall, to reject others before they reject you, but I'm really not scared. You're not scary. You're beautiful, not ugly. And I've seen some ugly things. I mean, I really have. Back in Ireland, I was attacked by this, by this *creature*, you know? It passed something on to me, the Deathmark. Wanna see it?"

"Not really."

He held out his right hand, proudly showing her his palm. Just below the surface of his skin, a tendril of darkness circled like a fish in a bowl. "Isn't it freaky? Ever since it happened, I've been meeting the oddest people. I met this guy in Dublin, this real weird guy, knows all about monsters and stuff. He said this thing will kill me in forty days if I don't pass it on to its intended target. That was, like, thirty-two days ago."

"You're going to die in eight days?" said Amber, frowning.

He nodded, and seemed oddly unbothered about it. "Unless I pass this mark on to a woman called Abigail. Apparently, she's a bad person. Like, really bad. Killed a lot of people, that kind of bad. I'll be doing the world a favour by passing this on to her. That's what I was told. She's supposed to be in a bar here in America that I haven't been able to find – The Dark Stair. You know it?"

"Sorry."

"Yeah, me neither. I looked it up online and nothing. I don't even know what state it's in. Maybe I'll find it, maybe I won't, but I'm here now, y'know? If I die, I want to die *here*. I want to see bigger things before I go, better things than the creature that attacked me. I want to see proper monsters. American monsters. I didn't think I'd see anything as beautiful as you, though."

"Right," said Amber. "Well, I better get going."

"Where are you off to?"

"Oh, uh, Springton. It's in Wisconsin. We have to find someone."

"We? Who's we? You and your boyfriend?"

"No, no. He's a… he's a guide, I guess."

"A guide to what?"

"Um…"

Glen's eyes widened. "Are you on the Demon Road?"

She hesitated. "No."

"You are!"

"We're not."

Glen was practically dancing in excitement. "I'm on the Demon Road, too! The guy, the weird guy, he said I should get on the Demon Road while I still had the chance, to see all the horrors the world had to offer. We're on the same road! What are the chances? Do you have a car?"

"No," Amber said automatically. Then, "I mean, I don't, personally. My friend does."

"Yeah? Do you think he'd let me tag along, like?"

"I… I don't mean to offend you or anything, but probably not. He doesn't know you and you *did* try to steal my money."

"I gave it back, though."

"Only after I caught you."

"That's true. But don't you think this is meant to be? I mean, what are the chances, really, of us meeting like this? Two people like us, cursed by darkness, meeting on the Demon Road?"

"According to my guide, they're actually pretty good."

"Oh. Really? Oh. Well, could you still ask him if there's room for one more?"

"Glen, you tried to rob me."

"Which turned out to be a mistake."

"And we're on a very dangerous journey, to be honest. We've got people coming after us and we're probably headed straight into even more danger, so I think it'd work out better for you if we just say goodbye here and now."

"But I don't have any other friends."

"You and me aren't friends, Glen."

He looked dismayed. "So I have no friends?"

"I have to get going."

She started walking again.

"I could help," he called after her. "And I wouldn't be a burden. I'd carry things, and I'd sit in the back and I wouldn't say anything, unless you needed me to say something, in which case I obviously would. Does your radio work? I could sing if it doesn't. I know a lot of songs. I don't have the best voice in the world and I might not remember every single one of the lyrics, or sing them in the right order, but I can carry a tune and I'll just make up the bits I forget. My dad used to do that all the time. It was like a gift he had, you know? Only he wasn't very good at it. I'm much better."

His voice eventually started to fade, and Amber left him behind. As she neared the edge of the woods, she focused on shifting back. What had Imelda called it? Reverting, that was it. She concentrated on her breathing, on calming down, on becoming her again, and, just when she thought it wasn't going to happen, an explosion of pain rocked her, made her stumble.

She put her shoulder to a tree and stayed there, blinking, her brown hair falling across her brow. She looked at her hand and noted the normal skin. She looked down and noted that her clothes fitted her once again. So that was normal, too, then.

Great.

15

A TANGLE OF BRIARS scraped across Amber's bare shin and she grimaced, bent down to rub it, then continued on. Moving through this little patch of forest had been easier as a demon – her red skin, even without the scales, was a lot hardier than the pale flesh she usually wore.

She felt the damp unpleasantness of her clothes more acutely now, too, as she did the embarrassment over a stranger seeing her naked. Both these sensations were washed away when she remembered what she'd done to that woman in the restroom. She could have killed her. She had *wanted* to kill Glen.

Amber forced herself to move on.

Emerging from the treeline further up from where she went in, she walked along the road back towards the truck stop. She kept her head down, really wishing she'd thought to grab the baseball cap as she ran from the restroom.

The throaty growl of the Charger's engine caught her by surprise, and she turned to watch it pull in sharply behind her.

Milo got out. He looked mad. She walked to the passenger side and he threw her the baseball cap. "Found this in the restroom," he said. "It was lying next to a woman who swore blind she'd been attacked by the Devil."

Amber put it on. "Um. Thanks."

They looked at each other over the roof of the car.

"I got you a sandwich," he said. "You can eat while we drive."

"It wasn't my fault," Amber said as Milo ducked to get in. "I shifted and she walked in. She pulled a knife, for God's sake!"

Milo straightened up. "She's fine, by the way."

Amber winced.

"A few nasty bruises. A dislocated shoulder. Maybe a fractured cheek. Definitely a concussion. But your concern over her wellbeing is touching."

"I get it, okay? You can stop now. I feel guilty enough as it is."

"I'm sure you do," said Milo. "But it isn't all bad. She's going to have a great story to tell, about the time she was attacked by a genuine, bona fide devil. A red-skinned devil with horns, no less. She's going to get some mileage out of that one. The cops have already been called, don't you worry."

Amber glared. "I just wanted to see what I looked like in a mirror. Is that so bad?"

"Not at all," said Milo. "Doing that in your bedroom mirror behind a locked door, no problem at all. Doing it in a truck-stop restroom, however..."

"Can we just go? Can we? Before the cops get here?"

"Sure." He hesitated, then looked at her again. "But I need you to understand something, Amber. This will catch the attention of your parents."

She blinked. "I'd... I'd..."

"You hadn't even considered that, had you?"

She frowned. "No. But I should have. What the *hell*?"

The expression on Milo's face softened. "What did Imelda tell you? Your demon side is more confident. You can take that to mean arrogant. And you can take *that* to mean self-centred. You're not going to be thinking too much of the consequences of your actions when you've got your horns on. That's what makes it so dangerous."

"Do you think they'll come here themselves?"

"I would, if I were them." A van passed on the road beside them. "We've lost our advantage. Up till now, they didn't know you were running; they just thought you were hiding. Now that they know, they'll be coming after you."

"I'm sorry," she said. "I'm so sorry."

He shrugged. "Come on, the sooner we get away, the better. At least no one here knows where we're headed."

Amber winced, and Milo froze.

"What?" he asked.

Dammit. Dammit, dammit, *dammit*. "Someone might know where we're going," she said.

Milo blinked at her. "I don't understand. Who did you find to talk to around here?"

"A guy. His name's Glen. I met him in the woods," she said. Then she added, "He's Irish."

"Oh well, he's Irish," said Milo. "That's okay, then. The Irish are renowned for how tight-lipped they are. What the *hell*, Amber?"

"I'm sorry, all right? I wasn't thinking."

"Some random guy in the woods?"

"He's not random," she responded, a little hotly. "He's like us. He's, you know... cursed by darkness."

Milo actually laughed. "He's what?"

"They're the words he used," she said, scowling. "And they're not too far away from what you said about the blackroads connecting points of darkness, whatever the hell that means. And, y'know, he's dying, actually. Glen. He's got the Deathmark."

"What's a Deathmark?"

"I... I thought you'd know."

"Edgar's the occult expert, not me."

"Well, the Deathmark is this thing that he has that's killing him, and he's on the Demon Road, too. He wants to see some real American monsters before he dies."

Milo rubbed a hand over his face. "He's going to get his chance."

"What do you mean?"

Milo folded his arms on the car roof and leaned on it. "People travelling the blackroads tend to meet, Amber. I told you that. Whether they're drawn to each other by some unconscious radar or it's all down to recurring coincidence or part of some grand scheme straight from hell, the fact is travellers tend to meet. That's why I'm confident of finding Dacre Shanks. But think who else is going to be on the blackroads. If your parents come here, and they will, and your new friend is still in the neighbourhood, the chances are they'll find him. And if he knows where we're going..."

"So... what do we do?"

Milo sagged. "We have two options."

Her eyes widened. "The first is killing him, isn't it? We're not doing that. We're not killing someone just because I made a mistake and said something I wasn't supposed to. What's the second option?"

"Convince him to come with us," Milo said. "Go get him. We'll take him as far as Springton and let him out there. If we have to tie him up and throw him in the back seat, we'll do that, too."

"I don't think convincing him will be a problem," said Amber. She turned, and started walking for the woods again.

"You have five minutes," said Milo. Amber didn't respond.

She retraced her steps until she found him. He was sitting on the same log she'd been sitting on, his elbows on his knees and his head down.

"Glen?"

He looked up quickly, but his hopeful smile vanished. "How do you know my name?"

She walked forward a few steps, and took off her cap. He regarded her suspiciously. Moments passed. His frown deepened, and then his eyebrows rose.

"You?"

"My name's Amber."

He jumped up. "But… but where's… what happened to you?"

"I told you, the skin and the horns are new. This is what I look like without them."

He couldn't take his eyes off her, but for entirely different reasons than before. "But what happened?" he asked. The look on his face was pure dismay.

Amber flushed with embarrassment and hurt. "I changed back," she said, putting the cap on again. "It doesn't matter. If you want to come with us, you can."

If she had asked him that while she was tall and red and beautiful, she knew he would have leaped for joy at the offer. As it was…

"Where are you going?" he asked doubtfully.

"Springton, Wisconsin," she said. "I told you."

He shrugged. "I'm terrible at place names. I forgot it the moment you said it. Couldn't have remembered it at gunpoint."

Amber stared at him. "Seriously?"

"I won't forget it again, though. Springton, Wisconsin. Springton, Wisconsin. Okay, it's embedded. Why are you going there?"

Anger coiled. "Because we are, okay? We're on the Demon Road, you're on the Demon Road, the Demon Road is taking us to Wisconsin, and we thought we'd be nice and offer you a lift that far. But hey, if you're inundated with other offers…"

She turned, started walking away, and after a moment she heard his running footsteps behind her, hurrying to catch up.

16

"THIS IS REALLY COOL OF YOU," said Glen from the back seat for the fourth time.

Milo nodded, and Amber felt him glance sideways at her. She didn't respond. She kept her eyes on the road as they drove past endless fields of white cotton pods, bursting like tiny puffs of cloud from all that green.

"So Amber tells me you're her guide," Glen continued. "You've travelled the Demon Road before, then?"

"We try not to talk about it," said Milo.

"Talk about what?"

Milo sighed. "When you're on the Demon Road, you don't really talk about the Demon Road. It's considered... crass. You can mention it, explain it, all that's fine... but just don't talk about it. And don't call it that, either."

"What, Demon Road?"

"Yeah. Try to be, you know... a little cooler about it."

"Oh," said Glen. "Yeah, sure. Blasé, like? Yeah, no problem. Kind of a nudge nudge, wink wink kind of thing, right? If you have to ask, you'll never know. First rule of Fight Club, that sort of vibe? Yeah, that's cool. I can do that."

"Good."

"So how long have you been on it?"

Amber turned in her seat. "He just said we don't talk about it."

"But how am I supposed to ask questions if I'm not allowed to talk about it?"

"Don't ask questions, then."

"But how am I supposed to learn?"

Amber went back to glaring out of the window.

Milo sighed again. "I haven't travelled these roads in years."

"Why not?"

"I didn't need to."

"Do you know them well?" Glen asked.

"I did. Once upon a time."

"So what are you?"

"What do you mean?"

"Well, Amber can transform into this beautiful demon girl, I'm dying of some monster's creepy Deathmark... how come you're here? What did you do or what was done to you?"

Milo didn't answer.

Glen leaned forward. "Could you not hear me?"

"He's ignoring you," said Amber.

"Why? What'd I say?"

"You're asking a whole lot of questions," said Milo. "I like to drive in silence."

"So do I," said Amber.

"You do?" said Glen. "I hate driving in silence. I always have to have the radio on, even if it's country music or something horrible like that. God, I hate country music. And I don't mean the country music you have here in America, I mean the stuff we have in Ireland. Country singers here sound like they've been in a few bar-room brawls, you know? Back home they're just blokes who walk around in woolly jumpers."

"Woolly what?"

"Sweaters," Milo said.

"Oh," said Amber.

"My dad was a country-music fan," said Glen. "At his funeral, they played all his favourite songs. It was awful. I wanted to walk out, y'know? Only I didn't because, well, I've never been one to walk out of places. Well, no, I mean, I walk out of places all the time, obviously, or else I'd never leave anywhere, but I've never walked out of somewhere on principle. I can't even walk out of a bad movie. My dad used to say I was just too polite for my own good. Suppose he was right." He quietened down for a moment, his cheerfulness dimming, then looked up again, smile renewed. "So, Milo, how'd you get to be a guide? What qualifies you? Do you have, like, a dark and tormented history or something? Are you a demon, too? What's your angle?"

"You writing a book?" Milo asked.

"Uh no. Just making conversation."

They lapsed into a short-lived silence.

"You know what this car reminds me of?" Glen asked. "You ever hear of the Ghost of the Highway?"

Milo was done talking, so Amber took up the reins. "No," she said. "Never have."

"It was this guy who drove around, years ago, with his headlights off," Glen said. "He'd drive up and down all these dark American roads at night, looking for his next victim."

"That's an urban legend," Amber said. "When someone passes

the other way and flicks their lights at him, he runs them off the road. We've all heard it."

"No, but this is real," said Glen. "Or, well, okay, maybe sort of real, but he *did* kill a few people back in the nineties. I looked it up. There are a load of websites about him."

"There are websites about everything."

"Yeah, I suppose. But it was a seventies muscle car he drove, I remember that much. Black, too. I think it was a Charger. Or a Challenger. So cool. Is this a Charger?"

Amber's gaze drifted to the window again. "Yeah," she said, hoping he'd shut the hell up now.

"There were a few survivors because he didn't, like, get out of the car to finish them off, or anything. All he was interested in was bashing them off the road. Though he did run a few down, but, if you ask me, anyone who thinks they're gonna sprint faster than a car kind of deserves to be run down, am I right? Ever since I heard about the Ghost of the Highway, I've wanted a car like that. And now I'm in one!"

"A dream come true," Amber muttered.

"Just to drive in something that cool... We don't have anything this awesome in Ireland. There are a few petrolheads who'll import the odd Mustang or whatever, but you wouldn't be able to drive around without people going, *Who does your man think he is?* – you know? But here you can drive a car like this and people won't automatically think you're a tool. People are more accepting here, y'know? But those police reports, in the victims' own words, describing what it was like to be chased down by this terrifying black beast of a car... One moment they're driving along fine, the road pitch-black behind them, the next these red headlights suddenly open up in their rear-view mirror..."

Amber stopped gazing out of the window, and looked at Milo out of the corner of her eye. His expression remained calm, but his hands gripped the wheel with such force that his knuckles had turned white. She suddenly had a knot in her belly.

"It was things like that, y'know?" Glen continued, oblivious. "Things like that that made me fall in love with America. A country so big you can do something as crazy as that as a *hobby* and never get caught... wow. I'm not saying I *want* to do something like that, but I appreciate the fact that I *could*. Land of the free, right? Home of the brave."

Glen settled back, lost in his own overwhelming sense of wonder, and Milo didn't speak again for another two hours.

By the time they stopped off at a Budget Inn in Jasper, Georgia, Milo looked a lot paler than he should have. His face was gaunt, his eyes distant. He got out of the Charger slowly, almost like it didn't want him to leave, and only when they had left it behind them in the parking lot did he regain a little of his spirit. He told Glen to shut up three times as they checked in.

For his own reasons, Glen attempted an American accent that sounded like a cross between John Wayne and John Wayne's idiot brother. Amber thought that the woman behind the desk would ask her for proof of age, but the woman seemingly couldn't have cared less. Amber went to her room with a small bag containing necessities, a vending-machine sandwich, and a lukewarm can of Coke. The water in her shower took forever to heat up, but eventually she stood under the spray and closed her eyes. She worked a full mini-bottle of shampoo and conditioner into her hair, which had dried out in knots and tangles following her dip in the river, and when she was done she stood in front of the bathroom mirror naked.

Unimpressed with what she saw, she resisted the urge to shift. She didn't see the point of feeling even worse about herself.

She turned on the TV. Every second channel had a preacher in an expensive suit talking about God and the Devil. She watched for a bit, hoping in vain to hear some words of comfort, but all she got was fear and greed. She flicked over to a horror movie, but that failed to distract her, so she turned the TV off, and all the lights, and climbed into bed. The mattress was uncomfortable and unfamiliar. The pillows were simultaneously too thin and too soft. She lay in the darkness. Voices came through the walls. TV sets played. Toilets flushed.

She thought about Milo and Glen and Imelda, and the trucker and Brandon. She thought about the Ghost of the Highway, and she thought of her parents, and how they were probably coming after her even as she lay there.

She got up, dragged a chair in front of the door, and jammed it up against the handle like she'd seen people do in movies.

She went back to bed. Sleep was a long time coming.

17

THEY SET OFF EARLY the next morning. Milo looked healthy and strong again, and he must have been up for a while because the Charger was gleaming when they got in. Glen told them all about his night. It wasn't very interesting.

When he realised nobody was answering him, Glen dozed for an hour in the back seat before checking on their location on his phone. "Ooh!" he said. "We're going to be passing Nashville! Can we stop?"

"No," Amber and Milo both said.

Glen looked hurt. "But... but this might be my last chance to see it. I'm dying, remember?"

"You haven't mentioned it," Milo said, making it the second joke he'd told since Amber had met him.

"Can't we even just drive through?" Glen asked. "You don't even have to go slow. Come on, please? Elvis started out in Nashville – it's where he recorded his first record. Elvis!"

"He did that in Memphis," Milo said.

Glen frowned. "Isn't Nashville in Memphis?"

"Nashville and Memphis are both in Tennessee. Which is where we are."

"Oh. Are we going to be passing through Memphis?"

"No."

"But I'm dying. Why are you in such a rush, anyway? Isn't it time you told me what's really going on? We're friends. We're on this trip together. That bonds people, y'know. We're bonded now. We're inseparable. We should have no secrets from each other. I've got no secrets from you. I told you all about the monster who attacked me and gave me the Deathmark and my quest to find The Dark Stair. What's your quest?"

"Don't call it a quest."

"But what is it?"

Amber turned to him. "We're dropping you off in Wisconsin. That's as far as you're going with us. Believe me, it's safer for you not to know anything beyond that."

He blinked at her. "But... but we're inseparable."

Amber turned back. "Not nearly as inseparable as you think."

Glen went quiet. A few minutes later, he was tapping away at his phone again.

He chuckled. "They have a Toledo in Ohio," he said. "Hey, do you think that's where the phrase Holy Toledo comes from? Do you? Hello?"

"There's also a Toledo in Spain," said Milo with dull exasperation. "It's a holy city."

"So that's where it came from?"

"I don't know, Glen."

"Makes you wonder, though, doesn't it?"

"I guess."

Glen nodded, went back to tapping.

*

They found a Walmart in Knoxville and pulled in.

"What're we doing here?" Glen asked.

"Need to buy some clothes," said Amber.

"Need help?"

She frowned at him. "No."

She ignored his look of disappointment, and got out. She pulled her cap down lower and turned her face from the security cameras on her approach. Once inside, she scanned the signs for the clothing section, and picked up a few toiletries on the way over. She added some fresh underwear to her basket and followed that with a pair of jeans a little longer than she usually wore. She grabbed a belt, a new top, a few cheap bracelets, and went looking for a light jacket. When she had everything she wanted, she took them to the dressing rooms.

Once inside the cubicle, she tried on the clothes, looped the belt through the jeans, and turned to the mirror. The jeans were comfortable around her waist but gathered at the ankles. She looked like a girl wearing her big sister's pants. Then she shifted, and her glorious red-skinned reflection grinned back at her. She tightened the belt, noting how the jeans were now the perfect length, how her T-shirt was now flatter around the belly and fuller around the bust. She added the jacket, turned and admired herself, imagining for a moment strolling back through Walmart like this, and wondering if the cries of alarm would dent her confidence. She doubted it.

But discretion, as ever, was called for, and she unbuckled her belt and reverted, and the jeans gathered at her ankles and her belly swelled to its usual proportions. Sighing, she changed back into her own clothes, put everything else into the basket, and left the cubicle, the cap once again pulled low.

She waited in line behind a woman who smelled really bad, and when she was gone the Hispanic boy at the till gave her a smile.

"Hi there," he said.

"Hi," she responded.

He started passing her items over the scanner – one at a time, slowly. "I like your eyes," he said.

Amber blinked at him. "What?"

"Your eyes," he repeated. "I like them."

She blinked. "These?"

He laughed. "You have any others I should know about?"

"No," she said, and blushed. He wasn't the best-looking boy in the world, but he wasn't bad, and he had a confidence that she could only manage when she was demonified. It was attractive. Hugely so. His name tag identified him as Eugenio.

"This is the part where you tell me you like my eyes, too," he said, in a mock whisper.

"Oh, sorry," said Amber. "I like your eyes, too." She did. She really did. They were brown like chocolate.

"How nice of you to say so," he said, giving her another smile. "So does a nice girl like you have a boyfriend? I only ask because if you say yes I will spiral into a bottomless pit of despair and loneliness, and you wouldn't want that, would you?"

"No, I wouldn't," she said. "And I don't have a, you know… a boyfriend."

"That seems highly unlikely. Are you sure?"

Before she knew what she was doing, she giggled. Dear Lord, she giggled.

"I'm sure," she said.

"Well then, how about we meet up later, if you're free? Do you live around here?"

"Ah, sorry, I don't. I'm just passing through."

"Oh no," Eugenio said, losing his smile and widening his eyes. If anything, that made him even cuter. "So I'll never see you again? Is that what you're saying?"

"Probably."

The last item to scan was a pair of socks. He held them to his chest. "So the moment I put these through and you pay, you're going to just walk out of here, walk out of my life, and never look back? But what if I don't scan these socks? Will you stay?"

"I'm afraid not," said Amber, packing the other stuff into flimsy plastic bags. "I'll just have to do without the socks."

He gasped. "But how can you do without socks? They are an integral part of any civilised society. A sockless person is no kind of person, that's what my father always says."

"He always says that?"

"He's not a very good conversationalist."

Amber laughed.

"Hey, Juan," said an unshaven guy standing behind Amber, "would you stop flirting with ugly chicks and do your damn job?"

Amber went cold with mortification even as her face flushed bright red. Eugenio lost his good humour in an instant.

"My name is not Juan," he said, "and be careful what you say about ladies, sir. You don't want to be rude."

The unshaven man had incredibly soft-looking curly hair, entirely at odds with the hardness of his face. "You wanna know what's rude, Pedro? Making paying customers stand in line while you try to get into this girl's pants."

Eugenio's jaw clenched. He dragged his eyes away from the man only when Amber held out her money. "I apologise," he said to her.

"It's okay," she said quietly.

He handed over her change. The rude man was now ignoring her as he dumped the last of his stuff on to the conveyor belt. Amber gathered up her things and walked away, eyes that were filling with tears firmly fixed on the floor.

By the time she reached the Charger, she was back in control again. She slipped the bracelets on over the numbers on her wrist, concealing them, then put the bags in the trunk and got in.

"I'm hungry," she announced, keeping her words curt, afraid that anything else might result in the others hearing her voice tremble. The topic of food set Glen off on some random tangent. Amber didn't listen. She replayed the scene in her head, only this time as she stood in the checkout lane she shifted, horns bursting from her forehead, fingernails turning to talons, and in her mind she watched herself tear the rude man's face off.

They passed into Kentucky, and by the time they stopped at a roadside diner with a startling view of the Daniel Boone National Forest, her embarrassment had been replaced with anger. And anger faded faster than embarrassment. She got out of the Charger and closed her eyes to the breeze. It was still hot, but the air was better out here. It moved through the great slabs of lush forest on either side of the road, brought with it all manner of freshness.

"Big trees," said Glen, and she had to agree with him. They were indeed big trees.

Inside the diner, the freshness was replaced by the smell of hamburger fat. There was a broken jukebox in the corner that played 'Here I Go Again' by Whitesnake on a loop. They sat at a plastic-covered table, and Amber ran her finger along the top, expecting to leave a trail in grease. The fact that it was perfectly clean disappointed her slightly.

They ate their burgers without speaking a whole lot. She could tell this was driving Glen insane, and it provided her with a glimmer of quiet amusement. He took some pamphlets from the stack beside the register and perused them while they ate.

"Did you know that the forest has one of the world's largest concentration of caves?" he asked.

"Yes," Amber answered, even though she knew no such thing, and cared even less.

Glen put that pamphlet aside, picked up another. "Hey, this is where Kentucky Fried Chicken was invented! Corbin, that is, not this diner. We should get some KFC! You want some?"

Amber loved KFC. "I hate KFC," she said.

Glen looked glum. Amber beamed inside.

Amber and Milo shared the bill, and Glen looked embarrassed. She actually had some sympathy for him, the way he sat there, all pathetic and grateful. She was about to say something nice to him when he shrugged, looked up and said brightly, "Well, I'm off for a wee!"

He practically skipped to the restroom.

"Curious boy," Milo muttered.

He led the way out of the diner, humming the Whitesnake song which was now firmly lodged in Amber's head, too. She was not looking forward to another half a day on the road. She wouldn't have minded staying here for a while, looking at the forest, enjoying the air. Apart from anything else, she liked the fact that Kentucky had mountains. Florida suddenly seemed way too flat for her liking.

A car pulled up, parking on the other side of a battered truck, and Amber glimpsed the occupants.

Terror stabbed her heart and she dived behind the Charger.

Milo stiffened. All at once his gun was out of its holster and held down by his leg.

Amber heard the car doors open and close. The *beep* as it locked. Footsteps on loose gravel.

And then her mother's voice. "Excuse me, we're looking for our daughter. Have you seen this girl?"

The driver of the truck. She could picture him in her head. Hispanic. Short. Wearing jeans and a T-shirt. He'd been eating at the counter when they'd ordered. Had he looked up? Had he noticed her?

"Sorry," she heard him say. "Can't help you."

The truck started, reversed all the way round the back of the Charger, and the driver happened to glance her way. She shook her head, mouthing the words *please, no*.

He hesitated, then pulled out on to the road and drove off.

"Hi," she heard her dad say, from the other side of the car.

"Hi there," Milo answered. He holstered his gun.

"We're looking for this girl," Bill said. "Would you have seen her, by any chance?"

His voice moved round the car. Milo opened the door, shielding Amber from view, keeping his feet planted to hide her own. He took off his jacket and threw it in.

She heard Bill and Betty stop walking suddenly. For a moment, she thought she'd been spotted.

"That's a nice weapon," said Bill. "What is it, a Glock?"

"Glock 21," said Milo. "You cops? I've got a concealed carry permit."

Betty had a smile in her voice. "No, we're not police. We're just looking for our daughter. Have you seen her?"

There was a moment while they showed Milo a photograph.

"Sorry," Milo said. "Don't think I've—"

The door to the diner opened and Glen came out. His eyes flickered over Amber and rested on her parents.

"Hi," he said, puncturing the silence. "Did we do something wrong?"

Betty laughed politely, with just the right amount of sadness. "No, we're not police officers. We're just looking for this girl. Have you seen her?"

Glen walked out of Amber's view. She shrank back against the Charger. If she had to trust in Glen's acting prowess, she wouldn't be hiding for very much longer. She got ready to shift. If she shifted before they did, maybe she could outrun them in the forest.

"Yeah," said Glen, "I've seen her."

Amber screwed her eyes shut. *No, you idiot.*

"You have?" said Betty, excited.

"You have?" said Milo. "Are you sure?"

"Sure I'm sure," Glen said. "They were at the table behind us when we got here. You'll have to excuse Milo – he doesn't notice a whole lot when Whitesnake is playing. I'm the brains of the operation. Name's Glen. How do you do."

"Hello, Glen," said Betty. "I'm Betty, and this is Bill. You've seen our daughter? You're sure it was her?"

"I think so," said Glen. "I didn't get a good look at her face, but I'm pretty sure. She was with a woman, a small woman with grey hair. They had a map out."

"When was this?"

"Milo?" said Glen. "When did we get here?"

"About an hour ago," said Milo, clearly resenting his role in this.

"Did they say where they were going?" Bill asked.

Glen hesitated. "Uh, listen, I'm sure you're good people, but if your daughter's run away, she probably has her reasons. No offence, but for all I know you might lock her in the cellar or something."

"We love our daughter," Betty said. "All we want is for her to be safe. That woman she's with, she's part of a cult. We have to get her back before we lose her for good."

"A cult?" Glen echoed. "Oh wow. Yeah, absolutely. My cousin went off and joined a cult years ago, so I know what that's like. It was a UFO cult. I hope your daughter's not in a UFO cult – they're the worst. I heard the woman say they were going to Toledo. I'm usually terrible with place names, but I remember that because, y'know, the phrase 'Holy Toledo'. Hey, you think that's where the phrase comes from?"

"Either that or the holy city of Toledo in Spain," said Bill. "Did you happen to see what they were driving?"

"A white van," said Glen, "in dire need of a wash. I didn't notice any UFO bumper stickers or anything, so you might be in luck. Like I said, they left about an hour ago."

"Thank you, Glen," Betty said, and Amber listened to their retreating footsteps.

"Hope you find her," Glen called.

Their car beeped and they got in, and Amber crawled on

her hands and knees to the front of the Charger as her parents' car pulled out on to the road and accelerated fast.

She stood.

"So," Glen said, "your parents, huh?"

18

THEY SPENT THE NIGHT at a Motel 6 somewhere in Indiana. Amber barricaded her door again, and she tossed and turned, but didn't fall asleep until a half-hour before Milo knocked. She didn't eat any breakfast and she kept her head down and her cap on while walking out to the Charger. It gleamed, the dust and dirt of the previous day's travel washed away like it had never happened.

If only that was true.

As they were bypassing Chicago, Amber relented and told Glen about Shanks. He'd earned the right to sit at the table with the cool kids, she reckoned. They drove through an endless suburban sprawl of strip malls and chain restaurants, the parking lots and signs repeating as if copied and pasted, and got into Springton, Wisconsin a little before three that afternoon. The day had dulled, become cold, and sporadic showers of rain splattered the windshield. They passed the high school, a building of red brick set a dozen steps above street level, and carried on to the town square. The library sat on one side, and opposite it, on the south side, sat the Mayor's Office – white, with pillars outside denoting its obvious importance. The buildings to the east and west housed various businesses and eateries.

They got out. Stretched. It was maybe ten degrees cooler than when they'd started their journey, and Amber was wearing jeans now. They felt weird on her legs. She pulled on a jacket and made sure her cap was secure.

"What do we do now?" she asked.

"We ask about Dacre Shanks," said Glen before Milo could answer. "We split up. We'll cover more ground that way. The sooner we get to him, the better, am I right? We've got your parents on our tail, Amber. I may have been able to throw them off the scent yesterday, but that won't stop them for long. Here, that guy looks like he might know something."

Glen strode towards an old man walking his dog.

Amber looked at Milo. "He's trying really hard."

Milo nodded. "You notice how quiet he was this morning? He didn't make one single stupid comment."

"And he *was* very useful yesterday."

Milo hesitated, then shook his head. "Doesn't make one bit of difference. This is where we cut him loose, *before* we talk to Shanks. The less he knows..." He trailed off.

Amber frowned. "What?"

"Nothing."

"What, Milo?"

Milo sighed. "Your parents know him now. If we leave him here and they find him, they might..."

"Do you think they'd kill him?"

"They killed those cops without a second thought, didn't they?"

They both looked at Glen, who was now arguing with the old man while the dog yapped and nipped at his legs.

"So," Milo said, "should we leave him, or...?"

They looked at each other and burst out laughing.

Glen jogged back. "What? What are you laughing about?"

"Nothing," said Amber, trying to contain herself. "Did you learn anything?"

"No," said Glen. "Turns out that old guy is German and doesn't speak a word of English."

"Then what were you arguing about?"

Glen looked puzzled. "How should I know?"

This set Amber and Milo off again. Glen tried to laugh along with them, then gave up and went for a walk.

A full third of the library was given over to computers, the bookcases crammed together in the space left. Amber walked the labyrinth until she found a section marked Local History. It was a single shelf with five books on it — four of them the same book. She flicked through the fifth — *Springton: A Legacy*, by a local author with a bad photo. She learned that Springton was established in 1829, and got its name from its wondrous spring-water reserve. She learned that the industry that built up around it polluted that reserve so much that the water became virtually undrinkable. The author called that 'ironic'.

Amber flicked through the rest of it, then checked the index. No mention of Dacre Shanks.

She replaced the book and wandered out of the stacks. Glen found her.

"They have a *Springton Gazette*," he said. "I asked the librarian if I could see the old editions, y'know, to read the articles on Shanks as they were printed? She said they're only available on microfiche."

"What's microfiche?"

"I don't know. Some kind of small fish, presumably."

Amber frowned. "Where's Milo?"

"Chatting up the other librarian. The cute one."

Amber looked around. Milo stood in that slouchy way of his, giving a smile she hadn't imagined he possessed to an attractive woman in her forties. She had brown hair with a streak of silver running through it. The librarian laughed and Milo's smile widened.

"I could do that," said Glen. "I just picked the wrong librarian to charm, that's all. I picked the old one. I thought she'd be the one to ask. If I'd known there was a younger one, I'd have called dibs."

"She's twice your age."

"Older women find me intensely attractive."

"Well, that's good, because younger women certainly don't."

Glen stopped glaring across at Milo, and switched his attention to Amber. "Oh, is that so? So you're telling me that you feel no attraction to me whatsoever?"

She blinked at him. "What? Where has this come from? No. None. None at all."

"Yeah," he said, laughing. "Right."

"Seriously."

"There have been studies carried out that say the Irish accent is the sexiest in the world."

"Who carried it out? Irish people?"

His smile faltered for a moment. "Maybe," he said, and then it was back. "I could charm you. You know I could charm you. The only thing stopping me is your age. You're too young for me. I prefer girls in their twenties."

"I will have to live with that crushing disappointment."

"Of course," he said, moving closer, "I could make an exception."

"Please don't."

"I could overlook the age thing if… you know."

Amber frowned. "What?"

"If you transformed," he whispered.

She lost all good humour. "Drop dead, Glen."

She made for the exit. He followed.

"Oh, go on! Just transform once for me. You're amazing when you transform. You're astonishing. Those horns are just the most beautiful—"

She spun round to face him. "Stop calling it that. Stop calling it transforming. You make me sound like an Autobot."

"Well, what's it called?"

"I don't know. Shifting. There isn't really an official term for it."

A slow grin spread across his face. "I've got one. Do you want to hear it?"

She walked away. "No."

"It's a good one," he said from right behind her.

"I don't care."

"You'll love it," he said. "I promise you, you'll love it."

They reached the exit. Milo was walking towards them. Amber couldn't help herself.

"Fine," she said. "What? What would you call it when I change?"

Glen's grin was immense. "Getting horny."

"Oh, I hate you so much."

Milo joined them. "She's hiding something," he said. "The moment she guessed where I was steering the conversation she closed down. You find anything?"

"Just a new level of annoyance," said Amber.

"She wants to join me in my utter hilarity," said Glen. "You can see it in her face, can't you? She wants to joke around. Give in to it, Amber. Give in."

She sighed. "Are you finished yet?"

Glen grinned, and turned to Milo. "What's microfiche?"

"Microfilm."

"Ohhh. So it's not a small fish."

"Come on," said Amber, "let's get something to eat. I'm starving."

They had lunch sitting in the window of one of the cafes on the square. They watched the high-school kids pass on their way home. A bunch of younger kids came into the cafe, and Amber looked at Milo with her eyebrows raised. He shrugged, and nodded, and she turned on her stool.

"Hi," she said, keeping her voice down. "I was wondering if you could help me? Have any of you heard of a man called Dacre Shanks?"

The name made the kids draw back in suspicion.

"Ask someone else," one of them said.

"So you've heard of him?"

"We're not talking about that."

"Why not?"

"Cos they're scared," said the smallest kid, black, with adorably huge eyes. "They're afraid their allowance might be taken away."

"Whatever," the other one said, and got up and walked out, followed by his friends. All except the little kid.

"You've heard of Shanks?" said Amber.

"Course," the kid said.

"And the others – they won't talk because they're scared of him?"

The kid laughed. "Scared of who? The boogie man? Naw, they're scared cos last year a bunch of us trashed two of those dollhouses they got up in the school, and when people found out they beat the hell out of us. I'm talking grown-ups here, y'know? Punching and kicking me while I'm all curled up on the floor, crying for my momma. Disgraceful behaviour, know what I'm saying?"

"I'm sorry, dollhouses?"

"I know, right? *Dollhouses*. This town's obsessed with them."

"What's your name? I'm Amber."

"Name's Walter," said the kid. "Walter S. Bryant. The S stands for Samuel. Had a teacher once, said my destiny was to become a poet with a name like that. But he didn't know what the hell he was talking about. I can barely spell, and most of the words I know don't even rhyme with each other."

"Walter, what's so important about a few dollhouses?"

"Where you from?"

"Florida."

"Florida," he repeated. "Wait, you mean with Disney World and all?"

"Yep, we have Disney World."

"You ever been?"

"A few times," she said. Always with friends, though – never with her parents.

"Aw man," said Walter. "Disney World. I'd like that, walking around and everything looking like it's out of a cartoon or something. Ever meet Mickey Mouse?"

"I have."

Walter laughed. "That's cool. You met Mickey Mouse. That's cool."

"I'm from Ireland," said Glen.

"I don't care," said Walter.

"Can you tell me about the dollhouses?" Amber asked.

"Oh yeah," said Walter. "I knew you weren't from around here, cos if you were you'd know already. There's this dumb story everyone's been telling us our entire lives, and they all expect us to believe it, y'know? Dacre Shanks. He *was* a real person, back in the 1970s, cos I looked him up. He was a toymaker, right? He had a little store down beside where the arcade once was, but he only made crappy toys like dolls and model railways and stuff. Nothing cool. But what nobody knew was that he was also this serial killer, and he killed a ton of people before the cops figured out who he was and came and shot him."

"I looked him up, too," said Amber. "I didn't see any mention of dollhouses."

"Course not," said Walter, "cos that's the part they made up, isn't it? The story is, he came back from the dead, right, ten years later, and kept killing and he, like, shrank his victims or something and put them in these dollhouses he made."

Amber frowned. "He shrank them?"

"How stupid is that, right? Not only do they have him come back from the dead, but they have him shrinking people, too. Anyway, the school had three dollhouses that supposedly held these shrunken victims – although officially they're just normal dollhouses with nothing weird about them at all. Cos every school has a few dollhouses in a huge glass cabinet right inside the door, don't they? I mean, *that* part's totally normal.

Nothing weird about that. Ask any of the teachers; they all say the story's a load of crap, but they say it in a way that's supposed to make you think they're lying. We had to pass those dollhouses every single day. I'm not stupid. I know why they were there. It was a message, wasn't it? *Stay in school. Keep your head down. Don't question authority. Or Dacre Shanks will get you.*

"Well, practically everyone else in my school were cool about going along with it, but me and a couple of others, and you just met them a few minutes ago, got talking one day and figured hey, we were getting a little tired of being treated like fools."

"So you trashed the dollhouses."

Walter nodded. "Stomped two of them to splinters before we were caught."

"What happened then?"

"Aw, everyone went insane. I knew the school would be mad and all, but they were threatening to expel us. It was crazy. Only reason they didn't is cos they didn't want the State Board to know about their dumb stories. But everyone, like, the whole entire town, was against us. Everyone except the old people. They didn't see what the fuss was about. But our folks, some of our older brothers and sisters, they just… I didn't know they'd take it so seriously."

"Is that when you were beaten up?"

"Yeah," Walter said, with an impressive amount of bitterness. "Broad daylight. Had to stay indoors the whole summer after that. People in this town are nuts, and they all worship that Medina chick."

"Who?"

"Heather Medina. She's the one who stopped Dacre Shanks from killing any more kids. According to the story."

"Does she still live around here?"

"Yeah, lives over on Pine Street. Works in the library."

"Brown hair?" asked Milo. "Silver in it?"

Walter nodded. "That's her. She won't even mention his name, though, so good luck trying to get anything out of her. She looks perfectly normal, but she's as crazy as the rest of them. That's why her husband left her, I heard. They expected us to believe a story like that, and then they were actually angry when we didn't. Moment I'm old enough to drive I am out of here. I may not be able to spell or rhyme, but I'm pretty smart. Smarter than everyone in this town, anyway."

"Definitely looks like it," said Amber. "Thank you so much for your help."

"Don't worry about it," the kid replied. "I'm assuming you'll take care of this?"

He held up his bag of doughnuts so the teller could see it, and Amber smiled. "Sure thing, Walter. See you around."

"Stay frosty," Walter said, and walked out.

Amber paid for the doughnuts, and rejoined Milo and Glen as they were putting on their jackets.

"You think you'll be able to get back in the librarian's good books?" Amber asked.

"Don't know," admitted Milo. "Women have a tendency to learn fast around me."

"Told you I should have talked to her first," Glen said.

They left the cafe and walked back to the Charger, where a stocky man in his late sixties stood admiring her. He gave them a quick smile as they approached, and when Amber saw the star on his shirt her own smile faded.

"Now this is a damn fine automobile," the man said. His

moustache was a deeper shade of grey than his hair. "A friend of mine had one, back in my youth. Light gold, it was. A thing of beauty. He crashed it not far from here, going too fast, and he just lost control. That's all there was to it. Nobody else was hurt, thank God, but my friend, he was killed instantly. I don't know, ever since then, I see one of these cars and I just think… death." He gave a little smile and a little shrug.

"Well, that is a story with a sad ending," said Milo.

"Isn't it just?" The man smiled at them, for real this time, though there wasn't much friendliness in it. "How are you folks? My name is Theodore Roosevelt, no relation to the big man, I'm afraid. You can call me Teddy. As you can probably tell by the badge, I'm the sheriff 'round these parts. If no one has bothered to do it, I bid you welcome to Springton. Now what brings you nice people to our little town, I wonder?"

"Just passing through."

"Ah, that old staple. Just passing through. It's hard to make new friends when everyone's just passing through, that ever strike you as a truism? I'm collecting them – truisms, that is. Collecting them, coming up with them, going to put them all into a book when I'm done, try and get it published some day. Kind of going for a homespun sort of feel, you know? Going to call it *Words of Wisdom*, something hokey like that. Hokiness sells."

"That another truism?"

Teddy smiled. "I guess it is. Might not include it in the collection, though. So is this a family trip?"

"That's what it is," said Milo.

"You and the kids, on a family trip. Your wife not come with you?"

"I'm afraid she's not with us anymore."

"Oh, I am sorry to hear that, Mr Sebastian. I am truly sorry." The air went quiet around them.

"You checked the plates, huh?" said Milo.

"One of the perks of being the sheriff," Teddy answered. "Funny, your details mention nothing about you having a family."

Milo nodded. "The kids were born out of wedlock. They're very self-conscious about it."

"Very," said Glen.

"Your kids don't look a whole lot like you," Teddy said. "Also, from what I hear from a certain elderly librarian, your son is Irish." He hooked his thumbs into his belt loops. "We get people like you passing through all the time. Oh, and by 'people like you', I don't mean the Irish. I mean gawkers. What I like to call bloodhounds. They hear about our town, hear we used to have a serial killer, and they come sniffing around, thinking how exciting it all is, how fun. But the wounds that man made still haven't closed over, and you walking around asking clumsy questions is just going to get people's backs up."

"It's my fault," said Glen, his shoulders drooping. "I'm not his son, I'm his nephew. Yes, I'm from Ireland. But I'm dying. I don't have long left."

"That so?"

"It is. I came over here to see America before I... before I pass on. And yeah, you're right, I asked to come to Springton because of the serial killer. I've always been fascinated with that stuff. A kind of morbid curiosity, I suppose. But I never intended to upset anyone, Sheriff. I'm really sorry."

"What's your name, son?"

"Glen, sir."

"Well, Glen, I'm sorry to hear of your ill-health. What have you got, if you don't mind me asking?"

"Lupus," said Glen.

Teddy frowned. "Is that fatal?"

"Oh yes," said Glen. "Very."

"You sure? I don't think it is."

"It's not always fatal," Glen said quickly. "If you get treatment for it, no, it's not fatal. Rarely fatal. But I have a rare form of lupus that is very fatal."

"Glen, forgive me for asking this, but do you know what lupus is? A friend of mine has lupus, a reverend. His joints get all swollen up, he gets rashes, he's tired all the time, and his hair even fell out."

Glen nodded. "I have the other kind of lupus."

"The kind that has none of those symptoms?"

Glen bit his lip for a moment. "I get the feeling you're not believing me."

Teddy sighed. "You're not too bright, son, and that's okay. There's no law against being stupid. There's also no law against being a bloodhound, but I'm going to have to ask you to stop pestering people with questions – especially my daughter."

"Your daughter?"

Teddy nodded. "She works in the library. She's the librarian who is not elderly."

"Ah," said Milo. "Heather called you."

"She may have mentioned it during one of our regular father-daughter chats."

"So are you going to run us out of town?"

Teddy chuckled. "I don't think I have to do anything quite so dramatic, do you? Quite the opposite, in fact. It's getting late in the day and, as you folks aren't from around here, I'd like to invite you to stay overnight in our little town."

"That's mighty Christian of you."

"And to save you some money, you'll be staying with us, my wife and I. Have a good home-cooked meal. That sound good?"

"We really couldn't impose," said Milo.

"It is not an imposition, I assure you," said Teddy. "I insist on you staying with us. That okay with you?"

Milo glanced at Amber, and nodded. "Sure," he said. "That'd be great."

"Excellent," Teddy said, beaming. "I'll tell her to make up the rooms. Our bed-and-breakfast rates are quite competitive, just so you know."

19

SHERIFF ROOSEVELT'S PLACE WAS a neat little house out on the edge of town. It had pebbles instead of grass in the front yard, and a path of cobblelock paving. Mrs Roosevelt – Ella-May – was a handsome woman who struck Amber as someone playing at running a B&B. She had a way about her, a way of asking questions and getting answers, that suggested a whipsmart mind, even in her advancing years. Running a B&B seemed a rather tame endeavour for someone like her.

The house looked like a picture-perfect amalgamation of various local tourism brochures. Everything was pretty, with a restrained, folksy charm. Milo and Glen had to share the twin beds in the double room, but Amber got a room all to herself. It had a small TV in the corner, the very opposite of a flatscreen.

Dinner was at eight. Amber had a bath to pass the time, and as she lay in all those bubbles she tried not to look at the countdown on her wrist.

438, it said now. Three days gone out of her twenty-one. Lots of time left. Plenty of time. Providing they find Dacre Shanks.

When eight rolled around, she was dressed and hungry. She went downstairs, following the aroma.

Teddy sat at one end of the table. Amber and Glen sat to his right, and Milo to his left. Glen kept his hand curled, hiding the Deathmark from sight in the same way that Amber's bracelets hid her scar. When Ella-May was finished serving the food, she sat opposite her husband.

Teddy interlocked his fingers and closed his eyes. "Lord, thank you for this meal we are about to enjoy. Thank you for our guests – after some initial frostiness, they have proven themselves to be nice enough people, and they've paid in advance, which I always take as a sign of good manners. Thank you for no dead bodies today and no real crime at all, to be fair. Thank you for my beautiful wife, my wonderful daughter, and for the continuing wellbeing of my town. Amen."

"Amen," Amber muttered, along with Glen. Milo and Ella-May remained silent.

"So, Milo," Teddy said as he reached for the potatoes, "what do you do for a living?"

"I get by."

"That it? That's all you do?"

Milo smiled like he was a normal, good-natured kind of guy. "I make ends meet, how about that?"

Teddy shrugged. "That's fair enough. A man who doesn't want to talk about his business shouldn't have to talk about his business. Where you from, originally?"

"Kentucky," Milo said.

"Aha," said Teddy. "The Bluegrass State."

"That's what they call it."

"You a farm boy, Milo?"

"Yes, sir."

"Pigs? Cattle?"

"Some." Milo's smile was easy and his tone was relaxed. He was like a different person. "Ella-May, this is one humdinger of a dinner."

Ella-May smiled. "Why, thank you, Milo. Humdinger, eh? Never heard my cooking called that before."

Milo actually chuckled. "How long you two been married?"

"I was nineteen," said Ella-May, "he was twenty-three. We were married in the summer. My father, who was sheriff, could not let his future son-in-law waste his natural gifts in an aluminum factory, so he made him a deputy and started him on the road to becoming the fine, upstanding law-enforcement official you see before you with gravy dripping down his chin."

"Goddamn it," Teddy said, dabbing at himself with his napkin.

"We were so in love."

Teddy winked at Amber. "She was besotted."

"Yeah," said Ella-May, "I was the one going all moon-eyed. I was the one blushing and stammering and falling over bushes…"

Teddy pointed his fork at her. "Hey. I fell over *one* bush."

"But it was a big one."

"Damn near broke my neck," Teddy muttered.

"I swear, my husband is brighter than he lets on."

"I'd have to be," said Teddy.

"Was your dad sheriff when Dacre Shanks was killing people?" Glen asked Ella-May.

Milo's smile vanished. "Damn it, Glen."

"What?"

"Boy, you have got to be the most tactless person I have met that I haven't punched yet," said Teddy.

Glen looked confused. "We were talking about cops and sheriffs and stuff. I'd have thought that'd be a natural segue into, y'know…"

"We don't talk about that man at the table," Ella-May said.

"Right. Um, sorry."

She nodded. Teddy shoved another forkful of food into his mouth and chewed. Milo looked pissed. Thirty seconds passed where no one said anything. Amber's wrist burned. She parted the bracelets and took another peek: 436 hours.

"We're looking for him," she said quietly.

"Looking for who?" Ella-May asked.

"Shanks," she said. "We need to find him."

Milo watched her, but didn't say anything. Glen shot her a glare and kicked her under the table. She kicked him back harder.

"Ow! God!"

"We lied to you," she said. Teddy put down his knife and fork and listened. "My life is in danger. I'm not going to tell you how or why or who is coming after me because, I'm sorry, but you're safer not knowing. And I'm safer with you not knowing. We lied. We're not family. We didn't even know each other until a few days ago."

"I'm not her cousin," Glen said, rubbing his shin.

"They don't care about that," said Milo.

"But I am dying," Glen added. "It's just I'm not dying of lupus. I'm not even sure what that is. I've got the Deathmark, see, and—"

"They don't care about any of that, either," said Milo.

"Dacre Shanks is dead," said Teddy. "Shot him myself. Me and three other deputies. One of the bullets caught him in the head. We never bothered figuring out who fired that one. But it took off the top of his skull."

"We know he's dead," Amber said carefully. "But we also know there's more to it than that."

"You've been listening to too many ghost stories," Ella-May said, getting up from the table.

"No," said Amber, "but I have seen too many monsters."

Amber went to bed and had a bad dream. Her demon-self was crouched over Ella-May's dead body, and she was scooping out and eating the woman's insides. Standing behind her were her parents, scooping out Amber's own guts from a gaping cavity in her back.

She woke up and cried for a bit. When she stopped, she heard a creaking – slow and regular. She got up, looked out of the window, saw an ember glowing in the dark. She put on jeans and a sweatshirt, went out on to the back porch.

"Did I wake you?" Teddy asked from his rocking chair.

She shook her head. "I haven't been sleeping too well, that's all. I've never known anyone who smoked a pipe before."

He smiled. "I didn't used to. Took this up in my forties when my hair started going grey. Thought it'd make me look wise and somewhat distinguished. Does it?"

"Somewhat."

He nodded, and puffed away.

"I'm sorry for the upset we've caused," said Amber.

"Ah, you seem like you're going through a lot, so I'm not going to hold it against you. Ella-May isn't, either, despite her silence earlier. That man has been a plague on our family, so we don't especially like talking about him at the dinner table."

"You knew him?" she asked.

Teddy nodded. "Everyone knew him. Nobody knew him well. Probably how he got away with it for so long."

"How did you find him? How did you figure out what he was doing?"

Teddy tapped the stem of his pipe against the chair, and put it back between his lips. "We didn't," he said. "Ella-May did. I'm a smart enough fella. I was a good deputy and I make a good sheriff. But Ella-May is my secret weapon. She paid attention to the little things, the little details. She added things together. She made enquiries. All under the radar. Not even her father suspecting for one moment that what she was doing was gathering evidence.

"Then her dad passed away. Nothing dramatic. He wasn't killed in the line of duty or anything like that. His heart just gave out one sunny afternoon while driving back to the station. He pulled over to the side of the road and had his heart attack and died. Responsible to the last. His replacement was not a particularly intelligent man. I brought Ella-May to him and she gave him all her evidence, told him her conclusions, and he ignored it all. He didn't want to imagine that a town like Springton could hold a horror like that. Dacre Shanks was a creepy little guy in a creepy little toystore. Sheriff Gunther, that was his name, was content with that. Creepy was fine. He could understand creepy. But serial killer? That was beyond him.

"So I started an unofficial investigation. My fellow deputies trusted me, and they trusted Ella-May. All the work she'd done meant we hit the ground running. We quickly had enough so that we could call in the Feds. Gunther found out, was not happy, threatened to fire us all. He called the FBI, told them it was all a big misunderstanding. That same night we got word that someone else had gone missing, a boy who fit the profile of some of Shanks's other victims. We convinced the judge to get us a search warrant – without Gunther's help – and we raided that toystore."

"Did you save the boy?" Amber asked.

"No, we did not." Teddy puffed on the pipe, but it had gone out. He didn't seem to notice. "We ran in on Shanks standing over him, though. All four of us opened fire. You know the rest. Gunther lost his job after that and I was elected in his place. For some reason, the folks around here have been electing me ever since. I don't think they're too smart."

"And what about after? There were other murders, weren't there? Ten years later, something like that?"

"Feds came to investigate. Thought there was a copycat. But, by the time they got here, the killings had stopped."

"Did your daughter have anything to do with that?"

Teddy struck a match, lit his pipe again. Gave it a few puffs. "The world is full of bad men, Amber. Bad women, too, I guess. Some of them hide in plain sight, and some of them don't. Some of them wear masks, and some of them wear smiles. I thought I'd seen the full extent of evil when we burst in on Dacre Shanks. Turns out I was wrong. There's another evil, a whole other layer of evil that I'd only read about in the Bible. I believe you know what I'm talking about."

She nodded.

"I've glimpsed impossible things," Teddy said. "I haven't seen them fully because I honestly don't think I'm able. But

I've seen enough to know that whatever path you're on, it's something I can't help you with."

"I understand."

"You get back to bed now, Amber. And you have good dreams, you hear me? The world's just about full up of the other kind."

20

S<small>HERIFF</small> R<small>OOSEVELT HAD ALREADY</small> left for work when Amber got up the next morning. She joined Milo and Glen at the table and Ella-May served them breakfast, but didn't eat with them. Amber ate in silence and Milo didn't say a word. Even Glen seemed subdued.

They threw their bags in the Charger and went back inside to pay. Ella-May gave Milo a handwritten receipt and walked them to the door and they stood there, waiting for someone to say something.

Ella-May was the one to puncture the quiet. "I'm not going to ask about your business," she said. "I'm not going to ask why you're interested in a man who has killed so many people, or how you know what you know. There's a dark underbelly to this country and I am well aware that there are people who have to walk through it – oftentimes through no fault of their own. If you're on that path… well, I'd pray for you if I prayed."

Amber gave her a small, pained smile.

Ella-May nodded brusquely. "I've called Heather. I told her to speak to you if she's in the mood. That's no guarantee that she will, mind you. My daughter is her own woman. The library opens late today, so she'll be at work at two. You could call in then, see if she's feeling talkative. Good day to you, now."

She closed the door.

At ten minutes past two, they walked into the library and found Heather Medina restocking shelves in the Self-help section. Up close, she was an attractive woman with plump, soft lips but hard eyes. There was a thin scar on her neck that disappeared behind the collar of her blouse. Everything about her, from her manner to the shoes that she wore – practical, like she was ready to run or fight at any given moment – screamed survivor. Amber liked her instantly.

"Your mother sent us," Milo said.

Heather nodded, and kept sliding books on to the shelves. "She told me you're a curious bunch, with a particular interest in our town's recent history. I told her I'd already been speaking to you. I told her you're not exactly subtle."

"She said you'd talk to us if you were in a talkative mood," Amber said.

"And you're wondering what kind of mood I'm currently in?" asked Heather. "It's Amber, right? And Glen? I used to have a boyfriend called Glen. Really good guy. I guess he was my first love. My high-school sweetheart. Dacre Shanks came back from the dead and killed him when I was sixteen."

She said it so matter-of-factly that Amber didn't notice the words sliding down her spine until they made her shiver. "It's true, then? Everything we've heard?"

"Well, I don't know," said Heather. "It all depends on what you've heard, doesn't it?"

The elderly librarian passed, gave them all a suspicious look, and Heather smiled, keeping her eyes locked on her until she'd moved out of earshot.

"When I was a kid, we all knew who Dacre Shanks was," said Heather. "I grew up hearing about the things he'd done and how my mother had been the one to figure it all out. In the playground, my friends used to re-enact the night he died. They'd take turns to be my dad and the other deputies, and they'd go in, guns blazing, and whoever was playing Shanks would howl and scream and whirl around and around as the bullets hit him. It was town history that quickly became town legend. My sister, Christina, she was older than me, looked just like my mom, so, even though my mother wasn't actually there the night Shanks died, the kids decided it'd be neater, more *satisfying*, if she were. Christina was in great demand during recess."

Heather smiled sadly, then shook the smile away.

"Christina went missing when she was sixteen," she continued. "The ten-year anniversary of Shanks's death, to the hour. She vanished, right out of her bedroom. Over the next few weeks, four others disappeared too – a man, a woman, a fourteen-year-old boy and a three-year-old girl."

"I'm sorry," Amber said quietly.

"It tore us apart for a while, my family. But my parents… I don't know. They're stronger than most, maybe. Then, exactly a year later, another five people went missing. Man, woman and three kids. Year after that, another five… They wouldn't be related, the five people, but they would all look vaguely alike in some way. It's what Shanks used to do. He'd make his grotesque little families."

"And everyone thought it was a copycat killer," said Milo.

"Everyone but me," said Heather. She rolled the cart of books to the Cooking section, started transferring them to the shelves. "Even my mom couldn't see what was happening. She has an amazing mind, but believing that a killer had returned from the dead was a stretch too far for her. I was sixteen years old and Shanks came after me – chased me through the old theatre where we used to hold our recitals. I ran straight into the janitor and we went flying, but, when I looked up, Shanks was gone. Me and a few friends broke into his old store and found a secret room that my dad and the other cops hadn't even looked for. There were all these dollhouses. They were fully furnished, but only half of them had any figures in them. These little people, like porcelain or something, sitting at the table or watching TV or playing with tiny, tiny toys on the carpet. I recognised my sister immediately. She was sitting on a bed upstairs, reading a book with a big smile on her face."

"Figurines of his victims," Glen said. "Creepy."

Heather shook her head. "You're not getting it. Shanks made the house, the furniture, all that stuff. But he didn't make the figures. He caught them."

Milo frowned. "Sorry?"

Heather made sure the elderly librarian wasn't within range, and she leaned in. "The figures *were* his victims. That was my sister sitting on the toy bed. My *actual* sister. He'd got her smile wrong, though. Christina always had this lopsided smile. He got that wrong."

"But you said the figures were made of porcelain," said Amber.

"That's what it looked like," Heather replied. "But I saw what he did to their bodies, when they were dead. He embalmed them. The cellar of his toyshop was one big embalming room. Then he dressed them and... and posed them. He'd stitch expressions on to their faces and arrange their arms this way or that... When he had them the way he wanted, he'd cover them with a kind of resin to hold them in place, and put them in the dollhouse."

"Yeah, no, still not getting it," said Glen. "Because the figures in dollhouses are tiny. It *sounds* like what you're telling us is that he killed them, embalmed them, and then shrank them, but you're a normal, sane lady so that can't be what you're actually saying."

"He didn't shrink them," said Heather. "Not really. Shanks called it doorway magic. He had this key, this special key, which acted as a tunnel, I guess, from one door to *any* other, whichever one he wanted. That's how he took people. That's how they vanished.

"When he took Glen – my boyfriend – he told him about it. Glen wrote it all down. I found it when I went looking for him, a scrap of paper soaked in his blood. Shanks was linking a normal door to the dollhouse doors – when you passed through, you became smaller. Shanks would work on the bodies here, get them into the proper poses, and then put them through into the dollhouse, where they'd be the size of figurines."

"I really don't mean any offence by this," Amber said, "but I hope you realise how nuts that sounds."

Heather smiled sadly. "I know."

"Because it really sounds nuts."

"And it is," Heather said. "But it's also what happened. People know it, too. Well – everyone of my generation. They've all heard the stories. They were there when Shanks started coming after me and my friends. They might not believe the story anymore, they may have come up with more rational explanations or dismissed the whole thing as nonsense, but a part of them still believes."

"That's why they beat up those kids last year," said Milo.

"Poor little Walter," Heather said, nodding. "I've heard his theory, that this is all some plot to get kids to behave themselves. If I were him, I'd probably think the same. But keeping the dollhouses at the school was our way of honouring Shanks's victims – remembering them even if we couldn't come right out and tell everyone what had really happened. The people who beat up those kids probably didn't even understand why they were so angry – not consciously, at least. But this entire town has been scarred by Dacre Shanks, and he still haunts us."

"How did you stop him?" Amber asked.

"First thing I did was steal his key. Then I trapped him. I managed to fool him into trapping himself, actually, in the fourth dollhouse. I was the only one of my friends to survive, and I barely did that."

She lifted her top to show them a jagged scar across her belly.

"Cool," breathed Glen.

Amber watched as Heather cast a furtive glance at Milo and then, almost like she'd just realised what she'd done, she blushed, and busied herself with tucking in her shirt.

"Where's the dollhouse now?" Amber asked.

"Why?"

"We… we need to talk to Dacre Shanks."

Heather stopped what she was doing. Thirty seconds passed in which nothing was said. Even Glen stayed quiet.

"Who are you?" Heather finally asked.

"We just need to ask him something," Amber said. "Just one thing and then we'll be gone."

"Who *are* you?"

Amber tried figuring out the best way to say what she had to say. "Some people want to kill me. They're monsters, I guess. Like Shanks. They won't stop until I'm dead. My only hope is to find this guy we're looking for and Shanks is the only one who knows his name."

"They're like Shanks?"

Amber nodded. "And there's five of them. Please, Heather, all I want is to ask him this guy's name."

"I'd like to help," Heather said. "I really would. But no one talks to Shanks. No one. Any opportunity to get free, he'll take it."

"We won't do anything to risk—"

"I'm sorry," said Heather. "He's killed too many people already. I've kept him trapped by not letting anyone know he's there, and certainly not letting anyone *talk* to him. You're just going to have to find another way to get what you need."

"There is no other way," said Milo.

"Then I'm sorry. I truly am. But if Shanks gets free it won't be you he goes after. It'll be me. It'll be people from this town. Springton will go back to being his hunting ground."

"Maybe we can help," said Amber. "He's trapped in a dollhouse – but how secure can that be? Those kids easily trashed two of the dollhouses kept at the school. He will eventually be found."

"And I suppose you have a better way?"

"We'll take the dollhouse away from here," Milo said. "Destroy it, bury it, burn it, whatever."

"Too risky. Sorry, but I'm not going to change my mind. My mom suggested I talk to you, and I've talked to you. If I had known you wanted to actually communicate with him, I'd never have agreed to it. If my mom had known that, I doubt she'd have even mentioned you to me. I can't help you, and I won't help you. I'm sorry about that, I really am. But I have to ask you to leave the library."

Amber had no argument left, and so she found herself walking out into the sunshine with Glen and Milo at her heels.

"Huh," she said. "I didn't think she'd actually say no. I mean, I should have but I didn't. We can't *make* her tell us where she's keeping Shanks, can we? I'm… I have no idea what to do now. What do we do?"

Glen shrugged. "How about we break into her house?"

Amber frowned. "Seriously?"

"Of course. This is life or death, right? You need to speak to this guy, so let's search her place and find him, then get the hell out of here before her dad comes after us with his gun. Do we know where she lives?"

"Pine Street," said Milo.

"There you go," Glen said, clapping his hands. "That's our plan, right?"

Amber looked at Milo.

"Sure," said Milo. "That's our plan."

Pine Street was a picket-fence affair: neat lawns and trimmed hedges and not one oil stain on a single driveway. They found the Medina house without a problem, passed it and drove down to the corner. Amber and Glen walked back, rang the doorbell and waited. They chatted about nothing, but they did so loudly and with much false cheer. A neighbour walking her dog glanced at them. They smiled politely, and rang the doorbell again.

The door opened, and Milo let them in.

While they searched, Milo did his best to patch up the window he had broken. He left money on the table for the damage. The dollhouse wasn't in any of the rooms. The attic was empty. The cellar was bare.

The dollhouse wasn't there.

They got back to the Charger.

"Okay," said Glen, "I'm out of ideas."

"It's in the library," Amber said. "It is, isn't it? Big old place like that probably has a hundred rooms that aren't being used. I bet they have big old locks on the doors, too."

"If the dollhouse is not where she lives," said Milo, "then it's probably where she works."

Glen sounded grumpy in the back seat. "It'll take ages to search that place."

Milo started the car. "Then I guess we'll have to do it at night."

21

THE LIBRARY WAS CREEPY when it got dark.

The staff turned out the lights and locked up. Heather Medina was the last to leave. When the silence had settled and ten minutes had passed, Amber and the others emerged from the restroom where they'd been hiding. The occasional bright sweep of headlights from the street outside was the only illumination they were granted as they made their way through the maze of bookcases. Those lights sent shadows dancing and flitting from floor to wall to ceiling, and each one set Amber's heart to drumming.

They split up, their task made easier when Glen found a set of keys lying in the office inbox. Locked doors swung open and revealed storage spaces, boxes of books and plaster busts gathering dust. They found desks piled on top of each other and a room full of broken chairs.

Finally, they found a door at the end of a dark and windowless corridor for which they had no key. Milo knelt and proceeded to pick the lock. It took a lot longer than Amber expected.

When the last tumbler slid into place, Milo pulled on the

handle and pushed. The door opened to a small room with a single table at its centre, and upon that table was a dollhouse.

Amber stepped in. They were deep enough in the library that she felt confident in turning on a light. The single bulb brightened slowly, its radiance dimmed by dust.

The dollhouse was magnificent. Front opening, with two stories and an attic space. It was the kind of thing Amber would have loved as a little girl, if only her parents had paid more attention to her subtle hints. If only her parents hadn't been planning to murder her from the day she was conceived.

She peered through the little windows, saw furniture. Beds and dressers. Downstairs, there was a hall with a staircase, and a kitchen.

"Can you see anything?" Glen whispered from beside her.

Something moved past the window and Amber recoiled sharply.

There was a moment, while she stood there, the hair on her neck prickling and every instinct urging her to run, when she genuinely considered just calling up her parents and imploring them to rethink their plans and let her come home. She was ready, in that moment, to forgive them, to carry on with her life as if nothing had happened.

The moment passed.

She cleared her throat. "Hello?" she said. She peered closer, but it was dark in there. "Are you there? Dacre Shanks, can you hear me?"

No answer. At least none that she could hear.

Glen hunkered down to look through the side windows. "Maybe he's sleeping," he said, then knocked heavily on the roof. "Hey, wake up in there!"

Milo took hold of Glen's wrist. "Please don't do that to the serial killer."

Glen took his hand back. "What? He lives in a dollhouse. He's the size of Thumbelina, for God's sake. You think he scares me?"

"It's not about whether or not he scares you," said Milo, "it's the principle of the thing. Wherever possible, you do not antagonise serial killers. That's just a general rule of life."

"I don't think it applies to serial killers you could fit in your pocket."

"Quiet," said Amber, leaning closer to the large upstairs window, the one looking on to the landing. Someone was standing there, very still. Someone who hadn't been there a moment earlier.

"Hello? Mr Shanks?"

Then she heard it. They all heard it. A man's voice. Quiet.

"Hello," it said, from inside the dollhouse.

If a voice could crawl, this one did. It crawled over Amber's face to her ears, scuttled in and burrowed its way into her brain. She could feel its legs, cold and frenzied. "You have my attention."

Her mouth was dry. Her mouth was so dry. "Mr Shanks, my name is Amber. I need—"

"Pleased to meet you, Amber."

For a moment, she couldn't talk. "Yeah," she said, feeling stupid and scared and childish. She was so very afraid. "I need your help. We've come—"

"And who are your companions?" Dacre Shanks asked in that creepy-crawly voice of his.

"Um, this is Milo and that's Glen."

"Hi," said Glen. Even he sounded scared.

"Mr Shanks," said Amber, "I'm here because I've been told you know of a man who tricked the Shining Demon – did a deal with him, then went on the run."

There was a pause. "Ah yes," came the voice from the window. "Indeed I do. I met him many years ago. Interesting fellow."

"Do you happen to remember his name, or where I might find him?"

"I remember his name, yes, and I also know the town in which he was born. Would that be of any use to you in tracking him down?"

"Yes," said Amber. "Very much so."

There was a moment of silence from inside the dollhouse. "How nice," said Shanks.

"Are you really tiny?" Glen asked suddenly, his curiosity overcoming his fear. "Can I see you?"

Milo put his hand on Glen's shoulder to shut him up.

Amber glared, grateful to Glen for allowing her to focus on something she could scorn. Reluctantly, she looked back through the window.

"Sorry about that," she said. "This man, could you tell me his name?"

Shanks said, "Forgive me for asking... Amber, wasn't it? Forgive me for asking, Amber, and forgive me for being so crude, but what exactly is in it for me?"

She frowned. "I'm sorry?"

"If I tell you what you came here to learn, what do I get out of it?"

"I... I don't know. What do you want? We can't release you."

"Why not?"

"Because you'll kill people."

"And?" said Shanks.

"And it'll be my fault."

"And this would upset you?"

"Well, yes."

"You are a curious girl. Tell me this – why do you want the man you seek?"

"I just want to talk to him," said Amber, aware how pathetic this sounded.

"About the Shining Demon?"

"Yes."

The man in the window moved slightly, and the light almost hit his face. He was wearing a short-sleeved shirt and a tie. "You want to make a deal? Or you've already made one and you're having second thoughts? Maybe I can help you. Release me and I'll speak to the Shining Demon on your behalf."

"I'm sorry, Mr Shanks, but you're not getting out."

"Then what else do you have to offer me? I am trapped in a dollhouse – what, apart from freedom, do you think I require? A pet?"

"We could get you a cute little convertible," said Glen. "Maybe throw in a Barbie if you're feeling lonely?"

Amber froze, awaiting Shanks's response.

"Your friend is very rude," he said eventually.

"I'm sorry," she responded. "And he's not my friend. Mr Shanks, you're absolutely right, there is nothing I can offer you. We're not releasing you. You've killed innocent people before and you will do it again. I can't allow that to happen."

"Then we are at an impasse."

"I guess we are." She bit her lip. "So why not just tell me?

You're not getting out, right? So we're not going to be making a deal here. If we're not going to make a deal, there's nothing you have to gain from this situation. And, if you have no chance of gaining anything, then you won't have anything to lose by telling me what I want to know, will you?"

A low chuckle. "I see your logic. Cleverly done, young lady."

"Thank you."

"But you're wrong about me not having anything to gain. You see, I've been stuck here for… I actually don't know how long."

"Thirty-one years," said Glen.

"Really? Well now… thirty-one years. Imagine that. In that case, I've been stuck here for thirty-one years. I can't go insane and I can't kill myself because I'm already dead. So I've been sitting here for thirty-one years, and I only rise out of my bored stupor when that door opens and little Heather Roosevelt pokes her pretty head in to make sure everything is still in place. Oh, but she's not a Roosevelt anymore, is she? She got married. She won't tell me to whom, but I saw the wedding ring – for as long as it was there. She's getting old, though, isn't she? Every time I see her, she is less and less like the troublesome teenager who trapped me in here in the first place.

"But here I sit. Bored. I don't need to eat or sleep. I don't age. I feel each and every one of those seconds as they drag by, too many to count, too many to keep track of. I haven't spoken to anyone in all that time. I talk only to myself these days, just because I like the sound of my own voice – as you've probably guessed. I haven't talked to anyone and I haven't interacted with anyone until you three walked in here.

"Your problem, as I have said, stems from the mistaken presumption that I have nothing to gain by not telling you what you want to know. The fact is, though, I do. I haven't spoken to anyone until you. I haven't interacted with anyone until you. But you know what else I haven't done? I haven't hurt anyone... until you. You need this information and you need it badly, or else you wouldn't be here talking to someone like me, but I'm not going to tell you simply because it makes me happy to disappoint you."

"Wow," said Glen. "You're a dick."

"I suppose I am, Glen, yes," said Shanks. "I take my pleasures where I can — small and petty as they may be."

Glen sneered through the window. "Well, why don't I just reach in there and smush your head?"

"Please do."

"Glen," said Amber.

He stepped back. "What? Am I the only one here who is aware of the fact that the big, bad, scary man we're talking to is, like, three inches tall? Am I the only one amused by that?"

"If you reach in there," said Amber, "you'll be opening the dollhouse. He can escape."

"Where to? A cartoon mouse hole in the skirting board? He'll still be only three inches tall."

"Are you sure about that?" Milo asked. "We don't know how this doorway magic works. You open that dollhouse and he might return to normal size."

"Don't listen to them, Glen," said Shanks from the window. "Reach in here and teach me a lesson."

Glen faltered. "Uh... no. No, I don't think so, if it's all the same to you."

"Are you a coward, Glen?"

"Only when threatened."

"Such a shame. My first impression of you was that you possessed a spark your companions lacked. But you have revealed your true nature, and your true nature, I am afraid to say, is a crushing disappointment."

Glen shrugged. "You're actually not the first person to say that."

"You are a coward and a dullard, just like the rest of your countrymen."

"Ah now, here," said Glen, "don't you go insulting my countrymen."

"What is Ireland but a land of mongrels, wastrels and whelps?"

"Ah, that's a bit strong…"

"Drunken buffoons stumbling through their maudlin lives, violent and thuggish and self-pitying, a nation of ungrateful—"

Glen laughed. "I'm sorry, pal, I don't care what you say. You're three inches tall. My mickey is bigger than you. And that was a pretty blatant attempt to provoke me, but what you're failing to realise is that Ireland is the greatest country in the world, you dope."

"Then why are you in America?"

Glen leaned down to grin straight into the window. "Because America has the best monsters."

There was a moment of silence, and then, amazingly, laughter.

"I like you," Shanks announced. "I like all three of you. And I will answer your question, Amber – but only to you. Not to your friends."

"We're not leaving," said Milo.

"That is my only condition," Shanks said.

"Why?" Amber asked. "Why not tell all of us?"

A chuckle. "Because I am tricky. Because I like pushing buttons. Glen may be a delightful buffoon, but Milo here is obviously your protector, and as such he takes things a lot more seriously. Since I am acquiescing to your request, I need to find some way of satisfying my quiet need to torture. Making your companions leave the room is a small triumph, but, as it has been pointed out, I am a small man."

Amber deliberated, then looked at Milo. He grunted, and left the room. Glen went with him.

Amber shut the door, and moved back to the dollhouse. "Yes?"

"Heather doesn't know you're here, does she?" Shanks asked.

"Why does it matter?"

"She has kept this dollhouse in this room for thirty–one years. My prison has many windows, but all I see are walls. She even took the other dollhouses to the local school, so I couldn't gaze at them for solace."

"And if I ask her to move it somewhere else? Somewhere with a view, maybe? If you give me the name of the man I'm looking for and the town he grew up in, I'll ask her. You have my word." Amber frowned. "Hello? Mr Shanks? Are you still there?"

"A view?" he said, even quieter than before. "You offer me a view?"

"Well, what do you want, Mr Shanks?"

"To be free."

"I told you, I'm not releasing you."

"There is more than one way to be free, Amber." Shanks

stood with his hands clasped at his chest, his face still in darkness. "I'll give you the name of the man you seek. I'll tell you where to find him."

Amber frowned. "And in return?"

A hesitation. "In return, you find a way to kill me."

She had to be honest – she hadn't been expecting that. "I'm sorry?"

"I'm never getting out of here," said Shanks. "Don't you think that's unnecessarily cruel? I know I've done bad things, evil things, but surely you understand that nobody deserves an eternity of this? Heather would gladly kill me if she could."

"I'm… I'm not killing anyone."

"Then get your protector to do it. He looks like he'd even enjoy the opportunity."

"This isn't why we came here."

"But you'd be doing the world a favour!" Shanks said. "What if I escape? The first thing I'm going to do if I ever get out of here is kill Heather Roosevelt. Then I'm going to kill her parents, and all of her friends. Then this entire town. So do the right thing, Amber. Find a way to finish me off now, while I'm vulnerable."

She shook her head. "We're not killers. We're not like you."

"Please," said Shanks. "You'd be putting me out of my misery."

"You've murdered innocent people," said Amber. "You deserve your misery."

"Then I'll give you something more!" Shanks said. "I'll give you his name, his address, and I'll even tell you how to get to him tonight."

Her heart beat faster. "He lives close?"

"No. He lives in Oregon. But distance doesn't mean a thing when you've got my key. It's on the wall behind you. See it?"

There was a single nail in the wall, and hanging from that nail was an ornate brass key. Amber took it down, tracing her fingers over the intricate etchings along its side. The head of the key was shaped like a lock.

"Heather hung it there to taunt me," said Shanks. "Always in sight, always out of reach. But that key can get you where you want to go instantly. Do we have a deal?"

Amber looked back at the dollhouse. "I'm not going to kill you, Mr Shanks."

"Then get Buxton to do it! He might even know how!"

"Buxton?"

"Gregory Buxton," said Shanks. "I first met him in the town of his birth, a bland little place called Cascade Falls. That's who you're looking for, and that's where you want to go."

"How do I know you're telling the truth?"

"See for yourself! Put the key in the lock of the door there. Turn it twice, but keep saying his name in your head, his name and the name of his town."

"Gregory Buxton," she said, turning to the door, "Cascade Falls."

"Try it," said Shanks. "Keep saying that, turn the key, open the door and walk through. That's all the proof you'll need. But then, once you've spoken to him, promise me you'll do as I ask."

"I'll... I'll talk to Milo about it."

"We had a deal!" Shanks shouted from behind her.

Amber didn't turn. "I didn't agree to anything." She put the key in the lock, repeating Buxton's name and the name of his town over and over in her head. She twisted the key and heard the door lock, then turned it again, heard the tumblers slide and settle. Then she opened the door and stepped through, but at the last moment the corridor became a dimly lit hall with a grand staircase and long shadows. The door shut behind her with a crash that reverberated through the floor itself. She spun. The door was now white and it didn't have a handle. She pounded on it. It was thin wood that shook under her fist.

And then Shanks's voice came drifting down from upstairs. "I told you I was tricky."

22

Amber lurched sideways, a fast-moving terror spreading outwards from the back of her neck to her fingertips and toes. She ran from the hall, seeing now how fake it all was, how flimsy the walls were. She skidded into the kitchen, with its table and chairs and stove and fridge, and her foot caught on something and she went stumbling, nearly falling over a sofa. The architecture was crazy. It made no sense. One half of this room was a kitchen, the other a living room.

She heard Dacre Shanks coming down the stairs.

"I fibbed," he called. "I tricked you. You can *use* the key, but only I control where it leads. I admit it, I played you for a fool. In my defence, though, you were an easy target."

Amber ran quietly into another room, a room with floor-to-ceiling shelves. Upon those shelves were rows of cardboard painted with the spines of anonymous books. This was the library, and it was also a utility room with a washing machine and a plastic bed for the dog.

She caught her foot again. A crack ran in a perfectly straight line between the dual rooms. It took her adrenalised brain another moment to piece it together. This was a dollhouse, after all. The front was a façade that split somewhere near the middle, and opened up like uneven wings, like the covers of a book, revealing the interior with its collection of half-rooms. Closed up like this, nothing made sense, and everything was folded together at an unnatural angle.

"Amber," Shanks called in a sing-song voice.

She ducked down in the dark behind a washing machine. Her hands were shaking.

"You're being silly," he continued. He was still in the hall, probably trying to figure out which way she'd run. "I'm not going to hurt you. You're the first person I'll be able to talk to, eye to eye, in all the time I've been here. Come out. Come on. You know I'm going to find you eventually."

She shuffled forward a little, and peeked round the edge of a bookcase. She glimpsed him, just enough to see the knife he held as he moved away. He was checking the other side of the house first. She'd been given a moment, a chance to think, to put her thoughts in order.

When he didn't find her over there, he'd come over here, and he'd find her within seconds. So she had to move. Upstairs. That was the way to go. Upstairs would have multiple bedrooms, which meant more places to hide. She gripped the bookcase, getting ready to pull herself up on to her quaking, trembling legs, but her gaze caught on her hand, and she looked at how soft and pink it was.

She'd almost forgotten.

She shifted. She felt that pain again, that peculiar kind of pain as the strength flooded through her and her limbs lengthened and her body reshaped itself. She had horns now, and her hands were long-fingered and tipped with black nails.

She forced the fear down and got up off her knees. She crept quickly and quietly back through the kitchen-living room, keeping her eyes locked on the darkness at the other side of the hall.

She reached the staircase. From a few steps away, the banisters had seemed ornate, but as she ascended she could feel the chips and inconsistencies in the wood beneath her hand. The steps didn't creak, though, and for this she was thankful. She sank into darkness and then plunged into light, a harsh light that cascaded through the circular window and bathed the second-floor landing in hellish reds and fiery oranges.

Amber moved to the side, into the shadow, and crouched, looking through the wooden railing and down into the hall. Seconds passed, then Dacre Shanks walked into view, crossing from one side of the hall to the other. She watched her enemy, marvelling at how easily the hunter can become the prey. All it takes is a new perspective.

To her right, a half-wall with a doorway leading into a bedroom, the wallpaper a dark colour, a blue or something like it. Maybe a green. Pressed against it, in the closed wing of the front of the house, another bedroom of a lighter colour. It was hard to tell in all this gloom, but it was probably pink.

To her left, the main bedroom and a bathroom with a Jacuzzi and a tub. No shower, though. There was also a toilet and a sink with a framed piece of reflective plastic that acted as a mirror.

Dacre Shanks strolled back into the hall, and raised his head. He was a narrow man, with dark hair turning grey and receding fast from his temples like it was afraid of his face. His face was something to fear. A long nose and a thin mouth and eyes in shadow. "Are you up there, Amber? Did you sneak by me? Oh, aren't you a clever one? Aren't you a sneaky one? But you know what you are, most of all? You are fun. You are a fun one. So come on down, Amber. You win our little game of hide-and-seek. I give up."

He raised his hands in surrender and chuckled.

"I'm waiting," said Amber.

Shanks swivelled his head to where she was crouched. He couldn't see her, though. His eyes passed over her.

"What was that?" he called. "I'm afraid I didn't quite hear you. Old age, you see. I'm not as young as I used to—"

"I said, I'm waiting."

Shanks zeroed in on her position, and gave her a smile that opened like a wound. "Waiting for me?"

"I'm not like the others you've killed," Amber said. "I'm not going to scream and run away."

"Ooooh," said Shanks, and laughed. "A fighter, are we? Heather was a fighter, back in her teenage years."

"And she beat you," said Amber. "So now I'm going to beat you."

"Wrong," said Shanks, a flicker of irritation crossing his features for the first time. "She tricked me. She didn't beat me, she tricked me into doing this to myself."

"So not only are you weak," Amber said, "you're also an idiot?"

Shanks made a sound she couldn't identify, and started up the stairs. "I've been doing this a very long time, young lady. I've hunted all kinds of people."

Amber stood as he approached. "You've never hunted anyone quite like me."

He reached the top, came towards her, and she stepped out of the shadows and smiled, giving him a flash of her fangs.

He froze, stared at her, and then his eyes narrowed. "You are a girl full of surprises, aren't you?" he said, starting to move to the side. Circling her. That knife in his hand. "So that's why you want Buxton. You have your power and now you want more. Funny the effect power has on a person."

"I suppose it is," she said, turning with him as he circled.

"Has it changed you, Amber? Apart from physically, I mean. Are you a different person now?"

"Like you wouldn't believe."

Shanks smiled. "I bet. I saw you and I thought to myself, *easy target*. Now look at you. Suddenly I feel very silly indeed."

"How did you get me in here?"

Shanks's chuckle was dry, and lacking good cheer. "You don't have to worry about that," he said. "You're never going to leave."

He lunged, jabbing low and then slashing high. Amber dodged backwards, barely avoiding the blade that whistled by her throat. Shanks didn't stop moving, however. In an instant, he was on her, pushing her back against the banister. She grabbed at his knife hand, fingers closing round his wrist. He was stronger than she'd expected. Not as strong as her but close enough. He headbutted her and pain flashed outwards from her nose. His other hand was on her throat and he was pushing her back, over the banister. She grew talons and raked his arm.

Howling, Shanks released his grip. They stumbled, locked

together. Blood ran from Shanks's forearm, but he ignored it and reached up for her horns. He suddenly stepped back and yanked downwards and Amber cried out, her knees hitting the floor. He kicked her, the toe of his shoe connecting with her chin, and Amber sprawled.

"You're all strength," Shanks said, kneeling on her throat, "but no finesse. No style."

"Amber!" came Milo's voice from all around them. "Amber, someone's coming. We must have set off an alarm. Amber?"

Through the window behind Shanks, she could see out into the room as Milo stepped in. He was a giant.

"Amber?" he said, his voice astonishingly loud.

Shanks smiled down at her. "Hush now. Don't spoil the surprise." He pulled her up, holding the knife against her throat, and moved her to the window.

Glen came in after Milo, closing the door. He noticed the key. "Where is she?" he asked, fiddling with it. The key twisted as he fiddled, locking the door.

"Oh my," whispered Shanks. "This will be even easier than I thought."

Milo came closer to the dollhouse, peering through the windows. "Shanks. I'd like a word."

Behind him, Glen turned the key in the other direction, and opened the door.

Shanks shoved Amber away, and ran for the stairs.

Amber toppled, still woozy from the kick to the head. She looked down through the banisters, saw Shanks sprinting for the front door. He vanished right before he hit it and she snapped her head up—

—as he smashed into Glen, throwing him violently off his

feet, then rebounded, went stumbling towards Milo as Milo turned. As the door slammed shut behind him, Shanks hit Milo with a wild swing boosted by his momentum, and Milo twisted and went down. Shanks got his feet under him, looked around and then through the dollhouse window, and a smile broke across his features.

Amber stood up, fresh terror mounting.

She heard footsteps, running footsteps from beyond the closed door.

"Get out of there!" came Heather's voice.

Shanks's face took on an expression of pure joy, and he darted behind the door.

"Heather, no!" Amber screamed, stumbling to the window. "Don't come in!"

Heather didn't hear her. She threw the door open and ran in and Shanks grabbed her, pushed her back against the wall and plunged his knife into her and Amber went cold.

Heather stared into Shanks's eyes, her mouth open, but no sound coming out.

"I told you," Shanks snarled as he dragged the blade across her belly. "I told you I'd kill you, you interfering little bitch."

He gave the knife another twist and Heather made a sound halfway between a sigh and a gag, and then a series of explosions filled Amber's ears. Shanks went stumbling, letting Heather fall as he scrambled out of the door. A moment later, Milo rose into view, his gun in his hand.

He helped Glen back to his feet, then tore the jacket off him. He crouched by Heather, pressing the jacket against her wound. "Keep applying pressure," he said. "Glen! Call an ambulance!"

Heather grabbed his arm. "Stop Shanks," she said, her voice weak. "Stop him."

Milo hesitated, then stood. "Glen, stay with her. When help comes, find Amber."

Then he was gone.

23

AMBER RAN FOR THE banister, leaped over it, and dropped to the floor below. The impact juddered from her feet to her hips, but she sprang for the white door the way Shanks had… and smashed straight into it.

She staggered back, landed on her ass.

She got up, hurried to the closest window. From there, she could see the huge figure of Glen pressing his jacket against Heather's wound as he talked on the phone, giving the address. There was blood everywhere. Amber looked past them, to the door, to the brass key still in the lock.

"Glen!" she yelled.

Glen looked around. "Amber?"

"Glen!"

He took Heather's hands, laid them on the jacket. "Hold this," he said, and hurried over, checking the windows. "Amber! You in there?"

She waved until she caught his attention. His face filled the window.

"Amber! You're red again!"

She stopped waving. "I'm also trapped in here."

"Yes," Glen said quickly. "Of course. How do I get you back to normal size?"

"The door. Close it and lock it, then unlock it and open it. Don't walk through."

Glen frowned. His eyebrows were massive and hairy. "Why?"

"The key! It's the key Heather told us about, the one that let Shanks travel between doorways!"

"Ohhh," said Glen. "Okay, cool. Hey, Amber? What does it look like when someone is dying? I think Heather might be dying."

"The door, Glen!"

"Right," he said, then hunkered down to peer in. "And listen, if this doesn't work, you can live in my pocket. I won't mind."

"The door!" she shouted.

Glen hurried to the door, stepping over Heather's outstretched legs as he did so. He locked it, unlocked it and opened it, and Amber ran forward, and right before she slammed into the dollhouse door it turned into the room outside, and she stumbled into Glen, who shrieked and spun as the door slammed shut behind her.

"Amber!" he gasped.

Relief washed over her, but then Heather raised her head, her eyes widened and she screamed.

"No, no, it's okay!" Glen said. "It's Amber! She's with us! She won't hurt you!"

Despite her wound, Heather scrambled away from them both, leaving a bloody smear on the ground.

"Glen, it's okay," Amber said. "I'm leaving. I'm going after Shanks."

"Well then, I'm going with you."

"No, you stay with her."

"I'm going with you," he insisted. "Heather's fine. Heather, aren't you fine? The ambulance will be here shortly, and all I'll be doing is soaking up blood. I'm going with you."

"Fine," Amber muttered, taking the brass key from the lock and pocketing it. She opened the door. The corridor looked perfectly normal.

"If you disappear again, I'll rescue you," Glen said from beside her.

She patted his shoulder, and then shoved him out into the corridor. He tripped, went sprawling, but at least he didn't disappear. She ran, jumped over him and kept going.

He did his best to keep up. "I don't mind that you did that," he called.

Amber ignored him.

She burst out into the night air just as Milo came striding back to the Charger, his gun held down by his leg.

"Amber! Where the hell were you?"

"Never mind that," she said. "Any sign of him?"

"No," Milo said as he opened the car door. "Get in. He's probably headed to the toystore."

"Maybe not," she said. "He mentioned the other dollhouses – he might be going there, instead. You check the toystore, I'll check the school."

"We're not splitting up," said Milo. "It's too dangerous."

"It's my fault he's out!" she shouted. "If he hurts anyone else, that's on me! I'll be fine – I'm a goddamn demon, okay? Go!"

Milo hesitated, then tucked his gun into his waistband and jumped in behind the wheel. Glen hurried up behind her as the Charger was speeding away.

"Come on," said Amber.

Glen panted and wheezed as they ran the block to the school, whereas she ran easily, giving a wide berth to every darkened doorway while Glen staggered by, oblivious to the threat Shanks posed. They got to the corner and paused, peering out across the street.

"It doesn't look like he's here," Glen whispered, still panting.

"Let's get closer."

Glen grabbed her arm. He could barely fit his hand around her bicep. "Maybe we should wait for Milo. He has the gun, right? I mean, you've got claws and you're amazing, but a gun's a gun."

"If we delay, he might hurt someone."

"So? Do you really care?"

She snapped her head round to him. "What?"

He held up his hands. "Hey, sorry. I just… You didn't exactly force me to stay with Heather, you know?"

She snarled. "You said she'd be fine."

"Well, yeah, but what do I know? I just said that so I could come along."

She leaned in. "Of course I care about Shanks hurting people."

"Right. Okay. I thought maybe you didn't really give a crap about that stuff. My mistake."

Amber wanted to hit him, wanted to take out her anger and frustration on his stupid face, but right before she made a move an alarm rang out, drawing her attention back to the school.

"Looks like we're the lucky ones," she said.

"I'll call Milo."

"You do that. I'm going to— *damn* it."

She ducked back as a police cruiser swept in, hopping the kerb and stopping right at the foot of the steps.

"Wow," said Glen. "Response time here is *fast*."

They watched Sheriff Roosevelt get out, and Dacre Shanks walk down the steps towards him.

Amber couldn't hear what Teddy was saying over the noise of the alarm, but Shanks kept on coming with his head down. Teddy backed away, his hand resting on the butt of his holstered gun.

Amber broke from cover, sprinting towards them, Glen at her heels.

She was halfway across the street when Shanks got close enough for Teddy to recognise him. Teddy jerked back, went for his gun, but Shanks took three quick steps and plunged his knife into the sheriff's throat.

Amber roared and Shanks turned to her, Teddy's gun in his outstretched hand.

She pulled up, stumbling a little. Glen ran into the back of her.

Shanks smiled at her. "Where's your friend?"

Amber hissed as Teddy sank slowly to the ground.

This just made Shanks smile wider. "He's a dangerous one. I could tell just by looking at him. Do me a favour, would you? Call out to him? Tell him to join us, and to leave his gun behind?"

"He's not here," said Amber.

"But he'll be here shortly," Glen added.

"Well then, I had better be ready for him, hadn't I?" said Shanks. "You are both going to accompany me into the school, if you please. Oh, and young lady, if you would do me the courtesy of changing from this beautiful red-skinned creature back to the dull little girl you really are, that would be simply marvellous."

She didn't want to. What she wanted to do was take her chances and dive at him. Maybe he'd shoot her, maybe he wouldn't. Maybe he'd miss. But she wouldn't miss. She'd carve his face up. Rip out his eyes. Tear his throat out with her teeth.

The gun in his hand didn't waver. Amber swallowed her anger, and reverted to normal.

"There," said Shanks. "Isn't that better?"

24

THE ALARM WOULDN'T STOP WAILING. It howled through the high school's wide corridors, an unrelenting assault on Amber's eardrums, and escaped through the open door that led out into the night.

Glen sat with one hand cuffed to the radiator. Amber herself was on her knees, both hands cuffed behind her back. She watched as Shanks opened the glass cabinet, and trailed a long finger over the contours of the dollhouse within, the last surviving dollhouse that contained so many of his victims.

He looked back at her, and smiled.

"This is my life's work," he said, his voice barely audible over the alarm. "This is everything that has ever given my existence meaning. What is your meaning, Amber? What is your purpose?"

Amber didn't say anything.

"Do you even know?" Shanks continued. "Do you have any idea? You probably don't. Very few do. I didn't – not when I was alive. I needed to die before I could see why I needed to live. The Shining Demon helped me. He granted me my new life, and he gave me the key that made everything so much *easier*. Do you have it, by the way? Did you bring it with you?"

"He wants you to help me," Amber said.

"Sorry? What was that?"

"The Shining Demon," she said, louder this time. "He wants you to help me."

Shanks laughed. "I don't think so, Amber. He plays games, as is his right as a Duke of Hell, but that is not a game he is interested in playing. He would rather we scurry about on our own, fumbling blindly in the dark. We arouse his curiosity only rarely, I'm afraid."

She shook her head. "I'm special. He said it himself. If you hurt me, if you harm me or my friends, he'll be—"

He hit her. It was a slap, an open palm, but it struck so fast and so suddenly that it rocked her, sent the world tilting and the floor rushing up to crack against her skull.

She lay on her side, the alarm in her head, tasting blood. Then she felt Shanks's hands on her as he pulled her back to kneeling position.

"My apologies," he said. "I don't like it when people lie to me. I shouldn't have lost my temper. That was rude. But try not to lie again, all right? It brings out my ugly side."

"Every side is your ugly side," Glen said.

"Do you really think it wise to taunt the man with the gun?"

"You think I'm scared of you?"

"Yes," answered Shanks. "You said as much, not fifteen minutes ago."

"That was then," Glen said. "This is now. You know what I think? I think you're the coward. You're a big man with the gun and the knife, but take those away, and you're a pathetic little loser."

Shanks said, in a bored voice that the alarm nearly drowned out, "You do realise I don't need you, yes? All I need is Amber here. You are quite disposable."

Glen laughed. "Of course I'm disposable. I've got four days to live. I'm practically dead already. Four days or right now – what difference does it make? Shoot me, or take these cuffs off and we'll settle this like men."

Amber watched them, waiting for her moment.

"I think I'll shoot you," said Shanks. "It'll be funnier." He raised the gun.

There.

A brief wave of pain washed over Amber as she shifted into her demonic form, and she charged into him, her shoulder catching him in the middle of the back and one of her horns scraping his neck. Shanks went down and she fell on top of him. She tried to snap the handcuffs that bound her wrists behind her – she felt the links strain – but her demon strength wasn't up to the task. Instead, she knelt on his hand and he let go of the gun, and she twisted and fell back, managing to kick the weapon. It skittered across the polished floor towards Glen. He reached for it with his free hand, but it stopped just short of his splayed fingers.

Shanks pushed her off. She got to her knees while he leaped to his feet. He darted for the gun and she threw herself at his legs. He fell sideways, smashing through the glass of the cabinet, narrowly avoiding the dollhouse inside.

Roaring, he clambered out, glass covering him in a thousand crystals. He grabbed Amber by the throat and threw her backwards, then reached down for the gun. In his fury, his clumsy attempt to snatch it up merely pushed it a few inches further away. Glen closed his hand around it, brought it up and fired three times, point-blank, into Shanks's chest.

The alarm cut off.

Shanks straightened up and kept going, toppling over backwards. He landed in a bed of glass and didn't move.

Amber stood up. Glen stared at the gun in his hand. The air carried a whine in the sudden silence.

"You okay?" Glen asked, his voice dull.

She nodded. "You did it."

"I did," said Glen. "I killed—"

Shanks sat up so suddenly it actually made Amber cry out in surprise. Glen tried to get another shot off, but Shanks tore the gun from his grip and pressed the barrel into his jaw.

Amber froze.

"You can't kill what's already dead," said Shanks. "Haven't you ever heard that?"

"I've always wanted to test that theory," said Milo from the door.

Shanks leaped up, grabbed Amber and put the gun to her temple. She felt her scales harden, but she doubted they'd be able to stop a bullet.

Milo walked slowly into the school, holding his gun in both hands, his head cocked slightly, aiming down the sights.

"Take one more step and I'll shoot," said Shanks. "Amber won't look so beautiful with half her face missing, now will she?"

Milo didn't lower the gun and didn't stop moving forward. "We're not letting you leave."

Shanks laughed. "Oh, Milo, I doubt that is your decision to make."

210

"You and me aren't on a first-name basis, Shanks. Let her go and I won't blow your head off. You remember what that feels like, don't you?"

Shanks's grip tightened. "I do indeed. But you may have noticed the last person to do that is now lying on the sidewalk outside with his life leaking away along with all that blood."

Milo gave a little smile. "I noticed, all right."

"Put the gun down. You know it can't hurt me."

"That's not exactly true, though, is it?" said Milo. "It can't kill you, no, but it can hurt you. Might even put you down long enough for us to take those cuffs off of Amber's wrists and put them on to yours."

"One more step," Shanks said. The cold steel pressed harder into Amber's head. "Take one more step."

Milo stopped walking.

"Good doggy," said Shanks. "Now toss the gun."

"Can't do that, I'm afraid. Against my upbringing."

"Toss it or your ridiculous Irish friend dies first."

"Glen is not my friend," said Milo. "And the moment that gun moves away from Amber's head, I pull my trigger. I'm a pretty good shot, I have to warn you."

"Then Amber will be the first to die."

"You kill her, I pull my trigger. Whatever you do, this trigger gets pulled."

"Unless I give up," said Shanks, "in which case you still put me back in that prison. You think you're giving me options, but they all end the same way. The only difference is how many of you I get to kill. Well, Milo? Which one will I start with? The rude Irish boy, or the red-skinned demon girl?"

Milo didn't answer for a moment, and then he spread his arms, taking his finger from the trigger. "You got me," he said. "Don't hurt either of them. I'm putting my gun down."

He laid his pistol on the floor and straightened up, his hands in the air.

Shanks shook his head. "I'm actually disappointed," he said. "I thought we were headed for a showdown."

Milo cracked a smile. "Like in *High Noon*, you mean?"

Shanks pushed Amber to her knees beside Glen, but kept his gun trained on Milo. "Something like that."

Milo didn't seem particularly worried. He was so casual, he shrugged. "Ah, I was always partial to *The Wild Bunch*, myself."

"Me too," said a voice behind them.

Shanks turned to see a shotgun levelled at his chest, and then Ella-May blasted him off his feet.

Shanks hit the ground, the front of his shirt obliterated. He rolled like a rag doll.

Milo holstered his pistol and ran to Amber, the handcuff key in his hand. She reverted to normal instantly, but Ella-May wasn't even looking at her.

Shanks chuckled, and stood.

Ella-May racked the shotgun's slide and blasted him again. And again. Each blast threw him further back, turned his clothes to rags, mutilated his flesh. But, every time he stood up, his skin was unmarked.

The fourth blast hurled him backwards through the door. Ella-May followed him out, and Milo, Amber and Glen followed.

Shanks got up, smiling. "You can shoot me all you want,"

he said, "you're not going to kill me. It's not going to change anything. Look at you. Ella-May Roosevelt. You got old."

"Maybe a few grey hairs here and there," Ella-May said.

"You look like them, you know. Your daughters. The ones I killed. Just like I killed your husband. You're not so smart now, are you, Ella-May? You led them to me all those years ago when you had your whole life ahead of you... and now look. You're old, with your life behind you, and I've taken every last one of your family from you."

"You took Christina," said Ella-May. "But that's all you're going to take from me."

Shanks narrowed his eyes and looked down at the street, where a blood-drenched Heather was helping a blood-drenched Teddy into the back of the cruiser.

"We Roosevelts are a hardy lot," Ella-May said, and blasted Shanks in the back.

For a moment, he flew, his spine arched and his arms flung wide. Then gravity found him, gripped him, yanked him down, hard, into the concrete steps. He bounced and twisted and tumbled and finally flipped, hitting the sidewalk with his head turned the wrong way round.

Milo walked down the steps after him, and calmly cuffed his hands behind his back as he lay there, unmoving.

A car pulled up and a man leaped out, carrying a black bag.

"Doc," Ella-May said in greeting as she handed the shotgun to Amber, "good of you to come so quickly. I need you to see to my husband and daughter while I drive us to Waukesha Memorial."

The doctor stared at the scene. "What the hell happened?"

"Heather has a stab wound to the abdomen," said Ella-May. "As far as I can tell, it missed the major organs. Teddy has had his throat cut. No arterial damage. Both have lost a lot of blood."

The doctor glanced down at Shanks. "What about this man?"

"He doesn't need your help," Ella-May said. She hurried down the steps and guided Heather into the passenger seat.

"Dad first," Heather said. She was corpse-pale and covered in sweat. "His pulse is barely there."

The doctor didn't ask any more questions. He climbed in the back and Ella-May got behind the wheel. She reversed away from the sidewalk and swung round.

"Guess you'll all be gone by the time I get back," she said through the open window.

"We will," said Amber.

"Good," said Ella-May, and she floored it, the cruiser's lights flashing.

Milo watched her go. "Passed her and Heather on my way here," he said. "Figured if she was half as tough as her daughter, giving her the shotgun might not be a bad idea."

Shanks moaned. His bones cracked and his neck straightened.

"Welcome back," said Milo, hauling him to his feet.

The streets were quiet in Springton. This didn't surprise Amber, not after the stories she'd been told. Tomorrow the townspeople would discuss the gunshots and the alarms and all this blood, and they'd let the theories settle in beside the legends and the myths they'd already stored up. She wondered what Walter S. Bryant would make of it all.

"What do we do with him?" asked Glen, keeping a respectful distance from Shanks as Milo forced him to walk.

"We're taking him with us," Milo said.

Shanks grunted out a laugh. "Are you inviting me to join your motley crew? I'll say yes, but only if I can be leader."

"Safest option," Milo said, ignoring Shanks and talking to Amber as they neared the Charger. "We can't leave him here, not after everything that's happened."

"We could chop him up," said Glen. "Or, I mean, *you* could chop him up. Bury him, maybe?"

"Maybe," said Milo. "But there'd always be the risk of someone digging him up by accident."

"I *do* have a tendency to return when you least expect it," said Shanks, chuckling.

They stopped at the rear of the Charger and Milo turned him so that Shanks's back was to the car. Amber noticed that all of their bags had been taken out of the trunk and were now in a pile on the ground.

The trunk opened silently, red light spilling out.

"So we'll take him with us," Milo said. "It'll be inconvenient for a few weeks, but the car will eventually digest him."

"What?" said Shanks, his face going slack, and then Milo shoved him backwards.

Amber's eyes played a trick on her then. For one crazy instant, it looked like Shanks was sucked into the trunk as the trunk itself *enveloped* him, the lid slamming closed like a great black jaw. Shanks kicked and battered and yelled from inside, and then all that noise turned down, like the Charger was slowly muting him.

Amber blinked. "Whoa."

Glen was frowning. "Did you see that? Did I see that? What the hell was that?"

Amber looked at Milo. "Were you serious? About the car digesting him?"

Milo trailed a hand lovingly over the Charger's contours. "She's a beast," he said.

25

They drove out of Springton, parked behind a billboard, and Milo took out the maps while Amber examined Shanks's brass key.

"Could we use that?" Glen asked, now sharing the back seat with their bags. "It took Shanks wherever he wanted to go, right? Can we use it?"

"He said only he controls where it leads," Amber said, trying to read the tiny writing along its side. She gave up. "I doubt he'd want to help us." She tossed it into the glove compartment and took out the iPad, started tapping.

Glen let a few moments go by before speaking again.

"I don't mean to whinge," he said, "but I am really uncomfortable with there being a serial killer in the boot."

"In the what?" said Amber.

"Trunk," Milo translated.

"Can he get me?" Glen asked. "What's separating me from him? Is it this seat? Upholstery and foam? What if he still has his knife? Does he have his knife? We didn't take it from him, did we? He might be burrowing through to me right now."

"You're safe," said Milo absently. "The car will take care of him."

"And that's another thing I'm uncomfortable with," Glen began, but Amber interrupted.

"Cascade Falls," she said, list on the screen. "There's one in Virginia, one in Michigan…" She frowned. "No, wait, those are waterfalls. I think. Well, they might be waterfalls *and* towns. What one do you think Shanks was talking about?"

"Found it," said Milo, laying the map across the steering wheel. "Cascade Falls, Oregon."

"How do you know that's the one Gregory Buxton grew up in?"

"It feels right."

She raised an eyebrow. "*That's* what we're going on?"

"You're on the blackroads, Amber. You've got to learn to trust your instincts."

"If you're sure…" A moment later, she had called up images of a sleepy little town beside a lake. "The town of Cascade Falls. Less than ten thousand people. How long will it take us to get there?"

"Don't know," said Milo, folding away the map. "Two thousand miles… Four days, maybe. Get there some time on Saturday."

Amber adjusted the bracelets on her wrist, sneaking a peek at the scars there: 406 hours left. Take four days away from that, and it would leave her with…

She scrunched up her face.

"What's wrong?" Milo asked.

"Nothing," she mumbled. "Doing math."

Three hundred and ten hours. Which was… thirteen days,

or thereabouts. Just under two weeks. Fully aware that time was slipping away from her, and equally aware that there was nothing she could do about it, Amber nodded. "Okay then, we better get going. Unless you want to find somewhere to sleep?"

She was quietly pleased when Milo shook his head. "Too wired after all that drama. I'll drive until morning, then we'll pull in somewhere for a few hours. That okay with you?"

"That's cool."

"I'll be dead by Oregon," Glen said quietly from the back seat.

She turned, but his face was in shadow. "Aw, listen, Glen…"

"Maybe I should go somewhere fun for my last few days, and let you go on without me." She could see the edge of a sad smile. "You've been to Disney World, Amber – do you think that'd be a good place to die?"

"I've… never really thought about it."

"Maybe on one of the rollercoasters," Glen said. "Or on that other ride, what's the really annoying one?"

"*It's a Small World.*"

"That's it. Go in alive, come out dead. That'd be something, wouldn't it? I wonder how many people die in theme parks every year."

"I don't know," said Amber. "But I do know that the chances of someone actually getting injured in the Orlando parks is, like, one in nine million or something."

"Wow. That's not bad. So someone dying on *It's a Small World* would be pretty rare, then?"

"Well, yeah… You're moving very slow and not a whole lot happens. Are you sure that's where you want to spend your last few days, though? Isn't it a bit…"

"Tacky?" said Milo.

"That wasn't what I was going to say. I was just wondering if it'd be better for you to spend time with your family."

"My family hates me," Glen said. "Why do you think I wanted to come here so badly?"

"I'm sure they don't *hate* you," said Amber.

"They might," said Milo.

Amber ignored him. "My parents want to kill me," she said. "I'm sure your parents aren't nearly as bad as *that*."

"Well, maybe not," said Glen, and he laughed, and Amber laughed, and then they remembered what they were laughing about and they both stopped.

"You two are a pair of idiots," said Milo, and he pulled out on to the road and drove.

They took the interstate west for a few hours, then slipped off on to the back roads. They drove through Sigourney, then Delta, and passed a sign for a town called What Cheer. Farmland and electricity pylons flashing by almost hypnotically. Amber started taking a mental note of the populations listed on each sign, testing her dreadful maths skills by adding them up in her head − 2,059, 328, 646... By the time they were in sight of Knoxville, Iowa, she was going to tell Milo that in the last hour they had passed 15,568 people, then she decided not to. It just wasn't that interesting.

They had breakfast at the Downtown Diner, then slept for a bit in the car. Exhaustion pulled Amber down deep into a dreamless sleep. Even her subconscious was too tired to play.

When she awoke, she cracked one eye open. Milo sat behind the wheel, looking through the windshield, unmoving. He wasn't blinking. His face was slack. She wondered if he slept with his eyes open, like a shark. She moved slightly and he turned to her, and that blank expression was wiped away like it had never really been there. He nodded to her, and started the car, and Glen sat up suddenly in the back.

"What?" He blinked. "Oh. Sorry. We're off again, then." When neither Amber nor Milo answered, he nodded to himself. "Another few hours closer to my death."

"Glen—"

"No, Amber. No. Don't try to comfort me. I'm beyond comfort. There's nothing you can do, nothing you can say, which would ease the weight I feel on my soul. It's heavy. It's so heavy. How much does a life weigh? Can you answer me that? No, I don't think you can. So thank you for your effort, Amber, and I truly mean that. But you won't see a smile from me today."

Amber felt bad. She had been about to tell him to shut up.

"You're not going to die," said Milo.

"Death is tapping me on the shoulder as I sit here."

"Nothing's tapping you anywhere. You're not going to die because we're going to stop off at The Dark Stair and you can deliver the Deathmark to this Abigail, whoever she may be, and then you can leave us alone."

Amber frowned. "You know where it is?"

Glen shoved his head between them. "You know where The Dark Stair is? You knew where it was all this time and you didn't tell me?"

Milo pulled out on to the road and started driving. "I wasn't sure if it'd be on our way. As it turns out, it is."

"Where is it?" asked Amber.

"Salt Lake City," said Milo. "It's a bar for people like… well, like us, I guess. People on the blackroads."

"Wait, wait, wait," said Glen. "If it wasn't in the direction you happen to be heading, would you have told me? Or would you have just let me die?"

"I'd have told you."

Glen gaped. "You'd have let me die!"

"I'd have told you," Milo said again. "I couldn't tell you before now because Amber's parents might have found you if you went off alone."

"I have less than four days to live, Milo! What if Shanks had told us that Gregory Buxton lived east instead of west? What then?"

"Then I'd have put you on a Greyhound."

Glen glanced at Amber. "A dog?"

"A bus."

He turned to Milo again. "And what if that Greyhound got a flat tyre? Or was in an accident? Or I got delayed somehow? I get lost very easily, I'll have you know! If you'd told me where The Dark Stair was at the very beginning, I'd have already delivered the Deathmark and I wouldn't be dying right now! Admit it! You don't care if I live or die, do you?"

Milo thought about it for a few seconds. "Not really," he said.

Glen gasped again.

They drove for another ten minutes without anyone saying a word, but Amber had to ask. She just had to.

"This isn't going to throw us off schedule too much, is it?"

"Ohh!" cried Glen, and Amber winced. "Oh, I'm sorry if my impending doom is throwing you off schedule, Amber! I'm sorry if my imminent demise is inconveniencing you! Tell you what, you let me out here. I'll roll over by the side of the road and die quietly without causing anyone too much bother!"

Milo waited until he had finished, then answered. "It shouldn't," he said.

"Are you still talking about this?" Glen cried.

"Salt Lake City is that weird place, isn't it?" said Amber. "Run by the Amish, or something."

"Founded by Mormons," said Milo. "And yeah, they're pretty strict with their liquor laws and they don't look too kindly on public profanity, but we're going to be well-behaved and we're not going to drink, now are we? Besides, The Dark Stair isn't exactly typical of Salt Lake City. It isn't typical of anywhere, for that matter."

"Do you know it well?"

Milo shook his head. "Been in there twice, for no more than half an hour apiece. There's a lot of kids running around. I remember thinking how weird that was. We'll spend tonight in Nebraska somewhere, get to Salt Lake City tomorrow afternoon or thereabouts. From there it's another eight hundred miles to Buxton's home town. It's Tuesday now – we're still on track to get to Cascade Falls by Saturday."

Amber nodded. "Okay. Yeah, okay."

"Bet if I died back here you wouldn't even notice," Glen muttered, but they ignored him.

They drove on flat roads through flat lands. A few trees here and there, though paltry things, and lonesome. Telegraph poles linked hands over green fields and brown, and carried on into the wide, never-ending distance. A train on the tracks, its carriages the colour of rust and wine, names and slogans painted on the side in indecipherable graffiti.

They stopped at an Amoco gas station outside of a town called McCook, and Amber and Glen went in to use the restrooms and get sandwiches while Milo waited in the Charger. It was just after two and it was warm. The smell of gasoline was on the air.

"How much do you know about Milo?" Glen asked while they were waiting to pay for the food. The old man in front of them was having trouble pulling his wallet from his sagging pants.

Amber shrugged. "I know I'm paying him a lot of money to get me where I need to go."

"So you don't know anything about him?"

She sighed. "No, Glen, I don't."

The old man got his wallet halfway out before it snagged on the corner of his pocket. Amber watched, with an interest that surprised her, the tug of war that followed.

"Remember that story I told you," Glen said, "about the Ghost of the Highway?"

"I don't want to talk about this."

He nodded, satisfied. "Then you suspect it, too."

"I don't suspect anything."

"Milo's the Ghost."

"Glen, seriously, drop it, okay? We've been driving for hours and I am sore and cranky."

"He's a serial killer, Amber."

"Don't be ridiculous."

The old man turned slowly, looked at them with frowning eyes. Amber gave him a pleasant smile, and waited for him to turn back round.

"What's ridiculous about it?" Glen asked softly. "He uses a car instead of a knife, but he's still a serial killer. And that isn't any ordinary car. You know it isn't. It's..." He leaned in closer, and his voice became a whisper. "It's possessed."

"Glen, you sound so dumb right now."

"You saw what it did. It swallowed Shanks. That wasn't my imagination running away with me, no matter how much I try to convince myself. It swallowed him. It's possessed."

The old man finally paid and moved off, and they stepped up to the cash register.

"Any gas?" the bored girl asked.

"Nope," said Amber, and paid.

They walked outside, looked across the forecourt to the Charger.

"We're at a gas station and he's not even filling the tank," said Glen. "How many times has he had to stop for petrol? Twice? Three times? Travelling all this way, he's had to stop for petrol three times? Do you know how much fuel a car like that burns?"

"So this car has good fuel economics. So what?"

"Aren't you wondering what else it runs on? He said it'll digest Shanks. How many other people has it digested? And look how clean it is. It's always clean and I've never seen him wash it. It's like it cleans itself. And what's the deal with him only being able to drive it eight hours a day?"

"On *average*," said Amber. "He's driven it longer."

"But what's the deal? Why that rule? Why eight hours? Because it's road safe? Or maybe it's got something to do with him not wanting to push his car too hard or else it'll get tired."

She turned to him. "Fine, Glen, I'll play this game. What does it mean? Huh? What does it all add up to?"

He hesitated before answering. "I think the Charger's alive."

"Oh my God..."

"Don't look at me like that. It's not just a car, is it? It's more than that. You know it is. You got him a sandwich, right? What's the betting he's not going to eat it?"

"And what will that prove? He's not hungry?"

"He doesn't eat when he's driving," said Glen. "I don't think he sleeps when he's behind the wheel, either. Did he sleep this morning? Did you see him sleep? I didn't."

She rubbed her eyes. "I was sleeping myself, okay? I didn't see much of anything."

"What about going to the toilet? We needed to pee — why didn't Milo?"

"Dude, I'm really not going to talk about anyone's bathroom habits."

"We've asked him to pull over so that *we* could pee, like, twenty times so far."

"You've got a bladder problem."

"I pee, you pee, he doesn't pee. Have you seen him pee?"

"No, Glen, I have not seen Milo pee. What the *hell* are you talking about?"

"I think the Charger sustains him. I think it takes his... y'know, his waste—"

"Ew."

"—and uses it, and when he's behind the wheel his body doesn't need to function the way our bodies do."

"That is disgusting. And stupid."

"He said the Charger would digest Shanks. That means some part of it is organic."

"He was being metaphorical, you idiot."

"Are you sure? He's the Ghost, Amber. He's a serial killer, and he's bonded to the Charger. Maybe he doesn't do it anymore, maybe he's reformed, I don't know. But you said he took it out of storage for the first time in twelve years? What if it's like an addiction? He's stayed away from it for all this time and he hasn't needed to kill. But now he's back using it again. How long before it takes him over? How long before he becomes the Ghost of the Highway?"

"This is a stupid conversation and it is ending right now."

She walked across the forecourt, black asphalt hot even through the soles of her shoes. Glen kept up.

"It swallowed Shanks. It's alive. You know what I think? I think the reason he doesn't turn on the radio is because he's scared of what the car might *say*."

She spun round to him. "If you're not happy with our mode of transport, you don't have to travel with us. No one's asking you to."

Glen looked her dead in the eye. "I'm not leaving you alone with him."

"He's not going to hurt me."

"You don't know him."

"Neither do you," she said, and stalked back to the Charger.

She got in, slamming the door. After a moment, she got out again, held the door open while Glen got in the back. Then she retook her seat and slammed the door a second time.

"Everything all right?" Milo asked.

"Fine," said Amber. "Here's your sandwich."

He took it. "Thanks. I'll have it later."

He turned the key and the Charger roared to life. It rolled smoothly across the loose gravel to the road as an eighteen-wheeler thundered by. Milo watched it go. While he was distracted, Amber reached for the radio.

Her fingers hovered over the dial. One turn. One turn, one

twist, and music would fill the car, or static, or someone complaining about something, or commercials, or preaching... or a voice. A voice unlike any she'd ever heard. The voice of the car. The dark voice of the dark car.

She dropped her hand, and the Charger pulled out on to the road, and they drove on.

26

THEY GOT TO SALT LAKE CITY the next day. Glen stared out at the snow-capped mountains that rose up behind the gleaming buildings like the backdrop of some insane science-fiction movie.

"They're *massive*," he breathed. "Are those the Rockies?"

"Yeah," Amber replied sarcastically, "because every mountain range in America is the Rockies."

"They actually *are* part of the Rockies," said Milo, and Amber glowered. "That's the Wasatch Range there."

"We don't have anything like this in Ireland," Glen said. "Like, we have some awesome mountains, like the Sugar Loaf, and MacGillycuddy's Reeks, and the Giant's Causeway up north, but... but that's less of a mountain and more of a... bit of rock. Are we anywhere near the Grand Canyon?"

Amber was pretty sure she knew this. "No," she said, with a slight hesitation in her voice.

Milo gave her a nod, and she relaxed.

Glen lost interest in the mountains pretty fast, and started paying attention to the streets. "This place doesn't seem that weird," he said. "Apart from their remarkably straight roads, that is. What did you say they were? Scientologists?"

"Mormons," said Milo.

"Which ones believe in the aliens?"

"Scientologists," said Amber.

"I'd love to have been a Scientologist," Glen said, "but I was never that good at science. I'll say one thing for the Mormons, though — they love their straight roads, don't they? I doubt Scientologists would have been able to build roads as straight as these, what with believing in aliens and all. Theirs would be all bendy."

Amber frowned. "Why?"

"Well, because they'd be looking up all the time, wouldn't they? Or maybe they'd try to build their cities around alien symbols, like crop circles, y'know? That'd be cool. Wouldn't be straight, though, and it'd be hell getting from one place to the other if all their roads were circular. The Mormons had it right, I think. Straight lines. That's the way to go. Who are the people with the beards?"

"Muslims?"

"No, the beards and the funny hats and building barns and stuff."

"The Amish," said Amber.

"And where do they control?"

"Nowhere. I mean, they have their communities, but they don't build cities or anything."

"They'd probably be better known if they built cities."

"Yeah. I'll mention that to them."

A few minutes later, they pulled in across the street from a run-down bar with a faded sign out front that showed a picture of a staircase. They crossed, and Milo pushed open the door. The place was as quiet as it was empty. By the looks of things, no one had been in here in years.

Milo didn't say anything, though, so Amber kept her mouth shut, and for once Glen wasn't yattering on about something. They came to a set of stairs and started down them.

Within moments, they were slowly sinking into ever-increasing gloom, and still no music or voices, no clink of glasses or sounds of laughter. They went further down, and further, and, just when Amber thought they couldn't possibly go any further, the wooden stairs turned to stone, and still they went down.

It was cold now, and pitch dark. The wall that Amber brushed against occasionally was now stone like the steps, cold and hard and wet. And then suddenly it wasn't there anymore, and when Amber went to touch it she reached too far and nearly toppled. Glen grabbed her, pulled her back from the edge.

All three of them stopped.

"We should go back," she said, though her voice sounded small and distant, like they were in some enormous cavern.

"Just a little further," Milo said. "Put your hand on my shoulder."

She did that, and Glen put his hand on hers, and they resumed their descent.

Gradually, Amber became aware of the darkness lightening to gloom again. Then a colour. Red. A hazy red. She heard music. And voices.

There was a wall beside her again. She could see it. It was painted a dark yellow, almost gold, and it blocked off the cold. Her fingers trailed over old fliers for old singers and old bands, her nails riding the bumps and the tears.

The stairs were wooden again, a dark wood, worn smooth by footfall. The music was fast – piano and trumpet music, the kind they used to dance to back in the 1930s or 1940s. The ceiling was low, and Milo and Glen had to duck their heads. Amber didn't. She kept her head up and her eyes open, as the bar was laid bare before her.

The place was packed. People drank and smoked and talked, danced and sang. The bar itself took up the centre of the room, the beating heart of the establishment.

"I'm too young to be in here," Amber said.

Glen looked nervous. "I think I am, too. Hey, no, look – they have children in here, like Milo said."

Amber counted maybe half a dozen kids wandering around.

"Should people even be smoking in a room that has children?" Glen asked. "I don't know if they should be doing that. They shouldn't even be smoking, anyway. Aren't they breaking the law?"

"Stay behind me and say nothing," said Milo, and led the way to the bar. The man serving was big, with a beard that spread from clavicle to just under his eyes. The sleeves of his white shirt were rolled back over strangely hairless forearms. "Hey," Milo said in greeting.

The big man looked up at Milo, then at Glen, and then at Amber, much as she tried to hide. But, instead of ordering her out or asking for ID, he said, "Three beers, then. Take a seat."

Glen beamed, and went immediately to a free table. Milo shrugged at Amber, and she followed him to a table near the back wall. Glen frowned, and joined them.

"What was wrong with my table?" he asked. Milo didn't answer.

The barmaid came over with their drinks on a tray. Amber

was pretty sure they weren't called barmaids anymore, but she couldn't for the life of her think what they *were* called. Besides, *barmaid* suited this place.

"Here you go," the barmaid said, setting their drinks down.

"Thank you," said Milo, putting a note on the tray. "I wonder if you can help us find someone. Our travelling companion—"

"Friend," Glen cut in.

"—is looking for someone. Abigail. If you can point her out to us, the tip's all yours."

The barmaid smiled. "Oh, no need, sir. Abigail's already found you."

Amber frowned. "She has?"

The barmaid walked away, and out of the crowd a little blonde girl in a pretty dress appeared.

"Hello."

"Hi," Amber said, forcing a confused smile on to her face. "What's your name?"

"I'm Abigail," said the girl, smiling back. "I'm the owner of the bar."

Glen paled. "*You're* Abigail?"

Milo frowned. "You're the *owner*?"

"Yep." She giggled. "Yeah, everyone has that look on their face when they find out. It's a funny look." She smiled again at Amber. "By the way, I *love* your horns."

Shock surging in her chest, Amber's hands went immediately to her head. No horns. Everything was normal.

Abigail looked at Milo, looked at him with eyes that saw more than what was there, and she smiled again. Amber wondered what she could see.

Lastly, Abigail looked at Glen. "You've got the Deathmark."

"Uh," said Glen.

"You're here to kill me, are you?"

Glen swallowed thickly. "No?"

Abigail nodded. "That's what I thought."

"I'm sorry," said Glen, "I didn't know you were a... a kid. Now I feel bad. I feel, like, really bad. I was told you'd killed people. Aw man. Now what do I do?"

"I can help you, if you want," said Abigail.

Glen brightened. "You can remove it?"

"Oh yes," the little girl replied. "It's quite easy."

She tilted her head, and the people around them surged, slamming Glen's head down on the table while they pressed a knife to Amber's throat. She froze.

Someone else had a knife to Milo's throat. "He really isn't a friend of ours," he said.

They gripped Glen's arm, straightening it out on the table, and a big man walked up, holding a butcher's cleaver.

"No!" Glen screamed. "No, no, please!"

"Don't be so silly!" Abigail giggled. "He's only going to cut your hand off. It's not like you're going to lose your entire arm!"

The cold blade pressed deeper into Amber's throat, like its wielder knew how much she wanted to shift into demon form.

"Please don't do this," said Glen, trying to sound reasonable. "I didn't know. I didn't know you were Abigail. If I'd known you were a little girl, I would have said no."

The big man tapped the cleaver on Glen's wrist a few times to test his aim, and then raised the cleaver high above his head.

Glen abandoned all attempts at appearing reasonable and started screaming again. "Oh God please don't do this please don't cut my hand off I need it I didn't know I didn't know the old man didn't tell me!"

Abigail held up a finger, and the man with the cleaver paused. She leaned closer. "What old man?"

Glen gasped. "The... the old man who passed the Deathmark on to me. He just said this was intended for someone who deserved to die. Said you'd killed people. Lots of people."

Abigail pursed her lips. "Did you ask his name?"

"No," said Glen.

Abigail shrugged. "Pity." She looked at the big man with the cleaver, was about to issue an order when Glen continued.

"But he had grey hair! And he was small! And Spanish! And he had a big grey beard!"

Abigail laughed. "*Lautaro Soto* asked you to kill me? That is so cute! He's not Spanish, though, he's Mexican. Or he *was*. He's dead now, right?"

Glen nodded. "Died as soon as he passed the Deathmark to me."

"He always was a sneaky one," said Abigail. "Hey, guys, you can let him up now."

Abigail's people released their grip. The guy with the cleaver looked disappointed. The knife was taken from Amber's throat and, like this happened every day, people around them went back to whatever they had been doing.

"Are you still going to chop my hand off?" Glen asked meekly.

Abigail laughed again. "No, you ninny! Everything has changed! This isn't the work of my enemies – this is Lautaro, one of my oldest, dearest, most recently departed friends."

"So... so you'll let me go?"

"Absolutely. So long as you deliver that Deathmark to someone else instead."

Glen's eyes narrowed. "But... but I thought it'd only work on you."

"Nope, it'll work on anyone."

"So I could have just given this away at any stage up until now?" Glen said, his voice rising. "Why didn't anyone tell me that? Why didn't the old man tell me that?"

"Lautaro probably didn't want you wasting it on some random person on the street," Abigail said. "But the guy I want you to pass it on to, he really deserves it. His name's Ralphie. He's a complete meanie, Glen, he really is. Him and his brother. Ralphie and Ossie. Oh, they are meanies. Drug dealers, too, and they have been known to kill a person for money. They're in on this for sure – they did everything Lautaro told them to. Make sure you kill Ralphie, though. He's the smart one." She paused. "Admittedly that's not saying a lot."

"Why did they want to kill you?" Amber asked.

Abigail shrugged. "Why does anyone want to kill anyone? It's just a thought that occurs, isn't it? Things happen and the thought occurs. They used to work for me, ages ago. Then they did something stupid, and I said things I regretted, but by then it was too late. They went and found God – I imagine He was between the sofa cushions, I'm always losing things there – and they hooked up with Lautaro. He was a preacher – he'd been after me for years. He was convinced I was the spawn of the Devil, which is just rude. Lautaro was the kind to look the other way when it came to Ralphie and Ossie dealing drugs and killing people, but still believe he was fighting the good fight when it came to me. Together they must have come to the conclusion that it would be a neat idea to kill me."

"So how did the old man end up in Ireland?" Glen asked.

"Educated guess?" said Abigail. "They figured out the Deathmark would be the only thing that could kill me, but making one isn't like reaching into a box of cereal and pulling out the cheap plastic toy, you know? Real, actual work is involved. Lautaro must have known someone in Ireland with the skill to do it, so over he goes, they make the Deathmark, and Lautaro intends to carry it back to America with him. Only he's an old man, and old men are frail, and the Deathmark can wear you down and wear you out if you're old and frail." She shrugged. "They miscalculated. It happens. So, right before he dies, he finds a healthy young man like you, Glen, and he gets you to agree to carry it over the ocean and use it to kill me. To kill... *me*."

Abigail's voice went very cold and very quiet.

Then that happy smiled returned. "But look at us! We're taking those meanies' plan and we're turning it back on them! How surprised are they going to be when you turn up on their doorstep, Glen? Can you imagine the look on their faces?"

"I... I don't know if I'm up to this," said Glen.

"Not on your own," Milo said. "But with our help you can do it. We'll make sure."

Glen blinked. "You'd... you'd do that for me?"

"Of course."

Glen started to smile, then stopped. "It's because you want me to go away, isn't it?"

"Of course."

Scowling, Glen turned back to Abigail. "I don't think I can do this. I can't kill someone. I thought I could, I thought I'd just pass it on to you, but... I can't. A few days ago, I shot someone — a bad man. For a moment, I thought I'd killed him. It was dreadful. He was a serial killer, but I felt dreadful, anyway.

I'm sorry, I just don't have it in me. But you have lots of people here that work for you, right? I can pass the Deathmark on to them and they can kill your friend for you."

Abigail shook her head. "The Deathmark can be passed on once, and no more. Lautaro Soto passed it to you. Whoever you pass it to next – they die. No loopholes. No exceptions. And, by the looks of it, Glen, you don't have an awful lot of time left."

Glen looked at his hand, at the black trail that was swirling faster. "I know."

"But, lucky for you, Ralphie and Ossie don't live far. Isn't that lucky?"

Glen stood up, clutching his hand. "We have to go! We have to go now!"

"Sit down, sit down," said Abigail. "I don't know where they'd be this early in the evening. I know where they'll be tonight, though."

"We can't wait that long," Glen said.

"Of course you can. You stay here and I'll be back when I know more. This is a busy bar and I am a busy lady. Enjoy the atmosphere."

She gave them another smile, swung her feet off the chair, and hopped off and walked away.

Glen hesitated, then sat back down, and Milo leaned in. "You *accepted* the Deathmark?"

"Did I?" said Glen. "Oh right, yeah. Yeah, the old guy may have said something about… uh, what was it? *In order to pass the Deathmark to another person, that other person has to willingly accept it. Or* something."

Amber glared at Glen. "You said you were *attacked*."

Glen looked hurt. "I was!"

"You said you were attacked by a *creature*."

Glen nodded. "Or a creature-like person, yes."

"I'm sorry? What? What's a creature-like person?"

"It's a, I mean, it's a person that looks like a creature, obviously. Like a, y'know… an old person."

"You said *creature*."

"I *meant* old person."

"And you accepted the Mark?" said Milo.

"I didn't know what it was!" Glen said. "This old guy comes out of the shadows and attacks me—"

"Attacks you?"

"—or talks to me, or whatever, and he says he's about to die, will I take this Mark of Death to its intended target, a terrible person called Abigail who's been hiding in this bar in America… What am I supposed to say? No?"

"Yes," said Amber. "You're supposed to say no."

"Well, I'd say no *now*," said Glen. "Obviously, I'd say no *now*. I'm in possession of all the facts *now*. But back then I wasn't. And he seemed so harmless and he… he reminded me a little of my granddad."

"Oh, for God's sake."

"What? My granddad was very important to me growing up."

"So just because he reminded you of your dearly departed grandfather—"

"Oh no, granddad's not dead. He's just living in Cork."

Amber glared. "He told you to kill someone in America and you said yes."

"My granddad?"

"*Soto.*"

Glen paused. "I suppose I did say yes, yeah. But I'd never

been to America and I'd always wanted to go. This seemed like the perfect opportunity."

"You," said Milo, "are an incredibly stupid person."

Glen slumped in his seat. "Whatever."

Amber stood, and Glen's mouth dropped open.

"You're abandoning me?"

"I'm going to the restroom."

"Oh. Uh. Carry on."

Sighing, she walked away from the table. She found the restroom, which turned out to be delightfully clean, and on her return trip she passed the dance floor. She saw Abigail, flanked by two burly members of staff, pointing to a woman doing her best to avoid eye contact. The staff members walked up either side of the woman, said a few words. The woman shook her head stiffly. The people she'd been talking to, her friends, took their drinks and moved away. She watched them go, pleading with her eyes.

The staff members took a firm grip of her elbows, led her to a room in the back. They nudged her gently through the open door and she immediately turned, tried to leave, tried to talk, but she was crying too much to get the words out.

Abigail was joined by the other children. The way they smiled sent actual shivers down Amber's spine. Six of them, six beautiful little children, walking for the room now. The staff members moved away. The woman stepped back, hands up to keep the children at a distance. Her knees buckled. She was in hysterics now. The little boys took thin knives from their pockets and the little girls took thin knives from their purses, and they went into that room and the woman started screaming and the door closed.

Amber hurried back to their table. "The kids are killers," she said, interrupting whatever Glen was saying to Milo. "The kids," she said again. "The children. Abigail. I just saw them go after a woman with knives in their hands."

Glen frowned. "Seriously?"

"Yes, Glen. Seriously."

"They're actual killers, like? Actual murderers?" The moment he said it, panic set in. "We have to get out of here. We have to leave. Don't we? Who goes first? We can't make it obvious that we're leaving."

"We're not going anywhere," said Milo.

"Did you not hear what she said?"

"We're waiting for Abigail's instructions. What she does here in the privacy of her own bar is her own business. It's got nothing to do with us."

"You don't seem surprised," Amber said to Milo. "About the killer kids."

"Of course not," he replied. "I recognised her the moment I saw her."

"You know her?"

"I've read about her. She's Abigail Gateling. Killed her entire family when she was eight years old. She was shipped off to an insane asylum while the authorities were figuring out what to do with her. She escaped the asylum and knocked on the first door she came to. She was found the next morning, drenched in blood."

Glen gaped. "And she's loose?"

"She's dead," said Milo. "This all happened in 1932."

Amber stared at him. Glen started crying. It kind of ruined the moment.

27

THE CHARGER WAS WAITING for them when they emerged from the bar. Night had fallen.

Milo took one of the maps from the glove compartment, planning their route from the directions Abigail had given them. When he was satisfied, he folded the map and passed it to Amber, and they started driving.

Glen sat in the back and didn't say much. If everything went according to plan, he would be free of the Deathmark by the end of the night. If everything went according to plan, he would be responsible for somebody's death.

The further they moved from the city, the wider the spaces became. Houses had room to breathe, and they drew in big, deep breaths. Thirsty lawns became crabgrass and scrub bush. The landscape exploded outwards, rearing up into mountains that loomed dark against the night sky. The roads became wide trails of dust.

They drove for another half an hour, until they had left all trace of civilisation behind, and Milo pulled over. Leaving the engine running, he opened up a map.

"Are we lost?" Glen asked.

"No, we are not," said Milo. "Just figuring out where to go. They should be around here somewhere, I just can't—"

Headlights lit them up from behind and something rammed into them. Glen screamed and so did Amber, and Milo thrust the map at her and while the creased paper filled her vision the Charger was already leaping forward, roaring. The light from behind was blinding and all Amber could hear was the growl of engines, and Milo twisted the wheel and the car spun, and something thundered by, clipping the driver's side mirror.

The Charger spun full circle and came to a stop, trembling with suppressed violence. Amber shoved the map down to her feet and only then did she become aware of Glen's curses. On the dusty road ahead of them, a dark-coloured pickup truck circled round, catching them with all of its many spotlights. Amber squinted.

"Seat belts on," Milo said in a quiet voice.

Amber knew hers was already fastened, but she checked anyway.

"There are no seat belts back here," Glen said, panicking. "Why are there no seat belts?"

"Lie on the floor," Milo said.

Glen whimpered, and slithered out of sight. He pulled the bags down on top of him.

The pickup shot forward and Milo kicked the Charger into reverse. Amber held on. The pickup's lights filled the windshield. Milo drove with one hand on the wheel, the other on Amber's seat, looking over his shoulder.

He braked suddenly, yanked the wheel, and the Charger spun again, throwing Amber against the door, but the pickup clipped them and the whole car jolted sideways. Milo's hand worked the gears and his boot stomped on the gas, and the Charger spat up dirt and dust and it was back under control and back on the road, the pickup right behind it.

"Who the hell *is* that?" Glen screeched from beneath all the bags.

Amber braced one hand against the dash and pressed herself back into her seat. To look behind was to be blinded, so she kept her eyes on the road ahead, the dirt trail almost indistinguishable at this speed from the land through which it cut. The pickup hit them and the Charger jumped and Milo fought to keep it under control. They were hit again and Milo hissed under his breath and the rear of the car started to slide sideways. The pickup slammed into Amber's side. She screamed, the scream barely audible over the roar of the engines and the shriek of twisting metal.

The Charger spun to a rocking stop. The engine cut out.

In the relative silence, Amber could hear Dacre Shanks, shouting from the trunk. His shouts were slowly muted.

The pickup looped round. For some reason, that loop seemed so casual, so playful, that it made Amber's anger rise in her throat.

Milo turned the key. The Charger spluttered.

"Oh God," Glen said.

The pickup came back at them, picking up speed.

The Charger spluttered again.

Amber pulled at the door handle, but the lock came down, sealing her inside.

She whipped her head round to Milo as he turned the key

a third time. The Charger roared, its headlights burning a devilish, hellish red.

It lunged out of the pickup's path a moment before impact, turned with a spray of pebbles and sand, and now they were speeding behind the pickup, closing in to slam into its tail lights. The pickup wobbled, almost hit a lonely tree, and Milo put his foot down. The Charger came up on the truck's right side. The pickup swerved into it. Milo responded in kind. The two vehicles battered at each other for a quarter of a mile or more, and then the pickup pulled away in front as the trail narrowed between two hills.

Milo commanded the Charger like he was a part of it. It was hard to see in the darkness and the quick bursts of light, but he seemed to be almost smiling. He looked darker, like the colour of the steering wheel was soaking into his hands and spreading through his skin. His jaw seemed more angular. The pickup's tail lights somehow reflected in his eyes, making them glow red. And were those horns beginning to protrude through his hair?

The pickup tried to get away and the Charger rammed into it once again. Milo's smile broadened and, when he opened his mouth, red light shone out between his white teeth.

Something bright arced in the sky. Amber tried to shout a warning, but it was too late, and the brightness exploded across the hood and flames covered the windshield.

Milo twisted the wheel and there was a new noise, a rapid popping, like fireworks. It took Amber a moment to realise they were being shot at. The bullets punctured the side of the car and cracked the rear windshield and Milo grunted, twisted in his seat. The Charger hit something and bounced and suddenly the sound of the road beneath them vanished, and they dropped, and Amber screamed and Glen screamed, and they were nothing but a fireball dropping into darkness—

—and then they crunched into the slope and Milo wrenched the wheel, using the brakes and gas pedal to propel them, slalom-like, round the trees and boulders that dotted the hillside.

The slope flattened out and the Charger crunched into the scrub and the earth and then rolled to a stop on a narrow little road. The last of the flames died on the hood.

Milo turned his head to Amber. The red glow faded from his eyes, as whatever was lighting him from within slowly extinguished. She stared at him. Didn't say anything.

"Glen," he said gruffly. "You okay?"

"No," said Glen, clambering slowly up. "Is it over? What happened?"

"We were led into an ambush."

"They knew we were coming?" he asked, and peered out. "Are we safe?"

Milo got out without answering. Amber unlocked her door, but had to lean back and kick it to get it open.

The Charger was wrecked. The hood, where the Molotov cocktail had hit, was a blistered mess of crumpled metal. Both doors were badly dented, the frame on the passenger side buckled. The rear windshield had two bullet holes in it. The driver's side had plenty more.

"Sorry about your car," Amber said dully.

Milo circled it, limping. The left leg of his jeans was soaked in something dark.

"You've been shot," said Amber. Then, louder, "Oh my God, you've been shot!"

"Just a graze," Milo responded. "I'll be all right by morning."

She ran over to him. "You've been shot, Milo! Look at the blood! You're leaving bloody footprints behind you!"

"I'll be all right by morning," he repeated, removed his arm from her grip, and got back behind the wheel.

Amber would have stayed where she was, but the adrenaline was wearing off and now she was feeling the cold. She got back in the car.

"What do we do now?" Glen asked.

"Get the blankets out," said Milo. "We're spending the night here."

"What if they come for us? They have machine guns."

"The car's not going anywhere," said Milo, "and neither are we. If they come for us, they come for us."

"And you expect us to *sleep*?"

"You do what you want," said Milo. "But me, I'm tired, and I want to close my eyes."

And, for the first time since Amber had known him, Milo did just that behind the wheel of his car.

There were moments, in the time it took her to fall asleep, where she thought death had claimed Milo without her noticing, and each time she'd freeze, coldness spreading from her heart until she heard, very faintly, the sound of his breathing.

Very faintly.

28

WHEN SHE WOKE, it was morning, and the sun was doing its best to get rid of the chill that the night had brought. Milo was outside, walking in a circle. He was wearing new jeans, and his limp was barely noticeable.

Keeping the blanket wrapped round her, Amber pulled the handle of the door. It swung open smoothly. She got out, stretched.

"How's the leg?" she asked.

Milo stopped walking. "Good," he answered. "It was just a graze, like I said."

He looked normal. Normal eyes, normal mouth, normal skin. No horns. He was lying, though, and, by the way he was looking at her, he was daring her to call him on it. But she didn't. He was entitled to his secrets. He'd earned that much from her.

She turned to get back into the car, and actually took a step back in surprise. "Jesus."

The Charger's hood was unblemished. Its dents were gone. No bullet holes and no scratches. It gleamed in the morning sun, not even a trace of dust on its glorious blackness.

"Turns out the damage wasn't that bad," said Milo.

Amber grunted as Glen sat up in the back and yawned. Milo got in, slid the key into the ignition and twisted.

The Charger woke immediately with a deep and healthy rumble.

It took half an hour, but they found their way back to the road they'd been on, and fifteen minutes after that they crested a dusty hill, and stopped. Below them stood a ramshackle house that looked like it had been built in stages by very different builders who only had a crooked eye in common. Parked outside was a badly damaged pickup truck.

"That's them!" Glen said needlessly.

Milo shared a look with Amber, and inched the Charger forward. He put it in neutral and turned off the engine. They rolled down the gentle hill, accompanied only by the crunch of wheels on dirt. They got to the bottom and Milo steered them behind the pickup, and stopped.

He got out with his gun in his hand, and as he attached his holster to his belt Amber and Glen climbed out after him. Amber kept low, remembering the sound of the machine gun from last night. Glen kept even lower.

They moved quickly but quietly to the house. Milo peered through the window for a few moments. Satisfied, he went to the door and got ready to kick. Something in his face changed, though, and instead he leaned forward, tried the handle. It turned, and the door opened, and he shrugged. Straightening, he holstered his gun and walked in, Amber and Glen at his heels.

The living room was barely habitable. An old TV sat huddled on a crate, cornered by a dirty couch and a filthy armchair.

They walked straight through to the kitchen, where two men sat eating cereal. Ralphie and Ossie, presumably. The brothers looked at them, frowning, like their arrival just didn't compute. The spoon in the bigger one's hand hovered halfway to his waiting mouth. He was a tall, stout man, his curly hair cut tight, fully dressed in jeans and an oil-stained T-shirt. The smaller one had his arm jammed inside the cereal box. He had a beard and a stupid Mohawk, and he only wore an old pair of boxers.

"Boys," said Milo, nodding at them.

The smaller man looked at all of them, one at a time. At no stage did comprehension dawn on his overfed face.

"You're the people from last night," said the bigger guy.

"Yes, we are," said Milo. "You're Ralphie, am I right? We were told you were the smart one." He turned to the smaller man, the one still wearing the look of dumb confusion. "And that makes you Ossie. So which one of you was in the pickup, and which one of you had the gun?"

"I don't know what you're talking about," said Ralphie, putting his spoon back in the bowl.

"That pickup outside says otherwise."

"That ain't ours. You can't prove nothing."

"Then it's a good thing we're not law enforcement, isn't it? Want to know what I think? I think you had the gun and the Molotov. I think Ossie here is the driver of the family. Would I be right, Ossie?"

Ossie glared at his brother. "Told you we should've finished them off."

"I thought they were dead," Ralphie replied.

"Who tipped you off?" Milo asked. "It doesn't matter to me

one way or the other, but I'm sure Abigail would like to know who betrayed her."

"Abigail is the Devil," said Ossie.

"She looks like a little girl."

"Looks are deceiving!" Ossie said, standing.

Milo's hand went to rest on the butt of his gun. "I'm going to have to ask you to sit back down, Ossie."

"She looks like a little girl, but she ain't!" Ossie crowed. "She's the Devil and we're the only ones brave enough to tell it like it is!"

"Be brave while seated, what do you say?"

"You don't scare me. I have seen with my own eyes the true face of evil, and it is that little girl. 'And the great dragon was cast out, that old serpent, called the Devil, and Satan, which... which...'" Ossie looked at Ralphie for help.

"Uh," said Ralphie, "'which... deceiveth'."

"'Which deceiveth the whole world!'" said Ossie. "'He was cast... he was...'"

He looked to Ralphie, who frowned and looked down, trying to remember.

Milo sighed. "'He was cast out into the earth, and his angels were cast out with him'. You fellas need to brush up on your Bible studies. Besides which, you used to work right alongside Abigail, did you not?"

Ralphie narrowed his eyes. "We were wayward, yes. But we were shown the true path."

"By the old man, right? Lautaro Soto? That the true path you're talking about? The one that allowed you to continue dealing drugs and killing people for money?"

Ralphie had nothing to say to that, so Ossie answered for him.

"She's still the Devil."

"Be that as it may, we came here to deliver something to Ralphie and, once that's done, we're going to drive away and hopefully never cross paths with you again. That sound good to you?"

The brothers shared a look of suspicion. "What've you got?" asked Ralphie.

Glen cleared his throat, and stepped forward. "I'm the one who has it, actually. The old man, he gave it to me, and now I suppose I'm returning it to you." He held up his hand and they saw the Deathmark.

Ralphie jumped to his feet.

"I'm really not happy with the number of people standing up right now," said Milo.

Ralphie jabbed a finger at Glen. "That is for her! You deliver that to Abigail! How did you even get that? Lautaro was supposed to—"

"Lautaro is dead," said Amber. "We get that you were trying to kill someone you think is evil. I believe you when you say she is. But you two are every bit as bad."

Ossie shook his head. "We'll kill you dead, but we won't damn your immortal soul."

"Dead's dead," said Milo. "Ralphie, you're going to stand there and let Glen lay his hand on you."

"You ain't touching my brother," Ossie said through gritted teeth.

Glen tried a smile. "Listen, I really don't want to hurt anyone, and this really isn't personal, but if I don't pass it on to you, Ralphie, it'll kill me."

"So die," said Ralphie.

"Well now, that's not really fair, is it? I don't have anything to do with any of this. So let's all be grown-ups here and do what has to be done," Glen said, stepping towards Ralphie.

What happened next happened way too fast and also way too slow. One moment Ossie was standing there, seething and tense, and the next he had the biggest hunting knife Amber had ever seen in his hand. Before she'd even asked herself where the hell he'd been hiding it, he was taking his first lunging step towards them. By this time, Milo's gun was already out of its holster. He fired twice, the gunshots loud in Amber's ears, and Ossie jerked as two small holes appeared in his chest, really close together. Even as he tumbled gracelessly to the ground – and here Amber realised he'd never even had a chance to complete that first step – Ralphie was bolting to the bedroom.

Glen yelled and ran in after him and time returned to normal, and then Glen came sprinting out of the bedroom, yelling even louder. The sound of that machine gun filled the house. Bullets peppered the walls in a shower of splinters. Milo dived, Glen dived, and Amber ducked and stumbled, and before she knew it her skin was red and she had horns again.

Ralphie strode from the bedroom door beside her, swinging the machine gun from side to side, firing the whole time, yelling and cursing and not noticing her as she straightened. She yanked the weapon from his hands, grabbed him by the throat, and lifted him off his feet. Ralphie dangled there for a moment, gurgling and struggling, finally registering who and what had a hold on him, and then Amber swung him up over her head and flipped him. He hit the floor and she raised her foot to turn his head to bloody splinters.

"Amber!" Glen cried, stumbling into view. "Amber, stop! What are you doing?"

Glen's stupid face sapped some of the rage from behind her eyes, and she froze, startled by both the depth of her viciousness and the suddenness with which it had overtaken her.

She threw the machine gun into the bedroom. "Whatever," she said.

Glen smiled at her, nodding like a lovesick idiot. She pointed a taloned finger at the man on the floor who was gasping for breath. "You going to do what we came here to do?"

"Oh yeah," Glen said, and crouched. "I'm really sorry." He pressed his hand to Ralphie's arm.

The blackness swarmed under Ralphie's skin, quickly spreading through his whole arm.

Glen straightened, checked his hand, and smiled in relief. "It's gone," he said. "I'm going to be okay. Hear that, Amber? I'm going to live!"

"Oh joy," she muttered.

Ralphie's breathing, already laboured, became a rattling wheeze.

"You okay?" Milo said to Amber.

She frowned at him. "Why shouldn't I be?"

He shrugged. "It's just, you haven't shifted back yet."

"So? What's wrong with staying like this for a while?"

"Exactly!" said Glen. "She's got nothing to be ashamed of! Look at her! She's beautiful! She's magnificent!"

"Yeah, Milo, I'm magnificent." She walked by Glen, heading to the door. "It's like breaking in a new pair of shoes, you know? You've got to give it the time it needs."

"Um…" said Glen. "I am *really* sorry about this."

She turned. Glen stood perfectly still, Ralphie behind him, holding that big hunting knife to his throat. Ralphie was sweating badly.

"Easy now," said Milo.

Ralphie started moving Glen around them, heading to the door.

"There was nothing personal here," Milo continued. "You get that, right? Your brother came at us. I had to put him down. There was no malice to it."

Amber resisted the urge to run at Ralphie and tear his face off. She was chock-full of malice.

"Gun down," Ralphie said, his voice sounding strangled. Inky tendrils of tattoo were writhing on his skin.

"Can't do it," said Milo.

Ralphie stopped with his back to the door, and spat out a mouthful of black phlegm. "I'll kill him."

"Then I'll shoot you."

Ralphie blinked quickly, and black liquid began streaming from the corners of his eyes. He said something unintelligible, then tried again. "Keys."

Milo hesitated, then took out his car keys. He tossed them and, when Ralphie reached out to catch, Glen slipped from his grasp. In an instant, Milo's gun was in his hand, but Glen came stumbling towards him and Ralphie ran out of the house.

"You didn't shoot me!" Glen cried, amazed. "We really are friends!"

Milo ignored him and walked for the door. Outside, the Charger roared to life.

Amber ran, beating Milo outside as Ralphie steered the Charger up the dusty hill. Milo strolled out after her, looking entirely too calm. He put his gun back in its holster, and started walking up the hill as the clouds of dust settled.

"You don't seem too upset," she said, walking beside him as Glen followed along behind, checking himself for injuries.

"Why should I be upset?" Milo asked.

She glared. "He's got your car."

"No," said Milo. "My car has him."

They walked up the slope. Glancing at her shadow on the ground and noting how cool her horns looked, Amber matched his pace, slow and leisurely, all the way up the hill – even though her entire body wanted to sprint and run and leap and fight. She wanted to tear faces off and bite through throats and pull out hearts. She wanted to rip and tear and decapitate and disembowel. She wanted violence. She wanted to kill.

They got to the top of the hill. The Charger was just ahead of them, one wheel up on a gentle mound of dirt, its engine still running.

As they neared, the door sprang open and grey smoke billowed into the open air. Ralphie threw himself out, coughing violently. He hit the ground and started dragging himself along by his elbows.

"She's got a tricky tailpipe," said Milo. "If you're not careful, it'll back up on you."

Once he was far enough away from the car that had almost killed him, Ralphie got to his hands and knees, still coughing, black spittle dripping from swollen lips. He spat. There was at least one tooth in all that dark phlegm. He got the coughing under control and, breathing loudly, he stood, swaying. He took the hunting knife from his belt. He looked sick.

"You want," said Milo, "I can shoot you now, put you out of your misery."

Ralphie gargled out a laugh, then pointed the knife at Amber. Grunts were all he could utter. She knew what he wanted, and she obliged. He wanted his chance to take out a demon before he went. There was something admirable in that, she supposed. She walked forward, and heard Milo sigh.

"Uh," said Glen, "should we be letting her do that?"

"She's not a kid," Milo answered. "She's dumb, but she's not a kid. She can do whatever the hell she wants."

Ralphie grinned at her. His lips were so swollen they looked like they might burst.

Even though he was dribbling blackness, Ralphie held that knife like he knew what he was doing. Excitement fluttered in Amber's belly. She didn't know how to fight, but she was being given a chance to prove herself by a man who was going to die, anyway. She had nothing to lose.

He darted at her and she jumped back. He came at her again and she slipped sideways. He was unsteady on his feet and he nearly toppled, but after coughing up a lungful of black ink he turned to continue.

She moved in close and he swiped. The blade skittered across the scales that were suddenly covering her forearm, and she hit him. It was a bad punch, but her fist sank into his soft side, and it hurt him nonetheless. Blackness began to seep into his T-shirt where she had broken the skin. He was rotting from the inside out.

He lunged but she moved and he missed. He stumbled and fell to his knees. Coughed. Spat. Got back up. Lunged at her again. Repeated the process.

He was done. Disappointingly, it was over before it had even begun.

He struggled to his feet and Amber ran forward and jumped. Powerful muscles launched her into the air faster than she'd expected, propelling her across the space between them just as Ralphie was turning to her. Her knee struck his chest and they went down, Amber on top. The knife clattered against a stone somewhere.

Beneath her, Ralphie's eyes were wide and blinking. He was trying to suck in air through his open mouth. Amber was kneeling on him. No, not on him. In him. She stood, removing her knee from the hole in his chest. Trails of blood and ink and rotten insides stretched between them like lines of spittle. She could feel it soaking through her jeans.

She reverted to normal without meaning to, and the cold realisation of what she had done washed over her. Milo and Glen were at her side now. The blackness was rising through Ralphie's skin, leaking from his pores. It weakened his flesh, turned it mushy. His arms and legs lost their form, like the bones themselves had dissolved. His ruined ribcage fell in on itself. A stench rose. Human waste and rotting meat. Then his face caved in. In another few moments, all that was left of Ralphie McGarry were his soaking, black-drenched clothes.

29

They got back to The Dark Stair a little before noon. The place was empty apart from Abigail, who sat on the bar with her legs swinging. Amber hadn't said anything on the ride over. She'd changed her jeans, though.

"It's done," said Milo.

"Never doubted you for a moment," said Abigail. "Did you encounter any difficulties?"

Milo took a moment. "You tipped them off."

Abigail's big eyes widened. "Me?"

"You led us right into an ambush."

She giggled. "You got me! You see right through me! I just thought, hey, wouldn't it be funny if Ralphie and Ossie got the drop on Milo Sebastian and his pals?"

"I don't remember giving you my name."

"I don't remember needing it." Abigail smiled. "I'm a huge fan of your work. I hope this doesn't mean we're not friends, though. I think we could all be great friends. Don't you?"

Milo didn't say anything. He just turned, walked for the stairs. Glen hesitated, then bowed to Abigail and followed.

But Amber stayed where she was. "What was his last name?" she asked. "Ralphie's?"

Abigail fixed her big blue eyes on her. "McGarry. Why? You like to know the name of your victims?"

Amber went cold. "He's not my... I just needed to know..."

"Oh, I didn't mean anything by it," Abigail said happily. "Are we going to be friends, Amber? I do hope so. From everything I've heard, you don't have many friends left."

"What... what have you heard?"

"Oh, sweetie, I know it all. I know all about your mean, mean parents. I know they're looking for you. I know they got halfway to Toledo, of all places, before they began to suspect that someone had lied to them. They're not very popular in places like this, with people like us, but they do have people who owe them, and people who are scared of them. They're coming for you, Amber."

"Are you going to tell them I was here?"

"I won't have to," said Abigail sadly. "Someone else will. It's inevitable. They're already looking for your car. A black Dodge Charger. That's a car that sticks in the memory."

"Can you help me?"

Abigail's smile was impish. "Help you how?"

"Could you... could you stop them for me?"

"You mean... kill them? You want me to kill your parents and their friends? But... but I'm just a little girl. What could I possibly do against big, bad monsters like that?"

"I don't want to kill them, I don't, I just... I want..."

"I'm not in the monster-stopping business, I'm afraid. But I will do you one favour. When they ask where you've gone, I'll pretend I don't know."

Amber frowned. "But you *don't* know."

That smile again. "Oh, Amber, I know everything."

Amber left The Dark Stair, found Milo and Glen waiting outside.

"She says my parents are back on our trail, and they know the car."

Milo nodded. "To be expected. Come on, then. No more detours."

"So," Glen said, chewing his lip, "here is where we part ways, huh?"

Milo said, "Bye," and walked to the Charger.

"Bye?" said Glen. "*Bye?* That's all I get, after everything we've been through?"

"Yep," said Milo.

Glen turned to Amber. "What if there *is* no bye? What if I didn't have to go?"

"But you do," said Amber. "You don't have the Deathmark anymore. You can go home."

"I don't have a home," said Glen. "My dad is dead. Everyone else despises me."

"Then explore America."

"I want to," he said. "With you."

"Glen…"

"Now just wait, Amber, okay? Yeah, there are times when we've butted heads, all three of us, but that's what makes us a great team. We each contribute. You're the brain. Milo's the muscle. Me? I'm the heart."

"No, you're not."

"Then I'm the soul."

"You're not the soul."

He frowned. "Then what am I? I'll be anything."

"You can be the appendix," said Milo.

"Then I'll be the appendix!"

"The appendix is a completely useless part of the colon."

"Whatever!" Glen cried. "I'll be the nose! I'll be the nose of this team! But I *do* contribute, you can't deny that. I helped against Shanks, didn't I?"

"Kind of," said Amber. "But Milo and me, we *have* to continue on this road. You don't. You can stop."

"I don't want to stop. I want to help. Please, Amber. I've never belonged anywhere before. Let me belong."

She looked over his shoulder at Milo.

"Don't look at him," said Glen. "He'll only shake his head. He's probably shaking his head right now, isn't he?"

She paused. "He's not *not* shaking it."

"I know you're shaking your head, Milo!"

"I want you to know that," Milo responded, sounding bored.

"Amber, please," said Glen. "We have something, don't we?"

"I'm sorry?"

"You and me. We have a connection. You feel it, too, I know you do. Especially… especially when you change. Especially when you get horny."

"Do *not* call it that."

"You can't abandon me," said Glen. "Ever think that maybe when we met it was meant to be? Fate has thrown us together, Amber. The universe has decided that we are to be a part of each other's lives from this moment on."

"But why does the universe hate me?"

"Amber, I'm asking you to let me help you on your quest. Let me help you stay ahead of your parents. If anything happened to you, Amber, anything that I could have prevented, I'd never be able to live with myself."

"Now you know how we feel," said Milo.

Glen ignored him. "You need all the help you can get. Don't try to deny it. I don't know why you're even listening to Milo's opinion. You're *paying* him to be here, but me? I'm here for free. I'm here because I care. We are a well-oiled machine, and do you know what we've been built for? Stopping you from being eaten. That's it. That's our purpose. That's my purpose. Don't deny me my purpose, Amber. Don't do it."

She sighed. "Fine."

His eyes widened. "Really?"

"Sure."

"Thank you! You will not regret it!"

"I better not."

"What was it that changed your mind? The team bit? The part about the well-oiled machine?"

"Mostly it was how pathetic you sounded."

"That'll work for me!"

"But don't call it a quest."

"Absolutely." He turned. "Hear that, Milo? I'm coming with you."

Milo ignored him and got in the car.

30

They left Salt Lake City and drove through a wide expanse of nothing. Mailboxes stood at the mouths of dirt trails that branched off from the road, trails that led to not much more than the rusted corpses of propane tanks and farm machinery. They passed a three-storey house that rose above the scattering of trailer homes around it, and a construction yard that had become a cemetery for old cars.

They drove until the flatness developed some hills. Amber preferred that. There was something so vastly empty about a featureless horizon, like they could drive and drive and the horizon would just fall away. There were moments when the earth seemed flat, and they were hurtling right to the nearest edge. Hills were good. Even the smallest and slightest of hills blocked her view of whatever lay beyond the next bend, allowing her some degree of hope. There was a certain kind of comfort in ignorance.

They got to a truck stop outside of Boise, Idaho, and Amber had a grilled ham and cheese sandwich and fries. She endured Glen talking about how everything in America came with fries – even when you didn't order them – and then they drove on for another two hours. They reached a small motel in Baker City with only two free rooms available. Milo decided to spend the night in the car and wouldn't change his mind, and they were on the road again before seven the next morning.

A little after midday on Saturday, their destination crept up on them. First there was nothing but trees rising up on either side, Douglas firs and red cedars mostly. The valley deepened, and there was a flower bed on a grass shoulder with a circular sign informing them that they were now entering Cascade Falls, and that the population was 9,243. A smaller sign beside that told them this was a Tree City USA. The first building they passed on their right was a nice-looking bar and restaurant – the first on their left was an Econ-o-Wash. They passed a feed and supply store, a used car lot, a drugstore, the Cascade Falls Heritage Centre, and a grand old hotel that stood tall and proud, looking out over the town.

"We'll stay here tonight," said Amber.

Milo nodded. His face was lined with tiredness, even though his eyes were bright. They parked in the front lot and got out. Amber and Glen eased the stiffness from their spines. Milo didn't have to.

They passed through the stone archway into the foyer. Lots of dark wood and old paintings. The woman behind the desk smiled. "Welcome to the Varga Hotel. My name is Ingrid. Do you have reservations?"

"We don't," said Milo. "Is that all right? Would you have three rooms for us?"

"You may be in luck." The smile stayed in place, like fresh flowers at a graveside, while Ingrid checked the outdated computer before her. "You're in luck," she said. "We do indeed have three rooms available. How long will you be requiring them for?"

"Tonight to start with," said Amber. "We may need them tomorrow night, but hopefully not."

Ingrid nodded. "Very well. But please do let us know at your earliest convenience, to make sure we can keep them for you if there's a sudden rush. Please fill out these forms." She slid them each a card and provided them with pens. "Have you been to Cascade Falls before?"

"First time."

"Oh, I'm sure you'll love it," Ingrid said as they wrote and lied. "We have a surprisingly diverse community. I know the town looks white bread through and through, but we have so many different cultures and people – it's a real American town, that's what my grandmother used to say. I was born here, you know."

"That so?" Milo asked.

"Born and raised," said Ingrid. "I moved away when I was twenty, got married and started a family in Boston. I liked it well enough, but I came back here for a weekend to visit my folks and realised I never wanted to leave again. I let go of my husband and my kids and all my stuff. I didn't need it. Didn't need any of it. Everything I needed was right here. This is a wonderful town. The people are lovely. Wait till you meet Mr Varga. He owns the hotel. You'll love him. Everyone does."

Her eyes had glazed over while she was talking, and her smile had stretched so wide Amber thought her skin might tear.

"We're actually looking for someone," Amber said, her voice cutting through whatever daze Ingrid was sinking into. "Gregory Buxton. Do you know him?"

Ingrid blinked, took a moment to process the question, then shook her head. "Sorry, I don't. I know an Althea Buxton, though. She's a nice old lady. Maybe she's related?"

"Maybe," said Milo. "She live around here?"

"Over on Bleeker Street. My mom and her used to be friends. Then she got all religious. Or maybe she was always religious. Althea, I'm talking about, not my mom. You'd never find my mom in church. She never had any time for organised religion, said it was all a big scam. Of course, she was visiting psychics every week and forking over most of her disability allowance, and if anything is a scam it's those crooks. She passed away two years ago. My mom, that is, not Althea."

"I'm sorry to hear that," said Milo.

"Thank you. Taken before her time, that's what everyone said. The Saturday after she died, one of the psychics she saw regularly called the house and asked why she'd missed her appointment. I said you can't be a very good psychic if you didn't see this coming. Know what she did? She offered her services as a medium at a reduced rate. I told her to go to hell, and hung up the phone."

"Nothing but vultures," said Milo.

Ingrid nodded. "That's what I said. I told Mr Varga about it and that's the exact word I used. I said she was a vulture. Mr Varga agreed with me. He's a very smart man, and he's been around the world, not just to Boston, like me. He knows a thing or two."

By this time, they'd all slid their cards back to her, and she scooped them up and placed then carefully into a narrow wooden box. She took three keys from the board behind her and handed them over.

"You're all on the second floor," she said. "Dinner is served from seven till ten, but, if you aim to be in the dining room at eight, you might even get a visit from Mr Varga himself."

"Well, that'd be lovely," said Milo, and smiled.

They dropped their bags in their rooms – Amber's had a four-poster bed and a heavy dresser with a huge mirror – and got back into the Charger. They drove to Bleeker Street, a pleasant road in a pleasant neighbourhood, up the hill slightly from a church. They found the house with Buxton on the mailbox and knocked on the door.

An elderly black woman answered, dressed in a bathrobe and slippers with a cross around her neck.

Amber smiled. "Althea Buxton?"

"Who are you?"

"Mrs Buxton, my name is—"

"What do you want?"

"We were hoping to—"

"What's this about? Who sent you?"

"Uh, no one sent us."

"I'm not going to invite you in."

"That's quite all right," said Amber. "We're looking for your son, actually. Is he around?"

"My son passed away."

Amber frowned. "It is *Gregory* Buxton we're looking for."

"I know who my son is," Althea snapped. "I only had one of them, and he passed, ten years or more. He's gone now and that's that. I can't help you."

She stepped back, and closed the door firmly, the sound coinciding perfectly with the plummeting of Amber's heart.

"That's it, then," she said dully. "It's over. He's dead. I have nothing to offer the Shining Demon. My parents will keep chasing me until they... they..."

Milo walked back to the car. "He's not dead," he said.

Amber looked up. "What?" She hurried after him. Glen followed. "How do you know he's not dead?"

"The Shining Demon would have known it," Milo said, leaning on the hood. "That old lady is scared."

"Of us?"

Milo looked back at the house. "Of someone."

They parked in the courtyard at the back of the hotel, and Amber took Milo's iPad to her room, using the free Wi-Fi to log on to the *In The Dark Places* messageboards. The very idea that she suddenly had some time to herself, plus an internet connection, filled her with such a feeling of warmth that it actually brought a tear to her eye. She refused to cry, though – to cry for something as silly as the ability to chat online would cheapen somewhat the things she genuinely had to cry about. Which were many. And dreadful. She didn't mind the tear in her eye, though. That didn't count.

She skimmed the users chatting, and her heart lifted when she saw names she recognised. This was a world she understood.

This was a community where she belonged, a place where she wasn't a monster. Wasn't a killer.

She shook her head, like the movement itself would be enough to shake the memory from her mind. Ralphie McGarry was dying, anyway. Glen had seen to that. She'd just helped him on his way, that's all. It had been a mercy killing. It had been the right thing to do. She wasn't to blame for any of it. She wasn't to blame for the circumstance she'd found herself in, nor the action she had taken. She wasn't even to blame for the brief flash of pleasure she had derived from killing him.

"Not me," she said aloud. "That wasn't me."

She pushed down the arguments brewing behind her words and instead focused on the words in front of her.

The Dark Princess said...
Hi BAC.

Balthazar's-Arm-Candy said...
Well hey there, stranger! Been a while! Y u no respond 2 my emails???

The Dark Princess said...
Been really busy, sorry. Family stuff.

Balthazar's-Arm-Candy said...
Problems?

The Dark Princess said...
You could say that.

Balthazar's-Arm-Candy said...
That's why we come here, right? To escape the
parental units and their insanity.
Hey, u hear that the full cast has
been confirmed for the con? 1st time EVER!

The Dark Princess said...
Doubt I'll be going actually. Plans have changed.

Balthazar's-Arm-Candy said...
Seriously?
U wanna talk about it?

The Dark Princess said...
It's nothing anyone can help me with.
Wow, that sounds dramatic! I'm doing OK, though.
Everything is messed up but I'm making new friends.
Kind of.

Balthazar's-Arm-Candy said...
Online or irl?

The Dark Princess said...
Real life. Weird, I know.

Balthazar's-Arm-Candy said...
Tres weird.

The Dark Princess said...
World's gone all upside down. Not able to email cuz

of reasons. Some pretty scary stuff happening.

Balthazar's-Arm-Candy said...
Sounds intense.

The Dark Princess said...
It is. Didn't want you worrying, that's all.

Balthazar's-Arm-Candy said...
Well I wasn't. I am NOW though.

Sith0Dude said...
OMG! Laurie killed Stryker! What the HELL?????

Balthazar's-Arm-Candy said...
Private convo, Sith0Dude.
(BTW spoiler warnings – heard of them??)

Sith0Dude said...
U shouldn't be having private convos in public forums.
How am I sposed to know?

(There's a spoiler warning at the start of this thread!)

The Dark Princess said...
Go away Sith0Dude.

Sith0Dude said...
U guys suck.

Balthazar's-Arm-Candy said...
You sound weird, Princess. Worryingly weird.

The Dark Princess said...
I'm sorry. Just wanted to log on, talk to you, get some normality back.

Balthazar's-Arm-Candy said...
Am I helping?

The Dark Princess said...
You always help.

Balthazar's-Arm-Candy said...
Wish I was with you. Why is Australia so far away? Wish I could just hop on a plane to Florida.

The Dark Princess said...
Not in Florida anymore.

Balthazar's-Arm-Candy said...
Gone travelling?

The Dark Princess said...
Yep.

Balthazar's-Arm-Candy said...
Where?

Amber hesitated. It was practically inconceivable for her parents to check these boards. They didn't know she chatted here, didn't know what her user name was... but even so. Even so they scared her so much that she wasn't about to take that chance.

The Dark Princess said...
Not far. Damn, have to go.

Balthazar's-Arm-Candy said...
Something I said?

The Dark Princess said...
Course not. It's late though. Need sleep. Early start tomorrow.

Balthazar's-Arm-Candy said...
Take care of yourself, OK? And check in regularly. U got me worried now!

The Dark Princess said...
Sorry! TTYL

Balthazar's-Arm-Candy said...
Peace.

Amber logged out, turned off the iPad, and let it drop on to the bed. Little by little, they were robbing her of every last semblance of normality, stripping her of every last link to her old life. She didn't even know who she was anymore. Everything her personality had been built on was a lie, and the more she examined it, the more it crumbled beneath her gaze.

If she wasn't a beloved daughter, and if she wasn't an only child, then who was she? Ten days ago, Amber Lamont had been a good person. But now she was someone who'd bitten off a finger. Now she was someone with a pair of jeans soaked in the black blood of a man whose chest she'd caved in.

Now she didn't know who she was.

31

WHEN AMBER CAME DOWN for dinner, her place was set at a large, long table, next to Glen's and across from Milo's. Another guest was joining them, an attractive, dark-haired woman in her thirties.

"Company!" the woman said, clearly delighted. "I haven't had company while eating for ages! Are you staying long?"

"Probably not," said Amber. "We're on a family road trip. This is my cousin Glen, my dad Milo, and I'm Amber."

"Very pleased to meet you," said the woman. "I'm Veronica. Have you travelled far?"

"We've been on the road for a few days," Milo said. "What about you?"

Veronica gave them all quite a beautiful smile. "I actually live here. Not in the hotel, but Cascade Falls. Well, I did. I thought I'd bought a place but it fell through at the last minute, and I've already sold my old house, so here I am, destitute. Destitute in a lovely hotel, but still... destitute."

"Why are you moving?" Amber asked. "It's such a beautiful place."

"It is," said Veronica, "it really is. And I'm going to miss it, but sometimes you just have to –" she fluttered her fingers – "leave."

"I noticed some closed-down stores," Milo said. "Does that have anything to do with it?"

Veronica shrugged. "Maybe. A few of my friends have moved away recently, a few more are about to follow them... No single reason, though. It's still a great place to live. We just... I don't know. We want somewhere new. So where are you from?"

"Georgia," said Milo. "My wife and I split up, and this trip is our father-daughter time."

"Father-daughter and cousin," said Glen quickly.

"How nice," Veronica said. "And your wife was okay with taking Amber out of school for this?"

Milo hesitated for just a moment too long, and Amber jumped in. "When he says they split up, what he means is, Mom passed away last year. Visiting all her favourite places is our way of saying goodbye."

"Oh no," said Veronica. "Oh, I'm so sorry."

"Not at all," said Milo, shooting a look at Amber.

"I'm from Ireland," said Glen.

Veronica nodded and smiled, and didn't say anything to that.

Glen looked mystified. He started to speak again – probably to repeat what he'd just said in the hope of a different reaction – when the doors opened and a man entered. Tall, astonishingly so, with broad shoulders and narrow hips, accentuated by the grey fitted coat he wore – tight around the midsection, then flowing to the floor. His trousers were black, his legs long, his arms long, even his fingers were long. He was handsome, had the complexion of a man who spent his time indoors, and his black hair was swept off his high forehead in an exaggerated widow's peak. He had a long nose, cheekbones like knife cuts, and twinkling dark eyes under a heavy brow.

"Miss Cartwright," he said, smiling. His accent was foreign, and unfamiliar to Amber. "It is a pleasure to see you, as always. And our newest guests – my deepest apologies for not being here to greet you upon your arrival. My name is Johann Varga, the owner of this hotel. I trust your time with us so far has been pleasant?"

"It has," said Milo. "Thank you."

"Have you travelled far?" Varga asked.

"It doesn't seem like it," said Milo, sounding genuinely friendly. "We've only been here a few hours, but even we can see that a town like Cascade Falls really rejuvenates a person, body and soul."

"Doesn't it?" Varga said. "A most peaceful place we have here. We are all quite rightly proud."

"You should be," Milo said, smiling.

Varga nodded his appreciation. "Alas, I have business to attend to. I hope to talk to you all again. For now, I bid you goodnight."

Amber joined the polite chorus that responded, and Varga left, drawing the doors closed behind him.

"Lovely man," said Veronica. "He does a lot for the town. It wouldn't be what it is today without him, and he never asks for anything in return. Sometimes I wonder what it must be like to be that selfless…"

"I like to do charity work," said Glen.

Veronica took her eyes away from Milo, and smiled like she was interested. "What kind?"

Glen shrugged. "It varies. I volunteer at homeless shelters

and animal rescue places, mostly. Cancer research. That sort of thing."

"You have no particular charity that's close to your heart?"

Glen adjusted his sitting position. "Well, I mean, yeah, I do. The main one, the main charity I do work for, is oil spills. Y'know when you see all those people in waterproofs cleaning seagulls and wildlife? That's me. I've always loved wildlife and I live near the sea back in Dublin, so it's pretty handy."

"Do you get a lot of oil spills in Dublin?"

"Uh, well, not really, no. But I'm always there if a whale gets beached, or whatever."

"Oh? What do you do when that happens?"

"Well, I… I push it back into the sea."

Veronica nodded, and waited for him to say more. When it became clear that he had nothing else to add, she turned back to Milo, and Glen frowned and sank a little lower in his chair.

After dinner, Amber took a shower in the bathroom down the hall from her room. It was a quaint affair and while, on the whole, she much preferred hotels that had bathrooms, it was still better than some of the motels they'd had to stay in so far.

She dried herself off, dressed in pyjamas, and bundled up her clothes, balancing her shoes on top. The carpet was soft under her bare feet as she walked to her room. Rounding the corner, she heard voices, and Milo and Veronica came into view, headed for Milo's room. They saw her and stopped. She blinked.

Eventually she said, "Just had a shower."

Milo nodded. "Good."

"How was the water?" Veronica asked.

"Hot," said Amber.

Milo nodded again, like this was an important piece of information he needed to file away. "Okay, well, see you in the morning."

"Yes, you will," Amber replied. "Goodnight."

Veronica gave her a beautiful smile, and Amber watched them both disappear into Milo's room.

She got to her own room and locked the door, then put her clothes on the chair. Then she stood in the middle of the room and frowned.

She had to admit, it was weird seeing Milo and Veronica... together. She found herself actually surprised, probably because the kind of things she associated with Milo were danger and fear and, to a possibly worrying degree, death. It had never occurred to her that he might have normal feelings behind all that alert coolness. She was even disappointed, in a way. She would have thought that someone like Veronica, as undeniably sexy as she was, would have had no effect on him. Amber had expected him to be above that sort of thing.

She laughed to herself at how prudish she sounded. He was a grown man, and he was allowed to do whatever he wanted, and it had nothing whatsoever to do with her.

She crossed to her bed, pulled the covers back, and slipped between them. The sheets were crisp, and she smiled. Nothing better than a freshly made bed. The pillow was cool, and she sank back into it. Not too soft, not too firm. Just right, as Goldilocks had said. She looked up at the ceiling, an off-white without any cracks.

Her smile faded.

She thought about Dacre Shanks, being digested in the trunk of the Charger. She thought about the Charger itself, and what manner of beast it was. She thought about Heather Medina and her father, wondered how they were. She thought of Gregory Buxton's mother, and what they were going to do if they couldn't convince her to help them. And she thought of her parents.

Most of all, she thought of her parents.

When tears came to her eyes, she rubbed them away and turned out the light. She dozed, then woke and lay there, changing position every few minutes.

Finally, she rolled on to her back again and listened to the hotel. It creaked softly. Groaned. Doors opened and closed. She heard muted footsteps. Muted voices. A dimmed world beyond these four walls, a world that was not about her, a world that didn't concern itself with her fears or her troubles. A world that would not mourn her passing, yet neither would it celebrate. An indifferent world. Uncaring. A world that reduced her to a speck.

Amber sat up. "Well, that's depressing," she muttered aloud.

She turned on the light and got up. She drew back the curtains, then opened the window and leaned out, breathing in the night air. She liked how cool it was. The air actually made her shiver. She allowed herself a smile, let herself enjoy the sensation.

There was movement below her – a window opening. Amber watched with mild amusement as someone else leaned out to experience the night in the same way as her. All she could see was the top of the guest's head. Maybe this was a thing people felt compelled to do here – look out across town and contemplate life.

Another window opened, and another head poked out. Then another, and the top of yet another guest's head. Amber stifled a giggle, remembering clips she'd seen from an old game show called Hollywood Squares. She resisted the urge to call out to them, let them share in the joke. But her smile faded when she watched the guests climb out of the windows, clinging to the wall, face down, before they let themselves drop into the darkness below.

Something blurred by to her left – someone dropping from a window above. She turned, looked up, straight into the face of Varga himself as he clung to the brickwork, his coat billowing behind him, his eyes wild and boring into hers. Then he released his hold on the wall and plummeted towards her.

32

AMBER SHRIEKED AND WHIPPED her head back, and Varga fell past her window.

She shut it quickly, backed away, then left the room, running to Milo's.

She slammed her fist against the door. "Milo, open up! Milo!"

Glen emerged from his room. "Amber? What's going on?"

"We have to leave. Varga's... I don't know what he is. But there's others like him, and we have to get out of here before they... do something."

Glen nodded. "You're not making a whole lot of sense, you know."

Amber ignored him, twisting the handle of Milo's door. To her surprise, it opened, and she ran in. The room was empty. The bed hadn't been slept in.

Amber's fingers curled in her hair. "Did you see him?"

"See who?" asked Glen.

"Milo! Who else? Did you see him?"

"Since dinner? No. Did you?"

"I saw him heading in here, with her."

"Her who?"

"The woman, Veronica."

Glen looked dismayed. "She went off with Milo? Aw man. She was giving me the eye all evening."

"She barely looked at you."

"That's called being coy."

Amber brushed past him, ran back to her room. Glen tried coming in after her, but she pushed him out.

"I'm getting dressed," she said. "Wait there. Tell me if you see anyone."

She slammed the door, ripped off her pyjamas and pulled on her clothes. When she was done, she left the room and hurried down the stairs.

"Can you please tell me what's going on?" Glen asked, right behind her.

Amber put a finger to her lips, and he scowled and shut up.

She crept through the hotel, noting for the first time how quiet it suddenly was, like it was holding its breath. There was no one at the front desk. She turned to share a look with Glen, but he was completely oblivious to how creepy it all was.

"Can I talk now?" he asked.

She hissed, and hit him, and he scowled again and rubbed his arm.

She led the way to the rear of the hotel. By now, even Glen had noticed how unnatural the silence was.

"Where is everyone?" he whispered.

Amber didn't answer.

They got to the small door leading to the parking area in the courtyard. The few feeble lights outside did little to dispel the encroaching darkness, but Amber really had no choice. She counted to three, then lunged from the hotel. Nothing jumped out at her, thank God. She ran to the hedge and stopped, her feet kicking up a shower of little stones. Glen almost bumped into her.

"Oops, sorry," he said. "What's wrong? Why— Hey, where's the car?"

"He's gone," Amber said softly.

Glen walked to the middle of the courtyard, like that would give him a vantage point from which to see the missing Charger. "Where? Where's he gone? Do you think he has Veronica with him? We should have a rule in future. The I *saw her* first rule. Y'know, it would have been me, but I'm too much of a gentleman to make a move so soon."

From overhead, a fluttering.

Amber looked up. The lights in the courtyard made the darkness above an impenetrable shroud of starless black.

She turned her head, following the fluttering as it moved from right to left. Then another, from in front to behind. More fluttering, getting closer and closer and then swooping up and away.

The fluttering not of feathers, or of wings, but of clothes.

"Glen," Amber whispered.

Glen stood there with his hands on his hips. "Milo knew I liked her. It was obvious. Maybe it's an Irish thing, but guys do not do that to each other. That is uncool."

"Glen."

"When he gets back, we're going to have a talk. Man to man."

"Glen, get inside," Amber said, her voice flat.

From above, a giggle.

Glen looked round. "You hear that?"

"Get inside, Glen."

Frowning, he watched her as she backed up to the door. The darkness was alive around them. On either side, a dreadful whispering, gleeful and mocking, while above, that fluttering. Always the fluttering.

Amber stepped backwards into the hotel, holding the door open for Glen as he came after her. He was frowning as he walked, kept turning his head. The darkness rippled above him. She saw shapes moving. The whispering got louder. Louder. There was laughter now – cruel and malicious laughter. Glen stopped looking around and fixed his eyes on Amber. He was terrified. His face trembled, like he was holding in a scream, like he was getting ready to bolt.

On either side of him, people were stepping from the shadows. An old man with white hair. A middle-aged woman with a pearl necklace. A young man with acne. More and more. They all wore identical smiles.

Then the shadows moved and something reached down from above and Amber grabbed Glen and yanked him inside, slammed the door and pressed her back to it.

Instant silence.

Except for Glen.

"Ohhhh my God! Holy crap! Would you look at my arms? See the goosebumps? What the hell was that? That was creepy! Oh *yikes*, y'know?"

He rubbed his arms and the back of his neck and laughed. "This place gets to you after a while, doesn't it?"

Amber stared at him. "Did you not see them?"

"See who?"

"The people."

"Where?"

"Out there! We were surrounded!"

"Uh, we were the only two out there, Amber…"

"They were about to grab you!"

"Who were?"

"The people! You heard them!"

"That was the wind. It was all creepy and spooky and scary and, y'know… The wind."

"That was voices. That was people whispering and laughing."

"It *did* sound like laughing."

"And what about the people flying?"

"Flying? What?"

"*They were going to grab you!*"

Glen put both hands on her shoulders, and said with an irritatingly soothing tone, "Amber, we're freaked out. The hotel is empty and Milo has taken off and we haven't a clue what the hell's going on, but we have to try to remain calm. If we let our imaginations run away with us, then we're—"

"Screw you," said Amber, walking past him.

"I didn't mean anything bad," Glen said, following. "Where are you going?"

"To my room. I'm going to barricade the door and wait till morning."

"Yeah, a good night's sleep is probably best."

"Shut up, Glen."

She climbed the stairs.

"Hey, I get it," he said. "You're scared. I get it, I do. Maybe if you change into your, y'know, other self, you mightn't be so freaked out. You might be able to calm down."

"Calming down is not a good idea when we're in danger. We have to stay frightened and alert."

"I agree," said Glen. "And I believe you. I believe that we're in danger. So I think we should go to your room, barricade the door, you should change into your other self, and we'll wait until morning."

Amber glared at him. "We?"

"I'm in danger, too, right?"

She sighed. "Yeah."

"Well then," he said, and walked into her room.

Gritting her teeth, Amber followed, and locked her door.

"I'll take first watch if you want," said Glen, moving to the open window. "You can change any time now."

Amber felt the blood drain from her face. "I shut that before I left," she whispered.

Glen rested his hands on the sill. "Hey," he said, "you can see Althea's house from here."

And then he was snatched away.

Amber screamed, found herself red-skinned before she knew what was happening. She ran to the window, looked out, saw nothing but heard laughter. She shut the window again, made sure the latch was secure, and closed the curtains. She pushed the dresser in front of the door. Finally, she dragged the bedclothes into the corner and sat, the duvet held tightly to her chin.

Something scraped against her door. Fingernails.

Someone whispered through the keyhole.

Amber waited for morning.

33

SHE DIDN'T SLEEP.

She was tired and her eyes wanted to close, but she didn't sleep, not with Glen having been snatched away, not with Milo missing, not with those... *people* out there. Nor did she change back. She kept her horns and fangs and talons, as much of a comfort to her as a gun to a soldier.

A half-hour before dawn, the silence left the hotel. Amber heard footsteps in the room above. She heard a window close in the room below. They were returning.

When dawn broke the darkness, the curtains let through a few weak strands of early morning sunlight. Gradually, she heard the sounds of normality seep through the floorboards. Doors opening and closing. Voices bidding each other good morning.

She waited until seven, until the sun was up and the day had properly begun. She got up. Opened the curtains. Cascade Falls lay fresh-faced before her.

She pushed the dresser back into place, and unlocked her door. When nobody came rushing in, she took a deep breath, and felt her horns retract.

She stepped out, careful to move as quietly as possible. She crept to Milo's room, reached for the handle, but the door opened before she touched it.

Amber yelped, and Milo jumped back.

"Jesus," he breathed, scowling at her.

She pushed by him, into the room.

"Where were you?" she whispered.

He looked at the open door, then at her, and then he closed it. "I'm sorry?"

"Last night, you disappeared. You took the car."

He nodded. "Veronica wanted to go for a ride. She'd never been in a Charger before. Why?"

"They took Glen."

"Who did?"

"Varga," she said. "Varga and the others took Glen."

"I'm not sure I understand."

"They were flying around last night and they dragged him right out the window!"

Milo looked at her.

She glared. "Don't you dare say I imagined it all."

"I wasn't about to," he murmured. He went to the bed, pulled his bag out from underneath, and removed his gun and holster from a side pocket. He clipped the holster to his belt and slid it out of sight. Then he put his jacket on over it.

He led the way out, and over to Glen's room. He listened at the door for a moment, then pushed it open. Glen's gentle snoring was the first thing to greet them.

Milo parted the curtains and Glen woke, turned over, gazing at them both blearily.

"What are you doing in my room?" he asked, his voice thick.

"What *happened?*" Amber asked.

"Sorry?"

"Last night," said Milo. "Amber, start from the beginning."

"I couldn't sleep," she said, "so I opened the window. I saw Varga and maybe five or six others climbing down the wall. No ropes, no gear, they were *sticking* to the bricks. Then they... then they let go and they *flew.*"

Glen frowned. "They flew?"

"Yes," she snapped, then ignored him and turned back to Milo. "Then I went to get you, but you were gone. Glen came out, and we went outside to look for the car."

"That was gone, too," said Glen unhelpfully.

"But there were people out there with us," Amber said, "and I could hear more of them flying overhead. They almost got Glen, but we got back inside, went to my room... I'd closed the window before I left, but it was open, and Glen went over to it and he was pulled out."

Glen frowned. "I was?"

She whirled. "You were pulled out the window, Glen."

He processed the information. "Ohhh," he said. "That's what happened."

Amber was ready to kill him. "*What?*"

"I woke up on the ground," said Glen. "I must have fallen out."

"You didn't fall. You were pulled! If you had fallen, half your bones would be broken!"

He shook his head. "Not necessarily. If my body had been completely limp on the way down, I'd stand a good chance of—"

"Shut up, Glen! How can you *not* remember?"

"I must have blacked out. I remember everything you said,

except the bits I didn't see, like, and I remember getting to your room and then waking up outside. I went back in, knocked on your door, but you were asleep—"

"I was not asleep."

"Well, then you didn't hear me, so I just went back to bed."

"And, if that was you, you did not knock. You scraped."

Glen's frown deepened. "Why would I do that?"

"Amber," said Milo, "you saw Varga, right? You're sure it was him?"

"Positive."

"Then we'll go have a talk with our gracious host."

She nodded. "Right. Good. Yeah."

"I have a question," said Glen. "What kind of a world is it we live in when a man will step between another man and the woman he obviously shares a deep connection and intense physical attraction with?"

"Are you talking about Veronica?" Milo asked, sounding genuinely puzzled.

"Yes, Milo, yes, I am."

"She doesn't like you, Glen."

"That is a lie."

"She said you reminded her of a startled meerkat."

Glen went quiet for a moment. Then he responded with, "That makes very little sense."

"Get up and get dressed," said Amber, leaving the room. "And bring your bag down with you. We're not staying here tonight."

Glen grumbled, but when he was dressed Amber led the way downstairs.

"Well, hello there," Ingrid said brightly when she saw them. Her eyes dipped to their bags. "Are you leaving us so soon? Did you have a good night?"

"Some of us had a better night than others," said Glen, strolling over.

Ingrid looked concerned. "Oh, that's a shame for some of you, then. Anything I can do to persuade you to stay?"

"Dunno," said Glen. "Do you have a younger sister?"

Milo stepped sharply in front of him. "Could we speak with Mr Varga, please?"

Ingrid gave another one of her smiles. "I'm sorry, Mr Varga is out on business for the day. We're expecting him back tonight, though, if that's any use to you?"

"Sure," said Milo. "We'll talk to him then."

"Wonderful," said Ingrid. "Is there anything else I can help you with?"

"No, thank you," said Milo, handing over his key.

Amber and Glen did the same, and they walked out to the Charger without saying another word. They got in.

"I don't like this town," Amber said. "We're leaving as soon as we get Gregory Buxton's location."

Glen nodded. "So we interrogate his mum. Force her to tell us where he is."

She turned to him. "What?"

He blinked. "We… we don't interrogate his mum?"

"She's, like, a hundred!"

"She's religious," said Milo, starting the car. "Today's Sunday. She'll most likely be going to church. Which means she'll be out of the house."

"We break in!" said Glen. "We're good at breaking into

places! Although technically we didn't break into the Springton Library, we just hid in the toilets, but the end result is the same."

"Shut up," Milo said calmly. "I'll break in, search through her stuff. There has to be a postcard or a letter or an address book or something."

"What'll we do?" Glen asked.

"We'll follow her," said Amber. "Make sure she doesn't come back early. If she does, we'll delay her."

"How?"

"You said that older women find you irresistible, right?"

Glen blanched. "You want me to... seduce her?"

Amber shrugged. "Only if you have to."

They parked a few streets away from Althea Buxton's house, and went walking. On their third time passing her street, they saw her emerging. Milo disappeared behind her house, and Amber and Glen followed her on the five-minute walk to the church.

Right before Amber stepped through the door, she wondered if she'd burst into flames the moment her foot touched the ground.

Thankfully, she didn't.

They chose a space on a pew near the back, where they could keep an eye on Althea. Amber tried to remember the last time she'd been in a church. Had she *ever* been in one? Her parents had never bothered with it — surprise, surprise — and her school was pretty secular. Maybe all she'd seen of the inside of churches had been from movies and TV. She looked up at a statue of Christ on the cross, noting how much he must have worked out to get abs like that, and thought for the first time about praying.

Was God the answer? Up until recently, she'd never had to think about it before, but having been faced with the stark reality of demons and devils – she only had to look in the mirror for proof of that – maybe now was the time to start.

Would it help if she got down on her knees and prayed? She contemplated, for a moment, the idea of praying for her parents, praying that they'd see sense, that they'd recover from whatever madness had gripped them. But she dismissed the idea almost as quickly. She might as well wish for a happy childhood where they hadn't ignored her.

"I don't feel well," Glen whispered. "I think I've got internal injuries."

Would a priest be able to absolve her of her sins? Amber wondered what this priest would make of her horns. If she stepped into a confessional box and she told him the truth, the whole truth, and revealed herself in all her red-skinned glory, what would his reaction be? Would it shatter his faith, shake it loose, or renew it? Would he have an answer for her, or would he cast her from this holy place, cursing her existence and damning her in the eyes of his Lord?

Was she *already* damned in the eyes of his Lord?

Jesus looked down at her, all rippling muscles and skimpy loincloth, and he didn't give a whole lot away. A sneaky one, that Jesus.

"My friends," the priest said. He was young and, even from where she was sitting, Amber could see the bags under his eyes like dark rings. He needed sleep. She could relate.

"Today brings us troubling times," he continued. "We turn on the news and we see civilisation crumble around the world. War and crime and terrorism and hatred. Poverty. Injustice. Everywhere we look, warning signs of evil. It is taking hold. It is taking root. But, you ask, why would I need to turn on the news to see evidence of this? Why would I need to open a newspaper, or go online? Have not the seeds of evil already taken root here in our very own town?"

A ripple of murmurings through the churchgoers, and Amber sat up a little straighter.

"I have God on my side," said the priest. "He is my shepherd. He guides me. He protects me. But, even so, I am afraid. I am beginning to doubt. Not God, however. He is as strong as He has ever been. No, my friends, I doubt myself. For my flesh is weak. And my heart is weak. Two weeks ago, we buried our great friend, Father Taylor, and suddenly I am standing up here alone. I find myself missing his comforting presence. I miss his words, his counsel. Most of all, though, I miss his bravery."

The priest glanced briefly to one side, and Amber noticed for the first time a large photograph, propped up on an easel. It showed a smiling, white-haired old man.

"He knew, you see," the priest continued. "He felt it. I denied it. And now it's too late."

"The man in the picture," Amber whispered to Glen.

"What about him?"

"I saw him," said Amber. "I saw him last night outside the hotel."

And then someone started singing. With a low voice, a quiet voice.

"Down in the willow garden, where me and my love did meet."

Disquiet spread softly.

"As we sat a-courtin', my love fell off to sleep."

Amber could see him now, the man who was singing. He sat with his head down.

"I had a bottle of Burgundy wine. My love, she did not know. So I poisoned that dear little girl, on the banks below."

The people on either side of him started to shuffle away.
He continued to sing. And then a female voice joined him.

"I drew a sabre through her, it was a bloody knife."

A third voice now, and more shuffling away, and the singing got a little stronger.

"I threw her in the river, which was a dreadful sign."

Another person joined the song, singing with his head down, and a fifth, and a sixth, and now people were getting up, their pushes becoming shoves in their attempts to create distance, and the panic was rising with the singing voices, and a seventh and an eighth person joined the song and the priest backed away with a look of horror on his face and people were crying now and running for the exit.

Amber saw Althea, pushed from behind and falling to her

knees. Amber sprang off the pew, barged into the surging crowd and was nearly knocked off her feet herself. But she made it, and she gripped Althea's arm and pulled her up, and now Glen was in front, clearing the way to the door.

"My race is run, beneath the sun. The scaffold waits for me."

Amber looked back, saw ten or twelve people now standing, but still with their heads down, and still singing.

"For I did murder that dear little girl, whose name was Rose Connelly."

And, just as Althea fainted and her whole bodyweight collapsed into Amber's arms, they burst out into the sun.

34

BETWEEN HERSELF AND GLEN they half walked, half carried Althea up the hill and back to her house.

She was, despite her modest height, quite a heavy woman, and the journey was slow and difficult. Althea came out of her faint twice, started muttering, then succumbed to it once again, the cross around her neck dangling beneath her chin. They got to the house and Amber knocked, calling Milo's name. A few moments later, the door opened and he let them in. On their way upstairs, they filled him in on what had happened, then laid Althea carefully on her bed. All at once the muttering stopped and Althea was sleeping deeply.

Milo and Glen shared a glance, then left the room. Amber frowned until she realised that she was expected to take care of the undressing.

Ten minutes later, she joined them both in the living room.

"Next time an old person needs to be readied for bed," she said, "one of you is going to do it."

The living room was modest, with a low-hanging faux-chandelier and wallpaper that hadn't even been in style when it was made. Rugs lay atop the carpet and the curtains were heavy and old. A sofa and an armchair huddled round the cold fireplace, the armchair facing a TV so stocky it would have crushed the old lady if it had fallen on her. Beside the window there was a small, circular table covered with a tablecloth. Framed photographs stood like privates in a parade. There was a painting of Jesus over the mantelpiece.

"I've been to church," said Glen, standing at the window and peeking out from behind the blinds. "That is not supposed to happen. That was creepy. It was more than creepy. It was... it was very creepy."

Milo was flicking through an address book, but paused long enough to glance at Amber. "Think it's got anything to do with what you saw last night?"

"Probably," she said. "The priest was talking about how the seeds of evil have already taken root here. I'm pretty sure those were some of the seeds he was talking about. Did you find anything?"

"Not yet," Milo replied. "But maybe Althea will be more willing to talk to us after this."

"She'll probably need one of us to be with her when she wakes, though," said Glen. "Just to make sure she doesn't freak out. I'll take first watch."

"Wait," said Amber. "You think waking up to find a strange Irishman in her bedroom will reassure her?"

Glen frowned. "What's wrong with that?"

Amber didn't bother answering. She just went back upstairs. She sat in an armchair, watching Althea sleep. After a few minutes, she closed her eyes. Just for a moment. Just to rest them.

*

When Amber awoke, the sunlight had a red tinge to it, like drops of blood in bathwater. She yawned, sitting up straighter in her chair. Mid-yawn, she froze. The bed was empty.

Alarmed, she hurried downstairs to find Althea sitting in the living room with Glen.

"Amber," said Glen, smiling broadly, "you're finally awake!"

"I didn't have the nerve to disturb you," Althea said. "You looked exhausted, so I thought to myself I'll let this poor girl sleep."

"Uh, thank you," said Amber. "I hope I didn't frighten you, or anything."

Althea smiled ruefully. "Takes more than a young girl to frighten me, let me tell you."

Milo came in, holding a saucer with a delicate cup of steaming tea. "Here you go, Althea," he said, passing it over.

"A saint, that's what you are," Althea said, taking it from him and sipping.

"Not too strong this time?"

Althea chuckled. "No, dear, it's perfect, thank you."

Milo sat in the armchair and looked at Amber. "Althea was just telling us who those people in church were. Some of them have been ill recently."

"That's right," said Althea. "I know Tom Prendergast hasn't been in work since Monday, and Rachel Faulkner didn't show up for her shift in the cafe yesterday or the day before. She didn't even call in sick. And I'm not one to listen to gossip, but that Stevens boy hasn't been well all week. They say he's got an infection."

She nodded when she said it, like Amber would know what kind of infection she meant.

"Do you think they were all sick with the same thing?" Amber asked.

Althea took another sip from her cup. "I'm sure I don't know. But it would appear so, wouldn't it? They were all complaining of weakness, and everyone who saw them remarked on how pale they looked. Then there were the..."

She trailed off.

"Then there were the what?" Milo prompted.

But Althea only smiled. "Nothing, dear. Worried people, that's all it is."

"You said something earlier about strange deaths?" Glen said.

"Oh heavens, no," Althea responded, her small eyes glittering. "Such talk is nothing more than salacious gossip, and I for one do not partake. But we have had a very odd year, a very unsettling year. People have died in mysterious circumstances and others have claimed to see them days or even weeks later, walking the streets. Always at night, though. Always at night. And it all began with that poor family."

"Tell us," said Glen. "Please."

The tip of Althea's tongue popped out from between her lips as she considered the request, and then vanished. She put her cup and saucer on the coffee table and sat forward on the sofa. Milo and Glen leaned in. Amber perched on the arm of Milo's chair and did the same.

"The Mastersons," Althea said. "Lovely family. The mother was a lawyer, her husband was a teacher. Mathematics, I think. They had two beautiful children. The boy was the youngest. A prodigy, they said. Sit him at a piano and he could play like Mozart. Hand him a violin and he could play like Vivaldi. The daughter, though, Rosalie, she was the one you'd remember. I daresay you'd have fallen in love with her at first sight, Glen. Beautiful and kind, intelligent and funny. She was the flower of Cascade Falls. She had many would-be suitors and, from what I've heard, they were remarkably well-behaved around her. No inappropriateness of any sort. Until Caleb Tylk.

"Caleb was a troubled boy," she went on. "Fights. Suspended from school three times. Vandalism. But, like every boy his age, he was in love with Rosalie Masterson. She was polite to him, which is testament enough to her character, wouldn't you say? But that was Rosalie. A girl much too lovely for this world."

"So I'm guessing something really bad happened," said Amber.

Althea nodded gravely. She reached for her cup, took a sip, and replaced it on its saucer. "Caleb Tylk's attentions were wildly, grotesquely inappropriate. He mistook her kindness for something more, and she was forced to reject his advances. He didn't take it well. They said he hanged himself on the old tree beside the Varga Hotel."

"They *said*?" Glen echoed. "They didn't know for sure?"

"My friend, Sally-Ann Deaton, insists that she saw him hanging there, but, by the time the authorities came, the body was gone."

"What happened to it?" asked Amber.

"Nobody knows," said Althea. "But three nights later, cruel and bloody murder paid a visit to the Masterson house. The mother had her head cut off. The father had his heart ripped out. The son, that poor boy, was torn limb from limb. And Rosalie was taken."

"You think Caleb did it," said Milo.

"Oh yes," said Althea. "Rosalie's bedroom door had been

broken down. On the wall beside the open window was *Caleb Tylk loves Rosalie Masterson*, written in Rosalie's own blood."

Silence followed her words. She took her saucer in her hand and had another sip of tea.

"Since then, things have gotten bad, and are getting worse. People are dying, and rising again. Oh, come now, wipe those looks off your faces. You know. I can tell. There's something out there… something evil. You can feel it, too. He is not of this world."

"He?"

"Varga," she said. "It's all centred around him."

"Why don't you leave?" Glen asked.

"I would've been out of here last week if my car hadn't broken down," Althea said with a chuckle. "At first, I was stubborn. I have lived in Cascade Falls my entire life and I was determined not to let any unholy creatures force me from my home. But then, well, my mind was changed. Vampires can do that to a person."

Glen blinked. "Vampires?"

"Well, of course," said Althea. "What did you think we were talking about?"

"I… have no idea," said Glen. "But vampires? Really?"

Althea nodded. "That's why I carry a crucifix with me wherever I go, and it's why I never invite anyone into my house after dark. Those people singing in church today were the vampires' human familiars – people who have been enslaved, but who have not yet been drained completely. I know my stuff, you best believe it."

"Are we seriously talking about Dracula-style vampires here?" asked Glen, an excited grin starting to spread.

"Of course we are," said Althea. "If you'd looked close, you would have seen that they all share two puncture wounds on their necks."

"Wow…" said Glen.

Althea looked at him sadly. "Just like yours."

35

GLEN'S SMILE FADED. "I'm sorry?"

"Your bitemark, dear," said Althea, tapping her collar.

Glen frowned, and his hand went to his own neck. His eyes widened. "*What?*"

He leaped to his feet, spinning so that Amber and Milo could see the puncture wounds.

Amber stood, almost stumbled. "Oh hell."

"What does it mean? *What does it mean?*" Glen wailed. "Oh God, am I a vampire? Does this mean I'm a vampire?"

"You're not a vampire," said Milo. "But you are marked."

"Not again! I can't be! I've already been marked! I had the Deathmark! I can't be marked again!"

"What does marked *mean?*" Amber asked.

"It means the vampire who bit Glen can find him anytime he or she wishes," said Althea, and then shrugged. "I've done my homework."

"I'm *marked,*" Glen breathed, his eyes wide.

"There's no need to make a big deal out of it," said Milo, but Glen was already moving towards the front door.

"I need to walk," he said. "I need to... I need to be *free!*"

And then he was gone, the door swinging closed behind him.

"What a dramatic young man," said Althea.

But, before the door had clicked shut, Glen was barging back through.

"They're here!" he cried, slamming the door and scuttling to the window.

Amber frowned. "The vampires?"

Glen looked back at her, real fear on his face. "Your *parents*."

She ran to the window before she knew what she was doing, in time to see her parents' car vanish round the corner. She went cold.

"Did they see you?" Milo asked, hauling Glen up by his collar. "They know your face. Did they see you?"

"No," Glen said. "No, they didn't."

Milo turned to Althea. "How many ways out of town?"

"Just two, I'm afraid," she answered. "The road to the east and the bridge to the west."

"They'll have them covered. Two on each, and the last two searching the town. We have to move."

"Wait," said Amber. It was all too much. All too fast. She needed things to slow down; she needed to be able to think. "They… they don't know why we're here, do they? I mean, they may have tracked us to this town, but they clearly haven't spoken to Shanks. They don't know about Althea or her son, and they don't know about the vampires. In a few hours, Cascade Falls will be crawling with the things, right, Althea?"

Althea nodded. "And every night it gets worse."

"There you go," said Amber. "That'll keep them busy. All we have to do is lie low until morning, then we'll just sneak past them. Althea, we'll take you with us. We'll pack your bags while we're waiting."

"That's a plan," said Milo. "But, if they've followed us this far, they know what kind of car we're driving. I'll have to hide it."

"There's a small barn just before the bridge," said Althea. "There's nothing inside and it's never locked."

"That's it, then," said Milo. "I'll get the car under cover and come back as soon as I can. Do not open the door to anyone. Vampires can't enter a property unless they're invited, am I right about that, Althea?"

"Yes, you are, Milo."

Milo turned to Glen. "What about you? Can I trust you not to do anything stupid?"

"I am a creature of the night," Glen whispered.

"That'll have to do," said Milo, and hurried out.

Amber locked the door behind him.

When Althea's bags were packed and sitting in the hall, Amber took her upstairs so she could get some rest. When she was gently snoring, Amber came back down and found Glen standing at the window, looking out.

"Have you seen them again?" she asked. "Glen? *Glen*."

He looked round, startled. "What? Sorry?"

"My parents," she said. "Have you seen them again?"

"Oh," he said. "No. Haven't seen them."

She nodded, and stood beside him. His gaze was once again on the town beyond the glass. He looked tired. Worn out. First the Deathmark and now this… Despite how much he annoyed her, she couldn't help but feel sorry for him.

"*There*," he said. "Did you hear it?"

She pushed down her worries about her parents, shoved them deep into a dark, dark hole, and made a big show of listening. "Uh no. I don't think so. Hear what?"

He frowned. "Nothing. Never mind."

"How are you feeling?" she asked gently.

He didn't look at her. "Feeling is something only the living do."

"Oh yeah?" Amber said, and punched his shoulder. "Feel that?"

"Ow!" He rubbed his arm. "How can you hit so hard with such small hands? God!"

She gave him a grin. "Don't be so dramatic."

"I think I'm entitled to be dramatic, actually," he said, glaring. "I'm the one bitten. I'm the one with the mark of the vampire upon his skin."

"*Upon his skin?*" she mocked.

He looked out of the window again. "You don't know what it's like for people like me."

"What, the Irish?"

"The damned. The doomed. Those with the vampire's kiss upon our lips."

"The vampire kissed you?"

"It's a metaphor."

"Barely."

His eyes widened. "There it is again!"

Amber frowned. "There what is?"

"A whisper," he said. "Or a… not a whisper, a call. But it's… it's soft. You're sure you don't hear it?"

"I'm pretty sure. Where's it coming from?"

"Out there," he said. He bit his lip. "Amber, would you promise me something?"

"Depends…"

"You… you won't let me die alone, will you?"

He looked at her, and all the pain he had ever felt was right there in his eyes.

"You're not going to die," she said. "You've been bitten. That means a vampire fed on you. You haven't been turned."

"I know, I know that, but… but you wouldn't let me die alone, right? We're friends, aren't we?"

"Yeah. I guess. Sort of."

"Well, even sort-of friends don't let each die alone, do they?"

She sighed, and took his hand. "No, they don't. You're going to be fine, Glen. We're going to wait till morning, and then we're going to leave. Easy as pie."

"Yeah," said Glen. "Yeah. Sorry. I've never really had much of a family before, except for my dad. He was like me, y'know? Sensitive. My mam, she used to slag him about it. Make fun of him, like. Then he lost his job and it was like all she ever did was slag him."

"How did he die?" Amber asked softly.

Glen hesitated. "Alone," he said.

"Do you have any brothers or sisters?"

"A brother. He's a dick."

"I had a brother," said Amber. "A long, long time ago. A sister, too. Never knew them. I always wanted a brother when I was growing up. A brother would beat up anyone who laughed at me or called me names."

"My brother was the one who laughed at me," said Glen. "He was the one who called *me* names."

"I don't think my brother would have been like that," Amber said. "I think he would have been nice. So you wouldn't go back to Ireland? Back to your mom?"

He smiled sadly. "She doesn't want me. Never did, I suppose. I wasn't the happiest kid growing up so I kind of… pretended I was? I got on her nerves a lot. Were you happy as a kid?"

"I thought I was," said Amber. "I mean, I knew my parents were different. They didn't hold my hand, they didn't play with me… I thought it was something I'd done, maybe something I was doing wrong. So I tried to act more like the other kids, but that didn't work, so I tried to act more like my parents, but that didn't work, either… It's only now that I can look back and realise they never noticed. All of my little efforts to please them or make them proud, anytime I changed my behaviour to get some kind of reaction out of them, they just… never noticed. Because they didn't care."

"So we were both sad kids," said Glen.

"I guess. The more I think about these things, the clearer I see what my life was really like."

"Scary, isn't it?"

"It is."

They smiled at each other, and she gave his hand a squeeze and went to let go, but he held on. His eyes found hers, and they softened, and he leaned in.

"I swear to God," she said, "do not try to kiss me."

He faltered. A moment passed, and then he hugged her arm and let it drop.

Another moment passed.

"That was so awkward," said Amber.

"I was just about to say that."

"That was weird and unsettling."

He nodded. "It was an ill-advised move, it's true."

"Were you seriously going to kiss me?"

"Apparently."

"Your eyes went funny."

"I've been told that happens."

"I thought you only liked me when I was all demony."

"You really think I'm that superficial?"

"Yes."

"You could be right," said Glen. "But isn't it possible that I might have grown as a person in the last few days? After all my brushes with death and everything?"

"I guess," she said.

"I think I might have," he went on. "I'm probably realising that, when it comes to beauty, it's what's inside that counts. Or maybe beauty is what my eye, y'know, beholds it to be? I think I might have turned a significant corner in, like, sorting out what's hot and what's not. This is a big moment for me. But I didn't mean to make things awkward between us. I just think you're really awesome and I thought we were having a moment and I made a mistake. I'm sorry."

"Listen, Glen, I want you to know—"

"I value your friendship, too."

"—that I am in no way attracted to you at all in the slightest."

He blinked. "I'm sorry?"

She winced. "I should have said what you said, about the valuing friendship stuff. Dammit. Can I go back and change my answer?"

"You don't think I'm cute?"

"I think you're reasonably good-looking, sure. But that doesn't mean I'm attracted to you."

"Why not?"

"It just doesn't."

"Are you sure that makes sense, though?"

She patted his shoulder. "I'm going to check on Althea. Maybe she'll be ready to talk about her son now. When I come back, we can hopefully pretend this never happened."

"Yeah," he said. "Okay."

She walked upstairs, feeling weird.

Althea was sitting up in bed. "Is Milo back yet?" she asked.

"No. But don't worry about him," said Amber. "Milo can take care of himself. How are you doing?"

Althea smiled. "I'm old, and I need a lot of rest, but apart from that I am as fine as I ever was. Or so I like to think." She chuckled. "Old age has a tendency to creep up on a person when they're not looking. It's sneaky like that." She sat back, folding her hands over her belly. "You wanted to know about Gregory, didn't you?"

"Yes," said Amber. "If you'll tell me. He's still alive, isn't he?"

Althea smiled sadly. "As far as I know. I don't know where he is, but maybe I can help you find him. How much do you know already?"

"We know he made a deal with the Devil."

"A lot of people would have trouble even uttering those words, but I think you've seen more of the truth of this world than you'd like. Would I be right?"

"I guess so."

"Figured," said Althea. "Gregory… Well. I understand why he did what he did, but that does not make it right. Not in the eyes of the Lord."

"Why did he do it?"

"Oh, it wasn't about greed or lust or power, if that's what you're thinking. My son isn't perfect, but he's a good man. It was because of my grandson, you see. Gregory made that deal out of love. And love is God's weapon. It's because of this that I pray, every night, that he finds his way back to the Lord, and I pray the Lord is willing to receive him. I'll add you to my prayers, if you like."

"Thank you," said Amber, oddly touched. "It'd be nice to have someone praying for me. What's your grandson's name?"

"Jacob," said Althea. "He had the cancer from a young age. By the time he was ten, his home was a hospital bed. He had tubes coming out of him and tubes going into him and then he needed help to breathe and then he couldn't see… Science failed him. It did its best, but it wasn't up to the job. I was praying, every day I was praying, but it seemed likely that God's plan was to kill that little boy and take his soul up to heaven. A fine plan, I supposed, in the overall scheme, though I couldn't for the life of me figure out why God was putting him through so much pain. I couldn't really see the point of that, to torture a little boy who'd never done nothing to nobody. If God had felt the need to torture, why not torture those folks who were just scraping into heaven, just barely? Maybe by making them suffer, they'd actually prove worthy of an afterlife? But by putting all that cancer into such a small boy, well… It just seemed cruel.

"But the Devil, you see, the Devil has no time for God's plans. The Devil and that Shining Demon of his are there to stir things up. Gregory made that deal and I'm glad he did it, because poor Jacob did not deserve what God was doing to him. I'm glad my son did what he did, even though he damned himself by doing it."

314

"What did the Shining Demon want in return?"

"Souls," said Althea. "What does he ever want? Souls, souls and more souls — the more innocent, the better. But my son is smarter than the Shining Demon. Jacob was healed, and Gregory disappeared without having to shed one single drop of blood. The Shining Demon doesn't know where to even look. So I doubt you'll be able to find him, if you don't mind me saying."

"You don't have any idea where he is?"

"I don't," said Althea. "Gregory probably thinks it's safer that way — safer for him and safer for me."

"What about your grandson?"

Althea shook her head. "Jacob doesn't know. Don't think he does, anyway."

"Could we talk to him?"

"I don't have a phone number for him, I'm afraid. He lives in Cricket Hill, that's in Colorado. Burkitt Road, I think. I might be wrong."

"He doesn't stay in touch?"

Althea smiled. "Young people have their own lives to lead, as you well know. No one has any responsibility to call me, or even write. Do you call your grandparents?"

"I, um, I never had any."

Althea patted her hand. "That's a shame. I have a feeling you'd have made a good granddaughter. What about your friend?"

"Glen? No, his family isn't anything to brag about, either."

"Well then," said Althea, "it's a good thing he has you and Milo, isn't it?"

"I guess."

Althea smiled. "Go on, now. Let an old woman get her rest."

Amber left the room, closing the door gently. She went to the bathroom, then made herself a sandwich in the kitchen. She made one for Glen, too, and took it to him. The living room was empty.

"Glen?" she called.

She searched the house, growing more and more panicked. Finally, she went to the window, looked in the direction Glen had been looking when he'd heard those whispers calling to him. In a darkened area across town, a single house was lit up.

Taking a heavy crucifix from Althea's wall, Amber followed him out into the night.

36

AMBER WALKED QUICKLY, sticking to the shadows, the crucifix clutched tightly in her hand. The streets were unnaturally quiet, the entire town of Cascade Falls holding its breath for morning. But morning was a long way off.

Halfway across town, Amber saw her first moving car of the night. She ducked behind a fence, scampered sideways, peering out through the leaves of a manicured hedge.

The car passed slowly, and so close that Amber got a good look at both Grant and Kirsty.

Her breath caught in her throat.

No demon horns for her parents' old friends. They looked perfectly normal, sitting there, scanning their surroundings like hawks, searching for prey. Amber had an irrational urge to stand up, let them see her.

She resisted.

The car moved on and Amber thought about what she'd seen. She thought about their faces. Calm but eager. Patient but excited. They knew she was close and they knew they were closing in. The urge to stand up faded quickly, replaced by a hatred so deep she now had to stop herself from screaming curses at them. Her heart pounded ever harder in her chest and she shifted without meaning to. This time there was no pain to accompany the transformation.

When the car had turned the corner, Amber moved on, still in her demon form, crossing the road quickly and slipping into shadow once again.

She got to the Varga Hotel without encountering anyone else, and skirted it. An image flashed into her head of vampires crawling all over the outside walls like flies on a rotting piece of meat, but so far there was nothing unusual – or unnatural – to be seen. She carried on through the darkened neighbourhood, to the only house with lights on.

Keeping to the shadows, she circled it, then crossed the road, and ducked down behind some bushes. She waited, making sure she hadn't been seen, then peeked back across the road at the front door, which gaped open like a hungry mouth.

Something bad had happened.

She bit her lip, feeling her sharp teeth. If there were vampires in there, she had the crucifix. If her parents were in there, the crucifix wouldn't make a damn bit of difference and she'd be walking to her death.

But she didn't have a choice. Glen was in that house, she just knew it, and she wasn't going to leave him behind – not if she could help it.

Keeping low, she jogged back across the road, straightening up as she approached the door. At the last moment, she reverted to her normal appearance – if she was wrong and everything was fine, she didn't want to give the owner of the house a heart attack.

Amber climbed the two small steps, pushed the door open the rest of the way, and, holding the crucifix out before her, she walked in.

The hall corridor was long and narrow, at the end of which was a door with a large partition of clouded glass. A doorway to her left led into a living room that was well maintained but barely lived in. Another doorway to her right opened on to a neat, bookshelf-lined study. She passed a small table on which sat a type of phone she'd only seen pictures of, the kind with a rotary dial. There was a bedroom on her left. A bathroom on her right.

The house was quiet and well lit. No shadows moved beyond the clouded glass ahead.

Amber stopped and listened. She counted to ten and, when she still didn't hear anything, she turned the handle and nudged the door. It swung open gently into a second living room, one that showed definite signs of having being lived in. The TV set in the corner, the logs beside the fireplace, the magazines and books scattered around on the various items of furniture – this was the room the owner of the house spent most of his time in.

He'd spent his last few moments in here as well.

His body lay crumpled beside the old sofa, his head twisted all the way round. His death had been quick – or at least it looked that way. Small mercies. Amber wondered if there would be anyone left in this town to gossip about it after tonight.

The living room connected to the kitchen. Amber crossed the carpeted floor silently. She got to the doorway and peeked inside, and a mournful weight dropped from her chest to her belly. Glen lay on the table, arms and legs flung wide, his eyes open and blinking. Dozens of small wounds punctured his body in perfect sets of two, and from those wounds trickled what little blood he had left. His skin was so pale. He looked empty. On the cusp of death.

His eyes flickered to her. He opened his mouth to moan, and all that escaped was a breath. A finger moved, and that's all he could manage.

A vampire stepped into the kitchen from the utility room ahead. She was middle-aged and as pale as Glen. She smiled at Amber, revealing her fangs.

Amber moved backwards out of the kitchen. The doors connecting the living room to the two main bedrooms were now open. Vampires stood there, watching her hungrily.

She backed up to the door with the clouded glass. They followed. Eight of them. She held up the crucifix. A look of physical pain passed over the vampires' faces. One of them actually recoiled, as if from a great heat. They hissed in anger.

The middle-aged woman was the bravest. With every step she took, Amber shrank back. The woman's eyes were astonishing. They blazed. Amber couldn't look away.

"Put down the cross," the woman said.

Her voice melted in Amber's head. The words sang. They tugged at every small corner of her mind, and brought with them a pleasing, numbing warmth.

Amber's arm dipped.

"Put it down," said the woman. "We won't hurt you."

Amber wanted to. She wanted to so badly. She didn't like holding the crucifix like this. She didn't want to hurt the woman's feelings. But the other vampires, she didn't like them. They scared her. Especially the way they were moving closer, their smiles spreading. In a matter of moments, one of them would be close enough to bat her arm down, maybe knock the crucifix from her hand altogether.

Would that be so bad? Maybe not. Maybe she should let them.

The woman's blazing eyes flickered briefly to the lowering crucifix, and Amber could think clearly again.

She bared her teeth, which became fangs, and her skin turned red and her muscles got bigger and her limbs lengthened and her horns grew and now it was the vampires who shrank back, their eyes wide as she stood before them, beautiful and terrible and snarling.

The middle-aged woman gaped. "What are you?"

Amber simply snarled, and stepped backwards into the corridor. Her free hand closed round the handle, and she slowly shut the door between them.

She backed off faster along the hallway. Shadows moved into the light beyond the clouded glass and bunched up, forming a solid mass. Amber reached the front door, put her foot out on to the first step.

The clouded glass shattered as the vampires came through. Amber spun, leaped off the steps and ran. They came after her, a cackling, spitting mass of bodies. She got to the street as a hand grabbed her shoulder and she shoved the crucifix behind her and heard a scream and the hand fell away as she ran on. They were in the air now, dark shapes flitting through the night sky. One of them swooped for her and she ducked, went stumbling. She jumped a low fence and ran through a backyard. The sudden fluttering of clothes from above and she felt a hand grasping at her hair, barely missing as it passed.

She ran to the next house, didn't slow down as she neared the front door. There was a whoosh of air behind her, and she just *knew* it was the middle-aged woman, the one with the honeyed voice. She leaped, putting her shoulder to the door, and it splintered and she went sprawling inside. She scrambled up. The door hung off its hinges, but the doorway itself was clear. They couldn't come in without an invitation.

She turned, saw a figure on the stairs, saw something glinting in the dark, and she dived to the ground as the shotgun blast filled the house. Then she was up, snatching the gun from the hands of its owner.

"What the hell?" she screamed.

The owner, a chunky guy in his forties with a bathrobe tied loosely over his boxers and T-shirt, held up his hands immediately. "Please!" he cried. "Don't hurt us! Just leave! God, please!"

"I'm not going to hurt you," she snapped.

He got a good look at her, he must have, because his face went slack. "Oh God… you're the Devil…"

"I'm not the Devil," she said. "My name's Amber. I'm not going to hurt you."

"Please," he sobbed. "Spare my family."

"I'm not going to hurt you," she repeated, louder this time. "You know what's going on, right? You know about all this craziness?"

He nodded quickly. "The… the things. The…"

"Go on. You can say it."

He swallowed thickly. "The vampires."

"There you go," said Amber. "Cascade Falls is overrun by vampires, right? Do I look like a vampire to you?"

"You look like the Devil."

"Still not a vampire, though. And I'm not going to hurt you or your family. Listen, they can't get in unless you invite them, all right? So you're perfectly safe."

"Are you going to eat us?"

"No," she said irritably. "I'm not going to eat you. Just do what I say and you'll live, got it?"

He nodded slowly. His eyes were moving now, darting to the front door as his thought processes came back online.

She handed him back his shotgun. "I'm going to trust you not to shoot me, okay?"

He hesitated, then took the weapon. "Thank you."

"I'm going to leave the first chance I get," she said. "If I can, I'll draw them away from you and your family. You want my advice? Get out of town first thing tomorrow."

"Yeah," he said shakily. "Yeah."

"I'm going to check the back," she said, "and see if I can get out there. Anyone even approaches that door, you blast them, understood?"

He nodded, and she patted his shoulder.

"You're all going to be okay," she said. "I promise."

She hurried into the dark kitchen, found the back door with the key still in the lock. She opened it, but didn't step out. She leaned, looking upwards. No sign of them.

She heard voices elsewhere in the house. She didn't want to freak out the guy's wife, but she really had no choice. She went back into the hallway.

He wasn't talking to his wife. He was talking to a vampire,

standing just outside the front door. The shotgun dangled in his hand. From here, Amber could see the vampire's blazing eyes.

The owner of the house stepped back. "Please," he said dully, "come in."

37

THE VAMPIRE WAS ON the man in an instant, mouth clamped round his jugular, and the other vampires poured in through the door. They half ran, half flew up the stairs, giggling in their anticipation. The screams of the family shook Amber out of her paralysis.

She turned and ran.

The town was a dark, jangled blur. She jumped walls and plunged through bushes. She trampled flowers and ducked under branches. She ran on road and lawn and sidewalk. The more she ran, the faster she ran. The oxygen she sucked in added fuel to her legs. She jumped over the hood of a parked car without touching it and smashed through a fence without feeling it.

She had reached Althea's house before she even looked back to see if they were following. They weren't.

She reverted to normal and nearly collapsed. Her muscles burned and she gasped for breath. Althea's door opened and Milo hurried out, took her arm and dragged her inside.

"Where the hell *were* you?" he asked as he closed the door behind her.

Veronica stood up from the sofa when she saw Amber. She was pale, and her clothes were dirty and her knee was bleeding.

But Amber didn't care about her. "Glen," she said. "They've got Glen."

Milo hesitated, and Amber sank into his chest and he hugged her.

She cried.

38

AMBER SLEPT AND DREAMED of dead things.

She awoke to sunlight and faint voices, coming from somewhere in the house. Calm voices. Quiet. She got up, and dressed by the window. From her vantage point on the hill, she had a pretty good view over the town. From here, Cascade Falls looked peaceful, the kind of peaceful only found in graveyards.

A car moved a few streets over, slipping in and out of view at a leisurely pace. Then it was gone.

She knew that car. She had travelled in it practically every day for the last three years, ever since her parents had bought it.

There was more movement, from another part of town. Two people walking. She squinted. Alastair she recognised immediately. The other person was momentarily obscured by a tree. Imelda emerged and Amber bit her lip to stop the sob from escaping.

She watched them walk up to a house. They shifted, their red skin and horns impressive even from this distance. Alastair kicked down the front door, and they strolled in.

Amber stood at the window, frowning.

Finally, there was movement, Alastair dragging someone out

of the house. He turned and threw the body on to the front lawn, and the moment sunlight hit him the man burst into flames. Amber couldn't hear his screams, but she could see Alastair laughing as he flailed. Imelda walked by Alastair and the burning vampire without looking at either of them, and went to the next house. Alastair reluctantly followed.

The burning vampire finally lay still, and the fire consumed him, flaring so brightly Amber had to look away. When the flames died, there were no remains left behind.

Imelda kicked in the door of the next house, and led the way in.

Door to door, killing the vampires that lay inside, searching for Amber. At the rate they were moving it'd take them until the afternoon to reach the hill – but they were coming.

Althea got the hell out of Cascade Falls by midday. They loaded up Veronica's car with her belongings and Veronica got behind the wheel. She hadn't said much the previous night. Amber knew that she had been running from vampires when Milo found her, and that was it. She had a look in her eyes, though – haunted. She was a different person from the woman who'd sat with them at dinner. Milo kissed her, and they said goodbye, and Althea waved at Amber as they drove quickly away.

"You liked her, huh?" said Amber to Milo.

He looked at her, and didn't answer.

"Thanks," she said.

Milo shrugged, and went back inside. Amber followed.

They watched from a window as Alastair and Imelda dragged vampires out into the sun. They were getting close.

Amber's parents passed the house. Amber started to duck down, but Milo grabbed her, held her in place.

"Movement attracts the eye," he said.

Her parents drove by without noticing them.

They couldn't see where Grant and Kirsty were.

"We have to leave," said Milo. "We go now and we have a few hours' head start. Maybe even a full day. Amber? What do you think?"

"We're going to leave Glen?" she asked quietly.

"There's nothing we can do for him now."

"We don't know that he's dead."

"You said he looked—"

"I know what I said," she snapped. "But I don't know for sure, do I?"

Milo let the silence settle for a few moments.

"We're not vampire killers," he said.

"I didn't say anything about—".

"You want to stop them. You want revenge. I can see it in your face."

"And along the way we can save the lives of whoever else is stupid enough to still be in this town."

He looked her dead in the eye. "What do you think we are? We're not the cavalry. This isn't our job or our responsibility."

"We stopped Shanks."

"Because we had no choice," Milo said. "Here, we have a choice. We get to the car and leave. Let your parents and their friends kill the vampires. They might actually do some good, for a change. Amber, you need to think about this. Jacob Buxton is a two-day drive away, and who knows how far we'll have to travel to get to his father after that?"

"Milo, I got an entire family killed last night."

"That wasn't your fault."

"How can it not be? I led the vampires right to their *house*. We have to do *something*. We stopped Dacre Shanks. We can stop these, too."

"Dacre Shanks was one guy with one trick," Milo said. "We don't know how many vampires there are – could be two dozen, could be a hundred, could be most of the town – but even one of them has the potential to kill both of us without thinking twice."

"So we do what Imelda's doing," said Amber. "We hit him now, during the day."

"Hit who?"

"Johann Varga," she said. "He'll be asleep, right? We get to the house I was in last night. If Glen isn't there, we go to the hotel, find Varga's coffin or whatever, and we stake him. It works, right? Staking them?"

"According to Althea's theory," said Milo.

"We stake Varga and, if Glen is there, we take him with us. If he's dead, we give him some kind of funeral. We're not going to just abandon him, Milo. I should have been here with him. I shouldn't have let him out of my sight. The moment he mentioned hearing voices I should have realised what it was and tied him to a chair or something."

"You didn't know."

"I should have. And now I owe him."

Milo looked at her, sighed, and walked from the room. A minute later, he was back, holding a hammer in one hand and a broken baseball bat in the other, the bat's broken end sharpened to a point. "This is what I was doing last night

330

while I was waiting for the coast to clear," he said. "This is our stake."

"That'll work?"

"It should. To be extra sure, we'll take a detour to the church, douse it in holy water. The hammer, too. We'll need to travel by foot, and take it slow. Amber, are you positive you want to do this? We'll be walking right into the vampires' nest, somewhere your folks are going to end up at, sooner or later. This is hugely, insanely risky."

"I know."

"You're not going to change your mind?"

"I can't, Milo."

He nodded. "In that case, bring the crucifix. We're going to need it."

By the time they got across town, the sun was dipping dangerously low in the sky. The body of the owner of the house was still in the living room, but Glen was gone. Amber knew he would be. They searched the house quickly, then moved on to the Varga Hotel. The only car Amber recognised in the lot was Imelda's. They went in through the rear door. There was no one around, not even Ingrid at the front desk.

"Where do we go?" Amber asked, her whisper oddly loud in the absolute quiet.

"Basement," said Milo.

They found the heavy door leading down. It got much too cold much too fast as they descended the stone steps. Milo went first, the stake and hammer in his hands, even though Amber was in full demon mode behind him. The very air down here made her want to turn round and run screaming, and never look back. There was a sense of something bad, something waiting for them beyond the wine racks. Something lurking.

They got to another door. Milo pulled his hand back from the handle.

"Cold," he whispered. He wrapped his sleeve round his hand and opened the door. A weak light flickered down another set of stairs.

Fear wrapped its fingers round the corners of Amber's mind and started to tug. She grew talons and bared her teeth, but that did nothing to bolster her courage.

The room below the basement was small, but even so the single light bulb had difficulty chasing the darkness away. Chained to the floor directly under the light bulb was a dried-out husk of a corpse, arranged in a cross-legged position with its head down. It wore rags and its hair was long. The sight of it was distressing, but it wasn't the source of Amber's fear. That came from something else.

The corpse looked up and Amber saw fangs.

The corpse, the vampire, didn't seem particularly surprised to see them, but his eyebrows rose as Amber stepped into the light.

"Huh," he said. His voice cracked. "And what are you supposed to be? The Devil? Has the Devil come to drive a stake through my heart after all this time?"

Milo approached him warily while Amber hung back.

"Hello, Caleb," said Milo.

Caleb Tylk managed a half-smile. "You've heard of me."

"We heard what you did to the Masterson family."

Caleb's smile soured. His skin was dry like parchment, and it flaked with every new expression. "And who are you?" he asked. "And why are you visiting me?"

"We're not here for you," said Amber. "We're here for your master. Where is Varga?"

"Varga's no master of mine," Caleb said. "He's kept me chained up here for two years. *Two years*. He won't let me sleep in a coffin, won't even let me sleep in the ground. Look around you. Concrete. Is that any way to treat your own kind?"

"What did you do?"

Caleb smiled. "Step closer so I can see you."

Talking in a normal voice soothed Amber's nerves, and she walked forward.

"Ohhh," said Caleb. "You're *wonderful*. A little closer, please."

"I don't think so."

"Just a little closer…"

Amber gave him a beautiful smile, and took another few steps. Then she slammed her right foot into his chest and knocked him on to his back. She kept her foot where it was, pinning him to the floor.

"What did you do," she said, smiling, "for Varga to chain you up like this?"

Caleb tried to push her foot off, but she ignored his feeble efforts.

"I broke his rule," he said at last. "I broke his sacred rule. I mean, what did he expect? That I'd wake up and be magically able to put my human life behind me without any second thoughts? He knew. He must have known. He's too old, you see. He forgets what it was like."

Amber put her weight on to her right foot. She heard one of Caleb's ribs crack. "What rule did you break?"

He snarled against the pain. "I didn't go elsewhere. I fed in the town where we lived." He paused. "Also, I don't know, something about being gauche, whatever that means…"

"You created more vampires than he could control," said Milo.

"Exactly," Caleb said. "It's all about control for him. He has to control everything and everyone. Well, I am not going to be controlled."

"You slaughtered an entire family."

"They had it coming."

Milo frowned. "How, exactly, did they have it coming?"

"I'd see them walking around town like they were too good for the likes of me. The parents, they never liked me. I called at the house one day and they looked at me like I was something they'd thrown up. And that kid, that annoying little brat—"

Amber twisted her foot in a semi-circle and Caleb grunted. "What about Rosalie?"

"What about her?" he fired back. "She was the worst of them. The biggest hypocrite of a family of hypocrites. She'd give it up for anyone with a bit of money, but the moment she realises I'm not going to be buying her diamond earrings, that's it. I'm shut out. Not all the way, of course. What fun would that be? No, no, she takes pleasure teasing me, promising me things and acting like she'll eventually give me a treat if I keep following her around like a little puppy…"

"So you killed her," said Amber.

"I should have," said Caleb.

"You turned her, didn't you?" Milo asked.

Caleb's lip, that dry, thin thing, curled. "She was supposed to be mine. I turned her for me. After all those years of her teasing me, laughing at me behind my back, leading me on…

I was going to be her master until the end of time. You want to know why? This is the truly funny part. Because, no matter what she'd done to me, I still loved her. Ain't that a riot? Even after everything she'd done."

"After everything *she* had done?" Amber said, her anger rising.

Caleb didn't notice. "But no. The moment Varga saw her, that was it. He took her from me. He said it was to punish me further, but he has me down here because he's afraid that Rosalie will choose me over him. I hear them together sometimes. He has no idea. She's using him, the same way she used me. It's pathetic is what it is. Let me out. Let me out of these chains and let me get my strength back and then I'll take care of Varga for you. I'll kill him myself, you understand? He fears me. He fears what I can do."

"Caleb," said Amber, "you're a pathetic loser and you're never getting out of those chains."

He glared at her. "I'll kill you," he said.

She moved her foot up to his throat, and pressed down. "Where is Varga?"

He gurgled, eyes blazing. Finally, he pointed to the wall beside Milo. She left her foot where it was while Milo examined the brickwork.

"Found something," he said, and a moment later a door in the wall swung open.

Once again, that terrible, freezing dread came over her, prying at her mind, and once again she wanted to run screaming from the cellar.

"Jesus," she whispered.

"Yeah," said Milo, and that's all he said.

Amber stepped off Caleb's throat and followed Milo into the corridor beyond. It got even colder. Even the light was cold. Milo turned the corner and stopped. Amber hesitated, then stepped out after him.

In front of them was a door. A big, thick, metal door, just like the ones they had in banks.

Amber stared. "Seriously?"

Milo examined the box on the wall beside it. "A time lock," he said. "Set to open when the sun goes down."

"How are we supposed to stake him when he sleeps in a frikkin' *vault*?"

"It does seem really unfair." Milo looked at her. "What do you want to do?"

"They must have Glen somewhere in this hotel," she said. "We have to find him. If he's alive, we take him with us. Any vampire we find along the way, you hammer that stake into their heart."

He nodded. "That I can do."

39

THEY STARTED AT THE room at the very top of the hotel.

Amber put her shoulder to the door. After three tries, she broke it down. The room was dark, the window boarded up from the inside. In place of a bed there was a coffin. Around it, flowers and framed photographs of a beautiful blonde girl. Rosalie Masterson. It had to be.

At Milo's nod, Amber lifted the coffin lid. Rosalie lay within, her head resting delicately on a satin pillow. Her perfect skin was pale. Her lips, plump and bow-shaped, were red. Her chest did not rise with her breathing. No pulse was noticeable in her throat. She looked dead and yet wonderfully, fantastically alive, like she was going to wake at any moment and break into a smile.

Milo pressed the tip of the stake over her heart. It sizzled against her skin, and Rosalie frowned in her death sleep. He raised the hammer, and hesitated. Amber had the irrational urge to leap forward, to stop him from doing what they'd come here to do, but her feet were stuck to the ground and she could only watch as he brought the hammer down.

The stake pierced Rosalie's chest with a sudden spurt of blood and her eyes snapped open and she screamed. Her eyes burning with hatred, yet clouded by confusion, she tried to grab the stake, tried to pull it out, but Milo hammered it down again and that was the one that did it. All tension fled from Rosalie's body and her arms fell by her sides and her legs stopped kicking and her skin puckered and burst and the stench of violent decomposition sent Milo reeling and Amber gagging. When Amber looked back, the beautiful girl had become little more than a skeleton, slick with its own blood.

Milo retrieved the stake, and they left the room and went into the next one. Room by room they went, coffin by coffin. Some vampires turned to skeletons, some to putrefying corpses, and some to dust. They all died with that same wide-eyed horror, though, that same look of disbelief on their faces.

The sun was dipping below the horizon and, just as they were about to abandon their search, Amber noticed a small door, tucked away in the eastern corner of the hotel. The key was still in the lock. Milo turned it, pushed the door open.

Glen lay on the bed inside. He was corpse-pale and his eyes were closed.

"Is he dead?" Amber asked softly.

Milo stepped in, and felt for a pulse. "Not yet," he said. "He's weak but alive."

Relief burst inside her, almost making her gasp, and she walked forward, shook Glen roughly. He muttered in his sleep but didn't wake.

"We have to leave now," said Milo. "We'll carry him out."

"I'll do it," Amber said, and hauled Glen to a sitting position. She ducked down, careful not to skewer him on her horns, and then straightened, Glen draped across her shoulders like a stole.

"You're smiling," said Milo.

"You're not," said Amber, "but don't pretend you weren't worried about him. He grew on you, didn't he?"

Without bothering to answer, Milo stepped out of the room and Amber heard Ingrid from the front desk say, "What... what are you doing?"

Milo looked at the hammer and stake in his hands, at his blood-splattered clothes, and before he could answer Amber stepped out to join him.

Ingrid cursed when she saw the horns, and bolted. Even with Glen on her back, Amber caught up to her easily. She kicked at her ankles and Ingrid yelped and went tumbling. She hit the stairs and rolled and spun and went flying again, finally sprawling on to the foyer floor below. Crying in pain, she started crawling. Her left leg appeared to be broken.

Amber and Milo walked down after her. Ingrid crawled by the front desk.

"You're not even one of them," Amber said. "You're still human. How could you do this?"

Ingrid turned on to her back. "The Master will kill you!" she screeched. "The Master will use you as—"

Amber kicked her in the face and Ingrid rolled over and shut the hell up.

Then a cold feeling came over Amber, slithering up her spine to tingle at the base of her skull. She turned, as did Milo, and they watched Varga sweep into the room. In a few quick strides, he had crossed to Milo, knocked the stake from his hand and pitched him over the desk. Next he turned to Amber, his eyes shining.

"You have the blood of my children on you," he said. Fury danced in his eyes. "You have the blood of my Rosalie on you."

Glen slipped off Amber's shoulders, fell in an unconscious heap. A series of nonsense words surged in her throat, jammed and wouldn't come out. She wanted to apologise, to threaten, to beg and to scream; she wanted to make noise and stay quiet. Instead, all she could do was raise her crucifix. Varga's lips curled back over his long, sharp teeth.

"Put that down," he commanded, and Amber recognised the authority in his voice, and she wanted so desperately to obey. Yet she was still thinking clearly enough to keep her trembling arm in place.

"This town is my town," Varga said. "You come here and you kill my children, my *Rosalie*, and you desecrate my home by bringing *that*," he sneered as he said it, and his eyes locked on to the crucifix in Amber's hand, "over the threshold. You have offended me in a great many ways, you foolish creature. Do you really expect to leave here alive?"

"You attacked my friend," Amber said, forcing the words out.

"I didn't touch a single hair on his singular head," said Varga. "In truth, I do not know who did. There are too many of us. We are best when we are few."

"Then we… we did you a favour. We—"

"You have murdered my children!" Varga boomed, and Amber stumbled back.

"The ones in this hotel were mine," he said, his voice calm once more. "The ones out there are… insubordinate things, never meant to be. The boy's doing. But they are no less my children."

Amber was so fixated on Varga that she didn't even notice Milo running at him. Varga did, however, and he spun, dodging the stake that was aimed at his back.

"Run!" Milo cried.

She did. She didn't think she would but she did. She ran, leaving Milo to face Varga alone. The moment she was out of the foyer, however, the fear drained away and she stopped, looked back. What the hell was she doing?

She turned back to see Milo slam into the wall. He dropped in a crumpled heap, the stake and hammer clattering to the ground nearby.

And then a familiar voice. "I hate vampires."

Fear surged once again, but this was not the supernatural terror that emanated from Varga's very pores – this was a fear much closer to her own heart. Her father's voice. Not even her demon form could keep that fear from infecting her. Now she really did want to run. She wanted to run and just keep running.

She made herself move up to the corner and peer round.

Bill and Betty led the demons into the foyer – tall and glorious with their red skin and horns. Alastair was the biggest of them – he had to duck when he came through, his horns scraping the top of the stone archway. Grant was the broadest, though – his jacket stretched tightly across his chest – and Kirsty's red hair had darkened to match the red of her skin. Imelda came last, eyes narrowed and focused on Varga.

"More mongrels," Varga said, distaste curling his lip. "You are not welcome here."

Bill smiled. "Unlike you, we don't need an invitation to walk in. That was always the problem with your particular breed, you know – you're just too polite."

"Ah," said Varga. "You think you have encountered my kind before."

"We have."

"No. If you had, you would be running right now. But my business is not with you. Leave here and I will forgive the transgressions you have made against my family."

"Family?" said Kirsty. "Oh, you mean all those nasty little vamps we've been dragging out into the sun all day? That family? That's a big family. You must get around."

Varga watched her without speaking as they slowly, casually, surrounded him.

"We'll leave," said Betty. "We'll walk out of here right this second, providing you tell us what we want to know. We're looking for a girl called Amber. She would have come in a black car. Do you know her?"

"I have seen the girl."

"You have? That's wonderful. Where is she?"

Amber prepared to run, but Varga smiled, and didn't say anything.

The demons raised their crosses, and Varga hissed.

"Where is she?" asked Bill, stepping closer.

Varga tried to back away, but the circle was too tight. His skin began to smoke. "All who have spilled the blood of my family are mine to kill," he said, his voice pained. "The girl. Her companion. And all of you."

Alastair laughed. "I'd like to see you try, bloodsucker."

Varga said something that Amber didn't catch and turned to him, locking eyes. Alastair swayed slightly, and his hand dipped.

That was all Varga needed.

He dived on Alastair impossibly, ridiculously fast, powering him backwards out of the circle. Next he tossed him as if he was a baby, hurling him with such force into Grant and Imelda that all three went down. Kirsty lunged, the crucifix held before her, and Varga turned to a man of smoke that burst apart when the cross passed through him.

Kirsty spun, sudden fear in her eyes, black scales beginning to spread across her skin as the smoke swirled and coalesced behind her. Varga's long-fingered hand closed round the back of her neck and he slammed her face-first into the wall.

He turned as Bill and Betty stepped closer together, their crucifixes up.

"You vampires and your magic tricks," said Betty. "The smoke, the bats, the hypnosis… You're like a bad vaudeville magician. You belong in a top hat on a crummy stage with a bored assistant, and instead here you are, bothering good, decent folk like us."

"Where is our daughter?" Bill asked.

"You will die first," said Varga. "Your mate will watch and cry for you, and only when grief has overtaken her heart will I end her life."

"You bore me," said Bill.

"And I have a name," said Betty.

"You are insects to me," said Varga.

"So rude," said Betty, just as Amber saw something in her other hand, a water bottle, and she flicked it and the water hit Varga and sizzled like acid against his face.

He recoiled, hissing in pain, and Bill was upon him in an instant. With black scales covering the fist that held the crucifix, Bill hit him, a right cross that sent the vampire stumbling over Glen's sleeping form. Bill ran at him, hit him again, and now Betty was there, pressing her crucifix to the side of Varga's head. They worked as a team, dividing the vampire's wrath between them, denying him focus and constantly driving him back. Betty squeezed the remains of the water bottle right into his face and Varga howled, hands over his eyes, and Bill's hands turned to talons that slashed at Varga's neck.

The swipe would probably have taken his head if he hadn't turned to smoke before it landed.

Varga solidified behind them, his skin already healed of the holy water's effects, his eyes burning with hatred.

He seized Bill and leaped upwards in a blur. The back of Bill's head hit the ceiling and he plummeted to the ground while Varga stayed up there. Betty moved instantly to stand over her husband, composure gone from her face for the first time, keeping the crucifix raised, and Amber realised with a sickening certainty that her mother had never shown her that protective instinct.

Varga scuttled across the ceiling and was lost to Amber's sight, but she was able to track his movements by the way Betty was keeping the crucifix between them. When Betty lowered the cross, Amber knew Varga had dropped to the floor. But, when Betty lowered her cross slightly again, she had no idea what was happening until she heard the growl.

Amber inched forward, searching for the source of the sound. Whatever the dog was and wherever it had come from, it was big, and it had shocked Betty so much she had almost taken a step backwards. But to move back was to abandon her husband, and Betty wasn't prepared to do that.

Amber moved slightly again, until she could see the animal. She'd been wrong. It wasn't a dog. It was a wolf. Huge and grey, it came slowly across the floor towards Betty, growling, its hackles raised and its teeth bared.

It barked once, sharply, and Amber flinched at the sound, and she saw her mother swallow and adjust her hold on the crucifix, and the wolf suddenly leaped. It burst into smoke before it hit the crucifix and hands reached from inside that smoke, knocking the cross from Betty's grip. She spun but the smoke had become Varga, and he had her, and he threw her into the wall.

She stumbled back and grew talons, but Varga moved so fast they were useless against him. He struck her with a lazy swipe across the ribs and she gasped, and he grabbed her round the throat. Betty clutched at his wrist as he tightened his hold. She sank to her knees, unable to breathe.

If Varga killed Betty, he'd kill the others just as quick. He'd kill Milo and Glen and then he'd come after Amber. She wouldn't have a chance of stopping him. The only chance she possibly had was to run right now, while his focus was elsewhere. Her parents would die. Milo and Glen would die, but she would get away. She'd be free.

It all made sense. It was logical. Practical. But logic wasn't why she crept forward, or why she picked up the hammer and stake. It wasn't logic that was burning at the very core of her being. It was anger. It was fury.

He was hurting her mom.

40

"Do you feel that?" Varga asked Betty, his voice soft. "Do you feel your vertebrae beginning to snap? How does it compare, do you think, to burning in sunlight? How does it compare to the deaths you have subjected my family to? Eh?" He leaned in closer. "When I take your head, little demon, I will mount it on my wall."

Amber charged and Varga heard her and spun, too late to stop the stake from piercing his chest. His back hit the wall and Amber swung the hammer, but he grabbed the wrist of the hand holding the stake and it barely moved. He smiled at her, showing his teeth.

She smiled back, showing hers.

She slammed the hammer into his face. He hissed in pain – the impact leaving a circle on his skin that sizzled like she'd just hit it with a clothes iron – and then she hammered the stake through his ribcage.

Varga stiffened, his eyes widening and his mouth opening. No blood, though.

She hammered again, and his surprise was overtaken by fury. He closed both hands round the stake, but could do nothing to stop her from hammering it in deeper, and deeper, and then she hit the stake so hard the head flew off the hammer. She dropped it, pounded at the stake with her fist, and now Varga was screaming and writhing, and she hit it one more time and a torrent of dark blood gushed from the wound, hit her full in the face, and drove her backwards. It blinded her, got in her mouth, got up her nose, and it covered the floor and she slipped, fell, spitting and coughing and wiping her eyes, and there was blood all over her, drenching her, flattening her hair to her scalp.

And then the torrent weakened, and shortened, and Amber blinked madly and looked up as the last of Varga's blood, which had turned black and thick, like tar, dripped slowly from his wound. He was nothing but a shell now, a dried-out husk, as grey as ash. He dropped to his knees and they cracked beneath him and his whole body crumpled, his suit flattening like a sail suddenly becalmed. His skull toppled, too heavy for his spine to support, and when it hit the ground it exploded into dust and fragments.

"Amber."

The voice, the tone, made her revert instantly, and she turned to see her mother – with her mother's face – struggling to her feet. She clutched her side like her ribs were broken. Or worse.

"You saved me," Betty said, her voice weak. "After everything that's happened, you saved me."

Amber stood, covered in blood, and couldn't find anything to say.

"We made a mistake," said Betty, leaning on the front desk for support. "We did. We have made such a huge mistake. But we're here now."

"I know what you want," Amber said.

Betty shook her head. "Not anymore. Whatever you've heard, things have changed. We changed them. Give us a chance, sweetheart. Let us explain."

"You'll just lie again."

"That's over with," Betty said, with a conviction in her eyes that made Amber believe her. "It's all over with. We've been doing this a long time, baby, and we're sick of it. We want something different."

"How many of my brothers and sisters have you killed?"

It was funny, but witnessing the hurt on her mother's face was almost enough to make Amber run to her.

"We're bad people," Betty said finally. "But we're trying not to be. Please, Amber, come back to us. We can start again. As a family."

Betty took a step towards her and her knee buckled, but before she hit the ground Amber was there, helping her hobble back to the desk.

"Thank you," Betty said, gritting her teeth against the pain. "Oh, sweetheart, you have no idea what we've been through. We thought we'd lost you."

"Can you stand?"

Betty managed a small laugh. "Always so considerate, aren't you? You didn't get that from your father, let me tell you. Didn't get it from me, either, I'm afraid."

Amber suddenly realised how vulnerable she was, but Betty released her hold of her as soon as she could balance on her own. Amber had gotten some of Varga's blood on her mother's top. It was an expensive top. Betty didn't even seem to notice.

"Do you know who you've always reminded me of?" Betty continued. "My mother. Your grandmother. I've never told you about her, have I?"

"You've never told me anything."

"Well, that ends today. From this moment on, no secrets between us. Deal?"

"Betty, you can't just—"

"Mom."

Amber frowned. "What?"

"I think I'd like you to call me Mom from now on," Betty said. "Do you think you could do that?"

"I... I don't know..."

Betty shook her head. "I'm going too fast, aren't I? I'm sorry, sweetheart. One step at a time, that's how we get our family back together."

"Betty... Mom... I don't know if I can believe you."

Betty's eyes glistened with sudden tears. "Right," she said. "Of course. I mean... obviously. We've put you through a lot and we have to... we have to earn back your trust. I get that. I do. But you have to see it from our perspective, Amber. You are our daughter and we love you above all else. Your safety and wellbeing are all we care about. You don't have to forgive us, sweetheart, not yet, but this family is not going to be split up anymore. We love you, baby."

Tears sprang to Amber's eyes and her mother pulled her in for a hug. She held her close and Amber sobbed, and when the sobbing was over Amber just closed her eyes for a few moments.

Just a few. That's all she needed for now.

"Go home," Amber said, moving back a little. She'd left a blood smear on Betty's chin. "I've got something to do and, when it's done, I'll go home, too, and we can go back to being a family."

"Wherever you go, we go," said Betty. "We are not leaving your side."

"I'll only be gone a few more days. I've started something and I need to finish it. But I'll see you at home, Mom. You and Dad."

Amber kissed her cheek, started to pull away.

Betty held on to her wrist. "What do you have to do?"

"Just something."

Betty's grip tightened.

"Mom, you're hurting me."

"Families stay together."

"Mom, please let go."

"We'll just ask your father, what do you say?"

And then Milo pressed the muzzle of his gun to the side of Betty's head and said, in a soft voice, "Let her go."

Betty's eyes widened slightly. Amber said nothing. Betty released her.

Keeping his gun aimed squarely at Betty's head, Milo moved to stand beside Amber.

"And just who exactly are you?" Betty inquired.

"I think you know who I am," said Milo. "I think you've already run a check on my car."

Betty half smiled. "Indeed we did, Mr Sebastian, but we could find precious little about you. Aren't you a bit old to be hanging around with sixteen-year-old girls?"

"And you're suddenly a concerned parent? You expect us to believe that?"

"So you're the one poisoning our daughter against us."

"No, you did that when she overheard you planning to kill her."

Betty stood straighter. Her ribs didn't seem to be bothering her as much anymore. "Amber, I've known men like him my whole life. He's nothing but trouble. You can't listen to a word he says. He doesn't know the facts. He doesn't know us."

"I… I trust him," said Amber.

"You can't," said Betty. "He's been lying to you this whole time. He's brainwashing you, can't you see that? He's turning you against us." She fixed her glare on Milo. "This is kidnapping. What you've done is kidnapping."

"Amber saved your life tonight," said Milo. "I'd remember that, if I were you."

"You don't matter," said Betty. "You don't matter to us. Amber, I forbid you to go anywhere with this man."

Milo picked Glen off the floor in a fireman's lift, and walked towards the door. Amber hesitated, then followed.

"Amber!" Betty said sharply, taking a few steps in pursuit. "Amber, you stay right here, young lady!"

Amber shook her head. "I have to—"

"You will stay with your family!"

Amber shifted, felt the power and the strength surge through her, and she snarled. "You're lucky I don't rip your head off, Mom. You think I believe a word you say? Do you?"

Betty met her glare with one of her own. "This is your one chance. The only chance you'll get. If you walk away, we'll come after you, and I *personally* will eat your heart, young lady."

Amber backed out of the door. "Love you, too," she said, and ran.

41

THEY DROVE FOR FIFTEEN HOURS. Every mile they clocked took a little something more from Milo. He was gaunt. He looked thinner. Amber didn't say anything. Glen slept. There were times when his breathing got so soft she thought he'd died. She didn't say anything about that, either. All she cared about was getting as far away from Cascade Falls as she could. They stopped four times in those fifteen hours. She'd been able to scrub her face and change her clothes, find her sunglasses and pee twice, and that was it. No time to do any more. No time to waste.

When they got to Death Valley National Park, it was past midday and the Nevada sun was a merciless thing. The asphalt stretched further than Amber could see and straighter than she could fathom. Heat rose in thick, hazy waves that shimmered and glimmered, but in the Charger it was cool. The air-conditioner was never on, but in the Charger it was always cool.

"How far are we from Colorado?" she asked.

"We're not going to Colorado," said Milo.

Amber frowned. "What?"

"Your parents expect us to run straight to wherever we're

352

headed next, now that we know they're right behind us. But we're going to meander. They're the ones in the hurry, not us. Let them overshoot us. We don't have a deadline."

Amber said nothing to this. They drove and she sat there. Her body was still, but her mind was whirling. In her head, arguments raged. Up until now, the one little secret she'd been keeping from Milo hadn't seemed like a big deal. It was the kind of thing she'd been planning to tell him once it was all over, the kind of thing she expected him to raise an eyebrow at, maybe shake his head in mild exasperation. But the events of the last few days had cleared her vision. She could see now that little details could have far-reaching consequences. She could see now that she didn't have the luxury of keeping secrets.

"What if we did have a deadline?" she asked softly.

"Sorry?" said Milo.

She took off her sunglasses. He kept his on. "You said my parents are in a hurry, not us. You said we don't have a deadline. But what if we did?"

Milo glanced at her. "Something you're not telling me, Amber?"

She looked away. "I… It seems silly now, but I didn't want you to think I was stupid."

The Charger slowed. "What are you talking about?"

"I'd just met you," said Amber. "I didn't know you, I didn't know Edgar. You gave me all these instructions for what not to do when talking to the Shining Demon and I followed them, I followed them all. But then he started talking about a deadline…"

Milo braked so suddenly she cried out and Glen slid off the back seat and into the footwell.

When he spoke, Milo's voice was barely above a whisper. "What did you agree to?"

She hesitated, then took off her bracelets and showed him her wrist.

He frowned. "A number?"

"A countdown."

"What the hell?" he said, voice raised. In the confines of the Charger, it sounded like a shout. "Why didn't you tell me? Why the hell didn't you tell me?"

"I'm sorry," she said, "I just—"

"Why did you keep this from me? You've had this since Miami and you're only telling me about it now? Why? You didn't want me to think you were stupid?" There was something going on behind his sunglasses, like his eyes were glowing. "Good going, Amber, because now I know you're stupid."

Suddenly the car felt too small. Too cramped. The cool air nipped at her face and crept down her collar.

Amber threw open the door and jumped out into the heat. She walked over cracked and dry ground, her legs stiff, her arms rigid by her sides, her shoes kicking stones. She started to think about her parents again, and she walked faster, but the thoughts kept up. She broke into a run, tears blurring her vision. When she was out of breath, she shifted into her demon form and ran on. In her demon form, she could run forever. In her demon form, she never had to worry about crying.

A racking sob took her by surprise and Amber stumbled, fell to her hands and knees. Tears dropped to the ground and the ground soaked them up thirstily. Not even her demon form could shield her.

She tried to get up but couldn't. She rocked back on her

haunches. Her eyes fixed on a spot on the ground and held it. It took her a good long moment to figure out that she was looking at her shadow. The way her shadow was, all bunched up like that, it made her horns look like Mickey Mouse ears, except thinner, and sharper. If Micky Mouse was a demon's shadow, she decided it'd be an exact match.

Walter S. Bryant, the kid back at Springton, had wanted to go to Disney World. She wondered if he ever would. He stood a good chance, she thought. At least Springton was still standing. How long did Cascade Falls have, now that the vampires were free to drain it dry? She wondered if it would rise from the dead, like so many of its other victims, but then decided not. Whatever it would be in the future, it would no longer be Cascade Falls, just like this shadow she cast was not Amber.

She reverted. Immediately, she began to sweat. The sun burned at her scalp. If she stayed here, the sun would eventually fry every last inch of her, she was sure. Fry her to nothing. Rob her of all liquids. Maybe she'd end up looking like Varga, right before he crumpled. She still had his blood on her. It was matted into her hair. She needed a serious shower before she'd be free of him. She'd need mouthwash, too. She could still taste it.

She stood, looked to the road. She'd run a long way. Her eyes dry now, she walked back to the Charger. Milo got out as she neared, looked at her over the roof. He took his sunglasses off, had to squint against the glare. His eyes looked tired, but perfectly normal.

"Sorry," he said.

"No, you're right. I was being stupid."

"You're allowed to be stupid. You're in a unique situation. There is no correct way to handle things."

"I still should have told you."

"How long do you have left?"

She looked at her wrist. "Two hundred and forty hours."

"Ten days," said Milo. "It'll take maybe fifteen hours of driving to get to Colorado. If Jacob Buxton can tell us exactly where his father is, we won't have a problem."

"Are you okay?" she asked.

"What do you mean?"

"You don't look well. You look sick. And your eyes…"

"I'm fine," he said.

"We're way above the eight-hours-a-day rule. Let me drive."

He shook his head. "I can keep going. I'm not tired. Remember, it's eight hours a day on *average*. I can handle a little more."

"We've been driving for double that."

"I can handle it, Amber. Besides, we're on a schedule. Now get in."

She hesitated, but he was already behind the wheel. She slid into her seat and buckled her belt, and the Charger ate up the endless road, the asphalt vanishing under its wheels.

42

WHEN THEY WERE ON the Beltway and making good time, Glen woke, and Amber bounced a crucifix off his head just to make sure he was still human.

"Ow," he said.

She examined him, then sat back and buckled her seat belt once more. "No burning or scarring," she said. "You're not a vampire."

She glanced at Milo, but he was staring straight ahead. Just like he had been for the last few hours.

Glen struggled to sit up. He was astonishingly pale, and every movement was slow and lethargic. When he was sitting up straight, he asked, "Where are we?"

"Nevada," said Amber. "How are you feeling?"

Glen licked his lips and worked his tongue around his mouth for a few moments. When he spoke again, his voice was clearer. "Awful," he said. "Really, really bad, like. Should I be in hospital? I feel like I should be in a hospital of some description."

"You're fine," said Amber. "You've just lost some blood."

"Oh," he said. "Oh yeah."

"How much do you remember?"

"Uh… bits. I remember being in Althea's house, and someone calling to me, and I went out—"

"You didn't think that was odd?" Amber asked.

"Sorry?"

"Someone calling to you from the other side of town," she said. "That didn't strike you as unusual at all?"

He frowned. "I didn't really think about it, to be honest. I just… went. Walked right into a house and there were loads of them, just waiting there. They were laughing at me. Then they…"

His frown deepened. After a moment of staring at nothing, he shook his head and looked up. "And you're sure I'm not going to turn into one of them?"

"Not according to Althea," she said. "You'll only turn after a vampire bite kills you. You're not dead, are you? So you're not one of them. But I'll throw the cross at you again if you want."

He held up a hand weakly. "No, no, you're fine, thanks. How did we get away?"

"We were outnumbered," she said, "and then you ran in and saved us."

His eyes widened. "I did?"

"No. You were asleep for the whole thing. Milo and I got us out."

Glen sighed. "So it was me being my typical useless self, then, was it?"

The look on his face robbed Amber of the joy of teasing him. "You're not useless," she said. "You were just bitten. It could have happened to any one of us."

"Yeah, except it happened to me." He rubbed a hand over his face. "Listen, can we stop for food, or something? I'm starving."

"We got you some nuts," said Amber, passing him a small bag.

He stared at it. "Nuts? Seriously?"

Amber glanced at Milo for help, but his face was set and he was looking straight ahead.

She gave Glen a smile. "Your body needs to make more blood. Nuts are a good way of doing that. When we stop, you can have fruit and meat and milk and whatever else you need."

Clearly unconvinced, Glen did his best to open the bag. Amber took it from him, opened it, and handed it back.

"Thanks," he mumbled, and started eating. After a moment of chewing, he looked up. "Nevada is where Las Vegas is, right? Are we going to be anywhere near it?"

"We're in Las Vegas now, dummy."

Glen brightened immediately and looked around, saw nothing but freeway. "Uh... where is it?"

"That way," she said, pointing.

They both looked out at the concrete border that separated the roads as they sped by.

"I can't see much beyond the, y'know, wall," said Glen.

"Yeah," said Amber.

"Are we going to see the Strip?"

"No."

"The hotels? Any of the casinos?"

"Probably not."

"Are we just... are we just driving round the city?"

"Yes."

"And we're not going to see anything of the city itself?"

"Yes."

"We are?"

"No, I mean, yes, we're not."

"So, after all these years of hearing about Las Vegas, and seeing it in movies and TV, I finally get here and… and all I get to see is a wall?" Tears sprang to his eyes.

Amber frowned. "Are you crying?"

"Am I?" Glen said, and sobbed loudly. "Dear Jesus, I am. Why am I crying? I'm not even that sad." He wiped tears from his cheeks like they were pesky insects. "It's just I really wanted to see Las Vegas."

"You've lost a lot of blood," said Amber. "You're very emotional."

"Apparently."

"I'm going to turn round now, and pretend you're not crying, because I don't know how to deal with that."

He nodded as he wept. "Sounds fair."

She turned round and looked out of the windshield and after a few minutes Glen stopped crying and fell asleep.

They carried on into Utah. By this stage, Amber had had enough of Milo's deteriorating condition. His skin was getting greyer by the mile. She demanded that he stop and he reluctantly obliged, and they stayed at a Super 8 in Green River. Amber slept like the dead that night. In the morning, Glen had some colour in his cheeks and Milo was back to normal and the Charger gleamed. As she got in, Amber was overcome by the feeling that it had been waiting for them.

She looked at her brand, not even hiding it now: 221 hours left.

They got to Cricket Hill, Colorado, a little after two that afternoon, then spent another hour trying to find Burkitt Road. It led them into the tree-covered hills, the way getting narrower the further they went. The road turned to a trail and the trail petered out, and they had to leave the Charger and continue on foot. A light rain fell, but the trees protected them for the most part and Glen didn't complain, despite the fact that he was obviously still very weak.

"Gregory Buxton doesn't sound like the kind of man I expected," Amber said, breaking the silence.

Milo glanced at her. "Meaning?"

"Meaning he's a good guy," said Amber. "From what Althea said, anyway. He made that deal to save his son, and he hasn't hurt anyone. He's not like Dacre Shanks or… or my folks. How can we offer him to the Shining Demon now that we know all that?"

Milo's strides were annoyingly long. "Offering him up is your best chance at survival," he said.

She hurried along beside him, leaving Glen struggling to catch up. "There has to be something else. There has to."

"So what now? You want to turn around?"

"No," she said. "I want to find him. He's managed to cheat the Shining Demon and stay alive for all this time. He sounds like someone who can help me."

"If Jacob will tell us where he is," Milo said.

"What do we do if he won't help?"

"Let's find him first," said Milo. "Whatever happens after that happens after that."

They followed the trail to a cabin. It may have been sturdy once, may have been proud and strong, may have stood in this clearing and proclaimed its toughness to all the trees that surrounded it, but time and circumstance had worn it down. It sagged like an old man now. The window to the right of the narrow door drooped sadly, and weeds burst from the rotten boards on the porch. A battered motorcycle was parked outside, its tyres flat, joining the cabin in its moroseness.

Amber and Glen stepped over a curving line of moss-covered stones, half buried in leaves, and followed Milo up to the door. The porch creaked dangerously under their weight. The door opened before Milo could even knock.

"What do you want?" Jacob Buxton asked. He was about forty, and skinny, only a little taller than Amber, and he needed a shave. He needed a good night's sleep, too. He looked awful. His eyes were bloodshot and his dark skin was irritated just under his jaw. He scratched at it absently with dirty fingernails.

"My name's Milo Sebastian, and this is Amber and that's Glen," said Milo. "You're Jacob, right?"

"I'm not interested in whatever you're selling," Jacob said. "Do yourselves a favour and go away."

He started to shut the door.

"We're looking for your father," said Amber.

Jacob paused, thought for a moment, then said, "Good luck with that."

"I'm in trouble."

"You will be if you don't leave," he said, threatening words that didn't sound like a threat.

"Please," said Amber. "Your father's the only one who can help me."

An expression passed over Jacob's face that may, on anyone else, have been mistaken for amusement. "You expect him to help? You've obviously never met him."

"No, but we were told about him."

He allowed the door to open a little wider, just so he could brace himself idly against the frame. "Believe me, the legend doesn't begin to even approach the man."

"Can you tell us where he might be?" Milo asked.

Jacob looked at them both. "Seriously?"

Amber frowned. "You're talking like you expect us to know something I don't think we know."

"Well then, let me enlighten you. I don't know where my father is," said Jacob. "That's why I'm here. That's kind of the whole point."

"Could I possibly use your bathroom?" Glen asked.

"No," said Jacob.

"Mr Buxton," said Milo, "we've travelled a very long way to talk to you. If you could just be straight with us, we'll move on and we won't bother you again. Those rocks we stepped over to get here – I'm assuming they go right around your property, yes? What do you need with a protective circle?"

Jacob examined him, then switched his gaze to Amber. She tried to look as knowledgeable as Milo.

"The girl doesn't know what you're talking about," Jacob said.

"She's new," said Milo.

"I'm learning," said Amber. "And I know more than Glen."

"I literally know nothing," Glen offered up happily.

"When you say protective circle," Amber said to Milo, "do you mean like the other one? The one I was in? So it's an occult thing, right?" She switched her focus to Jacob. "What's it for? What's it keeping out?"

"The witch," said Jacob.

Amber glanced at Milo to make sure he wasn't smiling. No smile, which meant no joke. She looked back at Jacob.

"There are witches?"

"There are."

"And why is she after you?"

Jacob ignored the question. "Who told you about me?"

"Your grandmother."

"She's still alive, then?"

"You don't know?"

"We had a falling out. She tends to skip over the unpleasant realities of our little family drama. Lovely woman, but stubborn as hell." Jacob started suddenly, like he'd seen something in the trees behind them. Amber glanced back, saw nothing but woodland.

"Listen," said Jacob, once his focus returned, "you want to know where my father is? I don't know. I'm sorry about that, but there it is. I don't know where he is and there's nothing you can do to *make* me know." He looked at Milo. "That's what you're planning, isn't it? Sorry, my friend. You look like you can dish it out, but I just don't have the information you're looking for. This is a dead end. You may as well go back to where you came from before you draw its attention."

"The witch," said Milo.

Jacob nodded.

"We're not going anywhere."

"I'm serious," said Jacob. "If it sees you, it'll go after you."

"Then you better invite us in."

Jacob sighed. "Whatever. Enjoy your walk back."

He closed the door.

Amber started to ask a question, but Milo held up a hand. She clamped her mouth shut and looked around. She wondered if it was a witch like the one in The Wizard of Oz or like the ones in that Roald Dahl book. She'd hoped it was a witch like the ones in *Harry Potter*, but she doubted it.

The cabin door opened and Jacob stood there, looking thoroughly pissed off.

"Get in, quick," he said.

43

THE CABIN WAS CLUTTERED with books and magazines and tied-off trashbags. Despite this, it was neat, to a degree, though a smell definitely lingered in the air.

"The witch is trapping you here?" Amber asked. "What happens if you try to leave?"

"It chases me back," Jacob answered, closing the door behind them. "It doesn't want to kill me. It just wants to plague me. It took me a few years to figure that out. It doesn't make things any better. Doesn't make it any easier to escape."

"The bathroom?" Glen asked.

Jacob sighed, and gestured to a door. Glen smiled his gratitude, and hurried in.

"How long have you been here?" Milo asked.

"Living here? Ten years," said Jacob. "Trapped in this cabin? Seven months. Stay away from the windows, please." He frowned. "You know, I can't remember the last time I had visitors. That says something, doesn't it? If I can't remember that? I'm not sure what it is I'm supposed to do now, though. Do people still apologise for the mess? I guess they do. In that case, excuse the state of things. My trash isn't picked up anymore. I do my best to recycle, but what I'd really like is to take all this junk outside and burn it. But like any Boy Scout I am well aware of the dangers of open fires in wooded areas. So tell me who you are or I'll kill you all with an axe."

Amber must have taken on a funny look, because Jacob gave her a smile.

"Not really. The axe is out back, and I've never killed anyone with it. But I am mighty curious as to who the hell you are and what you want with my father."

"We just want to talk to him," Amber said. "Your grandmother told us you might be able to help."

Jacob scratched his neck. "What else did she say?"

"She told us that when you were a kid you had cancer. Your father made a deal with the Shining Demon to cure you, but, when your dad was supposed to start repaying his debt, he ran, and the Shining Demon couldn't find him."

Jacob nodded. "She tell you what my dad had to do in return for saving my life?"

"She said he was supposed to harvest souls. But he never had to, because he ran."

Jacob looked to Milo. "You're a man of the world. You believe that?"

Milo hesitated. "Some of it has the ring of truth."

"And what part strikes that one bum note?"

"The fact that he never had to hurt anyone. I find that hard to accept."

"That's because it's not true," said Jacob. "When I was sick, my grandmother would pray by my bed almost every evening. She wasn't there to talk, wasn't there to chat, she wouldn't bring me any comic books or grapes, or *Get Well Soon* cards… It was like she wasn't even there for me. She was there to speak to God. She prayed so long and so hard, with the muttering and the clasped hands and the tears in the eyes, that she actually scared me. She was just so… fervent. Every night after she'd left, I'd lie there, hooked up to all those machines, terrified that right there, in that silence, when I was alone… God would answer. And I'd be the only one to hear it.

"Althea may have come to terms with one part of what my father did, but not the whole thing – not the parts that threaten her idea of who her son is. See, she was prepared to accept that what he did was necessary, but it only worked for her if he remained a saint. Anything other than that would have ruined everything."

"So your dad isn't a saint," Amber said. She had some experience of that.

"His intentions were good," Jacob replied. "I was dying. He was willing to do anything to save me. *Anything*. And he did. If he hadn't made that deal, I'd have been dead by the age of eleven."

"Where was the deal struck?" Milo asked.

"In my hospital room," Jacob answered. "My father and the Shining Demon, standing over my bed. The light was everywhere. There were no shadows. None. At first, I thought it was God, you know? I thought maybe He'd heard my grandmother and here He was to cure me. But then they started talking about the deal, and about what my father would have to do. Pretty soon the Demon didn't sound like God anymore. But my dad didn't sound like who I thought he was, either. He was talking to this Demon and he was negotiating the terms like he knew all the ins and outs. One thing I can say about my father, he is a smart man, and he likes to read. If a subject interests him, he'll read enough to make himself an expert, or as close to one as it's possible to get. And that's how he was talking to the Shining Demon – like an expert. I didn't know it at the time – how could I? – but he was negotiating a loophole in the agreement that not even the Shining Demon noticed."

Amber looked round as Glen walked in. "I think I broke your toilet," he said.

Amber closed her eyes.

"It has a difficult flush," said Jacob. "Wait until the water stops gurgling, and try again."

Glen responded to Amber's glare with a helpless shrug, then nodded and left.

Jacob moved into the kitchen – a lacklustre affair with a stove and a table. He boiled some water as he talked. "If you're going to ask me what that loophole was, don't bother. I don't know. But, after my dad had shaken the Shining Demon's hand, the Shining Demon reached down to me and his fingers – I remember them being long, long fingers – passed into my stomach. They didn't break the skin or anything, they just passed right through, and they hurt. I mean, they hurt like hell. My dad had his hand clamped over my mouth to stop me from screaming – we didn't want to alert the nurses – but I was thrashing and kicking and then I opened my eyes again and the Shining Demon was holding this grey lump of sludge and tissue. That was my cancer. The pain was gone; the sickness was gone. He just took it all away from me. I looked to my dad and for a moment, just the briefest of moments, I saw what the Demon had done to him. His skin was grey – the same grey as my cancer – but it was hard, and his eyes glowed, and he had fangs, and he had these two amazing, massive wings, like giant bat wings, growing from his shoulder blades. Just a glimpse is all I got of this, this *winged beast*, and then he was back to normal, but I'll never forget it. Never."

"Wings?" Amber pressed. "No horns?"

"Protrusions," said Jacob. "My dad had a headful of hair, but in that moment he was bald, and he had these short protrusions all the way around his head, like a crown. I suppose you could call them horns. Small horns. But big wings."

"What was the harvest schedule?" Milo asked.

"Three souls a year," said Jacob as he set about making four mugs of coffee. "For the first three years, he delivered. That's the part that Althea likes to forget. But then the excuses started. The Shining Demon sent out his representative, and Dad assured him he'd get back on track. But, while he was telling the representative that he found it difficult to go out three times a year, I was watching him go out every other *week*. There were people disappearing from all over our neighbourhood. The cops even came to speak to him. It got so bad, we had to move. He didn't have to tell me what was happening. I knew. He was harvesting a lot more souls than agreed upon, but he wasn't giving any of them to the Shining Demon. He had found a way, in all his research, to feed off those souls himself. He was making himself stronger."

"He'd planned to disappear all along," said Milo.

Glen joined them in the kitchen. "Sorry," he said, smiling, "would you happen to have a plunger available?"

Jacob frowned at him, then took one out from under the sink and handed it over.

"Any chance you'd have something bigger?" Glen asked.

"No," said Jacob.

"This'll do fine, then," Glen said, and left.

Jacob took a moment to look concerned, then handed Milo and Amber a coffee. Amber didn't like coffee.

"When I was seventeen," Jacob said, "my dad called me into the living room and sat me down and told me he was leaving. He said the representative had made it quite clear that unless he started making up for lost harvests, his own soul would be forfeit. He said if he told me where he was going, the Shining Demon would know, and he'd torture it out of me. He told me I was out of it. Obviously, he lied about that part." He sipped his coffee, leaning against the stove.

"So my dad left, and Althea took me in for a few years until I found a job and could manage on my own. I'd get the occasional postcard, but that was it. The representative started coming to see me, but, for all his threats, the cancer never came back."

"The Shining Demon must have been furious," said Amber.

Jacob shrugged. "He wasn't happy about it, no. But he knew that I didn't know where my dad was. Funny thing about Demons – and I mean proper Demons – they don't let anything cloud the subject at hand. He could have had me killed a thousand times over, just to appease his own irritation, but he kept his eyes on the prize. I think my dad knew that. I hope he did.

"Anyway, about fifteen years ago, the representative knocked on my door to tell me that this would be his last visit. He said he had better things to do with his time than trying to track down a cheat. Silly me, I took this for good news.

"Few weeks after that, I got the feeling I was being watched. Couldn't shake it. I was convinced someone – something – was following me. I started glimpsing it out of the corner of my eye. The witch. It started with some destruction of property. No big deal. Then it killed my neighbour's dog. Then it killed my neighbour. I moved. Had to move three times. The cops were getting interested, just like they'd been interested in my dad. It always found me. There's no way to stop it. I bought this place, where I didn't have any neighbours, and set up the perimeter to keep it out. I did learn *some* tricks from my old man. I used to drive into town every week, stock up on groceries and whatnot, but that got too dangerous, so now I get it all delivered."

"This has been going on for fifteen years?" Amber asked. "And the Shining Demon is hoping you'll wake up one day and, what, decide you've had enough? Tell him where your dad is?"

"I don't know where he is," Jacob said. "I keep telling you. The Shining Demon understands this. He didn't send the witch to get me to talk, but to torment — to try to get my dad to come to my rescue. Which, obviously, has not happened."

"Is there anyone who would know?" Milo asked.

"No one I'm familiar with. Why do you need to find him, anyway?"

"My parents made a deal with the Shining Demon that involves me," said Amber. "I'm trying to get out of it. I was hoping your dad might be able to help."

Jacob sighed. "For what it's worth, I believe you. And I'm sorry that I'm not able to tell you what you want to know."

"If you did know where he was," said Milo, "would you have told the Shining Demon?"

Jacob hesitated, then gave a grim smile. "Probably not."

"That's what I figured."

Glen walked in. They looked at him.

"The toilet is fine," he announced.

Milo sighed, and held out his hand to Jacob. "Thanks for talking to us."

Jacob shook Milo's hand, then Amber's. "Sorry I haven't been of any use to you."

"Thanks, anyway," she said.

Glen held out his hand to shake. Jacob gave him a nod instead. "Nice to meet you."

He led the way to the door, opened it, and they walked out. The light rain had stopped, though the sky was still overcast.

"Good luck," said Jacob. "Genuinely."

He closed the door, and they walked back towards the car.

"I broke his toilet," Glen said the moment they were back on the trail.

Amber ignored him, and looked at Milo. "Do you believe him when he says he doesn't know where his dad is?"

Milo sighed. "Yes, actually, I do. I wish I didn't."

"So what do we do now?"

"I… I don't know."

"We can't just stop. After all this, we can't just stop. There has to be some way of finding out where Jacob's dad is. What about the whole winged beast thing?"

Glen frowned. "Winged beast? There's a winged beast?"

"Surely someone has seen him flying around and posted it on some weird forum somewhere," Amber continued. "The internet would eat up something like this."

"You were talking about winged beasts? Seriously?"

"You're assuming Buxton is still harvesting souls," said Milo.

"Well, yeah," Amber responded. "I mean, why wouldn't he be?"

"Maybe he decided that killing innocent people is not something he wanted to continue doing."

"Guys, come on, stop walking so fast," Glen said. "I'm still weak."

"Or maybe he likes it," said Amber. "He killed who knows how many people in order to get strong enough to leave. I can't see how he'd be willing to lose that strength, can you? I'd say he'd want to get even stronger."

"I guess," Milo said slowly. "Especially if he thought the Shining Demon could turn up at any moment…"

"See, that's what I think," said Amber, snapping her fingers. "I think he hasn't stopped killing. Maybe it's not every other week, like Jacob said, but I bet it's still significant."

"Can you please slow down?" Glen said from behind them. "When Jacob finds out what I did to his toilet, he'll be coming after me and I'm too weak to defend myself. Also I don't know how."

"There's probably nothing about it online," said Amber, ignoring him. "Or, if there is, it's hidden away in some remote part of the web that we'd never find."

"Maybe not us," said Milo, "but someone who does this kind of thing for a living… Maybe."

Milo took out his phone and dialled a number. He waited till the call was answered.

"Edgar, old buddy," he said, smiling. "Looks like we're in need of your services yet again." His smile dropped slightly. "I'm not sure what you… oh, you mean the *powder flask*. Yeah, I think we may have accidentally taken that with us…"

Amber grinned, left Milo to explain himself, and carried on back down the trail to the car. Within moments, Milo and Glen were lost from sight. Another few seconds, and she could see the Charger.

Then a sound from somewhere to her left. The snapping of a twig.

Amber stopped walking, her eyes flickering from tree to tree. Nothing there. Nothing hiding, lurking, creeping... Nothing waiting.

And yet...

She walked off the trail a few steps, her feet crunching on dry twigs. Awareness prickled at the base of her skull.

She was being watched.

There were eyes on her, she was sure of that, and there was ill intent behind those eyes. Something out here wished her harm, and every step she was taking was one step closer to it, whatever it was.

But there was nothing there. Even in this failing light, she could still see clearly enough to know that. She took another step. The primal side of her, the unthinking lizard brain, would have commanded her body to spin and sprint at that moment, such was the spike of fear that shot through her. But she overrode it. Of course she did. There was nothing there. Nothing but trees.

Snap.

The sound, another twig breaking directly in front of her, turned her hands to talons, but she fought the change. The demon part of her was too confident, too assured. To start relying on it would be a mistake. She got herself back under control, and her reddening skin returned to normal. A twig had broken. That's all. No big deal. She glared at a tree as she approached, daring it to try and scare her again. It was just a stupid tree with stupid branches, with knots in its trunk that looked like a screaming face, eye sockets that gaped in hollow darkness.

The eyes opened.

Amber cursed, stepped back, her ankle buckling. Twigs cracked like bones as the tree untwisted, every sharp movement revealing another part of its body — a head, an arm, a hand, a leg. Not a tree but a thing, a thing of rough skin and knots, of bark and running sap and hair like twigs and leaves. A thing that stood and waited, straight and tall, but bent as it moved, its crippled spine curling gratefully, its long limbs reaching for Amber even as she scrambled backwards. Its mouth remained open, locked in a frozen scream, and a sound escaped like chattering teeth.

The witch.

It darted towards her and Amber fell back, hit the ground, and rolled desperately. When she looked up, she was alone.

She got up and went home, said goodnight to her parents and went to sleep. In her dreams, she was still in the woods, walking behind the witch, her senses dull. When she woke up, she went to school and sat in class. Her thoughts wandered back to the woods, where she was still walking. It seemed so real, in a way. After school, she worked her shift in the Firebird, then went home and went straight to bed. She dreamed of the gutted remains of an old house in the middle of the woods, and being led down into the basement.

In her dream, she went to sleep. In her sleep, she dreamed.

And in the morning she woke.

44

THE BASEMENT WAS STONE and cold. The ground was hard-packed dirt. Morning light sneaked in through the gaps in the wooden ceiling and the narrow window, set high on the eastern wall. The window didn't have any glass, but it did have metal bars, just like the cast-iron gate that was used as a door to the corridor beyond. Just like a prison cell. Amber sat up.

Five women looked back at her.

They were filthy. Their clothes had become dull rags. Their hair was long, unkempt. They looked like wild women, feral and dangerous, but they sat round her like they were waiting for a bus.

"Don't be afraid," one of them said.

Another one snorted a laugh.

"Fine," the first one said. "Do be afraid. But don't be afraid of us. We're not going to hurt you." She was in her forties, but her long hair was already grey. Down here, access to good hair dye was obviously limited. "I'm Deborah. You can call me Deb. This is Juliana, Honor, Faith and Iseul. What's your name?"

Amber put her back to the wall, and drew her legs in. "Amber," she said. "Where are we?"

"Somewhere we won't be found," said Juliana, the one who'd laughed. She was a little younger than Deb, with blonde hair that was once curly and was now merely knotted. Her face was hard but not unkind. "Do you have anything on you? A phone, something like that?"

Amber shook her head.

Honor, a girl in her early twenties with flawless ebony skin and a mouth full of metal braces, sat forward. "Does anyone know where you are? When it took you, were you close by?"

"I don't know how long I was walking, but I have friends who'll be looking for me," Amber replied.

"They won't find us," said Juliana. She got up, went to the barred gate, stood leaning against it. "You don't think people searched for us? Iseul over there is the niece of one of the richest men in the state – you don't think he had tracker dogs and helicopters looking for her?"

"My friends are different," said Amber. "This is the kind of thing they specialise in. One of them, anyway."

"I wouldn't get your hopes up," said Deb, her voice suddenly lifeless. "I don't think *anyone* specialises in this stuff."

Amber held her gaze. "What," she said, "witches?"

The other women frowned.

"Witches?" said Honor.

The Korean woman, Iseul, tossed a twig into the centre of the room. "The thing that brought me here was no witch," she said. "It was a tree-monster."

"And what's a tree-monster?" Amber asked.

"It's what took us," said Juliana. "It took you too, right? Looks like a tree until it opens its eyes? We don't know the technical term for it, but what it is, is a tree-monster."

"She's a witch," said Amber. "That's just how she looks."

"How would you know?" asked Deb.

"Because that's what she is. She was sent after a guy who lives in these woods, Jacob Buxton."

"Gretchen was right!" the fifth woman, Faith, suddenly exclaimed as she jumped to her feet. "She told us! The one person we all had contact with in the week before we woke up here! Gretchen knew he was in on it!"

"Who's Gretchen?" Amber asked.

Deb hesitated. "She was down here with us. Then she was taken away, and we haven't seen her since. There have been others, too. We were all that was left until you turned up."

By the looks on their faces, Amber knew that none of them harboured any hopes that Gretchen was still alive.

"Jacob's not responsible," said Amber.

"Bull!" cried Faith. "You don't think we've talked about every single possible thing that links us? Jacob Buxton is someone both Honor and I made deliveries to. Juliana called by his cabin to talk about the local elections. Iseul spoke to him outside her store. Deb went on two dates with him, for God's sake! We all spoke to him and, a few days later, we end up here!"

"Jacob wasn't the only thing we had in common," said Deb, sounding like they'd had this conversation a hundred times before. "There were six other people, there were eight locations... We live in a small town, Faith."

Faith jabbed a finger in Amber's direction. "But now she's saying Jacob Buxton is involved!"

"He's involved," said Amber, "but he's not responsible. He probably doesn't even know that you're missing. How long have you been here?"

"Gretchen was the first," said Deb, "a few weeks before me. It's April now, right? So I've been here ten months. Nearly eleven."

"I've been here four," said Honor. "I was the newbie, until you."

"How do you know all this about witches?" asked Juliana.

"The witch," said Amber, "because that's what she is, was sent by someone, it doesn't matter who, to basically make Jacob's life hell. The cabin is the only place he's safe from it."

"But why were we attacked?" Honor asked.

"I don't know," said Amber.

"Who are you? How do you know so much about this?"

"I needed to speak to Jacob. I didn't know him before yesterday. But does it matter? The only thing that matters right now is getting out of here."

"These walls are solid stone," said Honor. "The floor is hard-packed. We can't dig our way out, if that's what you're asking."

"And the shawl-women only ever let us out one at a time to use the bathroom," said Iseul.

Juliana smirked from the gate. "I love it that you still call it the bathroom."

Iseul grinned back. "I'm a civilised lady, what can I say? *Hole in the ground* doesn't have quite the same sense of grandeur."

"Who are the shawl-women?" Amber asked.

"They work for the tree-monster," said Juliana. "Or the witch, whatever. We've never seen their faces. They never talk. They bring us game that we have to skin and cook ourselves."

"How many of them are there?"

"At least five."

"Have you ever tried overpowering them?"

"Yeah," said Juliana, wincing at a painful memory. "I wouldn't advise it. Maybe if we all jumped on one of them at the same time… but they're never alone. We've never had the chance."

"Well, don't worry," said Amber. "You've got me now."

The sunlight glinted off the metalwork in Honor's smile. "I like this girl already," she said. "She's funny."

Amber stood, fighting a wave of dizziness that passed as quickly as it arrived.

"You're going to be woozy for a few minutes," said Deb. "We've all been there."

"What did she do to me?"

"It has a stinger," said Faith. "You've been poisoned. It doesn't last, don't worry. That's how it got all of us."

"And why is she keeping us alive?"

"Ah," said Iseul, "we're back on that cheery topic, are we?"

"We don't know," said Deb. "Why did it take Gretchen? Why did it take the others? Why not us? Why doesn't it just kill us and get it over with? Why doesn't it let us go? If we knew why we were here in the first place, we might be able to figure out an answer or two."

"Shawl-woman," said Juliana, backing away from the gate, and everyone who had been sitting got to their feet.

The shawl-woman came shuffling out of the darkness of the corridor, and Amber could see how the name had come about. Her clothes seemed to consist entirely of shawls, filthy, dirty and ragged, stitched together with twine, of varying fabrics and lengths. Her hands were lost in huge sleeves, and her face was hidden. A flick of her wrists and two skinny rabbits were tossed between the bars.

Juliana scooped them up, gave them a cursory examination, and called out after the shawl-woman as she shuffled back where she'd come from. "These are rabbits. I distinctly asked for duck!"

"She did!" said Iseul. "I remember!"

The shawl-woman didn't respond and didn't turn round.

Juliana held the rabbits out to Amber. "Dungeon tradition – the new arrival skins and cooks breakfast."

Amber's eyes widened. "Uh…"

"She's joking," said Deb.

"Oh, thank God."

"You guys are no fun," Juliana grumbled.

Amber watched as the women skinned and cooked the rabbits over a fire. They sat in a circle and ate, sharing cups of rainwater, collected in a bucket under a small hole in the ceiling. The rabbit was chewy. She did her best not to gag on the gristle. It occurred to her that her demon teeth would have no problem shearing through her meal, but thought it best not to shift in front of these women – not unless she had to, at least.

"Tell us about yourself, Amber," said Deb. "Where are you from?"

"Florida."

"And how come you know so much?"

Amber crunched on something. She pulled a bone from between her teeth, and swallowed the rest. "Me and my friend, we're looking for Jacob Buxton's father. My friend is the expert in all this."

"How does a teenaged girl from Florida fit in?" Juliana asked.

"I'm, uh, I'm in trouble. There are some people after me."

"Witches?"

"No. No, these are… different things. But they're after me, and that's why we came to Colorado, and that's why I'm here now."

"What kind of trouble are you in?" Deb asked.

"The bad kind."

Deb looked at her, gave a little shrug, and didn't ask any more. Amber got the feeling the real interrogation was yet to begin.

"I need to use the bathroom," she announced.

"You mean the hole in the ground," said Honor. "You sure? You'll be alone with the shawl-women. They won't hurt you if you don't try anything, but they're pretty creepy for someone who's just arrived."

"I really have to go," said Amber.

"A girl's gotta go, a girl's gotta go," said Deb, getting up and walking to the gate. She drank the last of her water, and rattled her cup against the bars. "Bathroom break!" she hollered. "Call of nature!"

She stayed where she was for a moment, looking out into the corridor, then she turned to Amber. "They're coming. Two of them. One's gonna walk in front, one behind. They'll take you straight to our luxurious hole in the ground, and when you're done they'll take you right back. You want my advice? Don't try to escape. They'll be expecting it, especially with someone new."

Amber stood, and nodded. "Thank you."

The shawl-women shuffled up. Without a word, the women went to the far wall, and stood with their foreheads pressed against the stone. The gate creaked heavily, and the shawl-women beckoned Amber out. Nerves sparking in her belly, Amber slipped out, and the gate was closed and locked behind her.

The shawl-women smelled of leaves and earth. They didn't say anything as they walked the length of the corridor, Amber between them. She tried to peek at their faces, but their hoods were too low. The darkness was punctuated by slivers of daylight. The wooden ceiling had been blackened by the blaze that had felled the rest of the house.

They passed the turn into another corridor, and Amber was brought to a small chamber. When they passed through the doorway, she was dismayed to discover that the hole in the ground was an actual hole in the actual ground.

The shawl-women stood in the door, waiting.

Amber hovered beside the hole. "Uh, would you mind turning around?"

The shawl-women didn't move.

Amber blushed as she manoeuvred herself into position. It took her half a minute to relax enough to pee. When she was done, she straightened up, careful not to fall into the hole, and pulled up her jeans. The shawl-women parted and they escorted her back the way they'd come, one in front and one behind.

When they passed the junction to the other corridor, however, Amber slowed to a stop. "What's down there?"

Neither of the shawl-women responded.

She did her best to keep it friendly. "Hello? Can you talk? I think I'm supposed to go down that way. Do you mind?"

She tried to step out of their little procession, but the shawl-woman behind blocked her way with one arm, while the shawl-woman in front turned.

"Please," said Amber. "I'm only sixteen. I'm a kid. All the others are women. Can't you let me go? Please? I promise I won't tell."

The shawl-women didn't respond.

Amber smiled. "I really tried to be nice," she said, and shifted, feeling the power flood her.

They grabbed at her, but she shoved them away, running down the other corridor. It widened to a room and she ran in and the smell hit her, made her stagger back.

The room was filled with flayed bodies. Here and there she saw animal carcasses, rotten and decaying, but it was the human remains that made her scream. They hung from the wooden beams, held in place by twisted and rusted nails. Their insides, the guts and organs, the meat and the bones, were nothing more than blackened heaps on the ground, long since picked over by rats and birds and maggots. It was the skins that the witch obviously valued, as shredded as they were.

No other door in here. No way out.

She turned and the shawl-women came at her. She swung, her talons digging into the first shawl-woman's chest. Panic biting her nerve endings, she ripped the shawls away, snarling into the face beneath. She was prepared for a human face, she was prepared for a monster's face, she was prepared for any face – as long as there was one. But instead of a face, instead of flesh and blood, she was greeted by a mass of tightly twisting sticks that writhed under her grip.

Something lurched in Amber's mind and her thoughts jammed for a long, desperate moment, and then the second shawl-woman wrapped an arm round her throat and pulled her backwards.

She grabbed at the arm, feeling nothing but more sticks through the fabric. The stick-thing in front of her reached out, those twigs lengthening, working their way around Amber's body, scratching and cutting her skin, tightening round her ribs. It was hard to breathe. Hard to stay upright. Her black scales did their best to protect her as thin branches wrapped around her head like vines, forcing her eyes closed. They were in her hair, coiling around her horns. Her arms were trapped, her claws useless. She wanted to shriek, but couldn't draw the breath that would let her. She wanted to shout, wanted to give up, wanted it to be over, but she didn't have a voice and there was no one to listen. She was going to die. They were going to kill her.

She fought against her own fear, fought the wave of panic that threatened to wash all rational thought away. A notion flashed through her mind – that of a Chinese finger puzzle, where the more you struggle, the faster you're caught. She focused on one thing. Just one thing.

She reverted.

The branches around her midsection tightened, but everywhere else they loosened, and she sucked in a breath. Amber resisted the urge to struggle and instead went limp, and gradually the pressure eased.

The branches moved from her face and she opened her eyes, just in time to see the witch enter the room.

45

THE WITCH APPROACHED LIKE a curious cat, her head tilted to one side. Even though her spine was curved, she loomed over Amber, her knotted hair almost touching the low ceiling. There was something behind her eyes as she examined Amber, a kind of intelligence, her long, sharp fingers poking and prodding. The shawl-women's branches moved subtly to clear a space in anticipation of every poke. No words were spoken, no obvious communication passed between them. The shawl-women moved independently of the witch but also with her, as if they were all part of the same body.

The witch peered closer. She scraped her fingers through Amber's hair, searching, Amber realised, for the horns that had just been there.

Her curiosity far from satisfied, the witch scratched and scraped deeper and harder, and Amber gritted her teeth against the pain.

There was a voice now, coming closer. One of the women from the cellar.

"Where are you taking me? Please. Please, let me go back to the others. Oh God, please..."

Faith came into the room, dragged by two more shawl-women. She saw the witch and shrank back, but was unable to stop the shawl-women from dragging her to Amber's side. She finally fell silent.

The witch reached out, her coarse fingers turning Amber's head one way and then the other. Dirty fingernails pried open her mouth, and Amber had to resist the urge to bite down. She nearly gagged as the witch explored. All of a sudden, the witch switched her attention to Faith, went through the same routine, and then came back to Amber, fingers prodding her chest and belly.

"What's it doing?" Faith whispered.

"Examining us," Amber said.

The witch snapped her head up and Amber shut her mouth.

Tears flowed down Faith's cheeks, but her soft voice was surprisingly steady. "Our Father, who art in heaven, hallowed be Thy name..."

The witch left Amber and moved to Faith, started squeezing and poking her body the way she had Amber's, but Faith didn't stop her prayer.

"Thy kingdom come, Thy will be done, on earth as it is in heaven, give us this day our daily bread, and forgive us our trespasses, as we forgive those who—"

All at once the witch stopped, and stepped back, and for one crazy moment Amber though the prayer was working. But then she knew. The witch had made her decision.

Tree roots burst from the dirt at Faith's feet and tore through her tattered jeans, burrowing into her legs. Faith screamed, nearly pulled free of the shawl-women, but they clung on and the roots kept coming. Amber cursed, cried out, tried to help and then tried to pull away, but there was nothing she could do but stand and watch as Faith's agony reached new heights, dragging her screams along with it. Branches bulged under her skin and twigs poked through, spraying blood, opening up gashes and wounds, from which fell her steaming innards. And then the screams were cut short and Faith made one last gagging sound and died.

Her chin dropped to her chest, but she didn't fall and she didn't stop moving. The roots continued to fill her, discarding the organs and the bones and the meaty essence of her body at her feet. The skin at her neck bulged, and a moment later she raised her head.

Amber stared.

The thing that had once been Faith took a step, breaking free of the roots that had pinned it to the ground. It dragged its other leg behind it. That one wasn't working right.

The witch examined the Faith-thing, inspecting her handiwork. As she did so, her mouth moved, like she was talking to herself. Then the Faith-thing's mouth started moving, a perfect mirror to the shapes formed by the witch. There were no words, however. Instead, a series of sounds became audible – a hollow rush of air and a distant creaking.

The witch turned her head towards Amber, and the Faith-thing mimicked the movement exactly. The witch raised her left arm and its new puppet did the same.

But the movement caused a tear in the skin along the underside of the Faith-thing's upper arm, a tear that joined with another rip and became a gaping hole from which sharp twigs protruded. The Faith-thing tried to hold itself together, but the rips were appearing all over now, and every tear led to two more, and in seconds the Faith-thing fell apart, the sticks tumbling to the floor.

The witch gazed down at her failed puppet, and the shawl-women dragged Amber backwards. She didn't resist as she was taken back to the basement. They flung her inside, then closed the gate behind her.

The other women rushed forward.

"What happened?" asked Deb. "Did you see Faith? They came in here and took her and then we heard screaming."

"She's... she's dead," said Amber. "I'm sorry."

There were no gasps and no arguments and no tears. The women just stood there, the reality settling upon their shoulders, almost too heavy to withstand.

"What happened?" Deb asked again.

"She examined us," Amber said dully. "The witch. She examined us both and then made her choice."

"What did it do to Faith?" Juliana pressed.

"Filled her with branches," said Amber. "Roots and twigs and branches. Filled her up. I found a room full of... full of that stuff."

"Gretchen?" said Deb.

"I don't know," Amber answered. "Probably. She's been doing this for a while. Experimenting. Trying to get it right."

"I don't get it," said Honor. "Filled her with branches? What does that mean?"

"The branches are alive," Amber said. "The witch controls them, or they're part of her or something. The shawl-women aren't women, they aren't people. They're just sticks. They're all extensions of her, I think. When she was finished with Faith, it was just Faith's skin, her face and her skin, filled with branches, doing whatever the witch was doing."

"But that's insane," said Iseul.

Amber nodded. "I think she wants to – the witch – I think she wants to be… us."

"Why?"

"I don't know."

"Why'd she let you live, and not Faith?"

Amber hesitated.

Juliana seized her arm. "What are you hiding?"

"Juliana," said Deb.

"No!" Juliana shouted. "She'd hiding something. Look at her. She's not even denying it."

Amber shook her head. "I don't know why—"

"Liar!"

The force of the word made Amber step back. The others looked at her.

"Why did the witch spare you?" Iseul asked.

"I don't know," said Amber. "I swear."

"Faith's been with us for *months*," Honor said. She had tears in her eyes, but her voice was steady. "Then you come in, and suddenly Faith gets killed? Why? Are we next? Am I next?"

"Why did that thing let you live?" asked Juliana. "Are you working with it? Are you? Answer me!"

Amber looked at them, saw the grim determination in their eyes, and knew she wasn't going to be able to talk her way out of this.

"I want you to be calm," she said.

"Just answer the question!" Juliana shouted.

Amber held up her hands. "I will. I'm about to. But I'm going to ask you to remain calm. I'm trapped here, the same as you. My life is in danger, the same as yours. We're on the same side. I'm not going to hurt you."

"Hurt us?" Deb said. "What do you—?"

Amber shifted, and the basement erupted in screams and shouts and curses.

"I'm not going to hurt you!" Amber said as they all scrambled back.

"Stay away from us!" Juliana screeched.

"I am!" said Amber, backing up to the far wall. "Look! I am! I'm not going to hurt you!"

They stared at her, and she did her best to appear non-threatening. She tried smiling.

"Look at her teeth!" Iseul whimpered, and Amber stopped smiling.

"Who are you?" asked Deb.

"I told you, my name's Amber."

"You're a devil!" said Honor.

"No, I am not. This doesn't mean anything. The horns, the skin, it doesn't change who I am. Not really. Not who I am inside. I'm still a good person, I swear to you!"

"You're working with the witch! That's how you know so much about it!"

Amber shook her head. "No, I'm not. And the only reason I know so much is because, well, this is the kind of thing I've been doing for the past two weeks."

Deb frowned. "You've been a devil for two weeks?"

"Please stop calling me a devil. It's a long story, how I got like this, but two weeks ago I thought I was totally normal and I didn't know anything like this even existed. Now here I am, and I'm doing my best to deal with what's being thrown at me, and I think I'm doing a pretty good job of it, actually, and I'm not a bad guy and I'm not a devil, and I don't want to hurt anyone except maybe the witch because of what she's done to Faith, and what she's doing to us, and… and I don't know what else to say."

They stared.

"So you're not a devil?" Juliana asked.

"No. My parents are kind of demons, though, and I inherited that from them, and now they're trying to kill me."

A few moments passed.

"Harsh," said Honor.

"Yes, it is," Amber responded. "Listen to me: I'm in at the deep end. I know this is freaky, I know this is terrifying, and it's very hard to believe someone when they have red skin and horns, but I'm not the bad guy. I'm really not."

Deb was the first one to take a step closer. "But this is why the witch chose you over Faith?"

"I think so," said Amber. "When I'm like this, I'm bigger, stronger… My skin might even be tough enough to stay in one piece if she takes me over. I'd be a better… vessel, maybe."

"If it wants to take you over," said Iseul, "then why didn't it?"

Amber relaxed a little more. "Like I said, she's been experimenting. She's been testing herself. It hasn't been going well for her."

"But now that you're here," said Iseul, "it might have found the vessel it's been waiting for."

"Yeah," said Amber. "Now she's ready to put all her experiments to use."

"So what happens to us?" Honor asked. "Do you think it'll let us go?"

"Hey," said Deb. "Hey. Before we start cheering too loud, let's figure out if we can help Amber, all right?"

Amber frowned. "You want to help me?"

"If we can."

"Thank you. Sincerely, thank you. But I don't know if you can do anything. The witch on her own is powerful, but add in those shawl-women and there's not a whole lot anyone could do."

"But what does it do, then?" Juliana asked. "Okay, it takes Amber's skin, takes her face, but so what? Now it looks like a devil — no offence, Amber — and so where can it go? What the hell does it want?"

"Oh my God," said Honor, practically running up to Amber. "When you're like this, and again no offence, yeah, you look evil and all, but you're also... I mean, you're beautiful. She's beautiful, right, guys?"

The other women nodded.

"Maybe that's why the witch chose you over Faith," Honor continued. "Not only because you're bigger and stronger and a more likely vessel, but also because you're better-looking."

"Uh," said Amber, "okay... I don't really know where you're going with this, though..."

"The one thing we never understood is what all this has to do with Jacob Buxton. You said the witch was sent to make his life hell, right? But none of this has any effect on him in the slightest. Amber, how long has the witch been doing this?"

"Killing people? I don't know. But she's been tormenting him for fifteen years."

"Fifteen years," said Honor, "this ugly old tree-monster witch-thing is making Jacob Buxton's life a misery. Fifteen years and it never stops. It never leaves. It doesn't go on vacation and it doesn't go home to its witch-husband and their little witch-kids. It's a single lady in an all-consuming job, and all it does – *all it does* – is watch over this one man. My brother was in the army; he worked in a sniper team. They had to stay in one place for days, watching their targets. He said the longer they watched, the harder it was to pull the trigger. Because they'd got to know the targets, they'd developed almost a fondness for them…"

"Holy crap," said Deb. "It's in love with him."

Honor snapped her fingers. "Exactly! He's all hidden away in his cabin and he doesn't talk to many people, does he? But every woman who has had contact with him, no matter how briefly, is snatched away and hidden in a dungeon."

"She's jealous," said Amber. "She wants her rivals out of the way and now she wants to take the form of one of us so that she can be with Jacob."

"B I N G and O," said Honor.

Juliana looked at them like they were nuts. "Seriously? The tree-monster's in love? That's our theory?"

"It's a good one," said Iseul.

"It's a tree-monster! What does it know about love?"

"More than some people," said Amber.

"Okay, okay," Deb said, "so we have a possible motive. If we were trying to solve a crime, this would be an important moment for us all. But it changes nothing. The lovestruck witch is still probably gonna take over Amber and then kill the rest of us. Knowing it has a softer side will not help us in the slightest."

"Wow," said Honor. "I know we've been living in a dungeon and all, and we're all in danger, but you are surprisingly depressing."

46

AMBER SLEPT ON A bed of leaves. It was exactly as uncomfortable as she'd expected.

In the morning, she woke to the sound of the gate opening. Two shawl-women stood there. Two more lurked beyond it. Their intentions were obvious.

Amber got up slowly. The other women stood beside her. It was a touching show of solidarity, but they couldn't help her. They couldn't stop what was about to happen.

"Don't change," said Deb. "If it's your red skin it wants, stay like you are."

Amber nodded, and passed through the gate, and it creaked shut behind her. The shawl-women brought her back to the room with all the carcasses, where the witch was waiting.

A long, gnarled finger reached out, poked Amber's shoulder. It poked again, and prodded her chest, but Amber didn't shift. The witch must have sensed her resolve, because she regarded her anew. After a moment, the shawl-women released their hold, and the witch struck her.

The force of the blow rattled Amber's skull and made her stumble, but she didn't fall. Holding one hand to her stinging cheek, she looked up at the witch and said, "I'm not going to change."

The witch hit her again, in the belly this time, doubling her over. Amber gasped and groaned, and fell to her knees. After a few panicked moments, she sucked in a breath, and the shawl-women hauled her up.

The witch was going easy on her. She couldn't afford to damage her vessel.

"I don't care what you do," Amber wheezed. "I am not going to change."

The witch observed her. Amber didn't like that. She could almost see the gears move behind those eyes.

She heard shouts of protests and curses, and Amber's heart plummeted. The shawl-women dragged Juliana in first, then Deb and Honor and Iseul. Despite their struggles, the captives were lined up along the wall.

"What's it want?" Honor asked, trying to free herself of a shawl-woman's grip. "It's not going to practise on me. No way am I letting that happen."

Amber sagged. "She doesn't want to practise," she said.

At Juliana's feet, roots cracked the hard-packed dirt, started twisting round her shoes. Juliana screamed, tried kicking, but Amber knew full well what was going to happen next.

"Okay!" she said. "Okay, just stop! You hear me? Stop."

The witch observed her a moment longer, and the roots retreated.

"They go free," Amber continued. "You let them go right now. That's the deal. Let them go, don't hurt them and don't go after them, and I'll change. You can... you can use my skin."

398

The witch considered the proposal for a moment, and then pointed at her. Amber hesitated, then shifted into her demon form. At once, the shawl-women released their captives.

The women shared a look of uncertainty, like they were expecting to be grabbed again the moment they started believing they were free. Iseul was the first to move to the corridor. No shawl-woman went to stop her. The witch didn't even look round.

Iseul ran.

Deb and the others started edging out.

"Up here!" Iseul yelled. "The way out is up here! Follow my voice!"

Honor hesitated. She looked at Amber, looked at the witch, and hurried out. Juliana went next.

"Thank you," Deb said to Amber, then she followed the others.

Amber waited to hear screams or shouts that would indicate they'd been recaptured. When that didn't happen, she looked back at the witch. "Seems we have a deal."

The witch stepped forward, and reached for her.

Amber's hand encircled her wrist. "I'm sorry," she said, black scales spreading across her skin, "you weren't expecting me to go without a fight, were you?"

She wrenched the witch towards her and slashed at her face. The witch howled, an unearthly sound that made Amber's bones quiver, and then they went tumbling. Roots sprouted from the ground, trying to hold Amber in place, but she was on her feet and moving, still tangled up with the witch as they crashed into the wall.

The witch's hair came alive and Amber shut her eyes against

a hundred stabbing splinters that scraped across her scales. She felt her way up from the witch's shoulder, found her neck and got two hands on it as they stumbled round the room. She started squeezing, then grew her talons and sank them into the witch's flesh. It didn't make any discernible difference.

There were shawl-women on her now, pulling her away, and Amber cracked her eyes open to find a target. When she found one, she swiped, and the shawls ripped cleanly and the branches underneath came apart. The clothes collapsed to the sound of falling sticks, but even as that happened another figure rose on the far side of the room. It wasn't even attempting to look like a person this time – the stick-thing joined the shawl-women and wrenched Amber's arms behind her back. They forced her to her knees, and she looked up as the witch stepped into view.

Amber's snarl turned to an angry, defiant roar.

The witch turned her head, and through that tangle of hair Amber saw an expression flash across her face—

Fear.

Amber smelled smoke moments before she noticed the flickering light. A fire. There was a fire raging, spreading fast. The shawl-women were loosening their grip as the witch's attention was diverted.

Amber heard shouting. The women. At first, she thought their voices were raised in panic – then she realised they were voices raised in challenge.

"Come get us!" she heard Deb shout. "Come get us, you monstrous bitch!"

Amber tore free and the shawl-women and the stick-things fell to the floor, nothing more than scattering branches. She launched herself at the witch and they fell back, hit the table and rolled off. Amber ignored the witch's long limbs and held her close. She bit down on an ear, tore a chunk out of it, and the witch shrieked and bucked wildly. Amber lost her grip, went tumbling, and only managed to get to her knees before the witch had scuttled round behind her. Hands gripped her. The world tilted and blurred and Amber hit the far wall and dropped.

The ceiling was on fire.

A beam dropped and the witch jumped back. Amber sat up, watching her panic, and a curious sense of victory took hold. Then she remembered that she was here as well, and the feeling vanished.

The witch ran.

Amber scrambled up and followed her, surging into billowing clouds of smoke that seared her lungs and burned her eyes. She groped blindly for the walls, letting them guide her, tripping on roots and banging her horns. She felt cool air on her skin and staggered towards that, before doubling over as coughs racked her body. She forced herself up, forced herself to focus on that cool air, and then she stumbled against steps. She climbed them on her hands and knees, felt more hands on her, dragging her up, and she emerged into fresh air and light.

The hands released her and she heard Deb and Honor, and she curled up, coughing, and dug her knuckles into her streaming eyes. She looked up, blinked against the sunlight. Juliana peered at her.

"Amber? You okay?"

She nodded, and coughed, and nodded again.

"People!" Iseul yelled. "Look!"

Amber looked to where Iseul was pointing, saw a dark figure move through the trees.

"Amber!" Milo shouted.

She forced herself up, wiped her eyes again, tried to answer, but coughed instead, made do with waving. Milo broke into a run, holding an axe in both hands. Something moved ahead of him.

Deb yelled a warning as a coughing fit bent Amber double and the witch sprang from cover. Milo went down, losing the axe, the witch all over him. She lifted him, threw him against a tree. He smacked into it horribly and spun and hit the ground. The witch moved in to finish him off, but Glen and Jacob Buxton were already there to help him to his feet.

The witch froze when she saw Jacob.

Amber sucked in a breath, broke free of Juliana's grip, and scrambled into a run. She scooped the fallen axe off the ground, jumped to a tree stump and leaped high. She swung, the axe cutting deep into the witch's neck and lodging there, and Amber landed empty-handed and went stumbling. The witch shrieked, arched her back and twisted, yellow blood spraying from her wound like sap. She found the handle, yanked it free and let it fall, but her head rolled to one side and she toppled, like she'd lost all sense of balance.

Amber ran back for the axe, but the witch caught her with a desperate swipe of her arm and Amber went rolling. She looked up to see the witch snatch up Jacob and run.

Amber grabbed the axe and took off in pursuit. The witch was easy to lose in the trees, but she caught flashes of Jacob's clothes and kept up. Her seared lungs burned.

She tripped on a log and stumbled and smacked her horns

off a branch and fell, cursing. She got up, ran to the last place she'd seen Jacob, ran on, shouting his name.

Then she slowed. The witch was on the ground, bent over on her knees with her arms out in front, like she was praying. Her head was turned sideways, with yellow blood slowly leaking from her wound. Jacob stood just out of her reach, looking down at her.

"She's dead," he said. His voice was oddly dull. "She was running and getting weaker, and stumbling, and then she put me down... and just sort of... sank to her knees."

He looked up, looked at Amber.

"Milo told me you were a demon," he said. "You don't look anything like the way my father did."

Amber reverted, and Jacob looked back at the witch.

"She was almost *gentle*," he said, sounding surprised.

47

Three minutes. That was how long Milo gave her to say her goodbyes. Any lead they'd had on Amber's parents had been eaten up by the witch. Her brand read 168 hours. They couldn't afford to waste any more time. Amber knew this. She agreed with it. And yet, as she was being ushered to the car, she realised that she didn't want to go. The women who had been held captive in that dungeon had welcomed her into their group even when she'd revealed the truth about herself. They'd accepted her. She'd belonged. They'd formed a family down there, formed bonds that would never be broken, and she'd been so close to being a part of that. Now they were standing there by Jacob's cabin, watching her go, their questions unanswered, her questions unasked.

Then she was in the Charger and she was leaving them behind.

"You okay?" Milo asked as they were driving away from Cricket Hill.

"I'd liked to have stayed a while," Amber said.

He nodded. "You understand why we had to get out fast, though, right?"

"My parents."

"Them," said Milo, "and we want to be far away from here when those women return home. The cops are going to be all over this. We can't afford to be delayed any longer than we already have been."

"Yeah," she said, looking out of the window. "I know. Where are we going?"

"New York!" Glen said excitedly from the back.

Milo sighed. "It didn't take Edgar long to find mentions of a winged beast. He found eleven in all, on obscure websites on something called the Dark Web. One sighting in Louisville, two in Baltimore, and the rest in New York."

"Is that where Gregory Buxton is?" Amber asked.

"We think so," said Glen, nodding seriously.

A flicker of annoyance crossed Milo's features. He'd had to deal with Glen for an entire night without Amber there to act as a buffer, and it was clearly taking its toll. "Edgar will be meeting us in Brooklyn," he said. "He'll get there ahead of us, snoop around, and hopefully by the time we get there he'll have something more solid."

"Okay," said Amber. "Good."

"Something else bothering you?"

She glanced at him. "Since when are you so eager to chat?"

"He was worried about you," said Glen.

Amber raised an eyebrow. "Really?"

"Don't know why you're so astonished," Milo said. "I looked away for one moment, and you were gone. I didn't know if you'd got lost, if the witch had grabbed you, or if your parents had tracked us down faster than I'd anticipated."

"We searched all night," said Glen. "Well, Milo did. I tried, but, until I've regained all my strength, I'm more hindrance than boon. At least that's what Milo said."

Amber suppressed a smile. "How did you find the witch's house?"

The road widened to become a highway, and Milo piled on the speed. "I knew we were in the right area when there were no more birds singing, but we could have been wandering for days if Glen hadn't seen the smoke from the fire those women lit."

"It was nothing," Glen said bashfully. "I shouldn't be called a hero just because I saw some smoke."

"No one's calling you a hero," Milo said.

"They're not? Really? But I saw the smoke."

Amber settled back and let Glen prattle on until his strength left him and he fell asleep. It was funny – when he wasn't talking, there seemed to be something missing, a vital element they'd left behind. She almost wanted to wake him and set him off again, like a wind-up toy, but she decided against it. He'd been through just as much as she had, and so she let him rest.

They stopped at a gas station for food and Amber and Milo got out, leaving Glen to snore gently in the Charger. As they were walking back across the forecourt, Milo said, "One of the women said you were there when the witch killed someone. Faith – was that her name?"

Amber nodded.

"I'm sorry you had to see that."

"Me too."

"We can talk about it, if you want."

The Charger stood before them, waiting to hear her story. She imagined her confession filling it like fuel, and she slowed.

"I killed her," said Amber.

Milo frowned. "Faith?"

"The witch," she said. "I killed her, just like I killed Varga."

"They were monsters."

She looked at him. "They were still living things. Almost living, anyway. One moment they could think and have opinions and do things, and the next... they couldn't. Because I killed them."

"They had both killed plenty of innocent people. You stopped them from killing more."

"I ended their lives."

"Yes, you did. And you have to live with that. But better you end theirs than they end yours."

"Have you killed people?"

Milo didn't answer for the longest time.

"Sorry," said Amber. "I didn't mean to—"

"My earliest memory is of murder," he said.

She looked at him. Didn't say anything.

"I woke up one morning in a motel with no idea who I was. I didn't know my name, didn't know where I was from... My life was a blank. The only memories I had were flashes of being in that car, driving at night. The only faces I could remember were the faces of the people I'd killed."

"Glen was right," Amber said softly. "You're the Ghost of the Highway."

"That's what some of the newspapers called me, yeah. I didn't know it, not when I was in that motel room that morning. I remembered everything about the world, but nothing about my place in it. I went outside, though, and I saw the Charger waiting for me. I could've walked away, I guess. Left it behind.

But I was terrified. I was alone, and lost. I didn't know what had happened, why I couldn't remember... But I knew, even then, that the car was a part of me. That I'm only complete when I'm sitting behind the wheel.

"I must have stood there for an hour, maybe longer, just looking at it. I knew what I was. I was a killer. More than that, I was a monster. I remembered fragments about a deal – vague fragments, from years before – and I remembered the Demon who spoke to me... Couldn't remember the words, though. Couldn't remember the terms, or even the reason why I'd summoned him in the first place."

"Is your name even Milo?" Amber asked. "Are you even from Kentucky?"

He gave a small smile. "According to the ID in my wallet. As far as I can tell, though, it's a false identity. Why I needed one, I don't know. But it was the only one I had, so I clung to it."

"What did you do? Did you get in the Charger?"

"I did," he said. "It was fine for the first few hours. I just drove. I was outside of Miami, so I headed for a hospital. Couldn't remember one thing about my life before the deal, but I remembered streets, oh yes. I remembered where everything was. But the more I drove, the more I began to slip away. I didn't notice it at first, how calm I was getting. How content. And then, just like that–" he clicked his fingers – "I knew that if I didn't get out of that car that I'd be gone again. So that's what I did.

"I stored the Charger, took a bus to the hospital. They couldn't find any head trauma. I went to shrinks, hypnotists... Hypnotists helped, actually. I started to remember more – but it was all about my time in the car, travelling the blackroads, choosing victims... Nothing about me. Nothing about my life before all that. I got in touch with Edgar to try to figure out more about the deal I'd done, or even just find out which Demon I'd done it with. It didn't work. I gradually accepted that my old life had been wiped away and there was no getting it back."

"You still don't remember anything?"

He shook his head.

"Jacob said the Shining Demon sent out a representative when his dad stopped harvesting souls. Did anyone like that ever come to you?"

"No. I'd have welcomed it, actually. Finally, I'd have some answers."

In the Charger ahead, Glen woke up. Amber saw him look around in sleepy befuddlement. He spotted her and waved.

"That was twelve years ago," said Milo. "Every few months I'd go by the garage, take the cover off and just... look at her. But I wouldn't touch. Wouldn't get in."

"Until I made you."

He looked at her, frowning, like he'd just remembered she was there. "You didn't make me do anything."

"You needed the car to take me on the blackroads."

"That was my choice," said Milo. "Besides, enough time has passed. I don't feel the same need as I did back then. I wouldn't have been able to handle the Charger before. I'd have been in danger of slipping right back into my old habits."

"And now you're not?"

"Of course not. It doesn't take me over like it used to."

"Sometimes it does."

"What?"

"When you've been driving too long, you kind of... You get weird. You look thinner."

Milo shrugged. "It can be a strain, sure. But I'm in control."

"You don't quit an addiction by going back to it."

"I'm in control, all right? Trust me."

"So... it really is alive? The car?"

"In a way."

"Can it hear us? Can it understand us?"

"Of course."

She looked over at the Charger, noticing how still it seemed, like a cat about to pounce.

Milo smiled. "She's not going to hurt you."

"How do you know?"

"Because I know when she doesn't like someone."

"It talks to you?"

"Sort of. Relax, Amber, okay? Things are different now. I'm older and stronger. I'm in control now, not the Charger. When you're in this car, you've got nothing to worry about, okay? It's everyone else out there," he said. "They're the ones who have to worry."

48

THEY STAYED IN KANSAS that night, and were gone by eight the next morning. Amber watched the landscape rise, flat land developing hills the further east they drove. They passed through Missouri and Illinois and got back into Indiana at five that afternoon. Tomorrow, Milo said, they'd be in New York.

They found a motel just like half a dozen others they'd stayed at, L-shaped, the rooms opening directly on to the parking lot. Amber got a room at the upper half of the L, Glen got one in the middle, and Milo got one nearer the corner.

They ate at a nearby diner and Milo and Glen went to their rooms. Amber took the iPad to hers, used MapQuest to work out that they had twelve hours of driving ahead of them. She really, really hoped that'd be the end of it. She couldn't handle any more.

At seven, she got so bored she went for a walk. She didn't know the name of the town they were in, but it was pretty big. Maybe it even qualified for city status. She got something to eat in a McDonald's, even though she wasn't hungry. Eating was something to do to pass the time.

When she was finished, she dumped the remains of her meal in the trash, slid the tray on to the stack, and walked out on to the sidewalk, nearly colliding with a pretty blonde girl who was passing. They smiled at each other, did that awkward dance where one moves round the other, and the girl walked on. Amber was going the same way, but she delayed for a moment, just to make it clear that she wasn't following this girl, and then she walked after her.

There was a guy up ahead in a crappy suit, slurping on a smoothie. He watched the blonde girl approach, then put the smoothie on top of a trash can and brought his hands together in an appreciative clap.

"Now that is how you fill a T-shirt," he said, grinning, as he fell into step beside her. "Hey there, baby, how're you doing today?"

The girl didn't answer, just kept walking.

Amber stayed a few paces behind.

"You are looking mighty fine, princess. Where you headed?"

"I'm in a hurry, sorry," the girl said.

"Where you rushing off to? Why don't you stay a while, talk with me?"

She shook her head, walked faster.

He kept pace. "I'm a nice guy, I'm a good guy. Ask anyone, they'll tell you." When she didn't answer, he lost his good cheer. "I'm just being friendly. Can't a fella be friendly these days? I'm paying you a compliment, for Christ's sake. Least you can do is say thank you."

The words left Amber's mouth before she realised what she was saying. "Leave her alone."

The guy swung round, his forehead creased in a frown, while the blonde girl took the opportunity to speed-walk away.

He gave Amber the once-over, and was not impressed. "What'd you say?"

Amber looked up at him and tried to keep the tremor out of her voice. "She didn't ask for the compliment. You gave it and she didn't ask for it or want it. She shouldn't have to say thank you for something she didn't want in the first place."

The guy stared at her, and laughed. "What the hell are you talking about? What does this have to do with you? We were just having a conversation." He turned, like he expected the blonde girl to still be there. "Aw man..."

He looked back at Amber. "What were you saying?"

"Nothing," said Amber, and walked by him.

He followed her. "You jealous, that it? Bet you never had someone come up to you out of the blue and compliment you, now did you? No. You know why? Because you are fugly. You are fug-ly."

"All right," Amber said.

He stopped following her, content to have the last word. "Next time, mind your own goddamn business, you goddamn troll-looking bitch."

Troll. That was it. That was the word that guy had used, back in the Firebird. Troll. What had his name been? Brian? Ben? Brandon.

Amber turned. The guy was just about to walk away, but when he saw Amber looking at him he squared up, eyebrow raised.

"We got a problem?"

"I get it," she said. "I'm short. I could do with losing a few pounds. I'm not as pretty as some other girls."

"And you look like a troll."

People passed them by, not giving them anything more than a cursory glance.

"So what?" Amber asked. "What if I do look like a troll? I don't think I do, personally, but let's say that I did — so what? What's it got to do with you?"

"Hey, you're the one started this," the guy said.

"That's right," she said, nodding. "I started this when you started hassling that girl."

"I complimented her!" he said. Almost shouted.

"She didn't want your attention."

The guy took a big step towards her. "Well, that's her problem, now isn't it? I compliment a girl, that's what it is. Not my problem if she takes it wrong."

Amber looked up at him calmly. "But you have eyes, right? You saw how quick she was walking? You saw how uncomfortable she was? So, even if your intention was to be nice, why didn't you back off when you noticed how uneasy you were making her?"

"So a man's not allowed to compliment a woman anymore, is that what you're saying? I swear, there's just no talking to people like you."

He stepped back, done, but she wasn't going to let him get away that easy. She just couldn't.

She grabbed his shirt, both hands bunching at his chest, and powered forward. He stumbled at first, too surprised to react, and then started laughing. Amused, he let himself get pushed into a narrow alley, then planted his feet and twisted. Amber lost her grip and tripped over his leg and fell to her knees. The ground was cold and wet.

"I'm not exactly sure what the hell is happening," he said,

"but it looked like you were trying to hurt me. Which is goddamn *hilarious*."

Amber stood, and met his gaze. "Just thought I'd give you what you're after."

"Ohhh, you mean with *you*? Not a chance, little girl. I like 'em tall and stacked, know what I'm saying?"

"I know," she said, and shifted into a tall, stacked, red-skinned demon. "So how do you like me now?"

His eyes widened and his mouth opened, but before he could yell she grabbed him, yanked him off his feet, and threw him deeper into the alley. He went rolling through a puddle and scrambled up and she shoved him back.

"Am I pretty enough now?" she said, smiling and showing her fangs. "Am I *sexy* enough now?"

She hit him, a backhanded swipe that sent him spinning, and stalked after him. "I've wanted to do this my whole life, you know that?"

"Get away from me!" he screeched.

He tried to run past her, but she caught him, of course she did, and she slammed his head into a set of filthy pipes running down the wall. He wobbled and fell, but his arms were still working and he started dragging himself away.

She lifted him off the ground by his ankle, swinging him into the wall. There was an awful crunching sound, and he landed heavily.

"What's wrong?" she asked. "All out of compliments?"

Her hand closed round his throat and she straightened, taking him with her. She held him off the ground with an ease that delighted her.

"Don't worry," she said, "I'm not going to kill you. I'm

going to let you go. But you're never going to forget this, are you? And so whenever you see a pretty girl walking down the street – or even a not-so-pretty girl – you're going to have to wonder to yourself – is she a demon? Because you wanna know a secret? There are a lot more than me out there. There are thousands of us, but you're not going to know who's who until it's too late."

"I'm... sorry," he gurgled.

"Shhh. It's almost over. I just want to leave you with something." Her free hand grew talons. "I'm just going to carve the word troll on your forehead."

He kicked, flailed, and she ignored him, and her smile grew wider as the tip of her nail touched his skin. She flicked downwards and he screamed and the scream pierced her calm like she'd been cut herself.

Amber dropped him in alarm and stepped back, and he curled into a ball with both hands pressed to his forehead. Blood flowed freely.

She looked at her hand, and watched as her talons retracted and her skin returned to normal and she was Amber again, the girl, the human, not the demon, and her thoughts were her own and all she wanted to do was puke.

She didn't, though. She swallowed thickly and stepped back. She hurried from the alley, keeping her head down, and half ran back to the motel.

Amber sat on the edge of her bed. A few minutes later, she realised she was shaking. She took a shower, dressed in pyjama bottoms and a T-shirt, and went back to where she'd been sitting.

"What the hell?" she whispered to the empty room.

She turned on the small TV to get her thoughts on to something else, and began flicking through the channels. She bypassed a *Two and a Half Men* marathon and found an old TV show where a man in a suit, tie and mask was fighting a werewolf. It wasn't very good, but it was better than *Two and a Half Men*. She watched it until she got bored, then flicked over and caught the end of a *Dark Places* rerun.

Her smile faded before it had even begun – the first time she'd seen this episode she had been at home, with her parents. It was the one where Balthazar was being stalked through an empty town by a trio of hunters. Bill had walked in just when they were explaining how they'd been tracking him. She remembered, with perfect clarity, the look on her father's face as he itched to tell her how ridiculous that explanation was.

To his credit, though, he had kept his opinions to himself. But then, she supposed, he always did. She tried to remember a time when he had criticised a favourite book or show, and wasn't surprised when she came up empty. In some ways, he'd actually been a good father.

Amber turned off the TV. It was dark now, almost eleven. She should sleep, or at least try. Instead, she picked up the iPad and logged on to the *Dark Places* forum. Nobody she liked was chatting so she skimmed the conversations and the GIFs. She looked into Balthazar's ice-blue eyes and found a piece of that old comfort, that sense of familiarity. She started to well up, and laughed at herself, but it was a laugh without humour. She dropped the iPad on the bed and went to the window, pressed her forehead against the glass. She watched a man walk from one of the rooms towards the street.

Bill had been right, of course. The scepticism on his face was entirely justified. The way the hunters had been tracking Balthazar was indeed stupid. She was just thankful that her parents had no such things as subdermal locators. The only way they could track her was by searching for the Charger – but looking for one car in all of America was an almost impossible task, even with their resources. Still, the car was a possibility, no matter how unlikely, but the people within the car were mere ghosts – Amber hadn't sent emails, she hadn't posted anything that could be traced back to her, Milo didn't use a credit card, and Glen didn't even *have* a credit card.

The man passed through a patch of darkness and she waited for him to emerge. When he didn't, she looked closer, trying to pick him out in the gloom. A bus's headlights swept the area, revealing its emptiness. She found herself looking up, like the guy was a vampire who had just lifted into the air and flown away instead of turning left or right or walking off down some lane she couldn't see. This was what she had been reduced to – seeing the supernatural when she should have been seeing the ordinary. In that direction, craziness lay.

Of course, the only way anyone could *possibly* track them was – according to Althea Buxton – if one of the vampires who had bitten Glen decided to come after him, but why the hell would they have done that? Why go after Glen, of all people? What was so important about him? The only reason she could think of, in all her wild imaginings, would be if her parents had noticed he'd been bitten. Then the smart move would be to either force or coerce the vampire who'd done it to lead them to him and, as a result, her. That'd be the smart move. That'd be the sneaky, unexpected thing that they'd probably think of.

Amber took her head away from the glass as her body very slowly turned cold. She felt sick and weak and she didn't want to move, but she went to her bag, took out the crucifix. Her hands were shaking.

She opened the door and stepped out. The parking lot was half full and still, lit by a street lamp that sprouted from a half-hearted flower bed along the sidewalk. Cars passed on the street beyond, but not many. The night was dark and it was quiet. It was holding a secret.

On bare feet Amber walked from her room, passing window and door, window and door, window and door.

She was paranoid. Of course she was. She was letting her imagination take over. This was natural. She was going to knock on Glen's door and he'd answer and she'd hand him the crucifix and the next morning he'd insist that she'd been sleepwalking, that he was irresistible to her, and she'd ignore him and they'd drive on and that would be the end of it.

Amber got to his room. His door was open. She stepped in.

The room was dark. Glen lay across the bed in his boxers. There was blood still dripping from his neck and his eyes were open but unseeing.

Amber dropped the crucifix and both hands went to her mouth as her knees gave out and she sagged against the wall. A whine escaped her lips that she quickly bit back before it became a scream.

He thought he'd got away from them. They all did. But Glen had been killed that first night in Cascade Falls – it had just taken this long for it to register.

She turned on to her hands and knees, finding it difficult to breathe. She needed to get out. Get Milo. Get in the car and drive. The vampire had found them, and if the vampire was here…

She looked up. From where she was, she could see through the open door, all the way across the parking lot, to where her parents and their friends were standing.

49

Amber clamped a hand over her mouth to keep from crying out. Her father emerged from the manager's office, talked with the others. Grant and Kirsty started walking towards Milo's room. She couldn't be sure, but it looked like they had guns in their hands.

Her parents and Imelda went left, headed for Amber's room. Alastair hung back, keeping an eye out. Amber left the door to Glen's room open – she didn't want anything to draw them to her – and forced herself to her feet. She stumbled to the window. Once her parents realised that her room was empty, they'd come straight here. Imelda would probably try to distract them, but she only had moments.

Alastair approached the Charger, running his hand over the bodywork admiringly. From where she was, Amber could see the trunk as it clicked open, spilling red light. Alastair frowned, moved closer.

Dacre Shanks lunged out at him.

They went down and there were shouts and curses and Amber backed away from the window, nearly falling over the bed, nearly falling over Glen's body. She caught a glimpse of herself in the mirror as she turned red and grew horns. She may have looked fierce, even in her pyjama bottoms and little T-shirt, but she didn't feel it. Outside in that parking lot right now was no mercy and certain death. The idea that she should stand and fight passed so fleetingly it was like it was never there. Which left only one course of action.

She hurried into the bathroom, shut the door and, as an afterthought, locked it. She stepped to the wall as her hands grew talons. Her first slash was pitiful – it barely scraped the plaster. But her second took some of that ridiculously light wood with it. She slashed again, and kicked, her bare foot smashing through to the other side. Another few slashes to weaken it further and then she took three steps back.

She heard gunshots. Grant and Kirsty had found Milo.

She charged, hit the wall with her shoulder, and exploded into the bathroom on the other side in a shower of splinters and cheap plaster. She stumbled a little but stayed upright, yanked the door open and hurried through. The room's occupant, a startled man with an alarming beard, was already on his feet, clutching a pillow to his chest. She backhanded him on her way past and he flew into the corner, crumpling into an unconscious heap. For his own good. Her parents would most likely kill any witness they came across.

Right before she left the man's room, she heard her father's voice somewhere behind her.

She ran out. Gaudy green neon lit up the small swimming pool in which dead bugs swam with cigarette butts. She jumped the railing. On the road ahead a patrol car was swerving into a U-turn, its siren suddenly blaring, coming back to investigate the sound of gunfire. For one crazy moment, Amber thought they could help her, but of course they couldn't. No one could.

She stuck to the darkness, running along the embankment beside the railing, keeping the motel on her left. The patrol car braked sharply and she looked back. Betty stood in the middle of the road, entirely calm in the headlights. The cops got out, yelled at her to put her hands up, and Bill landed on the car roof. He yanked the first cop off his feet and the second cop started shouting and then a shadow lunged at Amber and she went sliding down the embankment, tangled in arms and legs, catching the glint of a knife in the corner of her eye.

She hit the ground – cold, hard concrete – and Dacre Shanks squirmed on top of her. She grabbed his wrist, keeping the blade at bay. He hissed at her, trying to scratch through her scales with his other hand. He was thinner. His cheeks were sunken and his skin was pallid. The Charger had drained him and it showed. He looked ill, the kind of ill you don't recover from.

Amber rolled, shoved him off, let go of his wrist and kicked him away from her. He got up, slashing, and she kept back, out of range, her talons out and her fangs bared.

She would have spoken to him, would have told him to run now, while he still could, but there was something in his eyes that told her he wasn't going to listen. A madness. The reasoning side of Shanks's brain had shut down at some stage in that trunk and this was all that was left.

He came at her and the blade slid off the scales that had formed round her ribs. She hit him, a punch that lifted him sideways, that cracked his fragile bones. He gasped and she brought her fist down on his forearm. His fingers sprang open and his knife fell and he staggered back, clutching his hand and tilting to one side. She glanced behind her, making sure she was out of her parents' line of sight, and, when she looked back, Shanks was coming for her again.

She slashed at him, her talons gouging furrows into his cheek. He stumbled past, hands at his face, his bottom lip flapping against his chin. Moaning words she couldn't understand, Shanks tried reaching for her, but Amber grabbed him, took him off his feet. She slammed him against the wall and his head smacked wetly against concrete. Then she let go, and he dropped.

He tried to crawl, but that was all his body could take. With catastrophic speed, he came apart as she watched. His arms folded beneath him like they were made of rubber, and his face hit the ground, shattering his jaw. His eyes rolled up so he was looking at her when his flesh caved in. His hair, his scalp, his skin slid from his skull, and blood and bile and a dozen other noxious fluids sluiced from his pores. His eyes clouded and melted, dripped from their sockets while his face peeled back like the skin of a grape and his clothes flattened, soaked in the juices of all that remained of Dacre Shanks.

"What a way to go," Alastair said from behind her, and she spun.

In demon form, Alastair was seven feet tall, his shirt stretching to contain his mass. His beard was longer, and pointed. Behind it he smiled. "I don't know who he was, or why he was locked in the trunk of that car, but to die by melting? That is quite something."

Her mouth was dry. She'd never be able to outrun him. She didn't have a hope of overpowering him, either.

"You've led us on quite the chase, young lady," he continued. "I've got to admit — I didn't think you had it in you. Honestly. You've surprised me. Hell, you've impressed me. But it all ends here, I'm afraid."

She only had once chance — attack him now, while he least expected it. Attack him, put him on his back, and run. Sprint. Hide.

"Alastair," she said, "please don't hurt me."

He smiled, stepped forward, about to say something else, and she slammed into him. He grunted and she went for his eyes. When he grabbed her wrists, she tried to knee him in the groin, but he shifted position, took the knee on his hip, and a simple push sent her tumbling head over heels across the ground.

"It takes a while to get used to, doesn't it?" he asked. "The strength, I mean. It takes a while longer to stop relying on it, though."

She ran at him and he ripped a metal pipe from the wall and swung it into her jaw. The impact rattled her skull, and when her brain came back online she was lying face down on the ground.

"See what I mean?" Alastair said, standing over her. "You've got all this strength and so you figure hey, all I need to do is land a few punches, am I right? And then before you know it you've run headlong into a metal pipe and it's lights out."

Amber started to get to her hands and knees.

"I think it'd be a nice thing to tell you that I liked you most of all, out of all our children that we've killed. But that'd be a lie." He stomped on her back and her face hit the ground. "But you're a sweet girl, there's no denying it, and I hope you feel like you've had a good life."

"I'm sure she does," said Imelda, walking up to join them.

Alastair chuckled, picked Amber up by the scruff of the neck. "Look what I found."

"Doesn't she look beautiful?" Imelda said, sauntering closer. "Red suits you, sweetie."

She picked up the fallen metal pipe. "You hit her with this?"

"Indeed I did," said Alastair.

"And she's still conscious?"

"As it turns out, our little Amber is a bit of a tough cookie."

"Yes, she is," said Imelda, and swung the pipe into Alastair's face.

Amber dropped as Alastair staggered back. Imelda hit him three more times – once to get him on the ground, and twice more to keep him there – and then hurried back to help Amber to her feet.

"We have to run now," she said, and they ran.

They got a few streets over, reverting to normal, but still sticking to the shadows. They found a small park, the grass easier on Amber's bare feet than the sidewalks, and hurried to the group of trees at its centre.

"Milo," said Amber. "Where's Milo? I heard gunshots."

Imelda hesitated. "Me too."

"You think they… you think they got him?"

"I don't know, sweetie. We can't think about Milo right now."

"What? We can't just leave him. Glen's dead but Milo, Milo might still be alive."

"It's you they want, Amber, not Milo. The best thing we can do is get you as far away from here as possible."

"You're coming with me?"

"Well, I can hardly stick around after beating up my ex-husband, now can I?" Imelda said, and glanced behind them. She hissed, dragged Amber into the trees and ducked down. "They're behind us," she whispered.

"So we run."

Imelda bit her lip.

"Imelda, we run."

"They're faster than us," Imelda said. "We'd never make it."

"Then we hide," said Amber. "We stay here and we don't make a sound."

"They'll find us."

"Then what do we do? Do we fight?"

Imelda peeked out, and a soft moan of panic escaped her. Finally, she looked Amber dead in the eyes. "You're going to have to run."

Amber frowned. "You said you were coming with me."

"I know, sweetie, and I'm sorry, but I'll hold them off, all right? You get as far away from here as—"

"No," said Amber. "No. I am not leaving you. I'm not leaving Milo and I'm not leaving you. I already had to leave Glen and I'm not doing that again. I need you to come with me."

Imelda gripped Amber's shoulders. "Amber, please. All I care about in this world is you. Your safety is the only thing that matters to me. I have done awful, terrible, unforgivable things in my life, things I can't walk away from. All that bad stuff has finally caught up to me. Tonight is the night I pay for all the evil I've done. No, no, I'm okay with that. Do you understand? I'm okay with it. I deserve it. I... I think I even need it. But please, I am begging you, let the last thing I do be counted as a good thing. Let me help you escape."

"But I don't want you to die."

"I love you, Amber. I love you, sweetheart. I need you to live. I need you to be the one that lives. I couldn't do that for my own children. I can do it for you. That's what a parent is for. That's what it means. When you're older, you'll understand. When you have children of your own, you'll see. You're all that matters. You're all that should matter. You replace us. You carry on. You have to carry on, Amber."

And then a familiar roar, and the Charger screeched to a halt on the street ahead. The passenger door swung open and Milo pulled the seat forward.

"Move!" he yelled.

Amber glanced at Imelda, and Imelda grinned. "Of course, I'd like to carry on as well."

They started running.

Amber glanced behind her. The others were in pursuit, with Bill way out in front. He was moving so fast he'd be on them in seconds.

Milo revved the engine, like that would make them run faster.

When they were in throwing distance of the Charger, Amber heard a gunshot. Imelda grunted, lost her rhythm and stumbled, and Amber tried to stop, but Imelda shoved her on.

"Run!" Imelda snapped, and fell.

Amber ran. Milo pushed the seat back and she jumped in. Behind her, Imelda lunged at Bill as he tried to sprint by her. They went down in a snarling, snapping tumble. The Charger's wheels spun as Milo accelerated, but Amber twisted in her seat as the others descended on Imelda, claws slashing and fangs tearing.

"Go back," Amber said. "We have to go back!"

"They'd kill us," said Milo.

"I'll pay you! I'll pay you everything I have!"

"I can't," he said. "I'm so sorry."

She turned to argue with him, to scream at him, and only then did she notice how pale he was, how much he was sweating. He steered with his left hand while his right was pressed into his side. Blood darkened his T-shirt.

His head dipped and his hand dropped from the wheel and the Charger started to swerve off the road. Amber reached over, tried to correct their course, shouting for Milo to wake up.

The Charger hit the lamppost and Amber slammed her head against the dash.

50

THE SUDDEN PEACE AND quiet was unnatural, and it brought Amber back from the brink of unconsciousness.

She opened her eyes, sat up, looked around. A few seconds. She'd only lost a few seconds.

In the distance, she heard sirens.

She got out of the car, made sure her parents weren't anywhere in sight, and reached back in, pulling Milo on to the passenger seat and trying to ignore the amount of blood he was losing. When he was strapped in, she hurried round to the driver's side. As she reached for the handle, she had a sudden fear that the Charger would lock her out, but the door opened under her touch and she slid in.

Her horns scraped the car ceiling, and she reluctantly reverted to give herself more room.

She adjusted her seat, buckled her belt, and put the Charger into gear. They lurched on to the road and she hissed, wrenched the wheel, managed to get them going straight. This wasn't like the car she'd driven in Driver's Ed. This was a monstrosity, a heavy metal beast, and she was fully aware that any moment it could surge out of her control. She slowed at a

Stop sign, signalled, and turned on to a larger road. A larger road with other cars moving.

"Please don't let me crash, please don't let me crash," she muttered, not entirely sure if this was a prayer she was offering to God, to the Devil, or to the Charger itself.

An hour later, she pulled over, reached into her bag on the back seat, and pulled out some clothes. She put on socks and shoes and wrapped herself in a coat. The temperature in the car had plummeted. She covered Milo with a blanket, and drove on.

It took another hour and a half to get to Dayton, Ohio. She wasn't taking the smaller roads, like Milo had. She stayed on I-70 and just kept heading east. By now, her parents would have searched her motel room, found the iPad, found the MapQuest search. They knew where she was headed, so there was nothing to be gained now by sneaking. It was a straight blast towards New York.

She kept glancing at Milo as she drove. He slumped, pale and sweating, unconscious. Unconscious but not dead. Amber was okay with that. She trusted the car to heal him.

She picked up speed after Dayton, got to Columbus in an hour, picked up more speed, then had to pull into a gas station as the tank was verging on empty. This worried her, but she filled it carefully, with reverence, almost like it was a blood transfusion. Then they got back on the road and made it as far as Pittsburgh before sunrise, and morning traffic started to clog the lanes.

At eight, Milo woke.

Amber took an off-ramp, drove through a few quiet streets until she came to a parking lot behind a crappy-looking gym. She helped Milo out of the Charger and he stood in his bare feet, straightening up slowly. His blood had drenched the passenger seat.

"How're you feeling?" she asked.

"Bad," he muttered. "But I've been worse." He prodded the bullet hole in his ruined T-shirt, wincing every time. "I'll be okay in a day or two. Maybe even a few hours." He frowned, and looked around. "Where are we?"

"Somewhere in Pennsylvania," she said. "We passed Pittsburgh, like, an hour ago. Maybe more."

"You've been driving all night?"

"I wasn't exactly going to be able to sleep."

"No," Milo said, "I guess not. Okay, this is good. We should be in New York in another five hours. I'll drive."

"You're too weak."

"I'll be fine. Your turn to get some rest. Do me a favour — reach in there and grab my bag, would you? Get your own as well."

Amber passed him his bag and found his boots tossed on to the back seat. She walked beside him as he limped to the gym, and watched him bribe the guy inside. Milo headed off to the men's locker room, and she went to the women's. She showered, brushed her teeth, and put on the jeans that were too long for her. She turned the ends up, pulled on a fresh T-shirt and a jacket, and went outside to wait by the car. Milo joined her a few minutes later. He was moving easier now, dressed in clean jeans and a jacket over a dark plaid shirt.

"Glen's dead," Amber said when he reached the car. Blurted, really.

Milo hesitated. "Yeah," he said. "I figured."

"A vampire did it. It's how they tracked us."

He nodded, and she looked away.

"Do you think she got away?" Amber asked. "Imelda, I mean. She could have escaped, right?"

Milo put his bag in the trunk. "She wasn't getting away from that, Amber."

She glared. "We should have gone back for her."

"Then we'd both be dead, and my death would have been a lot quicker than yours. Keys?"

She handed them over. "Shanks is dead, too. The Charger let him out, you know."

"I know. If it wasn't for that, I would have been asleep when your parents' buddies kicked down my door. Get in, Amber. We can't afford to lose any more time."

She opened the passenger door. There was no blood on the seat. The car had soaked it all up. Absorbed it.

She got in. Milo lowered himself, carefully, behind the wheel.

And they drove to New York. The car felt empty without Glen.

Amber felt empty, too.

She woke to a yellow cab blasting its horn at a bike messenger who was giving it the finger. Sitting up straighter, she wiped the drool from her chin and watched the brownstones tick by in a rhythm she could hear only in her head. The afternoon sun glinted off stained-glass windows and she checked the scars on her wrist: 122 hours left. Five days.

She yawned.

"You were having a bad dream," said Milo.

"Was I? I don't remember." Plumes of steam poured out from orange and white pipes, twice the height of the people that passed them. This was the New York of the movies – not the gleaming skyscrapers of Manhattan, but scaffolding and cracked sidewalks, health-food stores and cafes and bricks and mortar the colour of chocolate. This was Brooklyn.

"Ever been to New York before?" Milo asked.

"Twice," said Amber. "When I was eight and then again when I was twelve. We all went. Imelda took me up the Empire State Building and we saw the Statue of Liberty and we went to see *The Lion King* on Broadway. I don't remember what my parents or the others were doing. Huh."

"What?"

"Before all this, I thought Imelda didn't like me all that much. But she was the only one who ever did anything with me."

Milo looked at her. "If she's still alive, and if it's at all possible, we'll get her back."

They found a place to park – which wasn't easy – and walked a few blocks to a pizzeria on Park Slope. Edgar Spurrier grinned when he saw them, half of his pizza topping spilling over and dripping on to his tie.

"Ah goddammit," he said when he noticed. As he dabbed himself with napkins, Amber and Milo slid into the booth.

"You two," said Edgar, dumping the napkins on the table beside him, "have been busy. Oh, I have been hearing about you and your adventures."

Amber frowned. "From who?"

"From the folks in the know," said Edgar. "Tittle-tattle. Scuttlebutt. The black Charger and the demon girl. This partnership of yours is garnering quite the reputation – and I've been sitting back and basking in the reflected glory of it all." His smile left him. "And you stole my powder flask."

"I meant to apologise about that," said Milo.

"Did you? Did you really?"

"I thought we might have need of it before you would."

"And you didn't think to ask? You didn't think that I would have gladly loaned you my powder flask, for which I paid more than a pretty penny, out of the goodness of my own heart?"

"Not really, no."

"Yeah, you're probably right," Edgar said, and shoved the rest of the slice into his mouth. Chewing, he said, "Do you still have it? You haven't lost it, have you?"

"We still have it."

"Good." He chewed on, and swallowed. "Amber, how are your parent troubles?"

"They still want to kill me, if that's what you mean."

"They haven't changed their minds about that, huh? A damn shame. My parents wanted to kill me when I was your age, too, but for entirely different reasons."

"Have you had any luck finding Gregory Buxton?" she asked, but a waitress came over before Edgar could answer. They ordered a few slices and she walked off, taking Edgar's crumpled-up napkins with her. Edgar leaned forward.

"I've been narrowing it down," he said. "I not only have the neighbourhood, I have the apartment building, and I'm pretty sure I even have the apartment. Buxton's been living under an assumed name – which I have naturally found out. All we have to do is stake the place out until he comes home."

"I'm impressed," Milo said.

Edgar shrugged. "I just do what I do. It's no big thing. I mean, you couldn't do it, and nobody you know could have done it, but I did it because I'm me, and I'm just that smart."

"And insufferable."

"That goes hand in hand with genius, my friend. I'm coming with you, by the way."

"Ah, Edgar, I don't know about that…"

Edgar dropped his pizza slice. "You are not leaving me out of this. You're about to go hunting a winged beast. *A winged beast*, for God's sake. How many people get to say that in their lifetime?"

"Probably not very many."

"*Exactly*. I've been studying this stuff for most of my adult life. Sure, I've tried to do things, practical things, every now and then, but none of them have met with any success. But this? Hunting a winged beast? This would be me *doing* something, instead of just reading about it. There are a multitude of untold horrors that lurk in America's shadows, and I want to start *stalking* them."

"You rehearsed that," said Milo.

"Did not," said Edgar. "It all came to me just then. Milo, come on – have I ever asked you for anything?"

Milo sighed. "No."

"And Amber, do you owe me for all my help?"

"I guess."

"Then it's settled," he said, and grinned wider.

"You," said Amber, "are a very strange man."

"I know," said Edgar. "And I love it."

51

GREGORY BUXTON'S APARTMENT BUILDING was right beside the East River. The other buildings on the street were redbrick, but this one was brown, the colour of dirt. The wall closest to the river was armoured with rusted scaffolding, and it was flanked by an auto-rental place on one side and the Kent Sugar Refinery on the other. The auto-rental place was devoid of any actual autos, and the Sugar Refinery was a flattened wasteland enclosed by barbed-wire fences.

Milo pulled over to the kerb on the corner. Night was falling, and New York was lighting up like a great beast opening its countless eyes. They crossed the street, took the stairs to the top floor. They knocked on Buxton's door, and when nobody answered they moved away to wait. A little under an hour later, a black man in his sixties came up the stairs, went straight to the door and slid a key in. They walked up behind him.

"Gregory Buxton?" Milo asked.

The old man froze. Amber thought for a moment that he might make a break for it, but he surprised her by turning. He was tall, looked strong, with broad shoulders and thick forearms. His white hair was cropped short, and his face was heavily lined. She could see the remains of a handsome man beneath all that wear and tear. His mouth had settled over the years into a calm, straight line, and his eyes, while wary, were not unfriendly.

"Nobody's called me that in years," he said. "Come on in."

He turned back to his door, opened it and walked inside. The door swung halfway shut, hiding him from view.

Milo took out his gun and they moved quickly but cautiously. Milo opened the door the rest of the way, and Amber watched Buxton leaning into his refrigerator.

"Got no beers, I'm afraid," he said. "I used to drink, then decided it wasn't worth the hassle. Got some juice and some soft drinks, though, if that tickles your fancy."

He straightened up, saw Milo's gun, and didn't react one way or the other as they walked in. It was a drab apartment, but neat, and well maintained.

"I'll have a juice," said Amber.

He poured her a glass, left it for her on the table, and sank into his armchair, enjoyed the comfort for a moment with his eyes closed, and then looked up. "So who might you be?"

Amber stepped forward. "My name is Amber Lamont. This is Milo, and that's Edgar Spurrier. They're helping me."

"Helping you do what, Amber?"

"My parents and four of their friends made a deal with the Shining Demon."

"Aha," said Buxton. "They're the children-eaters, huh? Yeah, I heard about them. Tough break."

"The Shining Demon said he'd renegotiate that deal so that I get to live… if I give him something he wants."

"Me."

"Yes."

"And this is why you're here? To ask if I'll go peacefully?"

"I'm pretty sure you won't."

"I'm pretty sure you're right. How did you find me anyway?"

"We just needed to know what to look for, and your son told us that."

For the first time, Buxton looked interested. "You talked to Jacob?"

"We did more than that," said Milo. "Amber took care of his witch problem."

"No kidding? That thing's been driving him nuts. How is he? He okay?"

"He's good," said Amber. "And so's your mom."

"You *have* been getting around. I do my best to check up on them from time to time, but there's only so much I can do from all the way over here. I guess I owe you my thanks."

Milo shrugged.

"How have you managed it?" Edgar asked. "Staying invisible for so long?"

"I did my research," said Buxton. "I know all the tricks, all the little symbols you've got to scratch and the words you've got to recite. It's limiting, though, I admit. I'm not as free as I'd like to be. Every move I make I've got to think of the possible ramifications. I've got to worry about stepping out of the shadows. One slip-up, just one, and the Shining Demon would be able to latch on to me and he'd never, ever let me go. I've stayed one step ahead of him all this time because I've been playing it patient and playing it smart. It's not much of a life, but I'd be willing to bet that it's better than death."

"You haven't stopped killing," said Amber.

Buxton fixed her with a look. "No, young lady, I guess I haven't. I didn't plan on killing anyone, not at the start. I thought I'd get him to cure Jacob and then I'd take my son and vanish. But I had to be sure the cure was permanent, which meant Jake had to go through all these tests, and suddenly I was sticking around for a lot longer than originally intended. So I harvested souls, just like I said I would.

"Eventually I came to the conclusion that Jacob would be better off without me. The refrain of the deadbeat dad, huh? Yeah, I'm aware, but that doesn't make it any less true. So I took off. All my tricks worked and the Shining Demon never came close to finding me. But, see, in order for my tricks to work, I needed some degree of… well, I guess you could call it mojo. And the only way I could get my mojo was to keep harvesting souls – only instead of passing them on to the Shining Demon's grumpy old representative, I kept them for myself. The more I kept, the stronger I got, and the stronger I got, the more I harvested."

"Then you must be pretty strong by now," said Amber.

Buxton gave her a small nod. "Strong enough," he said. "I try to harvest the guilty. Criminals, gangsters, corrupt officials, people like that… Their souls aren't as potent as the innocent, but they'll do the job. I've slipped up now and then – I ain't proclaiming to be some sort of saint – but I do all right."

Amber looked at him, sitting in his chair like he was chatting with his buddies. "How are you so calm?" she asked.

"Why wouldn't I be?"

"Because we've come to your door and told you we want to hand you over to the Shining Demon. If I were in your shoes, I'd be furious."

"What good would that do?" Buxton asked. "You haven't

handed me over yet, have you? And you haven't told the Shining Demon you know where I am or else he'd be here already. I figure I've got breathing space."

"And if we said we were going to summon him right now," said Edgar, "how would you feel then?"

Buxton shrugged. "Guess you'll have to try to summon him to find out."

Milo took his gun out again, and rested it on his knee. "You're planning to kill us," he said.

"I am," said Buxton.

Edgar went pale. "But there's three of us," he said. "And we've got a gun."

"I'll manage," said Buxton.

Milo gave a soft smile. "I'm pretty fast and pretty good."

"You'll have to be."

"If we don't hand you over," Amber said, talking quickly before the situation spiralled, "do you have any way to help me? If you know all the tricks, is there something we missed?"

Buxton took his eyes off Milo, and looked at her. "You've got two choices from what I know of your situation. You either keep running and hope they stop hunting you after a dozen or so years, or you hunt them. Personally, I'd hunt them down and kill them before they kill you."

"I don't want to kill anyone."

"You killed that witch, didn't you?"

"Well, yeah, but…"

"You don't think that witch was a living being? Sure, she might have been different from me and you, but she had a heartbeat. She drew breath. She had a life and you ended it. You've already killed, Amber."

"I know that," she said, a little too loudly. "I know."

Buxton shrugged. "So killing a few more is surely no big deal."

"What if she hides?" Milo asked. "You've stayed invisible to the Shining Demon for all this time – is there a way for Amber to do the same?"

"Sure," said Buxton. "There wouldn't be much mojo involved in that one. You'd just have to pick a small town, somewhere out of the way, somewhere off the Demon Road, and blend in. Spend the rest of your life there in this small, out-of-the-way place, never excelling in anything, never making a mark, never causing a fuss or creating a stir… Think you can do that, Amber? Think you can live a life of perfect ordinariness?"

She hesitated.

Buxton smiled. "Of course you can't agree to that. I don't care if you're the most boring person on the planet – nobody's going to choose a life of mediocrity."

"I just want my parents to stop."

"Then kill them."

"I can't do that."

"Then they're going to win."

"Isn't there *anything* I could do?"

Buxton sighed. "You could go to Desolation Hill."

"Where's that?"

"Alaska. I don't know the whys and wherefores, but that's the one place you'd be invisible to the Shining Demon and anyone he'd send after you. When I was starting out, I thought I could hide there for a few months, maybe even a few years – but I only lasted a week. I wouldn't advise making the journey."

"Mr Buxton, I was really hoping you'd be able to come up with some way to help me."

"Yeah, I get that. But, seeing as how my advice would be to kill your folks and their friends the first chance you get, I don't think you're going to be paying me too much heed. Which leaves us in an awkward situation."

"Uh," said Edgar, "what would that be?"

"Mr Spurrier, wasn't it? Mr Spurrier, what Milo and Amber here have decided in the last few minutes, quite independently of one another, is to hand me over to the Shining Demon. Milo doesn't really care what happens to me one way or the other, and Amber figures I've killed plenty of people already, so maybe I deserve to pay for my sins. To her credit, it wasn't an easy decision to make, was it, Amber?"

"I... Mr Buxton, I'm sorry."

Buxton waved away her apology. "Nonsense. And you may have a point. An argument could be made that I've done more harm than good in my—"

He moved without warning, kicking the coffee table into Milo's leg and knocking the gun from his knee. Milo's hand flashed and he caught the pistol before it hit the ground, but Buxton was on his feet now, slamming another kick into Milo's chest, driving him back and toppling his chair. In the three seconds it took Amber to grow horns, Buxton hurled her into Edgar, sending them both over the back of the couch.

Milo reached for his fallen gun, but Buxton kicked it away. He grabbed the back of Milo's jacket and threw him against the wall.

Amber ran at him, claws out. He dodged her swipe and kicked her feet from under her. He picked up the chair Milo had been sitting on and broke it across her shoulders. Amber dropped, struggling to stay conscious.

She heard Buxton grunt, saw Milo driving him backwards. They knocked over a lamp and hit the kitchen table, shifting it sideways. Buxton threw a punch and Milo covered up, moved in, responded with a headbutt and then an elbow to the bridge of the nose. Blood spurted. Buxton took an unsteady step. Milo kicked at his knee and spun him, got him in a chokehold, but Buxton powered backwards, slammed Milo into the wall. Milo didn't let go. Buxton's face was turning purple.

Buxton staggered to the middle of the room, to where Milo's gun had come to rest.

Amber cursed, tried to get up, but her legs were still shaky. She wobbled and fell as Buxton dropped to his knees. He stopped trying to break the chokehold and his fingers closed around the gun. He lifted it, but instead of aiming over his shoulder to shoot Milo, he aimed right at Amber.

Black scales rose on her skin. She doubted they'd do any good at this range.

Milo released the hold immediately and stepped back, leaving Buxton to suck in lungfuls of air.

"Is it over?" Edgar asked from behind the couch. "Did we win?" He peeked out. "Aw hell."

Scales retracting a little, Amber got to her feet slowly. Buxton did the same, moving so that he had all three of them covered. He wiped some of the blood from his nose.

"Hard luck," he said. "You almost got me."

He backed up to the door, opened it, gave them one last look, and ran.

Amber hesitated. She looked at Milo, and he looked at her, and together they sprinted for the door.

"But he's still got the gun!" Edgar shouted after them.

They burst out on to the landing, caught a glimpse of Buxton running up the stairs. They followed. Halfway up, Buxton dropped the gun. Milo scooped it up without slowing.

Amber reached the door to the roof before Milo and she charged through. Buxton was running for the edge. Milo fired a warning shot into the night sky, but Buxton didn't slow down. Amber piled on the speed. There was nowhere for Buxton to run.

But, of course, he had no intention of running.

He changed suddenly, from tall, broad-shouldered old man to taller, broader-shouldered demon. Wings, massive wings, split the back of his shirt. His dark skin turned grey. He reached the edge of the rooftop and those wings unfurled and he dived upwards, wings beating the air. Amber stopped running and watched, her mouth open. Buxton twisted, looked down at her. His grey face looked like it had been carved from granite. He had a crown of small horns circling his skull, just like Jacob had described.

Milo ran up beside her, fired two more shots as Buxton's wings closed over and he plummeted. Just before he fell out of sight, his wings opened and he swooped, disappearing into the darkness.

"What do we do?" Edgar asked.

"We chase," said Amber.

She ran to the roof's edge and leaped.

52

EDGAR CRIED OUT AND Milo called her name, but then rushing air filled Amber's ears and she slammed into the fire escape of the auto-rental building across the alley, her strong fingers wrapping around the wrought-iron railing. She turned, braced her feet, and flung herself back to the other side, dropping lower as she did so. She flipped, curled her body, hit the bricks with her feet, and once again she powered back to the fire escape. Down she went, clinging to the railing one side and bounding off the other, until she dropped to the alley floor. Someone cursed in the darkness, a homeless woman huddled in a sleeping bag, and Amber jumped over her and sprinted for the street. A car passed, didn't see her, and Amber ran out, eyes on the sky.

There.

She took off in pursuit, reverting when she approached people and shifting when she was clear. She cut across streets and alleys and car lots and barged through dogwalkers and couples out for a late-night stroll. She kept Buxton in view.

Then she lost him. Of course she did. She knew she had to, she knew she couldn't keep this up, but even so it stoked her anger, made her run faster, made her more determined to catch sight of him again.

She caught glimpses that sent her hurtling in different directions. The more she ran, the less inclined she was to revert. As plain old Amber, she slowed down, she got out of breath, she puffed and panted and wheezed – but as the demon, she was relentless, her muscles were strong, and she never weakened.

Let the people of New York wonder about her. Let them wonder if this was just another weirdo New Yorker going to some costume party or a real-life demon running through their streets. She didn't care. The only thing she cared about was tracking down Buxton and tearing his goddamn wings off.

Light behind her and her shadow lengthened and she whirled as the Charger braked. Edgar was already in the back seat. She jumped in and they took off. Amber had to duck her head so that her horns fitted.

"You were running around in public," said Milo as they turned a corner, drifting slightly. "What the hell were you thinking?"

"I'm thinking, if we let him get away, I'm dead," she answered. "That's what I'm thinking."

Milo craned his head out of the window. "You were seen."

"I'd rather be seen than be dead."

"Hold on," said Milo.

He turned the wheel sharply and they spun 180 degrees, the seat belt biting into Amber's shoulder. She could see Buxton's dark silhouette, barely visible beyond the street lights. The Charger pursued.

"I'd just like to take this moment to apologise," Edgar said from the back. "I know I was not the best use back there. Violence has never been my thing."

Amber lost sight of Buxton.

"It's fine, Edgar," said Milo through gritted teeth.

Edgar continued. "I just want to assure you that, were we to find ourselves in a similar situation again, I would do my very best to be a good source of backup."

Neither Amber nor Milo responded this time. They were too busy trying to spot Buxton.

"It's just," Edgar went on, "I've never been that athletic. Even in high school, I was always considered to be on the slower side of fast. I preferred books and TV to going out and doing stuff. I blame my parents, to be honest. They rarely encouraged me, and when they did it was lacklustre and, I felt, disingenuous."

Amber pointed. "There!"

Milo swerved, almost hitting a yellow cab coming the other way. Amber locked her eyes on Buxton's beating wings. The beating was getting slower. He was tiring. Then he vanished.

Amber frowned. "Where's he gone?"

"He dropped," said Milo. He gunned the engine. "I'm going after him on foot. Edgar, you drive. Circle round the block, make sure he doesn't slip away."

"Uh," said Edgar, "you want me to drive this car?"

"She won't hurt you," Milo said. "She likes Amber."

"What does she think of me?" Edgar asked.

"You don't want to know."

Edgar looked dismayed. "Rejected by an automobile. A new low."

"I'll come with you," said Amber as Milo undid his seat belt.

"You stay with Edgar."

"No, I'm coming with—"

"I can't have you running around looking like that," Milo said. "Stay in the damn car and I'll chase Buxton towards you."

Amber stared at him, but Milo was already turning the wheel. He braked, then leaped out and ran between two buildings, his gun in his hand. She forced herself to remain in the car.

It was a good plan. Despite her anger, despite her sudden fury, it was a good plan.

Edgar grunted as he climbed out of the back seat and got behind the wheel. "Okay then," he said. "Off we go."

The Charger moved away from the kerb slowly, and didn't pick up a whole lot of speed.

"Faster!" Amber snapped.

"Driving a car is like riding a horse," Edgar said patiently. "You've got to get to know her over time, figure out her—"

Amber snarled at him. "Faster."

Edgar swallowed thickly, and put his foot down.

They were just rounding the block when Edgar glanced up, hissed and wrenched the wheel in the opposite direction.

Amber's horns knocked heavily against the ceiling. "What the hell, Edgar?"

They were speeding along now, Edgar spending more time looking out of the window than he was looking at the road ahead. "Buxton," he said. "He's got Milo."

"He's what?"

They turned on to a busier street.

"You didn't see? He's carrying him," Edgar said. "Milo looks unconscious. Oh God, you don't think Buxton's going to drop him, do you?"

Amber ignored the question. "Where are they? I can't see them."

"Straight ahead of us," said Edgar, swerving round traffic. "See them? Straight… oh hell. Where are they? They were right there, they were — *aha!*"

Another wrench of the wheel and once again Amber's horns scraped the ceiling. "Little bit of warning," she said, growing angrier.

"Sorry," said Edgar. "They're over my side. Can you see them?"

"I'll take your word for it."

Edgar's driving was attracting a lot of attention. Car horns blasted them when they passed, and Edgar shouted an apology to each one.

"Stop doing that," Amber said.

"Driving?"

"Apologising."

"Oh," said Edgar. "Sorry. But this is exciting, isn't it? I mean, if he doesn't drop Milo, it'll be exciting. If he drops Milo, it'll be tragic and terrible, but right now it's exciting. Can you feel it? Can you feel the excitement?"

"I can feel it," Amber said, wanting to kill him.

"Look at me," Edgar continued, "driving a demon car, hunting a winged beast… Danger is all around, but do I turn and flee? Does my courage fail me? It does not."

"Are you *still* talking?"

"I talk when I'm nervous. I guess I talk when I hunt demons, too. This is my first time hunting a demon, and I'm talking, so I guess I must talk when I hunt demons. Ha! These are my demon-hunting pants. I always wear them when I'm hunting demons."

She wanted to tear out his throat, but didn't. If she tore out his throat, he might crash.

"This car is something magnificent, isn't it?" he asked. "You hear people talking about how engines growl — well, this one actually does, doesn't it? You can hear it, right? That growl. That power. This car is alive. Hey, I wonder if I'll be affected. You know, because of... uh..."

"Because Milo is the Ghost of the Highway and this car is possessed?"

"Oooh," Edgar said, "he told you, cool. Yeah, I wonder if I'll suddenly get all possessed and dark and stuff."

"I doubt it."

"Yeah, you're probably right." Keeping track of Buxton and Milo through the open window, Edgar swept round a corner. Less traffic here. More closed-up businesses and art galleries. A hell of a lot of art galleries. They were heading towards the harbour. "It would be quite something, though. To feel that kind of power. When you're like this, Amber, in this form, what's it like? If you don't mind me asking, of course."

She gave up trying to spot Buxton. "I'm better. Stronger. Faster."

"Beautiful."

She glared at him.

"Sorry," he mumbled. A moment later, he slowed.

Amber tensed. "What?"

"They're landing," he said. He turned another corner. No cars here now. No pedestrians. Boarded-up businesses and warehouses. He killed the headlights and they cruised slowly through an open gate.

They passed cargo containers, stacked high like building blocks, and massive cranes that loomed over temporary offices.

Edgar drove so close to a pyramid of broken pipes that their jagged ends almost scraped the Charger's bodywork. They crept by it all, to the warehouse on the yard's east side, and Edgar cut the engine and looked at Amber nervously. She sighed, and got out. She could smell the sea.

Beyond the yard's high walls, New York rattled and hummed. But within them it was quiet.

"I think they're in there," Edgar whispered, eyes on the warehouse ahead.

Amber nodded, started walking towards the door.

"I'd feel better if I had a weapon," Edgar whispered beside her. "I should get a weapon. Maybe there's a gun store nearby that's still open."

"Get a weapon," Amber responded, "don't get a weapon, it's all the same to me. I'm going in."

Edgar puffed out his chest. "And I'm going in with you." He looked around, and picked up a rusted crowbar. "And I'm going in armed."

Amber shrugged. She really didn't care.

With Edgar on her heels, she passed through the door. There was a small corridor with stairs leading up. She skirted them, made straight for the door at the other end. It creaked slightly when she opened it. Beyond it was the warehouse proper. It was empty, apart from an engine block in the middle of the floor.

"They're not here," she whispered.

Edgar nodded. "Might be upstairs. Might be on the roof. I can't go on the roof. I'm afraid of..."

His voice trailed off.

She followed his gaze to the engine block. The light from

a street lamp came in through the high windows, and glinted off something shiny amid all that rust. She walked closer. Were they handcuffs?

She turned, and Edgar swung the crowbar into her head.

53

THE WORLD TILTED.

Amber was aware – somehow – of being dragged. Unconsciousness pulled at her, but instead of going down, instead of sinking into its depths, she managed to stay afloat, managed to keep her head above the waterline. Something cold encircled her wrist. Something metal. Then her eyes were flickering open, and Edgar was walking away and she lay back, looking up at long bars of brightness. She wanted to rest. Staying awake was so hard. And it hurt. Her head hurt, where Edgar had… where he had… what had he done?

Hit her with a goddamn crowbar, that was it.

Amber frowned. The pain was already receding. Her thoughts were beginning to clear. The bars of brightness above became strip lights hanging from the warehouse ceiling. The coldness on her wrist became a handcuff. She listened to a curious hissing and waited for her brain to sort itself out.

She ran her tongue against her fangs and bit down, letting the pain sharpen her further. Then she sat up. Slowly.

Edgar had cuffed her to the engine block. Of course he had. She didn't know how much an engine block weighed, but it was a hell of a lot more than she could lift, even in her current state.

She looked over at him. The hissing sound was the fine black powder being poured from the powder flask. Edgar moved sideways, close to joining up the large circle he was making around her.

"You're working for my parents," Amber said.

He glanced up, just long enough to smile and shake his head, then went back to work. "Nope. I understand why you'd think that, but I've never even met your folks. Don't think I'd want to, either. What kind of people would eat their own children? I swear, there are some sick and twisted individuals in the world, are there not?"

He moved sideways again, close to completing the circle.

"Then what are you doing?" she asked, standing.

"Hold on for just one moment," he said distractedly. "Need to get this just right… There. Done."

The circle complete, he straightened up, a hand on his back. "Not as young as I used to be," he chuckled, and stoppered the flask. "Amber, I really hope you understand that none of this is personal. It's not that I don't like you. I do, I really do. I think you're a smart, interesting person. To go through the stuff you're going through and still remain so positive and good-natured? That's a rare gift you have, Amber. Value it. Truly."

"What are you doing? What's the circle about?"

"Come now," he said. "You're not stupid. You know what this is."

"You're going to summon the Shining Demon?"

"Finally, we're on the same page."

"But we were going to do that, anyway."

"This isn't for you, Amber. This has never been for you. Despite everything, you're still just a teenager, yes? You think the world revolves around you. Sorry to disappoint you, kiddo, but this is for me. I've tried to summon the Shining Demon in the past, but I guess I'm just not interesting enough for someone like him. But this time I think he'll appear. I think he'll be willing to deal once he sees what I intend to offer as a blood sacrifice." He stepped over the circle and came towards her. "It's a shame, really. Getting a good look at you like this, even I'm hesitating. Killing you is going to be like killing something on the endangered species list, a tiger or leopard or something." He moved a little closer. "You truly are magnificent."

Amber lunged. The handcuff held her, but Edgar flinched back anyway, then laughed.

"Look at those fangs!" he said. "Look at that snarl! You, Amber, are a truly scary girl, if you don't mind me saying. But beautiful, too. Undeniably beautiful. How does it feel, to know that the monster version of you is the beautiful one? That skin. Those horns…" He pursed his lips. "I wonder how much I'd get for them…"

"Edgar, please…"

He waved her words away. "Don't bother, Amber. This has been a dream of mine ever since I heard about our bright and shiny friend. I see people like you, people like Milo and Buxton, and I wonder — why not me? What's so wrong with me that I don't get to share in all this wonderful, unholy power? I don't even want anything, that's the funny part. I'm not asking him for anything — all I want is the power to harvest him some souls."

"You're going to kill me?"

Edgar nodded. "Blood sacrifice. The clue's in the name."

"You think he'll want to talk to you after you've killed one of his demons?"

Edgar laughed. "Oh, so now you *are* one of his demons, eh? You changed that particular tune pretty darn quick."

"Edgar, you need to think about this," said Amber. "In the past few weeks, I've made mistakes and people have died. I killed—"

Edgar laughed. "It's really touching to see how concerned you are for my conscience, but you're hardly the first girl I've killed. Oh dear, I'm sorry, did you think that you were? Oh Lord, no. I've been killing lovely young ladies for a long time now. Some of them in situations like this, as a blood sacrifice. Some of them because they deserved it. Some of them just because I felt like it. America's monsters don't all have horns, you know. Some of them are just ordinary people. Like me."

"Milo will find you."

"I'll deal with Milo."

"He'll kill you," Amber said, through clenched teeth.

"I have his car. Separate Milo from his car for any length of time, and what is he? He's just a man. But me? I'll be a demon."

He slid a knife from his jacket.

She forced a snarl on to her face. "You think he's not on his way here right now?"

"He's busy tracking Buxton. Besides, he doesn't know where we are."

"He's the Ghost of the Highway," she said. "He's linked to that car. It's a part of him. Wherever it is, he's able to find it."

For the first time, she saw a brief flicker of doubt in Edgar's eyes.

"You kill me," she said, "and it works, and you arrive in the

Shining Demon's castle and he gives you what you want, you know what's going to happen then? You're going to arrive back here and Milo will be waiting. And he's not going to give you even a moment to test out your brand-new demonic powers. He's just going to shoot you right in the face. You think you stand a chance? You think he's going to miss?"

Edgar didn't say anything.

"He's a good shot," said Amber. "And you've got a big frikkin' head."

Edgar put the knife away. "Then I'll just move the car down the street," he said. "You don't go anywhere, you hear?"

She watched him walk out, keeping the snarl on her face, but the moment he was gone she reverted. The handcuff didn't get any looser around her wrist, but her hands, those small hands of hers…

She gritted her teeth against the pain and started to pull her hand out. For a moment, it felt like her bones were going to pop, or she was about to scrape all her skin off, but then her hand moved, and she bit her lip to stop from crying out. It was working. It was going to work.

Headlights moved across the walls, but the engine she heard didn't belong to the Charger. The idea flashed into her head that maybe Milo had found her, that everything she'd said about him being able to track down his car was true.

She redoubled her efforts to free herself. She was not going to let him rescue her. She'd never hear the end of it.

With a hiss of pain, Amber pulled her hand free and immediately shifted to get rid of the pain. Picking up Edgar's crowbar, she ran to the door, just as her father called her name.

54

Amber threw herself down, scrambling behind cover.

"We know you're there, Amber!" Bill shouted. "We know you're listening!"

She took a peek. Two cars, engines off but the headlights still on, and Bill and Betty walking into the blinding glare, taking centre stage in full demon form.

"Come on out, honey!" Bill shouted, his long shadow dancing around the yard. "We'll make it quick and painless, I promise!"

Amber moved slightly so she could see the Charger. She glimpsed Edgar, cowering in the darkness behind it.

"It's me, Amber," said Betty, clasping her hands and holding them over her heart. "It's Mommy. We are so sorry for scaring you. We really are. And we feel so, so bad for everything that's happened – but you know why we had to do it, don't you? You understand. I know you do."

"Come on out, honey." Bill wrapped his arm round his wife, and she rested her head against his shoulder. He kissed her horn. "You won't feel a thing, and then it'll all be over."

Amber moved backwards, and took the stairs up. Even there, she could hear their voices.

"It's the Shining Demon," Betty said. "The deal we made with him, the things we've had to do to fulfil our end of the bargain… None of this is what we wanted, Amber. None of it."

Amber emerged into a large, empty space that smelled of sawdust. Windows lined each side, and she crossed to the nearest one, peeking out. In the darkness behind the headlights, she saw Alastair and the others, but the gloom was too pervasive to make anyone out clearly.

"We didn't want to scare you," Betty continued, "or chase you. We didn't want to drive you to associate with the… the people you've been associating with. We just wanted our baby, in her short life, to be happy. To be loved. This has all gone so wrong." Betty turned, buried her head in Bill's shoulder.

He patted her back. "It's okay, sweetheart. Amber understands. Amber, you understand, don't you? Come out here right now. The life we gave you is ours to take away. It doesn't belong to you."

"Please, baby," Betty cried. "Don't make this any harder on me."

Anger boiled in Amber's throat as she watched her parents look at each other sadly.

No one's buying this, she wanted to shout. *No one's believing this. Why are you bothering to pretend?*

But she kept quiet.

Bill turned slightly, beckoned with a finger, and the others came forward out of the darkness.

Amber stiffened as Imelda was shoved into the light.

Imelda fell. Her hands were bound behind her and she had a gag over her mouth. Her clothes were torn and, even from where she sat, Amber could see the bloodstains. Most distressing of all was that the tip of one of Imelda's horns had been snapped off.

Bill dragged her through the dirt. They got to the pyramid of broken pipes and he held her face mere inches away from a jagged piece of metal. "If you don't come forward right now, young lady, we're going to kill your dear Auntie Imelda. She had us fooled, she really did. I genuinely thought she despised you from the moment you were born. We all did. But we couldn't see into her nasty, treacherous little heart."

"Does Imelda deserve to die?" Betty asked, walking with her hands out, imploring the entire dockyard. "Yes, she does. But does she deserve to die tonight? Does she deserve to die in your place, in unbelievable pain? Well, that is something only you can answer, Amber. What do you think?"

"We're going to count down from ten," Bill shouted. "Nine. Eight."

Amber couldn't let it happen. She just couldn't. Imelda was the only person in the world who loved her. She thought she'd lost her before – she couldn't handle losing her again.

Amber ran back down the steps. They didn't see her running towards them until she dropped the crowbar and stepped into the light. Bill stopped at the count of three.

"I'm here," said Amber.

"Well now," said Kirsty, "don't you scrub up well?"

"I told you she was beautiful," said Betty.

"My daughter," said Bill. "Who would have thought it?"

"Let her go," Amber said. "Let Imelda go and you can have me."

Bill smiled, pulled Imelda to her feet, and led her back to the group. From this close, Amber got a good look at the beating they'd given her.

"Wait," said Alastair, stepping forward. "Bill, Betty... I have an alternative. We don't have to kill Amber. You hear that, Amber? You don't have to die. You impressed me, back in Indiana. You're strong. Fierce, even. You're someone to be admired. You're like us."

"Ooooh," said Grant. "I get it. You dog." He laughed.

"With your permission," Alastair said to Bill and Betty.

Amber's parents looked at each other.

"I don't like it," Bill said.

"What other choice do we have?" asked Betty. "Amber, honey, would you consider it? Joining us?"

Amber frowned. "What?"

"Imelda's a traitor. She can't be trusted anymore. She's out. And so the six of us are cut down to five."

"Unless you join," said Alastair. "You wouldn't have to do anything right now. Grant and Kirsty have already stepped up to the plate."

Kirsty beamed, and patted her belly. "We're just thrilled."

"And seventeen years from now," Alastair continued, "it would have been my turn with Imelda. But with Imelda gone... I'm going to need a new mate."

"I'm really not comfortable with this," Bill muttered.

"Why not?" Alastair said. "She's strong, she's beautiful, she's formidable. In seventeen years, she'll be thirty-three – a good age to start a family."

"No," said Amber. Astonishingly, after everything that had happened, she was shocked. "Just no. No to joining you, no to being a part of this... this sick cycle of murder, and definitely no to mating with you."

Alastair held up his hands. "I'm not saying it won't be weird, but you'll get used to the idea if you just give it a try."

"Screw you. I'd rather you eat me."

"Sweetie," said Betty, "you're not thinking this through. It might be for the best. Wouldn't it be nice, to be a family again?"

"A family?" said Amber. "With you and Bill? After what you've done? After what you've tried to do? We're not a family anymore, Betty – we never were. You're my parents by some unfunny cosmic joke, but we are not family."

"She's made her decision," said Bill. "We kill her, we eat her, just like we'd planned."

"Bill, wait," said Betty. "Give her a chance to think about it."

"She's not going to change her mind," Bill said irritably. "Have you ever known her to change her mind when she's in a mood like this? She'd rather die than admit that she's wrong. She'd rather die just to spite us. You know how wilfully obstinate she is, Betty."

"Bill, come on," said Alastair.

"Don't come on me. In a lot of ways, all this is your fault. You couldn't keep Imelda happy and now—"

Alastair dived at Bill, and only Grant and Betty held him back.

"Each couple looks out for each other," said Bill. "You think I'd have let Betty stray so far? You think I wouldn't have noticed her attitude changing? You think she wouldn't have noticed a change in me? Has Grant let Kirsty totter out on the precipice?

Has Kirsty been so inattentive that Grant finds himself alone with his doubts? We back each other up, Alastair. That's the deal we made, *ourselves*, when all this started. We would be each other's rock. We stayed true to that idea. You didn't."

Alastair pushed himself free of the hands restraining him. "You're not going to blame this on me," he said. "You and Betty were married before we ever talked to the Shining Demon. Grant and Kirsty were in love. But me? I barely knew Imelda, and yet suddenly she was a part of our group and I was told, hey, this is the woman you have to spend the rest of your life with. This is your mate from now on. There will be no others. I never loved her."

"She never loved you, either," said Kirsty.

Alastair glared. "I don't care. You get that? I don't give a damn. I was forced into this with her by my side and the rest of you were too busy gazing into each other's eyes to notice that Imelda was the weak link in the chain. But now we have a chance to replace that link with someone stronger."

"From the look on her face, I don't think my daughter loves you," said Betty.

"She'll grow to."

"If Imelda didn't, why would Amber?"

"What's our alterative? Kill them both? We don't know what that would do to how the power is divided between us."

"You're not killing Imelda," said Amber, "and you can shut up about all that other stuff. Bill's right. I'm not going to change my mind. Let Imelda go, and you can take me."

"We could take you, anyway," said Kirsty. "You really think you can outrun us all?"

"No," said Amber, "but I'd fight you all the way. If you let

Imelda go, I won't resist, as long as you promise not to make it painful."

The demons looked at each other, and Bill glanced at Imelda.

"You heard her. Get going. You want my advice, you won't stop running."

They stood aside, opening up a way out. Imelda looked at it, then back to Amber. She had tears in her eyes.

"Go on," Amber said. "You've saved me enough. Now it's time for me to save you."

Imelda sobbed behind her gag, and reverted. Amber felt a sudden wave of affection for the woman, the only person who'd ever shown her real, genuine love, and her heart broke as Imelda turned away.

But, at the last moment, Imelda whirled, broke into a sprint, running not for the way out but for the pyramid of broken pipes and steel rods. She ran straight into it. Amber screamed her name as Imelda came to a sudden stop, her impaled body hanging limply, her head lolling forward.

The demons stared in shock.

Tears streaming down her face, Amber backed away.

Alastair reached out slowly, like he couldn't believe what Imelda had done. He pulled her body from the pipes and laid it gently in the dirt. Then he knelt, and the others did the same. For a moment, Amber thought they were genuinely saddened by what had happened.

Then Imelda moaned softly, and Amber's hand flew to her mouth as the demons began tearing at Imelda's clothes, rending and ripping her flesh with their claws, biting and tearing with their teeth, blood flowing as they feasted.

A wail escaped from between Amber's lips when Imelda

turned her head, her eyes still open, almost as if she could see Amber hidden in the darkness.

They were eating her alive, and she only died when Bill plucked out her heart.

55

SHE WATCHED THEM FROM the darkness as they gorged themselves on Imelda's body.

Once they had finished, they tossed the remains into the dirt and staggered away. It took Amber a few moments to realise they were drunk. Bill and Betty lay on the hood of their car while Grant and Kirsty waltzed through the yellow light, giggling and singing as they tried not to step on each other's feet. Alastair stumbled around them, muttering to himself. He tried using one of the cars to prop himself up, but he lost his balance, fell slowly and awkwardly, and once he reached the ground he stayed there, curling up and going to sleep.

Drunken demons, their red skin splattered with red blood.

Another set of headlights approached. Round headlights, and close together, much closer than any modern car. Amber moved, crouched over, to get a better look as the car neared. She didn't know what it was called, but it was an old one – from the 1930s or 1940s, the kind with the long fronts and the running boards, the kind that gangsters used to stand on after robbing banks.

Her parents were on their feet, scrubbing dried blood from their mouths and straightening their clothes. Grant kicked Alastair and Alastair woke, saw the car and scrambled up.

The car stopped and the engine cut off. A bald old man got out.

He was small, and stoop-shouldered, and he wore a woollen cardigan over his shirt and tie. He reached back into the car, taking out a big black case, the kind doctors used to carry. Next, he pulled out a folding table, carrying both into the brightly lit circle, to where the demons were waiting. He gave the table to Bill, who set it up. When it was done, the old man placed the bag on top.

He took out a neat pile of bandages and then six small jars, one at a time, and laid them in a row on the table. Bill stood before the first jar. Betty stood beside him. Only the last jar didn't have anyone standing before it.

The old man handed them each a long-bladed scalpel. He was left with one over.

Bill removed his jacket and rolled up his shirtsleeve. He ran the blade along his red skin and held his forearm over the jar. The blood fell in a steady stream. The others did the same.

When the jars were full, they placed wooden stoppers in the necks and wrapped their wounds with the bandages.

The old man looked at the jars. He eyed the sixth one disapprovingly.

"We are dreadfully sorry," said Bill, "but Imelda, she... she turned on us."

"The deal was for six jars," said the old man.

"You can have more of my blood," said Bill, but such a look

of disgust rippled across the old man's face that Bill actually took a step backwards.

"Your blood is already losing its potency," the old man said. "The terms of the deal were quite specific."

Betty smiled her million-watt smile. "We'll fill the sixth, I assure you. We're going to find our daughter. She's here, she's close. We'll feed again, and we'll give you enough for *another* six jars."

Amazingly, her words still hurt. Amber would have laughed if she didn't feel so much like crying.

"I have no interest in another six," the old man said. "I only require enough to fill this empty jar, as per the deal."

"We know," Bill said quietly. "You have our unreserved apology for the inconvenience. If you would like to stay here, we'll find her. We'll find her right now."

The old man sighed, and they took this sigh for agreement.

Amber ducked down as they spread out to search for her. They were sobering up fast, but they passed her hiding spot without even glancing down.

She circled round, came up in the shadow of the old man's car. She peered out at him and his glass jars. She could sneak over there, offer him her blood, get close, and then smash every one of them. Then he'd go back to the Shining Demon empty-handed, and the Shining Demon would be so furious that he'd smite Amber's parents and take care of her problem for her.

It was a good goddamn plan. It was also her only goddamn plan.

The old man turned in her direction. Impossible. He couldn't see her. He couldn't possibly—

His eyes locked on hers. He didn't say anything.

She stayed where she was, crouched down. "My name is Amber," she said, keeping her voice low. "I... I'm the one they're looking for."

"I have nothing to say to you, child."

"But I'm here to... I mean, I'd like to give blood. You need that jar filled, don't you? No matter how fast I run, eventually my folks are going to find me, catch me and... and kill me."

"Your fate is none of my concern."

Amber straightened up. She figured she could reach that table in six, maybe seven strides. "I understand that," she said, "I do, but since my blood is going to be used, anyway, I thought I'd give it voluntarily. Maybe that way I can take Imelda's place in the group. Maybe they'll let me live."

The old man had unsettling eyes. She didn't like the way he looked at her. "Perhaps. But I am merely the Shining Demon's representative – I do not speak with his voice."

Amber nodded. "That's good enough for me."

She stepped forward, but the representative held up a withered hand.

"When you have fed, you may approach."

He was a frail old man. One shove would be all it'd take to send him stumbling. And yet there was something about him, something about those eyes, that stopped her from making a move. He turned, then, stood with his back to her, but this only made her hesitate further. He'd called her bluff and now he was dismissing her, and so her only choice was to tackle him right now or start running.

She turned, and started running. She passed a prefabricated office and was almost to the gate when something charged at her from the darkness. A hand slammed into her chest and sent her crashing through a door. She fell backwards over a desk, sent a chair spinning, heard a heavy old computer hit the floor.

Alastair walked in after her.

"It didn't have to be this way," he said. "You could have joined us."

She got up. The office had only one door, and Alastair was blocking it.

"If you had said yes," he continued, "I wouldn't have to kill you. If you'd taken part, your blood would have been bubbling and boiling with all this incredible power and the representative would have gone back to his master with six jars."

A part of Amber wanted to plead with him, reason with him, get down on her knees and beg him — but he still had Imelda's blood smeared across his face, matted in his beard. And that made her angry.

Oh, that made her so *angry*.

"And all I'd have to do is have sex with you in seventeen years' time?" she said. "I think I'd rather you kill me."

Alastair shook his head as he came forward. "It's not a good idea to taunt me, Amber."

"Why? Are you going to try to kill me *more*? Jesus, no wonder Imelda dumped you."

"Watch it…"

"You're not exactly much of a man, are you?"

Alastair gave a roar and swung a punch that Amber ducked under. She raked her claws into his side and he bellowed, tried to grab her, but she dodged away.

"You little bitch," he snarled.

"Imelda told me about you," she said, backing away. "You

know the way we women like to gossip. She gave me every last detail, and she was not complimentary. Not that she had a whole lot to be complimentary *about*."

"I'm going to rip your head off," Alastair said, stalking after her.

"Did you really think I'd say yes?" Amber asked. "I may not be anything to look at normally, but check me out now. I am beautiful. My own mother pales in comparison beside me, doesn't she? I wonder how that makes her feel. How does it make you feel, Alastair?"

"Keep on talking," he said. "Won't make a bit of difference."

"My point is, I'm way too good for you. Even if I had wanted to join your club, you really think I'd settle for you? Grant, though, now he's a good-looking man, and from what I've heard he wouldn't disappoint…"

Alastair stopped walking. He smiled coldly. "You think I was born yesterday? You think I don't know what you're doing?"

"Of course you know what I'm doing," she said. "I'm goading you."

"It's not going to work."

"You moron, it already *is* working. You know why? Because you and I both know that everything I'm saying is one hundred per cent true, you pathetic excuse for a man."

He came at her too fast to dodge. One hand grabbed her while another punched. Her scales did nothing to dampen the pain. She fell back against another desk and flipped over it, landing badly. She tried to get up and he helped her with a kick to the ribs.

Suddenly she couldn't breathe, and he grabbed her jacket and hauled her to her feet when all her body wanted to do was curl up. He hit her again, and again, and when she tried to hit him back he laughed, and slammed her face into the wall.

Two people walked by the window. She tried to shout, but all she managed was a desperate gasp, and neither Milo nor the demon that was Gregory Buxton heard her.

Alastair's hand closed round the back of her neck, and he pinned her in place while he peered out. "Who was that?" he whispered in her ear. "I recognised your friend, the car guy, but who was the guy with the wings?"

She had no breath with which to answer.

"It doesn't matter," said Alastair. "We'll kill them both. Do you know how strong we are right now? What am I saying? Of course you don't. Our kind is always strongest right after feeding. If your friends want a fight, we'll pull their damn wings off. Especially after we eat you."

He dragged her towards the door.

"Why share?" she moaned.

He stopped, twisted her head so that he could look at her. "What was that?"

She sucked in a sliver of air. "Why share? Why not just… eat me yourself?"

"Because that's not how we do things."

She could take shallow breaths, but it was enough.

"Wouldn't you get even stronger?" she asked. "Is that how it… works? The more you eat… the stronger you get?"

"Yeah, that's how it works."

"So don't you… want to be the strongest?"

"I'm sharing you because that's what we do."

He started dragging her again.

"Sure you're not scared?"

He pulled her closer, tightening his grip on the back of her neck. "What did you say?"

Her breathing back under control, she gazed up at him. "I was just wondering if you're scared of what the others would do if they found out you'd eaten me by yourself."

"This has nothing to do with being scared. This is all to do with how we do things, and we share the—".

"Just so long as you're not doing this because you're scared of my dad."

He slammed her face down on to a desk and pain exploded behind her eyes. She crumpled to the floor. "You're getting transparent, Amber. You're not as sneaky as you seem to think you are. And is this really the route you want to go down – to goad me into killing you up here, right now? I don't think you've thought this through."

"Maybe not," she mumbled.

He grabbed her horns and hauled her up. "Be a good girl, and shut your mouth, and maybe we'll kill you before we eat you."

He pushed her ahead of him and she stumbled a little. She hit a desk with her hip. Her knees almost gave way.

"If I have to knock you out and carry you, I will," said Alastair. "Keep going."

"I'm seeing double," she said. "You hit me too hard."

He laughed. "Maybe that's because this isn't a game we're playing. If you think I hit you too hard, are you going to think we killed you too much? Go on, quit your complaining."

She let herself drop to the ground.

He stared down at her. "What do you think you're doing? Get up."

"Make me."

He kicked her and she cried out, rolled across the floor.

"Getting up now?"

She sat up, rubbing her back, but went no further. "Screw you."

He took hold of her arm, but she let her jacket slip off. Sighing, he threw it to one side, then grabbed her horns, started dragging her to the door. Her fingers closed round the edge of a desk.

"Jesus Christ," Alastair muttered. "Have a little dignity, would you?"

"I don't want to die."

"I don't give a crap." He yanked back on her horns and crouched, jabbing his finger into her face. "I will beat you into a coma, you little brat, and then we'll eat you. You got that? You hear me?"

She whimpered.

He let go of her horns, but kept the finger there. "You give me one more ounce of trouble and I swear to you I will—"

She bit his finger off.

Alastair squealed and fell back, clutching his hand. Amber spat out the finger and he lunged, grabbed her, slammed her against the wall, his fangs bared. She brought her fist down on his injured hand and he recoiled, and then she sank her own teeth into the meat of his throat.

Hot blood gushed into her mouth. She swallowed it instinctively, even as Alastair was staggering backwards. Amber clung on. He tried desperately to detach her, but he was weakening with every moment. He fell to his knees and Amber's weight came forward and he fell on to his back, and Amber wrenched her head to the side, coming away with a chunk of flesh.

She swallowed that, too.

A small part of her recoiled, but she ignored it. The taste was too good. The taste was amazing. Intoxicating. She tore out another chunk, dimly aware of the gurgling sounds Alastair was making. She chewed and swallowed and went back for more. The taste was better than anything she'd ever experienced. The blood was charged with energy, with raw power. She ate the flesh and drank the blood and it filled her and it was glorious, and the more she ate and the more she drank, the less she could hear of that small part of her, that pesky human part, that cried out in fear and disgust and dismay.

Alastair was dead. Amber didn't care. She ripped his shirt open and kept eating.

That's what demons did.

56

IT DIDN'T SEEM ALL that bad anymore.

The whole demon thing was weird, sure, but hell – so what? And as for her parents trying to kill her... that was just funny. It *was*, though. It was, like, the most unfortunate thing that could possibly have happened to her. Probably. She didn't know. It was kind of hard to take anything seriously right now, if she was being honest.

Was she laughing? She may have been laughing. She was pretty sure her laughing caught the attention of Milo and the big grey guy with wings, because they walked in to find her on the floor, covered in blood.

"Oops," she said.

Milo had the strangest look on his face. Half horrified, half concerned. It was funny, and she giggled. Yup, definitely a giggle.

"What happened?" Milo asked.

She stopped giggling and frowned. "What do you think happened? What does it look like happened? I got the munchies."

"Who is that?" he asked, looking at the remains scattered around her.

"This is Alastair," she said. "*Was* Alastair. *Is* Alastair? It *was* Alastair, and it will be again, when I poop."

That was funny, and it made her laugh.

"You okay?" Milo asked.

Amber did her best to stifle her giggles. She was still in an extraordinary amount of danger, after all. "I'm great," she said in a loud, loud whisper. "Peachy keen, jelly bean. I thought you were dead. Or Edgar told me you were dead, anyway. Hey, did you know he's a dick? He tried to kill me."

Milo's eyes widened in alarm. "Edgar?"

"Yep. Wanted to make a blood sacrifice of me to Big Shiny. Hey, what happened to you? How come you're palling around with the scary grey wing-monster?"

"You can just call me Gregory," said Buxton.

Amber shook her head. "That's a silly name for a wing-monster. From now on, you shall be known as… Steve."

"I prefer Gregory."

"Phillip, and that's my final offer."

Milo stepped forward. "Are you drunk?"

She clambered to her feet. "High on life, my dark and mysterious friend. Also, eating demons apparently gets you hammered, so… Who knew? I may not be able to operate heavy machinery for a little while, just to warn you."

"We have to get you out of here."

"No, no, no, Milo," she said. The words tumbled delightfully from her mouth. "No, no, no. No. I have a plan, you see, and it is as ingenious as it is clever. Did you happen to see an old man outside?"

"We saw him," said Buxton. "The Shining Demon's representative."

Amber nodded. "Very *good*, Phil. Can I call you Phil?"

"My name's still Gregory."

"That old man is indeed Big Shiny's representative. He comes to collect their offerings of blood. He currently has five jars." She listened to herself. She liked her voice. She liked how it sounded. Her whole life she'd been stifling that voice, choking on her own intent, but this feeling, this incredible feeling of speaking and being *heard*, was like the real her, the *true* her, bursting forth.

It was like being born again.

She frowned, and looked back at Milo and Buxton. "Where was I? Sorry, lost track. There are the words I'm saying and the words I'm thinking, and they're not the same. Kind of hard to keep everything where it's supposed to be. What was I saying?"

Milo hesitated. "Jars of blood?"

She snapped her fingers. "Yes! Thank you! He has five jars. He needs one more. My plan, as clever as it is ingenious, is to offer to fill that last jar myself. Once I am close enough – BABOOM!"

Milo looked unsure. "You explode?"

"What? No. I break the other jars."

"Oh."

"I thought she exploded, too," said Buxton.

"How come you two are friends?" Amber asked. "How did that happen? Did you bond over how scary you can be?"

"I caught up to him," said Milo, "and we got talking. He's going to help us."

Amber frowned. "So he wasn't flying around, carrying you? Edgar said that's what was happening. Though now I understand why Edgar was the one who kept on seeing you and not me. Guess he needed some way to get me here. He is a sneaky little fella, isn't he?" She shrugged, then grinned. "So now you're buddies. Super duper."

Milo winced slightly. "You've got, uh, something in your teeth."

"How embarrassing," said Amber, using her claws to rake between her fangs. "Is it gone? Is it?"

"It's gone," said Buxton. "And we should be too."

"Not yet," Amber said. "I am smashing those jars. The Shining Demon's going to be so mad at my parents and their dumb friends that no one's gonna give two hoots about my fine red ass. So what do you say, Phil? You in?"

"If you call me by my actual name, then yes."

"Cool," said Amber. "What's your actual name again?"

"Gregory."

She frowned. "You sure it's not Steve, Phil?"

"I'm fairly certain."

"Okay then, it's your name, you should know. What's the plan?"

"First we get the Charger," said Milo. "We need a fast getaway, and Gregory isn't able to carry us both."

"The creepy car it is," Amber said, nodding. "We get the Charger, I smash the jars, we drive away. Nice plan. Good plan. Let's do it." She held out her hand. "Go, go, Demon Squad."

Buxton looked unsure.

"It's what we do, Gregory," she explained. "It's a thing. A tradition. Now that you're fighting by our side, you've got to say it, too. Go ahead."

"Uh," Buxton said, placing his huge grey hand on top of hers. "Go, go, Demon Squad."

Amber laughed, dropping her arm. "Only kidding, we don't say that. You have no idea how dumb you just sounded."

"She's usually a lot more sensible than this," Milo muttered.

He led the way out and Amber followed, with Buxton coming behind. He looked so odd with his wings folded up behind him. She wondered how he sat down, or leaned against stuff. She wondered if a gust of wind had ever snatched him away like a kite. She planned to ask him. These were things she needed to know.

They gave the representative a wide berth on their way to the Charger. Milo took them the long way round, and they passed behind stacks of pallets and crates and splashed through stagnant puddles that waited in the dark. Amber could have complained, but this was very serious business, and so she kept her opinion to herself. Feeling very proud of how responsible and adult she could be sometimes, she walked into Milo.

"Oops," she whispered, "excuse you."

He didn't answer, which was rude. She looked beyond him, to where her mother was standing in front of the Charger.

Kirsty was there as well, and Grant, and of course Bill, who had his arm round Edgar. Edgar stood rigid like the slightest movement would cause Bill to tear his head off – which was probably true, now that Amber thought about it. But, as Amber stepped into the light, Bill smiled, and let go, and Edgar scuttled away.

"Hello, sweetheart," Bill said. "You're grounded."

"Aren't you going to introduce us to your friends?" Betty asked. "Mr Buxton, please forgive my daughter's manners. I thought we'd raised her better than this, I truly did. I love your wings, by the way. I'm a big fan of wings. Kirsty, haven't I always said how much I love wings?"

"For as long as I can remember," said Kirsty.

"For as long as Kirsty can remember, I have always said I love a good pair of wings. And they are a fine pair, Mr Buxton."

"Wait, wait, wait," said Grant. "One of these kids is definitely doing their own thing, aren't they? Here we have our beautiful Amber, resplendent in red, and Mr Buxton here, gracious in grey... but Mr Sebastian, I am afraid, is distressingly dull."

"Come now, Milo," said Bill, "we're all friends here, aren't we? After all, you drove off with my daughter – I imagine that makes us practically family. And your good friend Edgar has told us all about you, so why don't you join us? Show us your true face."

"This won't end well for you," said Milo.

Bill lost his good humour. "Grant, do me a favour, would you? Shoot him in the head."

Grant smiled, went for the gun tucked into his waistband, but Milo's gun leaped into his hand and suddenly the night was filled with gunfire and Amber was stumbling sideways, Buxton's arm round her waist.

She fell to her knees and Buxton was gone, and she felt a tremendous gust of wind and heard the beating of his wings. More gunshots, and shouting, and, just as Amber was making sense of it all, Kirsty was standing in front of her.

"You little pest," she said, and rammed a knee into Amber's face.

Amber fell back, the world a crazy place of tilting horizons and bright spots exploding before her eyes.

"You insufferable little bitch." Kirsty lashed a kick into her side that sent Amber rolling. "I never could stand you, you know that? Out of all of them, you've been the most annoying.

Just so goddamn glum all the time. Always watching that ridiculous TV show with all the pretty people moping around."

Amber tried getting up, but Kirsty's fist came down like a rock.

"Why'd you have to be so glum? What do teenagers have to be glum about?" Kirsty picked her up by the throat. "Why couldn't you have just learned to have fun?"

Kirsty headbutted her and Amber staggered back until she toppled.

In a daze, she watched Buxton throwing Bill against a cargo container, and Betty charge into him from behind. He was bigger than them, and probably stronger, but there were two of them, and when they worked as a team they were a lethal partnership.

Kirsty grabbed Amber's hair and yanked, and Amber cried out as she scrambled to her feet. Kirsty twisted her head round, till Amber was watching Grant pummelling Milo.

"Want to know a secret?" Grant said when Milo dropped. "I hate you guys. You know who I mean, right? You car guys. Your whole act just seems so self-conscious. You drive a cool-looking car. That's your entire thing. Where's the sense in that?"

He kicked Milo across the ground.

"How close do you have to be to it to get the full benefit of your deal? Closer than this, am I right?" He looked up at Kirsty. "Hey, honey, how close do car guys have to get?"

"Fifty paces is the standard, last I heard," said Kirsty.

"Fifty paces," Grant repeated. "You're, what, sixty paces right now, yeah? Around that? So close. So very close."

Milo started dragging himself towards the Charger.

"That's the spirit! Never say die!" Grant stood on Milo's leg. "Well, never say die until you do die, and by then what's the point, am I right?"

Kirsty laughed, and Amber slammed her elbow into her nose and broke free of her grip.

While Kirsty bellowed her anger, Amber went stumbling. Whatever high she was experiencing was beginning to ebb, but it had already lost its appeal. She was truly terrified, and she had no idea what to do.

She should have run. They all should have run when they had the chance.

Kirsty rammed into her from behind and Amber hit the ground, but managed to roll, managed to get up before Kirsty could grab her. She ducked the grasping hands and now she did run, but Kirsty was right behind her and sounding very, very angry.

Kirsty's hand found her hair and yanked again, even harder this time. Amber's head snapped back and she fell to one knee, and Kirsty had a hold of her now and Amber hurtled into a stack of pallets and they tumbled down around her, the edge of one smacking into her skull. The world spun and darkened. Hands on her. Kirsty's voice. Kirsty's face, hazy and bloody and furious. Pain blossomed and Amber fell against something. The Charger. She felt a tinge of surprise somewhere in the corner of her mind when it rolled backwards a few inches.

Amber's vision cleared in time to see Kirsty closing in. She braced herself against the car, got a hand to the hood, and pushed herself off, experiencing the dizzying notion that such a push was all the Charger had been waiting for. It rolled backwards at an unnaturally steady pace.

Amber swung a punch that Kirsty dodged, and got a swipe of her talons in return. They cut through her clothes, cut through her skin before her scales had a chance to form, and Amber made a noise like a wounded cat and Kirsty laughed.

Amber backed away, watching the Charger as it rolled silently along the even ground. Kirsty frowned, turning to see what was commanding her attention. Her eyes widened.

"Grant!" she yelled. "The car!"

Grant looked over, and Milo straightened up and Amber saw him, saw Milo, for the first time.

He was glorious. He had grown no taller and no broader, but his skin had darkened to an impossible black, a black that drank in the light around it so that his outline merged with the shadows behind him. The horns on his forehead were curved and sharp, three or four inches long, and when he smiled the same red light spilled from his mouth as shone from his eyes.

Grant turned and Milo plunged his talons into his gut, lifting him off his feet even as Kirsty screamed her husband's name.

57

AMBER MOVED THROUGH A small maze of crates, away from the fighting, got to the crane and ducked behind the control cabin. She lifted her blood-drenched T-shirt. The claw marks across her side were not that deep, but the pain still made her grimace. She took a deep breath and moved on, keeping low until she neared the representative. He watched her approach, seemingly unimpressed by the sounds of violence from the other side of the stacks.

"You've eaten," he said.

"Yes, I have," she responded.

He peered at her. "You haven't got long before your blood is useless to me. Make haste."

Amber walked to the table, to the five jars of blood and the single empty one. The representative handed her a scalpel.

"Looks sharp," she said.

He didn't answer.

"Do I have to cut my arm? I'm already bleeding. Could I use that blood?"

"You may."

She nodded, moved the jar to her side, then looked up.

"What does he do with it all? The Shining Demon, I mean? Does he drink it? Bathe in it?"

The representative didn't answer.

Amber smiled nervously. "Not going to discuss your boss's personal habits, are you? I can understand that, I guess."

"You are wasting time."

She nodded. "Where'd your boss come from, anyway? Is he from hell? Was I in hell when I spoke to him?"

"Questions are irrelevant."

"Oh. Right. Yeah, okay."

"Your blood."

"Yes. My blood."

She put down the empty jar, and picked up a full one.

The representative frowned. "Be careful with—"

"I'm sorry?" Amber said, and flung the jar against the same pyramid of pipes that Imelda had impaled herself on.

Blood burst from exploding glass and the representative gasped, too stunned to move. Amber turned her hands to claws and destroyed two more jars before he barged into her. He was surprisingly strong for someone so old, but she scooped up one of the remaining jars while he grabbed the last one. He held it close to his chest, his eyes narrow.

"Why?" he snarled.

She tossed her jar into the air, caught it one-handed. "My parents are monsters. Your master's a Demon. Why would I ever want to be part of that?"

"You have no idea what you've done," the old man said. "You have no idea what this means for you."

Amber shrugged. "I imagine a lot of people are going to be very angry with me. But I don't mind that, because your boss is going to be very angry with *you*, too. You let this happen, after all. You were stupid enough to let me get this close. Looking at it like that, all this is kind of your fault."

"Give me the jar."

She held it up. "What's the point? Big Shiny won't be happy with two jars. It'd be an insult, right? So come on – I'll smash this one, you smash that one. Let's see who can throw it further."

"My master requires six jars," said the representative. "When your parents and their friends eat you, four more jars will be filled."

"Huh," said Amber. "I hadn't thought of that."

She went to throw, but the representative lunged, snatching the jar from her hand a split second before his shoulder rammed into her chest. Knocked off her feet, Amber hit the ground and rolled to a stop. The representative carefully placed the two jars back on the table.

"You're pretty spry for an old guy," Amber muttered.

"You have caused much disruption," he said.

"Yeah." She stood, the harbour wind playing with her hair. "So what are you going to do about it, old man?"

The old man looked at her, and grew. His arms and legs lengthened, tearing his clothes, reducing them to rags. He loomed over her, ten feet tall and rake-thin. His skin turned grey and smooth, almost rubbery like a shark, and his eyes closed over and his nose sank in and his lips stretched, impossibly wide, turned black and parted, revealing a second mouth that was no more than a hole ringed with curved teeth.

It wasn't a man anymore, it was a thing, a creature, and it shrieked at Amber, but she was already stepping backwards as a thousand different nightmares flooded her memory. She tried to run, but her foot slipped on some of Imelda's remains and then the creature was upon her.

With her left arm jammed under its chin, she tried to keep it at bay. The teeth of its second mouth were moving, undulating in their eagerness to get at her. Protective scales formed on her skin. Its breath was cold and foul, and it was strong, stronger than her, and no matter how hard she pushed, it drew closer and closer, and with one final surge it clamped its mouth on her shoulder.

Amber screamed as the teeth sank in like her scales weren't even there. Beyond the pain, which was exquisite in its striking clarity, she could feel those teeth beginning to bore through her flesh. She grew talons on her free hand and tried to plunge them into the creature's ribcage, but couldn't pierce its rubbery hide. She toppled, fell, the creature on top. Blood ran down her arm, her back, her chest. She screamed and raked and clawed and battered, but it didn't notice. It just drank.

She brought her knees in, got her feet against its body and tried to straighten her legs. The creature was too strong. Its grip was too secure.

"Please," Amber cried, "stop!"

The pain reached new heights as the creature adjusted its position. She turned her head away, looking desperately for something to use, something to fight it off with. Imelda's shoe was right there, but it didn't even have a sharp heel. Beyond it, no more than ten paces away, was the table.

She grabbed the shoe, doing her best to ignore the agony, and took careful aim. She threw, but the shoe sailed high and wide, missing both of the remaining jars.

She saw Imelda's other shoe. Her last chance.

She reached for it with her foot, managed to nudge it back towards her, then got her heel behind it and bent her leg, dragging it across the ground to her waiting hand. This time she didn't even bother to aim. She just lobbed, and the shoe missed the jars but hit the table, and the jars fell off the edge and smashed.

Instant relief as the creature snapped its head up, shrieking its fury when it saw what Amber had done.

She immediately pushed herself away, scrambled up, leaping to avoid its attempts to reclaim her.

Clutching her shoulder, she plunged into the stacks of pallets and crates. Didn't look behind her. Didn't want to and didn't need to. She heard it coming. It skittered and clattered and scraped and shrieked. She imagined it reaching for her with those long arms, those grasping hands, and pulling her towards its terrible funnel mouth. It wouldn't release her again, she knew that. The next time it clamped that mouth on her, it would be the end.

She darted left, wincing against the pain as she squeezed through a gap between cargo containers too narrow for the creature to follow. It reached for her, almost snagged her, but she kept moving, her horns knocking against the metal, preventing her from turning her head.

She emerged the other side, went stumbling, wanted nothing more than to curl up in a ball and cry, wanting this pain to just go away, but she kept running, across an open space now, trying to find cover before the creature found her.

She ran right into a dead end, whirled to try another route, and froze.

The night was cold. The night was freezing. Amber could suddenly feel every particle of air pressing against her skin. She could feel every strand of hair that the breeze played with. She could feel every bruise and laceration. She could feel everything now, on this cold night in New York, as the creature closed in.

Amber backed off. The creature moved closer.

An engine started up and she glanced to her left, saw Milo at the crane controls. There was a heavy whine behind her, a cargo container lifting off the ground, and she spun and ran right for it. She jumped, caught the edge with her good hand, looked down to see the creature leaping for her. Its fingertips grazed her leg, but it lost its grip. It hit the ground, scrambled up, screeched its rage as she heaved herself on to the top of the container. The crane took her higher and she clutched her shoulder, blood still pouring through her fingers. Higher she went, and higher, the sea breeze brushing past her skin, and she looked down, saw Kirsty throwing Milo into a pillar.

She lay back, grimacing in pain, looking up at the light-polluted night sky. The container swayed the higher it went, the breeze becoming a wind that was getting stronger and colder, but at least she was safe up here.

The container eventually stopped rising. Turning her head to her left, Amber could see the Statue of Liberty. She could see Manhattan, and across the Hudson into Newark. She could see tugs on the river, bright lights bobbing on blackness. What a sight.

She rolled on to her stomach and inched towards the edge. She'd never had a problem with heights before, but this was different. She wasn't strapped into a rollercoaster at Disney World here. She wasn't strapped into anything.

She looked down, down, all the way down. Whoa, that was a long way. Amber suddenly felt very vulnerable and very light, as if one of these strong gusts could just nudge her over the edge. She watched the people below fighting, couldn't really tell who was who with the way they kept moving in and out of the light. She looked for the creature, and frowned when she couldn't see it. Then she caught movement out of the corner of her eye – there it was, climbing up the crane arm.

Coming for her.

She moved back from the edge, got to her hands and knees, and crawled for the nearest steel cable. Gripping it tightly, she stood, watched as the creature reached the top of the crane arm and started across.

"Milo!" she screamed. "Gregory!"

The wind whipped her words away. She stood there, hanging on to the cable, watching the creature get nearer. She couldn't run, couldn't hide, couldn't escape and couldn't fight. She couldn't fight that. The only thing she could do was die. She looked down. She could end it now. Step off and plummet. Terrifying but painless, and infinitely better than what was to come if she stayed where she was.

Sobbing, Amber lifted one foot, or tried to, at least. But it wouldn't budge. She tried to fling herself forward, but her body disobeyed. Her legs wouldn't move and her hands wouldn't let go.

"Please," she whispered to herself, but her body didn't listen. It refused her commands. It wasn't going to go to its death quietly, no matter how much she might want it to. It wanted to fight. It wanted to *survive*.

Her body buzzing with an energy like electricity, an energy that could send her sprinting or make her seize up like jammed machinery, she watched the creature get closer. It was practically overhead now. Soon it would drop down, and she had nowhere to run, and it would clamp that mouth on to her again, and it'd kill her. There'd be no surviving that. Without a doubt, it would kill her where her parents had failed, and the witch had failed, and the vampires had failed, and the serial killer had failed, and that guy had failed, back at the diner. What was his name? The name of the guy whose finger she'd bitten off? What was his goddamn name?

Brandon, that was it. *Brandon*.

The creature dropped to the container and while it struggled for balance Amber let go of the steel cable and ran at it. She jumped, both feet slamming into its chest, knocking it back off the edge. She twisted, reaching for a handhold, but the creature's flailing arms caught her leg and then she was falling too.

They both fell.

Plummeting.

Spinning in rushing air.

Then something slammed into her and suddenly there were strong arms around her and she heard the beating of great wings, and she watched the creature hit the ground, so far below, and come apart in a wretched explosion of blood and body parts, and she was swooping upwards.

Buxton let go and her momentum took her through the

air, her arms and legs pinwheeling. She touched down and crumpled and went rolling, coming to a wonderfully painful stop.

She lay there for a moment, a nice long moment, then raised her head, saw her parents coming for her.

58

AMBER RAN INTO THE warehouse, started up the stairs, but then remembered that up there she'd be trapped, so she jumped back down, ran across the warehouse floor. Nowhere to hide here, nowhere except behind the engine block.

She went to duck behind it, found Edgar cowering there. He looked up at her with tears in his eyes and she hit him and he crumpled. She crouched over him, and listened to her parents' footsteps.

"We're not mad," said Betty, "are we, Bill?"

"Not mad at all," said Bill.

"You've proven yourself," Amber's mom said. "We're impressed. We are. Come on out, sweetie. We've got a lot to talk about."

Amber's shoulder was still bleeding badly. She couldn't fight them, and she couldn't run. They were stronger and faster and better. She had one option. Right here, right now, she had one way to escape.

She dug a hand into her pocket.

"We're going to need to make plans," said Bill. "The Shining Demon isn't going to be pleased with any of us – least of all you. We're stronger if we stick together."

Amber tore a match from the matchbook she'd taken from Edgar's house, back in Miami. She dropped the match on the ring of powder, and stood.

Her parents smiled, and Bill opened his mouth to say something, but Betty saw the flames at the last moment and she grabbed him, yanked him into the circle with her just before the flames met and turned blue.

And then they were in the Shining Demon's castle, with its five arched doorways and its obscene tapestries and stained-glass windows.

Bill and Betty whirled, confused. In their day, a summoning would mean the Demon appeared to them. Amber didn't bother telling them that times had changed.

Her breath crystallised as she adjusted to her new surroundings. Now she could hear the distant screams, and she could see better in the gloom.

"Hello, Fool," she said.

Her parents stood together, watching as Fool emerged from darkness. Thin rivers of sweat streaked its ash-pale make-up, but its glass-shard smile was as fresh as ever. "I've been waiting for you," it said. "Do you have him? Is that him there?"

It tried to peer at Edgar as he stirred, but Amber blocked its view. "First you give me what I want," she said.

Fool shook its head. "The Master's instructions were clear. First you hand over Gregory Buxton and then I give you this." It took a small vial of yellow liquid from its patchwork robes.

Her eyes locked on to it. "And what about the countdown?"

"Drink this," said Fool, "and the scars will fade."

She took a moment. "No, Fool," she said sternly, like she was talking to a child, or a dog. "I don't trust you."

"Where are we?" Bill asked.

Fool looked at him, started to answer.

"Your master's business is with *me*," Amber snapped. "Forget about them. They mean nothing. It's *me* you need to address. I don't trust you, Fool, so I am not going to give you Gregory Buxton until *after* you give me the vial."

"But the Master—"

"The Shining Demon wants Buxton," Amber interrupted, "and the only way that's happening is if you do what I say."

Fool licked its red lips. "Same time," it said. "Yes, yes, same time."

She couldn't put it off any longer, so Amber grabbed Edgar by the collar and hauled him to his feet. He moaned, almost toppled. "Here he is," she said. "Here's Gregory Buxton."

Fool looked at Edgar.

And nodded eagerly.

He held out the vial with one hand. In the other, he clutched a metal collar attached to a chain.

Amber nudged Edgar out of the circle as she snatched the vial from Fool's hand, and Fool snapped the collar around Edgar's neck with practised ease.

Edgar straightened up at once. "What? What's going on?"

"What *is* going on?" said Bill. "Creature, what did you give our daughter? What is that?"

"Seasoning," said Fool, and giggled. "It'll turn her blood to poison."

Bill reached for the vial, but Amber backed away. Betty moved behind her.

"Give it to me," said Bill. "Give it to me right this instant, young lady."

Amber snarled. "Screw you, *Dad.*"

He dived at her and she held him off with one hand while she thumbed the stopper from the vial. Her mother was grabbing her from behind, trying to tear the vial from her grip. They had her wrist pinned so she leaned down, took the vial between her teeth and threw her head back. The yellow liquid splashed down her throat and burned. It reached her stomach and sent out hot jabs of pain, and her parents stepped away as she fell to her knees. Her vision dimmed. She couldn't feel her fingers or toes. Her blood boiled in her veins. Through blurred eyes, she watched the scarred numbers fade from her wrist.

And then, just like that, it was gone, and she gasped and blinked and looked up in time to see Fool tugging angrily at Edgar's chain.

"You *are* Gregory Buxton!" it said. "I know you are him! You are just trying to confuse me!"

"Gregory Buxton is a sixty-five-year-old black man!" Edgar cried. "I'm a forty-six-year-old white guy!"

Fool frowned at him, then its eyes widened. "You all look the same to me," it mumbled.

From one of the corridors, a rapidly intensifying glow. Amber's parents turned away instantly, and Edgar clamped his hands over his face. Amber screwed her eyes shut as footsteps thundered on the stone floor, so heavy she felt the vibrations through the soles of her own feet.

"You dare cheat *me?*" the Shining Demon roared. His brightness was blinding, even with her eyes closed, and his voice came from above. He was towering over her, towering over them all. "You come to *my* castle and you dare try to cheat *me?*"

Amber's legs were shaking and she desperately wanted to curl up in a ball and cry, but she forced herself to stay standing.

For a long time, there was not one other sound to be heard. Even the distant screams quietened.

Then the Shining Demon softened his voice. "Look at me," he said.

Amber didn't move for a few seconds. She certainly didn't open her eyes.

But then the brightness began to retract, and when it stopped hurting Amber dared to look up. For a moment she thought she saw a being of terrifying proportions and impossible appendages, but her squinting eyes adjusted as the brightness was reined in, and now she saw that the figure was of normal height, and not the monstrous thing she had glimpsed. The Shining Demon blazed with a fierce light from within. Tattoos dotted his translucent skin like archipelagos, black islands in a sea of burning orange. His face was calm. He had black eyes.

"My Lord Astaroth," Edgar said, falling to one knee, "the Duke of Hell whom we mortals call the Shining Demon, I ask of you only that you remake me, sire. I have so far been unworthy of your attentions, but look, I have brought to you a curiosity, a girl of—"

The Shining Demon looked at him like Edgar was something he'd stepped in. "You? You have brought me nothing."

"But... but I have everything to offer," Edgar countered, bowing his head. "I offer you my soul, sire. All I have ever wanted in my entire pathetic life was the power you have bestowed upon mortals like me. I offer you my flesh to remake how you see fit. I offer you my soul to sculpt, and my mind to twist, and—"

"You offer me nothing I do not possess," said the Shining Demon. "You are outside the circle, little insect. You have nothing to bargain with. Your soul is mine already."

Fool tittered, and yanked on the chain. Edgar fell back.

"No!" he cried. "Wait, it's not meant to be like this! All I want is power! Please, just—"

Another tug and the last of Edgar's words were choked from him. Fool started walking for the nearest of the arched corridors, and Edgar was dragged after him, kicking and spluttering. He reached out to Amber, but she just stood there, on her side of the blue flames, and watched him go until he was lost to sight.

Amber turned back to the Shining Demon to find his eyes fixed on her parents, who were still averting their gaze.

"Look at me," he commanded, and this time they obeyed. "Two of your brethren are dead, along with my representative on Earth. And I have received no tribute."

"We… we can make it up to you," said Bill. "We can—"

"You have failed to fulfil your part of our deal," said the Shining Demon. "You had better start running."

Bill and Betty clutched each other's hands.

The Shining Demon turned his gaze upon Amber. "And finally you. You have cheated me, you foolish, foolish girl. You think, because Buxton has eluded me, you stand a chance? Buxton made himself an expert in the arcane arts. Can you say the same?"

Amber swallowed. "No," she said. "But I found him in less than three weeks, and you've been after him for fifteen years. So it occurs to me that maybe you're not so hot at finding *anyone*, you dumb shit."

The Shining Demon stared.

"I don't care what your excuse is," she continued while a

significant part of her brain screamed at her to shut the hell up. "I don't care if you regard time differently or if you've got endless patience or what. Fifteen years is fifteen years. You've had all that time to learn how to google and instead you kept trying to find him on Demon radar. I mean, seriously? You might be shiny, but you're not too bright, are you?"

"I will make you pay for every insolent word."

"You sure you can count that high, you moronic pile of crap? Screw you. I'm not scared of you. Come after me. Send another representative after me and I'll kill him just like I did your last one."

She thought that'd make him explode. Instead, he just smiled. Which was worse.

"Amber," he said, "you are a brave girl. You are even a clever girl, in your way. But you are also an ignorant girl. I could command your parents to force you from that circle and then you would be my plaything for all eternity. But there is a certain way to do things. Deals. Negotiations. Collecting debts. Wreaking vengeance. All these things I have been doing for centuries upon centuries. Technology means nothing to me. If I want you, I will get you. Your body may fade, but your soul will burn as bright.

"Yet you have cheated me and insulted me. I do not easily forgive insolence. Your parents will run as they must." The Shining Demon smiled. "But you must run faster, for the Hounds of Hell will be coming for you."

The blue flames spluttered and went out, and they were suddenly back in the warehouse.

59

Amber took a moment to adjust to her new surroundings, took a moment to absorb what the Shining Demon had said, and then she turned and Bill lunged at her and Milo said, "Stop."

Bill froze, though his body practically hummed with restrained violence. Milo and Buxton stood over the unconscious forms of Grant and Kirsty. Milo was back to normal, and his gun was pointed straight down into Grant's face.

"We'll pay you ten times what Imelda was paying you," said Bill. "Just walk away, Mr Sebastian. We'll pay you, too, Mr Buxton. This is a family matter."

"Indeed it is," said Milo, and he didn't budge.

Amber watched as the space between the two men became charged, and then Betty was there, her hand on Bill's arm.

"We have to go," she said. "We have to go now."

"Don't forget your friends," said Buxton.

Moving slowly, her father approached Grant and her mother went over to Kirsty. Amber just stood there, waiting for them to look at her. Her dad hauled Grant off the ground by his shirt collar. She was being ignored. They were going to walk out and walk away and she was being ignored.

"Apologise!" she screamed.

Everyone looked at her.

"I beg your pardon?" Bill said.

"Apologise," Amber repeated, trying to get her voice under control. She would not cry. Not in front of them. Not ever again. "After everything you've done, the least you can do is—"

"You ruined everything," her mother said.

Her words robbed Amber of her voice.

"We gave you life," said her dad. "For sixteen years, you wanted for nothing. We provided for you, we kept you safe, we let you have friends, go to school… We didn't have to. We could have locked you in the attic. But we allowed you to live. And this… this is how you repay us."

Her throat was so tight. "You wanted to kill me," said Amber.

"That was always going to be how it ended," Betty replied. "We knew you only had sixteen years so we decided to let you spend it however you wanted. We allowed you happiness, Amber."

"You think… you think I was happy?"

"You didn't know any better. And we were good parents."

Bill nodded. "We were very good parents. Did we ever shout at you? Did we ever ground you? We let you live your life however you wanted to live it. Do you think it's our fault that you never made any real friends? Are you blaming us for that? Not that we're complaining. One good thing about you being socially inept – we've got no one probing too deeply into your disappearance. We've been wonderful parents, and all we've tried to do is give you a good life."

Amber frowned at how incredible this was. "You think you've done me a favour?"

"Every minute," said Betty, "every second of your sixteen years was possible only because we needed you to boost our power. That is your *purpose*, Amber. That has *always* been your purpose. You were meant for nothing else, just like your brother and your sister were meant for nothing else but to sustain us, to keep us going. This isn't about you. This isn't your story, Amber – it's ours. We're not going to hand over the reins to the younger generation – not when we're better, faster, smarter and stronger. We deserve our power and our life because we carved it out for ourselves. You? Your generation? You expect to have everything handed to you. You never had to work, to really work, for anything. So what do you deserve? Really, what do you deserve?"

"A chance," said Amber.

"You've squandered it," said Bill. He put Grant over his shoulder. "You've ruined everything for everyone. Imelda's dead because of you. You killed Alastair. Now we have to run, and you… You have no idea what's coming for you."

He walked out while Betty took Kirsty's hands.

"You should have just let us kill you," Betty said, and followed her husband, dragging Kirsty behind her.

60

THEY WERE SIX DAYS into their drive to Alaska, and they were staying in a bed and breakfast outside of Edmonton, Canada. Amber's bag was by the door. She slept in her jeans and socks. That evening, she'd eaten her first real meal in days, and for the first time in a week she'd been able to shower. These were things she was beginning to view as luxuries. She already considered a good night's sleep as an extravagance she couldn't afford, and as for a general feeling of safety...

At the slightest noise her eyes would spring open and her body would tense. The house creaked and groaned around her and she hovered like this, on the edge of sleep, as the hours slouched by. She wondered if Milo was finding it as difficult to sleep in the next room. He'd been even more taciturn than usual, ever since they'd fled New York. She would have liked to believe he was angry with her, maybe for the mess she'd dragged him into, but she knew he wasn't, and she knew the truth.

He was scared.

The Hounds were after them, and Milo was scared.

She heard a voice call her name and she nearly screamed.

She didn't move. She didn't sit up. She just went rigid,

and she listened. Maybe she'd gotten it wrong. It could have been the wind, or the pipes, or her imagination. Amber lay there, a statue made of nerve endings stretched like bowstrings. She stopped breathing. She waited.

But she couldn't close her eyes. She couldn't allow herself to believe it had been the wind. Not without checking.

She got out of bed, standing in the cold, cold room, her bare arms prickling with goosebumps. It took seven steps to get to the window. She wished it had taken more. She parted the curtains.

Her room was on the second floor. Glen was outside her window, standing on darkness and nothing else. He looked so pale. He looked so sad.

With trembling hands, Amber closed the curtains.

She stayed where she was for five minutes.

When she looked again, he was gone. The half-moon struggled out from behind some clouds, did its best to cast a silver light on the buildings and homes around her. The people in those homes slept, whole families warm in their beds. In the morning, they'd wake and the kids would go to school and the parents would work or do whatever it is they did, and they'd have their arguments and their fights and the parents wouldn't understand and the kids would storm to their rooms, and life would continue on as normal, or as normal as it ever got.

But, of course, normal was subjective. And so was life, now that Amber thought about it.

She reached for the cord to draw the curtains closed once more and she happened to glance to the east, to the long dark road they'd driven in on. In the distance – way, way in the distance — she saw tiny lights coming closer. Five of them. Motorcycles.

Amber grabbed her sneakers and her jacket and her bag. She hammered on Milo's door and he rushed out, fully clothed.

They got in the Charger and they drove.

DEREK LANDY

DESOLATION

THE DEMON ROAD TRILOGY

Reeling from their **bloody encounter**
in New York City, Amber and Milo flee north.
On their trail are the **Hounds of Hell** — five
demonic bikers who will stop at nothing to
drag their quarries back to their unholy master.

Amber and Milo's only hope lies within
Desolation Hill — a small town with a
big secret; a town with a darkness to it, where
evil seeps through the very floorboards. Until,
on one night every year, it spills over onto the
streets and **all hell breaks loose.**

And that night is coming...

READ ON FOR A SNEAK PREVIEW...

THEY WERE ALIVE WHEN SHE WALKED IN.

Fourteen people, including the short-order cook and the waitress with the badly dyed hair, in this little rest stop just outside of Whitehorse in Yukon. Everyone looked tired, this time of night. They ate pie or drank coffee or read newspapers or sat in their booths, focusing on their phones. Nobody glanced up when Amber entered. Nobody talked. Music played, drifting through from the small kitchen. Something by Bon Jovi. It was safe in here. None of these people wanted to kill her. She was getting good at spotting the telltale signs.

She went straight to the restroom. It was chilly, and not very clean, but she didn't mind. She'd had to pee in worse places these past few days.

When she was done, she washed her hands. In the cracked mirror above the cracked sink, her hair was a mess and there were bags under her red-rimmed eyes. Her pale skin was blotchy. She looked like she needed a shower. She looked like a scared girl on the run.

Funny that.

Her belly rumbled and Amber turned off the faucet, wiped her hands on her jeans, and left the restroom.

They were all dead when she walked out.

She went instantly cold. All moisture left her mouth, her knees weakened, and every nerve ending jingled and jangled and screamed at her to run. But she couldn't run. Her legs wouldn't obey. She could barely stay standing.

Some of them had been attacked where they sat – others while they tried to escape. Bludgeoned to death, every one of them. A woman in a brown cardigan was slumped over her table, blood leaking from the mess in the back of her head. A trucker in a plaid shirt had half his face caved in. The waitress had been dragged across the counter. Blood dripped from the dented gash in her temple, forming a growing pool on the floor beneath her. Amber couldn't see the cook, but knew he was lying on the floor of the kitchen. She could see his blood on the wall.

Fourteen people when she'd walked in. Fourteen corpses. But now there was a fifteenth person. He was sitting in the booth next to the door, his back to her, wearing a baseball cap and a grey, faded boiler suit. He was singing along to the radio. 'Every Rose Has Its Thorn' by Poison.

The booth moved closer to her. Closer still. No, it wasn't the booth that was moving – it was Amber. She frowned, looked down at her feet as they took another step. Apparently, they were on their way out of the door, and they were taking the rest of her with them. She was okay with that. She didn't want to stay here, anyway, not with all those corpses. She just had to pass this guy and then she could run out into the quiet street, shout for Milo, and he'd come roaring up in the Charger and they could get the hell out of there. Easy. No fuss, no muss.

The man in the boiler suit had a claw hammer on the table in front of him. It was bloodstained. There was a chunk of scalp hanging off it.

"How you doing?" he asked.

Amber froze.

He didn't have a nice voice. It was curiously strained, like he'd spent most of his life shouting.

She kept her eyes on the door and took another step. And another.

"Amber, isn't it?"

She stopped.

"Yeah," the man said. "It's you. I expected something else, to be honest. All the things you've done, I expected someone a little more…" he licked his lips, "…impressive."

She looked at him. She had to. Her gaze moved slowly, and reluctantly, from the door to the booth. First she looked at the claw hammer, then at the remains of the pie he'd been eating. Then at his rough, worn hands, and the blood-splattered sleeves of his boiler suit. He was thin. Wiry. He had a narrow face and a pointed chin and a nasty smile. No hair. His cap had a faded logo Amber couldn't make out. Her eyes finally settled on his and she had the strangest feeling of vertigo.

"You're the one killed the Shining Demon's representative, right?" the man asked. He had an accent. Southern. Georgia, maybe. "Made him go splat? I like your style. I'd been searching for the best way to kill that prick for years, but you got there first."

"What do you want?" Amber asked.

"It ain't what I want, little girl. It's what you can give me." He slid slowly out of the booth. He wasn't tall, he had maybe two inches on Amber, but she took a step back nonetheless. "You're my ticket," he said.

"To what?"

He breathed in, and spread his arms. "All this." His right arm dipped, and he picked up the claw hammer.

"Why did you kill these people?"

He gave her one of those nasty smiles. "No one told me I wasn't supposed to. Besides, it's been way too long since I got to kill new folks. Do you know what it's like, little girl, do you have *any idea* what it's like to be trapped in a middle-of-nowhere town where the biggest challenge is to find someone worthy to stalk? Jesus H. Christ, what is it with the young people of today? I'm old-fashioned and I make no apology for it. I like to stalk and kill teenagers. I like a challenge, you know what I mean? Teenagers are fit and strong and they're surrounded by family and friends... but do you know what makes them so perfect to stalk? They run to parents, they run to cops, they tell them a bad man is trying to kill them, but no one takes them seriously. The look on their faces when they realise they're alone − that they are truly *alone* − after a lifetime of being told they'll be supported no matter what... Well. It's just heaven, is what it is. But these days, trying to find one one who can put up a decent fight is an impossible task. Worthy teenagers are a dying breed, and that is a sad state of affairs."

That smile of his broadened. "So what about you, Amber? You gonna put up a fight? You've got that look about you. It's in the eyes. Man, isn't this just typical? I find a teenager who may actually be able to mount a challenge and I'm not allowed to kill her."

Amber frowned. "You're not allowed?"

"Nope. No killing the girl, those are my orders. I'm just here to bring you back."

"You're working for Astaroth."

"On a first-name basis with the Shining Demon, are you? Must be nice. But yes, I am guilty as charged, as I said at my trial. Now you've managed to stay ahead of the Hounds, which is a feat that few have accomplished for this long, but now the professional is here to take care of business and to stop all this silliness."

"I have money," said Amber. "I can pay you to walk away."

The man laughed. "Money? I don't have any use for it. Besides, you can't match what he's offering."

"Try me."

"Freedom, little girl. See, I made a mistake when I made my deal with the Devil. A lot of us do. We get fixated on the people who caught us. All I wanted was to get my revenge on that Podunk little town – but when I was done? I couldn't leave. I didn't exist beyond its borders. The Shining Demon will, ah, broaden my remit. I'll be able to travel. Kill people in new places. And this is just a taster of that. Look at me – Elias Mauk – killing in Canada. I'm gonna take my show on the road."

"I... I read about you."

"I'm flattered."

"You're dead."

"That too."

"You were executed."

"Fried," he said, whipping off his cap. A thick band of still-sizzling flesh wrapped around his head where the electricity had been focused. Amber could smell the burning skin from where she stood.

Mauk put his cap back on, and grinned. "They said I murdered twenty-two people. It was more like forty, but that was back when I was alive. Ever since the chair, my body count has grown. And after this? It's gonna skyrocket."

He took a step forward and she took a step back, holding up her hands.

"I don't want to fight you," she said.

"Oh Amber, don't you dare disappoint me now. Killing a room full of people is distressingly easy for someone like me. You gotta put up *some* resistance, at least."

"You're not the first serial killer I've faced," Amber said. "You're not even the first returned-from-the-grave serial killer I've faced. I killed Dacre Shanks."

"Shanks ain't got nothing on me."

"Not anymore he doesn't," she said. "He came after me and I killed him. Now he's dead and it's the kind of dead that you don't come back from. I'll kill you, too."

"I am liking this confidence," said Mauk. "You're definitely making the butterflies flutter, I'm not gonna lie to you. But Shanks was nothing. Take his precious little key away from him, and what did he have to offer? Tell me if this is true – when you found him, was he stuck inside one of his own dollhouses? I've heard he was stuck inside one of his own dollhouses. That's funny. How'd you kill him? You step on him? Hell, you're heavy enough."

"Oh, I wasn't like this when I killed him," said Amber.

"No?"

"No," she said, and she shifted.

Her bones lengthened and realigned and she grew taller. Her excess weight spread throughout her body and she became slimmer. Her brown hair turned black and her flushed skin turned red and two ebony horns blossomed from her forehead and curled back.

"There you are," breathed Mauk. "Oh, you are magnificent."

Amber didn't bother agreeing as she grabbed him. She knew she was magnificent. He swung the hammer, but she ripped it out of his hand and tossed it aside. She picked him up, her newly formed muscles not even straining with the effort, and hurled him across a table. She caught a glimpse of her reflection as she stalked after him, and her sudden beauty was almost enough to make her pause. She still wasn't used to it. A slight reconfiguration of her features was all it took to turn her from ugly human to mesmerising demon.

Ugly. There was a word she'd never used about herself before. Plenty of others had, in their crueller moments, but never her. She didn't stop to wonder what it meant, as she watched Mauk take a steak knife from a dead patron, and it didn't bother her. Precious little did when she was a demon.

Incredibly, Mauk was smiling as he came forward. Her skin tightened and black scales formed, and the knife skimmed across her armour without drawing blood. He tried stabbing at her again, but she was much too fast. She gripped his wrist and twisted. The knife fell and she hit him twice and he wobbled, and she took hold of the back of his head and sent him sprawling across the floor.

"Told you you should have walked away," she said, and her fingers grew to claws.

Mauk groaned, turned over, and looked at her. He was still smiling. She didn't like that. She was used to people dismissing her when she was herself, when she was ordinary old human

Amber, but not when she was like this. When she was like this, she demanded *respect*.

"Oh, I'm sorry," said Mauk, "you think you're winning this little exchange? There's a lot more to beating me than hitting me a coupla times." He got to his feet. "See, when I kill, I like to… play. And my playmates, well… they just do whatever I tell 'em. Ain't that right, my friends?"

The corpses stirred, and all the dead people in the rest stop slid out of their booths and stood, and Amber heard some distant part of herself scream.

ALL HEADS TURNED AND dead eyes opened. Amber backed off as the patrons came at her, their faces blank and splattered with their own blood.

"Stay back," Amber warned, shoving the waitress. "Don't touch me. Don't you dare—"

They grabbed her and she cursed, struggled. She didn't want to hit them, didn't want to hurt them, but they were dead, they were already dead, and it was too late for them so she started slashing with her claws, punching, headbutting, and they kept coming, and now her arms were pinned and one of them had her by the throat and they pushed her back, this solid mass of corpses working as one, and they forced her into a booth and started crawling on top of her until she could barely breathe.

"Get them off me!" she screamed. "Get them off!"

Through the tangle of limbs, she watched as Mauk put the claw hammer on the table. Then he stepped back, taking a small pouch from inside his boiler suit. He dipped his fingers in, drew out a handful of black powder, and crouched. Amber lost sight of him, but she knew what he was doing. He was making a circle.

"We're gonna be taking a trip," he said.

"I swear to God, I'll kill you."

He stuck his head up into her line of sight. "Hey, you be nice to me and I'll be nice to you. The Shining Demon only told me to bring you to him alive. Now there's *alive*, and there's *barely alive* — I don't much care which one it ends up being." Then he ducked down again.

She listened to the soft hiss of the powder. There were six or seven people lying on top of her, but they were still. They didn't even breathe. Her eyes settled on the claw hammer. She tried to reach for it.

Mauk stood, put the pouch back into his boiler suit, and slid into the seat opposite. He pulled the hammer a little closer to him.

"Your parents were after you, ain't that right?" he asked. "Yeah, I heard all about your folks and their friends. They actually wanted to eat you? That's messed up — and I should know. But you evaded them — you, a sixteen-year-old kid, evaded a bunch of demons a hundred and something years old. Not only that, you killed the representative, smushed that overrated pile of crap Shanks, *and* you've managed to stay ahead of the Hounds of Hell."

He whistled in admiration. "I mean, they'd have caught you eventually. It's what they do. Astaroth sets the Hounds on you, they don't give up till you're caught, and there ain't nothing you can do about it. You don't fight the Hounds. You can't beat 'em. Never heard of anyone managing that. You can't hide from 'em, neither. They got your scent. But look at you. You're still running. That says something about you, little demon. Says you are not to be underestimated. Under different circumstances, I would have been honoured to have stalked and killed you."

He put a pair of handcuffs on the table. "But, seeing as how I'm gonna be delivering you to the Shining Demon, I gotta take precautions."

The corpses moved on top of Amber, and they stretched out her right arm, pinning it to the tabletop.

"You'll be wearing these," said Mauk. "I don't like to do it. I was in chains when they caught me and I didn't much like it, and putting shackles on such a beautiful beast as yourself seems to me a crime of some magnitude. But I ain't gonna underestimate you." He opened the cuffs, then laid them to one side. "And with that in mind I gotta think about those claws of yours. No telling what manner of mischief you could get up to with those things. So we're gonna have to do something about them, too."

He picked up the hammer as the corpses flattened her hand fully against the table.

Amber started to panic. "What are you doing? What are you going to do? Tell them to let go of me. Tell them!"

Mauk's free hand pinned her thumb. She turned it into a claw, tried to slash at him, but he laughed, and raised the hammer.

"Don't," she said. "Please don't. I swear I—"

"This little piggy," said Mauk, and brought the hammer down.

Pain rocketed through her and Amber screamed, tried to kick and flail, but the weight of all those bodies on top of her made that impossible. Tears came to her eyes, rolled down her cheeks. The pain was so immense that she almost didn't feel him singling out her next finger.

"No!" she cried. "Please!"

He didn't bother saying anything this time. With a happy smile on his face, he smashed the bones in that finger, too.

"You bastard!" Amber howled. She was sobbing. She was actually sobbing. "You bastard, I'll kill you, I'll kill you, I'll rip your—"

The third finger was smashed and Amber lost her words to the screams that were being ripped from her throat. The fourth followed. Then the fifth. Finally, the corpses released their hold on her. She tried to retract her arm, tried to clutch it close to her, but to do so it'd have had to pass through the tangle of corpses. She held it in mid-air while she cried and struggled to breathe.

Then the corpses moved again. They had her left hand in their grip.

"No!" she screamed, trying to keep it underneath her, jammed between her chest and the cheap upholstery. But now they were turning her, turning her on to her back, and as her left arm was being pulled out of the tangle her right arm was being pulled in, and her broken fingers jolted and sent fresh waves of pain straight into her thoughts, blinding them, freezing them, slicing through them and leaving them in tatters. When the wave crested and her thoughts became her own once more, her face was pressed tight into someone's torso, and she could feel the surface of the table beneath her left palm and Mauk's grip on her thumb, and she squeezed her eyes shut.

The hammer found its target and she gasped.

It found its next target. And the next one. And now she was screaming once more, but it didn't change anything, because she only had two fingers that weren't broken and Mauk quickly reduced that to one. Amber fought the urge to puke. If she puked, she'd choke on her own vomit.

"And this little piggy went wee, wee, wee, all the way home," said Mauk, and smashed her little finger.

While she screamed, the corpses climbed off her. One by one, the weight lessened, and she could turn her head now, and breathe in lungfuls of air to help her cry. Someone – Mauk, probably – had her hands in his. His skin was rough. Calloused. She barely felt the handcuffs slide around her wrists. The last corpse climbed off her and she sat up.

"There," Mauk said. "That wasn't so bad, now was it?"

She ran her forearm over her eyes – that movement alone was enough to bring fresh tears – then blinked at him as he sat there, smiling.

"I didn't wanna have to do that," he said. "But I'm a cautious fellow. I see that you have sharp teeth, too. Let's do each other a favour, okay? You try not to bite me, and I won't smash each and every one of those pearly whites. I'd hate to have to ruin your beautiful smile. It is beautiful, ain't it? I bet it is. Smile for me. Go on. Just a little smile."

Her demon side wanted to snarl and snap and sneer, but her human side, the ugly, ordinary, weak side, just wanted to be spared any more pain.

She raised the corners of her mouth in a twitching, pathetic smile.

"I knew it," said Mauk. "I've often wondered how much better looking I'd be if Astaroth had made me a demon, instead of bestowing upon me the gifts I'd asked for. I'd be taller for a start, huh?" He chuckled, then slid out of the booth. "Come on now, girlie. The Shining Demon don't like to wait."

It took a few moments, but Amber got out of the booth,

stood on shaky legs. The circle of black powder Mauk had made was just big enough for the two of them to stand in.

"Hop to it," said Mauk. "And don't scuff the edges, neither."

She wanted to turn, run, but the corpses were watching her. She couldn't fight, not with the handcuffs on and not when the slightest touch would bring her to her knees.

Mauk held out his hand. "Come on, Amber. Time to give this Devil his due."

KEEP YOUR EYES ON THE ROAD

by following Derek @
po.st/demonroad
🐦/dereklandy